Books by Callie Hart

Brimstone
Quicksilver

BLOOD & ROSES

Vol. 1

Callie Hart

FOREVER
LARGE PRINT

This book is a work of fiction. Names, characters, places, and incidents are the product of the author's imagination or are used fictitiously. Any resemblance to actual events, locales, or persons, living or dead, is coincidental.

Copyright © 2014 by Callie Hart

Cover design by Daniela Medina
Cover images © Shutterstock
Cover copyright © 2026 by Hachette Book Group, Inc.

Hachette Book Group supports the right to free expression and the value of copyright. The purpose of copyright is to encourage writers and artists to produce the creative works that enrich our culture.

The scanning, uploading, and distribution of this book without permission is a theft of the author's intellectual property. If you would like permission to use material from the book (other than for review purposes), please contact permissions@hbgusa.com. Thank you for your support of the author's rights.

Forever
Hachette Book Group
1290 Avenue of the Americas, New York, NY 10104
read-forever.com
@readforeverpub

Originally published as the novellas *Deviant* / *Fracture* / *Burn*
First Forever edition: January 2026

Forever is an imprint of Grand Central Publishing. The Forever name and logo are registered trademarks of Hachette Book Group, Inc.

The publisher is not responsible for websites (or their content) that are not owned by the publisher.

Forever books may be purchased in bulk for business, educational, or promotional use. For information, please contact your local bookseller or the Hachette Book Group Special Markets Department at special.markets@hbgusa.com.

Library of Congress Control Number: 2025944950

ISBNs: 9781538778494 (trade paperback); 9781538782026 (International trade paperback); 9781538778739 (ebook); 9781538782934 (large print)

ONCE THERE WAS A BOY WHO LIVED IN THE DARK...

AND HE LIKED IT THERE JUST FINE

Content Guidance

Blood & Roses is a dark romance series that contains explicit content and heavy themes intended for mature audiences. Readers are strongly encouraged to consider their personal sensitivities.

This book contains: graphic violence, human trafficking, murder, psychological abuse, coercion, child abuse, substance abuse and addiction, and BDSM.

1

SLOANE

WHEN I SAY I'M A GHOST, I'M NOT BEING literal. I'm very much alive, or at least some days I hurt just enough to know I'm still clinging onto a heartbeat. No, when I say I'm a ghost, I mean people rarely see me. I'm the girl in the background. The average height, average weight twenty-something people look *through* instead of *at*.

I slip silently through the world without smiling. Without having to greet anyone for days at a time. It's been this way for the last six months. It's rare that I have to speak to strangers, but when I do it's perfunctory. Instinctively, people seem to know I'm not primed for small talk. Today is no exception.

"Here's your room key, Ms. Fredrich." The receptionist in Downtown Seattle's Marriott Hotel slides the plastic key card across the marble countertop. Once she's withdrawn her hand a safe distance, I reach out and palm it.

"Thank you." Eyes down, the receptionist staples my paperwork together. "So. Business or pleasure?" The warmth in her eyes dies when she looks up at me and registers my void expression—her smile slides away like butter from a hot knife.

"Business," I say, because nothing has ever been truer.

"Okay, well...I hope you enjoy your stay." She looks away as soon as she's done with her front desk script. She doesn't ask why I've turned up at her hotel with no bags or why I'm only booking in for one night. Nor does she ask why I've left a spare key card at the front desk for a Mr. Hanson. She isn't supposed to. Eli's given me a rundown of how this thing will play out, and so far, everything's going to plan. I lift my purse from the desk and head to the elevator, straightening my coat.

Twenty-two, twenty-one, twenty, nineteen, eighteen...

I watch the numbers light up one by one. Each disc, the size of a dollar coin, flares and darkens in turn, and the elevator descends while I wait, impatient and unblinking. Others wait for the car to arrive. If this were an office building or a shopping center, I'd take the stairs. Me and closed spaces? We're not friends. But since this hotel is forty-seven floors high, and I've booked a room on the forty-second floor, it looks like I'll have to tolerate the presence of strangers for a beat.

The doors slide back, and I walk in first, moving to the back of the car. I don't want the four businessmen who follow brushing past me as they exit. They're staying somewhere mid-level. It's easy to label them as mid-level guys. They're wearing mid-level-guy suits. All four of them have mid-level-guy haircuts. An accounting department booked their accommodation, and accounting departments don't spring for penthouses. They spring for twin rooms with en suites that have access to the gym and not much else. *No mini bar for you, Mr. Corporate.*

The lift doors roll closed, and I retreat within myself, pressing my back against the rear wall of the elevator. I close my eyes, exhale down my nose. This will all be over soon, but my heart still dances in my chest all the same. The fear of being trapped, of what I am about to do, is a coiled snake, wreaking havoc on my insides.

"Hey. You okay? You look a little freaked out."

One of them talks to me. He thinks my nerves are because of the elevator ride, which they are, but only partially. The guy has brown eyes—a warm color that reminds me of melted chocolate. He has dimples, too. Probably twenty-eight or so. Around my age. He looks nice. The kind of nice I might have dated once upon a time, before...well. Before dating became an impossibility.

I force myself to look at him. "I'm fine. Thanks."

"Good." The guy with chocolate eyes smiles. "Deep breathing sometimes helps my sister. She isn't a fan of elevators, either."

He's sweet. Way sweeter than I deserve considering my purpose here today. I reward him with a watery smile—he grins back—and then the doors open, and the four of them leave. I jam my hands into my pockets to stop them from shaking. I'm alone for eighteen floors (better than being trapped with four strangers, but still not great) and then finally it's my turn to alight.

This hotel is much like any other I've stayed in. The only thing that sets it apart from any other hotel, the thing that will forever define it, is my purpose for coming here today.

I'm about to have sex with a total stranger.

And I'm doing it to find my baby sister.

2

SLOANE

BY THE TIME I'M INSIDE AND I'VE HUNG my coat on the back of the door, I'm almost ready. I'm wearing what I've been told to wear: black lace. Eli, the private investigator I hired to find my sister, wasn't any more specific than that. He's the one who set this whole thing up.

"*Sometimes money just isn't enough to buy what you're looking for, sweetheart. Sometimes it takes a little more*... persuasion *to procure information like this. I tell you what. I'll share what I know in return for a little favor.*"

"*What kind of favor?*"

"*You spread your legs for a paying customer, and I'll*

tell you everything you need to know." The disgusting pig had actually *smiled*. The audacity. *"Oh, come now, Ms. Romera. Don't look at me like that. You want to find your sister, don't you?"*

And in the end, I'd agreed. He was right. I do want to find Lex. I want her home, safe and sound, and I'll do anything to make that happen. Even if I won't be able to live with myself afterward.

Aside from the lingerie, Eli told me to bring something else with me today. Something hidden in the pocket of my jacket. I take it out and put it on. The mask is a black satin, trimmed with blood-red lace edging. It makes me a feel a little more disguised, at least. I hit the bathroom light switch and rummage in my purse for my life raft. The bottle of Valium rattles when I pull it out. The thing about being a fifth-year resident at a large hospital is that there's *always* someone available to prescribe medication when you need it, no questions asked. The Valium isn't even in my name. It'll never appear on my medical record. I pop one—just enough to keep me calm. Not enough to make me drowsy—and then I peer into the mirror, fixing the mask's band underneath my hair.

You look like shit, Sloane.

I tell myself this every time I look into a mirror these days. Maybe it's true. Then again, maybe it isn't. I've been staring at myself in mirrors for so long now that my reflection doesn't make any sense anymore. Lex was always the beautiful one. Oh, sure, I know I have a nice body. Eli said that was the only reason he was willing to do business with me. Because my tits were real and I had a nice ass.

Your height might make some guys uncomfortable, but hey... not a lot you can do about that.

I focus on the dark rings under my eyes, trying to remember that this is all temporary. It isn't forever. I'm a medical student, after all. The body is just a machine, full of cogs and intricate parts all ticking away, working in harmony to keep you moving. Intercourse is a function of that machine, nothing more.

You can do this, Sloane. You can do this.

And then, not even two seconds later...

Lex wouldn't want this. She wouldn't want you used and abused, selling yourself for so little.

I hate that voice inside my head. It makes it so hard to justify going through with this, but I'm not auctioning off my most valuable possession for drugs or money, or even fame and fortune like some girls do. I am doing it out of love. Love for *Lex*. Any sister would do the same.

It's been six months and I'm still no closer to finding Alexis. This really *does* feel like my last resort. And Eli's smart. He's given me just enough information to keep my hope alive, but nowhere near enough to risk me backing out of our little arrangement.

Thud, thud, thud.

"Holy shh—" The door. I suck my bottom lip into my mouth, trapping the curse word behind my teeth. It's go time.

Mr. Hanson will have collected his key from the chirpy concierge downstairs, but I was told to expect the knock. Lets me know the guy I'm going to be sleeping with is here and I have to wait in the bathroom until he comes to get me. I pull the door closed, and for a second, I grapple with a wave of fear. If I lock myself in here and refuse to come out, how long will he wait until he gets pissed off and leaves? I can't do that, though. Eli will never hold up his end of the bargain, and besides, none of this matters. *None* of it. This is a means to an end.

An electronic beep sounds as a key card is accepted into the door. The rough catch of the lock sliding back follows. Then silence. The edge of the sink digs into the back of my legs as I lean against it, frozen, before I remember I shouldn't do that. It'll mark my body, and that's against the rules. Even temporary marks like that. My stranger wants me in perfect condition.

Thankfully the drugs begin to kick in as a flat sense of peace washes over me. A good thing, too, because whoever is out there takes their sweet time in making themselves at home. Without it, I'd have been on the verge of making a run for it by the time a knuckle raps against the door. "Come on out. Turn the light off first," a voice commands. It's gruff and full of gravel, maybe the voice of a smoker? Fucking great. I'm going to have to spend the next two hours with my tongue down a smoker's throat, and then I'm gonna have to bleach my mouth out. I turn the light off and open the door, and I'm perplexed by what I see beyond.

Nothing.

Absolutely nothing. The room is pitch black.

"Couldn't find the light switch?"

"Don't touch it. Just come here," the voice tells me. He sounds young enough, and he's alone. Not that I was expecting more than one guy, of course. Eli swore it would only be the one guy. And only this one time. I step gingerly into the room, wishing I'd paid more attention to where the furniture was positioned before I'd shut myself in the bathroom. I immediately stub my toe on God only knows what and hiss with pain.

"You okay?" There's an amused lilt to his voice, which is irritating. Who gets off on a girl breaking her toes?

"Well...I can't see a *thing*," I mutter.

"That's the point, I'm afraid. Come here."

If I knew where *here* was, I'd probably be a little less turned around. I try again, and this time I manage to stumble to the bed without colliding with anything else. The mattress dips as I climb onto it, wondering where the hell he is. I'm not half as scared as I should be. In fact, I feel almost a little giddy.

"Sit in the middle of the bed with your hands behind your back," he whispers. Is he going to tie me up? That thought should bother me. *Would* bother me any other time.

"Do you need a name?" Eli said I should ask.

A low rumble, deep and throaty, breaks the silence, and I realize he's laughing. "Are you offering to tell me your *real* name?"

"Eli said that's against the rules."

"Then, no." The mattress dips again. He's moving, coming closer. His hot breath grazes across the skin of my neck when he speaks. "I'm not gonna call you Melody or Candy or some other fake-ass name. We'll just be strangers for a while. That square with you?"

"Yeah, I—I guess."

In the darkness, my skin is alive. So are my other senses. My nose keeps on whispering to me, hints of mint and the ocean. Whoever he is, this guy smells incredible. Not a whiff of cigarettes on him at all, which means that voice…that voice is one hundred percent natural. I find myself curious about him in the most detached way.

"You done this before? Like this?" he asks me.

"Never." My breath actually catches in my throat.

I'm so spaced out that I can barely think straight, but the lack of lighting in the room is making my heart race. This guy could be a serial killer. He could still be a serial killer with the lights on, but at least I'd get the opportunity to see it in his eyes and run for my life.

Mystery Guy exhales, sending another warm breath across my chest. My nipples harden even though I'm not cold. I've never experienced that before. Never. Probably because I've never been this close to a guy before. "Place your hands in your lap," he tells me.

I do it, and jump a little when I feel his hand touch my leg.

"Scared?"

"No."

He laughs, and it's a cruel and wicked thing. His hand gently trails up my leg until he finds *my* hand, where his fingers curl around my wrist. "You're braver than most girls."

"You do this with a lot of girls?"

"Some."

Well, at least he's honest. He lifts up my hand, brings it toward himself, and stubble prickles against the sensitive skin on the inside of my wrist.

"You smell like flowers. What perfume do you wear?"

"Afresia," I tell him.

"It's clean. Not too heavy. I like it."

So glad you approve. I feel like giggling. His nose brushes against my wrist and then the soft touch of his lips follows soon after. The kiss is barely even there, soft and gentle, but I can read a lot from it. His lips are full, and he's gentle with his mouth. That's unexpected. I fidget on the bed, wondering where this is going. Where his *mouth* will be going next.

"Have you ever thought about what it would be like to be blind?" he rumbles.

"Why? Are *you* blind?"

"No. Answer the question."

"I suppose so. Sometimes."

He guides my hand upward and takes it in both of his, uncurling my fingers so that my palm is open. He does it slowly, running calloused fingers down the length of my own, and I can't help but shiver. It's a simple thing, but the way he does it feels intimate and considered, not just grabbing and touching for the hell of it. I hold my breath as he guides my hand again, until my fingertips meet his hair, and then down to his face.

"Tell me what you think I look like," he says, his voice a resonating growl. He lets go of my hand, and I have to lean forward to reach him properly. I shimmy closer, tucking my legs under my butt so I can balance properly, and then I raise my other hand to his face, too.

His hair is short, a little stiff from his styling product. His facial features are strong. Pronounced. Jaw's a little square, nose mostly straight apart from a slightly flattened part near the ridge of his brow. His eyelashes are surprisingly long, and his lips...I was right. His lips are full and way softer than any guy's lips have a right to be. Especially a guy with a voice like his. From the tingling pads of my fingers, I can sense this guy has the face of an angel. A barbaric one—maybe like one of those guys who did a lot of smiting back in Babylon.

"What do you think?" he asks.

"You're probably very attractive," I admit.

He grunts. "And what about the rest of me?"

He applies a little pressure to my forearms so that they travel down to his chest, where my fingers meet with smooth skin and hard-packed, rippling muscle. His pecs twitch as my hands brush lightly over them, and then downward. I come across three horizontal ridges in his skin that shouldn't be there, to the right of his abs spaced a couple of inches apart, and my fingers draw circles over them, trying to tease their story from them, trying to figure out where they came from. There's an untold history of violence here, written in the planes of his formidable body. He twitches a little as I explore him, probing with a feather-light touch until I've traced my way across his washboard stomach and up over his obliques. He sucks in a sharp breath and tenses when I do that, and I smile a little. I actually smile. This guy's ticklish. He doesn't laugh or tell me not to touch him there, but his body tightens further still when I go over the area one more time to test the theory.

I move up to his shoulders, which are powerful and strong, and I lace my arms around the back of his neck, feeling over his shoulder blades. He's huge, but I'm not really afraid of him. Of course I should be, yes, but I'm not. The Valium has flattened out my fear, and besides, the way I'd imagined this, the guy was going to come in here and want to lay his hands on me. He'd poke and prod and examine every inch of me, and he'd most definitely want to see what he was paying for. So far, this guy has touched me sparingly, and that was *on the hand.*

"Well?" he asks.

"Where did the scars come from?"

"I was stabbed." He just comes right out and says it. Wow.

"Did you nearly die?"

"Yes."

"Did it hurt?"

"Yes."

I let my hands fall from his shoulders and find the scars again, one, two, three of them. They feel jagged and terrible under my fingers. "What happened to the person who did this to you?" I almost don't want to ask. Mystery Man's been unnervingly candid since we began this interaction five minutes ago, and I'm afraid his answer will finally put the fear of God into me.

"He got what was coming to him," he says softly. The bedsheets rustle when he moves, his stomach muscles contracting under my hands. When he touches my hair, tangling his fingers into it, I'm still trying to decide whether he means he killed whoever did that to him.

"I'm very particular about what I want. Do what I ask without question and this will go nicely for both of us, okay?" he breathes.

A shot of adrenaline finally lights up my nerve endings—an appropriate reaction to my situation. What the hell have I gotten myself into here? Valium or no Valium, I know that sounded like a threat. I'm in way over my head, but there's little I can do about it. Besides. Alexis. *Always* Alexis. "I can do that," I whisper.

"Good. Lie on your back."

I let go of him, and suddenly I feel like I'm afloat in the middle of an ocean, drowning, with no way of saving myself. The smart part of my brain—the part still focused on self-preservation—screams that I should get the hell out of here, and for the first time the wrath of Eli almost isn't enough to keep me pinned to the bed. But the thought of finding Alexis is. My muscles are jumping, ready to explode into action, when the guy gently takes hold of my right ankle.

"Did you touch yourself today?"

"Do...do you mean—" I'm no fool. I *know* what he means.

"Have you made yourself come today? Have you played with your pussy?"

Heat flares in my cheeks. No one has ever asked me that before. "No. No, I—I haven't," I stammer.

"Good. Then you'll taste so much sweeter." Rather than hooking his fingers under the waistband of my panties and pulling them down, he draws them to one side. My legs lock up when his hot breath skims over my exposed flesh. What am I supposed to be doing with my hands? This is untrodden ground for me in a very big way. When a guy gives you head, it's usually because he's done something very, very bad and needs to make up for it. At least, that's what Pippa says.

"Do you want me to lick you?" His voice is even deeper now, laden with the promise of sex.

"I want whatever you want," I gasp. That's what he's paying for, after all. That's what's going to help me get Lex back. He grips me hard around the top of my leg, squeezing until I cry out.

"We're not playing that game. Own me, or I'll own you. And trust me...you don't want that."

Shit. "Yes! I want you to lick me."

He makes a satisfied grunt and moves, pushing his way between my legs. When his tongue darts out and laps at me, my leg muscles tense up. It feels hot and… and *good*. What the holy hell? I shouldn't be reacting like this. Embarrassment prickles at my cheeks. What sort of person am I, enjoying a complete stranger giving me head? And under these circumstances? I can't help it, though. From head to toe, my body feels like it's being caressed.

His tongue moves expertly, applying a subtle pressure to my clit, stroking up and down in a rhythmic pattern that sends waves of heat crashing through me. I'm on the precipice of letting go, the tension in my arms and legs relaxing, when he stops lapping and *sucks*.

"Fuck!"

He doesn't stop. He growls when I push back against him, rocking into his mouth shamelessly. I've never felt anything like this before. It feels…incredible. I'm panting and moaning like an animal when he pulls away, running his hands from the very tops of my knees, down the insides of my thighs to my panties. He rips them off in one swift motion.

"How badly do you want me to fuck you?"

I'm not here because I want to fuck him. It's my job to make him *think* I do, yet the lines between acting and the truth are so blurred when I murmur, "Really badly. I want you really bad."

"Spread your legs," he commands. I spread them, wondering what's coming next. The room is like a black void, so dark I can't even make out the shadow of him as he moves around the bed. I hear a zip being undone and then the rattle of metal, like a buckle being unfastened. Sucking my bottom lip into my mouth, I wait for him to do whatever he's about to do, piqued with worrying curiosity. He restrains my left leg first, strapping something wide and tight around it and then affixing it to the bed. My right leg is next, and then he carefully does the same to my wrists. I'm star-fished on the bed and completely vulnerable. His restraints aren't the kind for show. They're the kind made to stop people from getting away, and I'm sure as hell not going anywhere. Six months ago, I might have said a prayer. Now, I whimper, half from fear, half from anticipation.

He climbs up onto the bed, kneeling at my side, his breath playing across me again. I tense when something cold and hard presses against my stomach. "Are you still a brave girl?"

"Yes," I exhale.

He doesn't tell me what he's going to do. The cool, sharp object pressing into my skin travels slowly upward until it's poised directly under my breasts. I gasp like a fish out of water, trying to keep still, because I know what he's holding now: It's a knife. A really fucking *sharp* one to boot.

He lifts my bra by the underwire in the middle, and then in a single, clean sweep, it springs apart, freeing my breasts. He cut through *my bra*? Exposed. Terrified. Exhilarated. *Confused.* I can't fucking think straight. My Mystery Man straddles me, and the material of his pants, rough, slides against my sides. He lays the flat, cool edge of his knife against my right nipple, sending a bolt of panic through me.

"Don't move," he whispers. I don't. I am the stillest still thing ever. He leans down and touches me, his hand finally finding my breast. "You're so fucking perfect," he breathes. "So well behaved." And then his mouth is on my nipple, licking and sucking, hotter than anything I've ever felt before. My back arches up off the bed, and he chuckles. "You want me inside you?"

"Yes."

"You sure? Be careful what you wish for."

I wish for death on a daily basis. I wish for pain and suffering and blood and misery upon the heads of those who took my sister. Wishing for this feels just as dangerous but somehow safer than all that at the same time. He wanted me to own him, and despite the fact that he's tied me up now, I still think that's what he wants. I brace, hoping this is the right thing, and I demand, "Do it. Fuck me now. Don't make me wait."

The knife vanishes. He shifts off the bed, and I hear

him undoing his pants, slipping them off. Panic sings through me again when I hear the rattle of another buckle.

"Ready?"

There's no backing out of it now. "I'm ready."

And he does something I hadn't even considered. Not even for a second. He threads a loop of leather over my head—his belt—and cinches it tight.

Oh, fuck. I'm in trouble now.

"Open your mouth."

"I—"

"*Do it.*" The tone of his voice is firm yet gentle at the same time. He brushes a hand down the side of my face. It's designed to be a reassuring gesture—*this is scary right now. Trust me.* But *trust* him? I'd be fucking *mad* to trust him. And yet I do what he tells me to. He pushes forward and guides his cock into my mouth. I have no experience in this arena. God, this is my first time at the fucking circus. What the hell I'm supposed to *do*? He's rock hard and tastes clean and slightly musky... and he's massive. He barely fits inside my mouth. I suspect only half of his length slides past my lips before he hits the back of my throat.

"Shit!" He hisses as I suck, forming a vacuum around him. I think I got that part right. His hips rock back, and he draws out of my mouth, causing a wet popping noise. "Still think you want me inside you?" He knows just how big he is. He's fucking *smug* about it. This is going to hurt like nothing else, but I don't want him to realize I'm a virgin. Even Eli doesn't know that part. I'm sure he would have charged this guy a whole lot more if he did, and that thought turns my stomach.

"Yes," I tell him. "Yes, I want you."

"Good. But you're gonna have to exercise a little patience first. We aren't done here." He fists a handful of my hair and lifts my head closer to him, and then he pushes back inside my mouth, thrusting in and out while applying a gentle pressure to the back of my head. I writhe on the bed, surprised by how much this turns me on. I'm floored when he tugs on the belt strap, though.

Floored.

Even in the dark, I see stars. I can't breathe with my windpipe cut off and his cock pulsing in and out of my mouth. "Stay with me, okay?" he grunts.

Fear and excitement pool in my stomach. It's the same kind of anticipation I experienced as a child, suspended over the drop of a roller coaster, only a thousand times worse. And a whole lot scarier. Between my legs, my pussy tightens as he works his hips back and forth, keeping just enough tension on the belt strap so that I can drag the tiniest amount of oxygen into my lungs.

He shivers as his erection turns granite hard. If he doesn't stop now, I think I know what will happen. But he *does* stop. Breathing heavily, he withdraws and crouches down beside the bed, easing his fingers beneath the belt and loosening it. His face is so close to mine, I can feel the intensity of his gaze as he stares at me in the dark. I still can't see a thing, but then maybe he has better night vision than I do.

"Your mouth is perfect," he whispers. And then he does two things that surprise me. First, reverently, he strokes my sweat-soaked skin, sweeping my hair out of my face. Second, he softly kisses my forehead.

"For being such a good girl, I'm going to make you come now," he breathes. A tremor of anticipation shimmers across my skin, and he chuckles. "You are being a *very* good girl."

He climbs up onto the bed and positions himself, hooking his arms underneath my hips, hoisting me up to meet him. The position is awkward with my ankles still bound to the bed, but all thoughts of my discomfort are forgotten when he buries his face between my legs and starts sucking on my clit again.

"*Ahh!*"

It's too much. I climb, ascending higher as an unfamiliar, unfathomable feeling builds between my legs. It unfurls in gentle pins and needles throughout my body, growing more and more intense. And then…

I'm screaming. A wordless release. I'd scream for God, but I doubt He would approve of this situation. I have no idea who this guy is, so I can't scream for *him*. I scream for myself and for the fireworks going off inside my head, the inferno licking over my skin, burning me out, leaving me hollow and spent. I fall slack, trembling as he continues to sweep his tongue over and over my clit.

"Stop! Oh my God, stop, please, that's so—sensitive!"

"Mm, so selfish." He hums into my pussy, making me clench. "Don't forget. It's *my* turn." He fiddles around for a moment—condom? Fuck, I hope that's a condom—and then he drops my hips and thrusts into me, hands tight on my pelvis, trapping me.

Oh…

My…

The pain is almost crippling. An uncomfortable feeling, a buildup of pressure and then a stinging release, lets me know that it's done.

He stops.

"What…?" He inhales deep. Exhales. "You probably shouldn't have kept that from me," he says softly. He sighs, then, as though he's disappointed in me, which is the most messed-up thing ever. "Are you ready?"

I whisper a faint response. "Yes."

"Try to relax." He fills me up, stretches me, makes

me whole. He starts off slow, gentler than I think he would have done if he hadn't just deflowered me. After a while, the pain subsides, gradually transforming until I no longer tense with every thrust but lean into it. By the end, he's fucking me like a freight train—unstoppable and raw with need. He comes so hard, he roars.

I don't, of course. It's my first time, and the pain outweighed the pleasure. My mind is too fogged to understand what's going on as he climbs off me and slides down my body. His lips caress the inside of my thigh, and I shiver as his fingers carefully stroke over my core. The touch isn't designed to excite me—it's more of an apology. Moving around in the dark, he unshackles my wrists and my ankles.

"You enjoy that?" The bass of his voice makes my legs press together.

"Yeah, I—I did." The most startling thing, the thing that makes me most sick, is that I'm telling the truth. What the hell is wrong with me?

He grunts, unthreading his belt from around my neck. The release of pressure makes me feel like I'm floating two feet off the bed.

I lay very still as he packs up his things. I sense him next to me pulling on his clothes. Then, when he's dressed, he stands beside the bed. He brushes his fingertips against my cheek again, so soft it's not a touch at all.

"Be seeing you." He heads for the door, and the light from the hallway nearly splits my skull apart when he opens it. And there my mystery man pauses, and I catch the one and only glimpse of him I ever get. Wearing a worn leather jacket, his back to me, a black duffel bag in his right hand, he tips his head down to his shoulder. He doesn't look back at me. He hovers there long enough for me to make out the silhouette of his profile, his dark, mussed hair, the bruised pout to his full lips.

And then he goes.

I never find out his name.

3

SLOANE

ELI ISN'T ANSWERING HIS PHONE. I'VE been calling for three days, and Eli—lying, manipulative, disgusting Eli—isn't answering his phone. I've only been to his PI office once—a dark, depressing studio above a liquor store in Rainier Valley that stank of stale Chinese food. But I've been losing my shit since I left that hotel room, and I can't take it anymore. I've skipped rounds at the hospital this morning and trekked all the way across the city to find out what the hell is going on.

You're a stupid fool. He tricked you. You slept with a complete stranger, gave up a part of yourself you're never going to get back. Ever. And now what?

And now what? I'll only have an answer to that question once I speak to Eli.

The stairs up to his office are slick with hard-packed ice. I navigate them with the greatest of care, holding my breath with each step. His piece-of-shit car is parked in the lot below, so I know he's here. I just don't know what I'm going to say to him. I can hardly threaten to go to the cops if he doesn't give me the information he promised me. That wouldn't work. I have zero proof that I have an arrangement with him, and besides, Eli's a private investigator. Would the police even take my word over his?

I go straight in, knowing that if I knock, I'll only chicken out and run. I start talking as soon I see the man sitting in his chair.

"What the hell, Eli? I've been call—" My tongue sticks to the roof of my mouth at the same time my brain shorts out. This...this can't be happening. "Oh...Oh, my God."

The smell hits me first. Oh God, the *smell*. I try to breathe in through my nose, but the air stings my sinuses. I cover my face with my hands, trying to process the scene in front of me. Eli was a large man before, but now his distended stomach has bloated to obscene proportions, pressed up against his desk. As an intern, I've witnessed the same thing before, primarily in the morgue. *Bloating*. All of that gas and bacteria wants out, and by the looks of things, it'll have its way sooner rather than later.

Eli hasn't been answering my phone calls for the past three days because he's dead. His office looks like someone went on a rampage in here. Blood covers the walls and his desk. It's crusted and dried in the stained carpet. Eli's mouth hangs open in a grim yawn, his eyes rolled back in his head. His skin is a sickly gray color everywhere apart from his hands. They rest on his desk, his fingers tinged purple-black by all of the blood coagulated in his palms.

My tears fall thick and fast, but I regain control of myself enough to enter the room properly and stand in front of the man who cheated me out of my virginity. I'm not crying because I feel bad that Eli's dead. Call me cold, but I'm *glad* he's been stabbed to death with his own letter opener (still sticking out of his chest). I'm crying because he's dead. Now, he'll never be able to tell me where Alexis is. I'll never know if he was telling the truth. If she's even alive.

But it can't be over just like that. It *can't*. There has to be something here, some way of figuring out whatever he was going to tell me. My mind locks up as I realize what I'm going to have to do. I've seen far more horrific things than Eli's dead body, but it isn't his appearance that makes me feel like passing out. It's my anger. I'm *so* angry, *so* cheated, *so* furious that

I'm scared of what I might do if I have to go near him. He's already dead. I couldn't be arrested for stabbing him again, but still...

I don't want the dead man's blood on my hands.

I suck in a lungful of air and hold it, then take a small step forward. I just need to get through this. For Alexis. This is *all* for Alexis. Maybe Eli kept the information in a file somewhere. That's something a regular personal investigator would do, surely? Eli was more than a PI, though. He was a drug-dealing pimp, too. Admin probably wasn't very high on his list of priorities. My head spins as I pick my way through the devastation of his office, climbing over an upturned chair to reach the small, three-drawer filing cabinet. It's unlocked. The top draw is buckled and dented, as if someone took a crowbar to it. Inside, there are files. My heart soars when I yank open the middle drawer and find one labeled with my sister's name: Alexis Romera. Missing Person. With trembling fingers I take it out of the cabinet and almost sink to my knees. It's empty. There's nothing inside. Not a *single* sheet of paper.

"No, no, no, come on!"

The other files all have paperwork inside them. Regular information about bail bonds and cheating spouses. Only Lex's is empty. What the fuck? There are no papers on Eli's desk and none on the floor either.

No hidden drawers that could contain the information I'm looking for. It's gone. Someone's taken it, and I have no idea who. I suddenly can't hold it in anymore. The past three days take their toll at last. I throw up the piece of dry toast I ate for breakfast so violently that it strips my throat raw.

I sob as I leave Eli's office. I feel useless. Powerless. Weak.

"I'm sorry, Lex. I'm so fucking sorry." She can't hear me, but I say the words anyway. Admitting them out loud makes me own them instead of hiding them away, letting them burn me from the inside out. I've let her down. All hope of finding her is gone. The very worst part of acknowledging that is the relief. It courses through me like a single exhaled breath, rushing from my head to my feet. There's nothing more I can do. The responsibility is no longer mine.

I am the very worst of people. I don't even bother to report Eli's death.

I leave him there to rot.

4

ZETH

Two Years Later

"YOU'RE *SCANDALOUS*, ZETH MAYFAIR."

Lacey's laughter is grating the fuck outta me this morning. She's been riding me all morning about the two girls she caught me escorting out of the warehouse in the early hours. Cracking bad jokes. Making sly comments. The woman just doesn't know when to shut the hell up. We've been stuck in the car for the past twenty minutes, and sometimes, twenty minutes in an enclosed space with Lacey is tantamount to twenty minutes in hell.

"How 'bout we don't talk for the next while, huh, Lace?"

"How about you tell me what this guy's done, and I'll be quiet? That sounds like a fair trade."

Lacey's tiny. She was malnourished as a kid and didn't get the nutrients she needed to grow, which means her head barely hits me mid-chest. Her long, blond hair is straight as straight comes. Her eyes are pale cornflower blue. Combined with her fine features and high cheekbones, she looks positively angelic, but *I* know better. The girl crawled straight out of hell to test me.

I'd have left her at home today, but then again, she's not a fan of her own company. Bad shit goes down when she's left to her own devices, and a trip to the hospital is the last thing I need tonight. Not after I've done what I'm about to do.

"Matthew's been bad. That's all you need to know."

"When *isn't* Matthew bad?" Lace pouts. Apparently, she and Matty fucked a couple of times, back before she showed up at my doorstep like a stray cat and refused to leave. Since then, she's been focused on more delicate prey, namely the female of the species. Most times, I have to be careful about the chicks I bring back to the warehouse. I let 'em out of my sight for ten minutes, Lace'll have their panties around their ankles and her face buried between their thighs. The girl knows no bounds.

But anyway, I think she's still got some sort of grind for Matty. She went quiet for a moment when I told her where we were headed, and that doesn't happen too often.

"Just don't cause a scene, okay? Wait in the car like I told you. I'll be five minutes max." Truth is, even I don't have a clue what Matty's done. All I know is that I've been sent to pay him a visit, and that only happens when someone has grade-A fucked up.

Charlie isn't exactly a lenient man, but he only brings out his most expensive toys for his most expensive problems. Miss a payment on a loan? Charlie sends Sam out to relieve you of a few fingernails. Lose a shipment of coke with the equivalent street value of a five-bedroom house, and you get a visit from *me*. Horses for courses, that's what Charlie says.

We pull up outside Stanton Farm Markets, and I slam the gear stick into neutral. It's raining. Surprise sur-fucking-prise. Welcome to Seattle. The windshield turns opaque, blasted by raindrops as soon as the wipers quit. For a moment, it's just me and Lace inside our own little messed-up world. "You hear me, right? Stay in the car."

She gives me the three-finger Boy Scouts salute—the one that means she's feeling a hundred percent noncompliant but doesn't want to argue. "Gotcha, Boss Man."

She's called me that since the day I started paying her to launder my money for me. I could have hired the Vondys to wash my bills, but everyone hires the Vondys. One family having access to the financials for *every* crooked organization in the Pacific Northwest has never sat right with me. And besides, Lacey needed a purpose, even if it was an illegal one.

"Be right back." I jump out of the car, collect the black duffel from the back seat of the Camaro, and head into Stanton's without looking back. Doubt Lace will disobey me today, actually. The rain'll wreck her hair.

Inside, Archie Stanton, Matty's brother, stands behind the counter, double-bagging for an old woman with a stooped back and perfectly styled white hair. Probably a wig. He drops the bag when he sees me, tomatoes bouncing out onto the counter and rolling away.

"Matty ain't here today, Zeth. He's outta state with Cindy."

I ignore the kid. He's paid (barely) to keep the front-of-store charade respectable, believable, if you will, and that includes running interference when a member of the family's in trouble.

Looks like I'm expected.

I head straight for the swinging doors to the rear of the store, while Archie scrambles over the counter, green apron thrown over his shoulder. "Zeth, I mean it, man. Matty ain't here."

But when I slam through the office door hidden out back, Matty most definitely *is* here. His beat-up, junkie wife is on her knees, blowing him good. Her black-and-white striped dress is hiked up so high I can see her ass cheeks. The look of surprise on Matty's face is priceless. He's so stunned that it takes a second for him to slap Cindy's shoulder. Another two seconds for her head to stop bobbing.

"Put your dick away, Matty. We're having words." The last thing I need to see right after dinner is his fucking cock. I roll my eyes to the ceiling while he zips up. Cindy stands, one hand balancing herself on Matty's desk, the other hand tugging her dress down. Her eyes are bloodshot, totally vacant. In other words, she's baked.

"The fuck you think you're doing, Zeth?" she drawls. "You can't just barge in here whenever you fucking feel like it."

Her husband slaps the back of her leg—*crack!* "Watch it, bitch. Careful how you speak to my business associates." He might as well have thrown a bucket of water over her. A spark of life reignites in her eyes.

"Well, fuck *you*, Matty. I got better things to do than stand around defending you all day."

"You were on your knees if I recall. Now get out of here. Me and Zeth gotta talk." He either has no idea why I'm here or he's trying to ingratiate himself to me. It doesn't matter. There's no sweet-talking me. No point in brown-nosing. I curl a lip as Cindy storms out of the office. She shoulder barges me, and I raise an eyebrow at Matty.

"Bad attitude," I tell him.

"Bad everything," he replies. Matty and Cindy were like Bonnie and Clyde ten years ago, but now he's a two-bit womanizer and she's an addict. Matty still has his looks, though—the only reason Lacey looked at him twice. She's shallow like that. It's part of her charm. Matty leans back in his leather chair, eyeing me.

"You know why you've been given this ticket, Zeth?" he asks.

"Am I supposed to?"

Matty shrugs. "Most times, people know why they're killing a man."

So he *does* know why I'm here. Hardly surprising. You don't piss off Charlie to this degree without realizing you're gonna reap the consequences. "I'm not what you'd consider… *inner circle*. I get an address and a set of instructions, nothing more."

"And a suitcase full of cash, too, right?"

My turn to shrug. No point in being shy. "Right."

"Well, how 'bout I offer you two suitcases full'a cash instead, Zeth? Hire you to go right back where you came from and put an end to this once and for all?"

"You want to hire *me* to kill Charlie?"

"Why not?" Matty is one composed motherfucker. He's richer than God—the eighties might be long gone, but cocaine is still Seattle's drug of choice—and I doubt this is the first time he's offered to buy his way into someone's good graces. No doubt he's never had anyone tell him no before, though. See, the thing is I don't *have* good graces. And I don't need his money. I dump the duffel onto his desk. Unzip it. Pull out my go-to duster.

Matty's still not blinking. The fucker must have cast-iron balls. "I'm Charlie's man. You know that, Matt. Now, I have other jobs to get to tonight. Let's tidy up these loose ends, huh?"

The reason for Matty's calm appears in hand a split second later. The little shit's had a gun on me under his desk the whole time. Desert Eagle .50 caliber. Nice. He holds it up at shoulder height, arm straight out. "Shame you won't just do the job for me. Charlie's been running this place into the ground for years. Time for him to move on. And time *you* were leaving, Zeth. Okay?"

I've had a lot of guns aimed at me over the years. A man's intent is always right there, shining in his eyes, easy to read like the pages of a book. Some of them just wanna scare you enough that you back off. Some of them are so desperate to hide their own fear that they forget to make you believe they mean it. You *gotta* mean it. And some of them are sharks. Stone cold. People who've pulled the trigger countless times before and haven't thought twice.

Matty, the little fuck, is a shark.

I'd never have called it. I clench my fingers around the duster, staring down at my fist. Not much to do about it now. Things will play out the way they're meant to. "This is where you shoot me, then?"

"I guess," he answers.

Someone, somewhere, said something I felt compelled to have tattooed onto my chest when I was drunk once: *So it goes.* I know it was Billy Pilgrim from Vonnegut's *Slaughterhouse-Five* who said that, but I pretend that I don't. That would mean admitting I actually read something in high school before I dropped out. But never mind that. As the bullet zips through the air, I realize how absolutely fucking perfect that saying is. So it goes. There's something so inevitable about me getting shot here tonight. Something so obvious and unavoidable.

Pain ricochets through my body like a hot, white lance. The bullet hits me in the chest, two inches below my collarbone...and suffice it to say, it hurts like a bitch. Matty seems stunned that I'm still standing. If I were him, I'd have already shot me another five times and emptied the clip just to make sure I was dead. Fucker's gonna wish he had. I launch over the desk and grapple the gun from him, ripping it free from his grip.

"Big mistake, Matty. *Big* mistake." I smash my fist into his face with a brutal force. The crunch of metal crushing bone, skin and muscle separating, isn't something I ever get used to, but on occasions like this I allow myself to enjoy it a little. Just a little. We have to try to enjoy our work, after all, and pain always awakens my dark side.

Matty's head rolls back as I pound my fist into his face over and over and over again. My hands, T-shirt, jacket, jeans, everything is covered in blood by the time the guy falls slack. I laugh hysterically as blood bubbles form on his lips.

"It wasn't my fault," he mumbles. I've broken his teeth and his speech is distorted, but I get the gist. "You lock people inside a sealed shipping container for th-three days, they're gonna d-die, Zeth. How is that *my* fault?"

The burritos I ate an hour ago churn in my stomach. What the fuck is he talking about? I raise my fist to smash it into his mouth again, but… I can't. This is just fucking perfect. "What *people*?"

"The ones Charlie's been bringing in through the docklands. Girls. Girls in con...containers."

I let Matty go. *Girls in containers?* Charlie promised me two years ago that he didn't deal in girls. Drugs and guns, yeah, but he swore no skin trade. "What's he moving girls for?" I press my hand to my shoulder, wincing. My own pain is growing now that I'm not inflicting it on someone else.

"Why do you *think*?" Matty rasps. "He gets twenty grand a pop if he can prove they're still...still in... intact." He chokes on the blood welling in his mouth. It runs down his chin, dripping onto his ruined shirt.

"You're lying."

"I ain't," he says, and I believe him.

Fuck.

Charlie's the one who's been lying to me all this time. A part of me wants to believe this is a new development, but I know my boss. He's got a degree, a masters and a goddamned doctorate in lying. Especially when it comes to money. No way he'd pass up twenty grand for a nobody kid he could have snatched off the street. My head spins, disoriented from the pain radiating from my shoulder. Through the mist slowing down my mind, I still think it, though. *Was I right about the girl, then? Did Charlie take the girl's sister nearly three years ago?*

The first time I saw her, she was working a night

shift at the hospital. My sack of shit uncle had just been eighty-sixed—badly. The body wasn't supposed to be *found* after something like that—and it had been on me to identify the body. Well, what was left of it. I could tell Sloane was a broken bird. Beautiful in an understated way. Luminous brown eyes. Wavy brown hair. It was the fight in her eyes that had captured me, though. Captured and enthralled me in the space of ten seconds flat. We'd stood face-to-face in the corridor as she waited for the elevator, and her eyes had met mine. I felt like I was being gutted stem to sternum, and yet I knew she wasn't seeing me at all. She was seeing some distant horror that I could only guess at. And I didn't like guessing.

I'd made it my business to find out everything there was to know about her. That was when I'd discovered her sister had gone missing. Snatched off the side of the road, only twenty-one years old. Sloane's family were Christian to the core. Promise rings, hymns every Sunday, no cursing, no drinking, the whole nine yards. Except when her sister had been kidnapped, Sloane had stopped going to church. Didn't wear the cross I knew her mother had given her. She'd given up believing because it was just too hard to keep her faith alive when something so terrible had marred her life.

And then on top of everything else, and in keeping

with the truly vile motherfucker that I am, I'd taken her virginity. But that had been a mistake.

I'd found out Eli Harris was bribing her when he'd shown up to pay his dues to Charlie. Like everyone else in Seattle, he owed Holsan protection money. He'd been bragging about the trade he'd made with her as he'd settled his account. The sick bastard thought it was hilarious that he was about to sell Sloane to the highest bidder—a guy I knew from reputation alone. A guy who liked to beat his women black and blue while he screwed them. I'd paid big to take his place. Double Eli's month's protection money. Eli had told me she was no stranger to selling her body for information. That she enjoyed it. That *she'd* been the one who suggested the trade.

And I had no beef with sex workers. It was the most honest trade there was. Only Eli had fucking *lied*, hadn't he. Of *course* he fucking had. The woman had never even been *touched* by a guy before. Eli had manipulated her into the deal, as he'd manipulated me into believing the arrangement was something it was not, and I had taken Sloane Romera's virginity as a result.

That was on me. But it had *also* been on Eli…and, oh *boy*, he had paid for that lie.

Before he died, I'd made him spill everything he'd known about Alexis Romera's disappearance. The pimp had said it was Charlie all along. I hadn't believed him, but I'd still confronted my boss about it. Charlie had been mortally offended that I'd even suggested such a thing.

You know me better than that, son. I'm signed up for some questionable dealings, but I ain't interested in pussy. Karma on that shit's too raw, now go on. Get the fuck out my face.

I'd had my one night with Sloane and then severed all ties. Left her with no way of knowing what Eli was promising to tell her. It had been harsh, yeah, sure, since she'd carried out her end of the bargain and never gotten the lead she was after. But fuck, I'd at least made sure she'd enjoyed it. Made sure she wouldn't have nightmares about my face every second she closed her eyes. I could have just walked away. Left her in that hotel room still a virgin, unspoiled. But then again, I couldn't have, could I? I hadn't *known* she was a virgin. By the time I'd figured that out, it had been too fucking late.

"You're sure about this?" I tighten my grip around Matty's neck, and his eyes damn near bug out of his head.

"Yeah, man! Yeah, I'm sure!"

Screw you, Charlie. I stoop and pick up the piece from off the floor where Matty dropped it. Desert Eagle. I don't usually kill with guns, but sometimes, for a work of art, you've just gotta make an exception.

"Zeth! Zeth, man, don't! I'm sorry, okay? I'm—I'm sorry I shot you!"

Begging makes me feel queasy. I do it. I pull the trigger and Matty's head kicks back like a Rock'em Sock'em robot, except there's blood. A whole lot of blood and fragments of bone, like little pieces of smashed porcelain.

"Why am I right all the time?"

I turn and there is Lacey in the doorway, the heel of her right palm pressed into her sternum. She's soaked to the skin and panting.

"Lacey—"

"Don't worry about it," she tells me. "I already knew." She stumbles into the room and looks down on Matty, eyebrows banked together, mouth drawn down in a confused pout. I'd like to think this is her first dead body, only I know better. She faces me. Holds her hand out. "Come on. Let's get you to the hospital."

I don't take her hand. "No. Not the hospital. I'm not going there."

I won't risk seeing Sloane again. Not until I hear the truth come out of Charlie's mouth. Even if I have to beat it out of him, I *will* learn the truth.

5

SLOANE

"TEN CCS OF EPINEPHRINE. CALL AHEAD to the OR, let them know we're coming up."

"Yeah, I... I got it."

I look up and the skinny intern with the bad haircut is still standing there, staring at the guy bleeding out on the gurney in front of him. *The guy I'm buried wrist-deep inside.* "What are you waiting for? RUN!"

The fresh intake of interns is always a nightmare. They're so green they're absolutely no use to anyone, and yet in between the severed limbs, and the gunshot victims, and the world falling down around our heads, we are supposed to teach them how to fix people. *I'm* supposed to teach them, which is insane because I've only just learned how to do all of this myself.

"He's crashing, Dr. Romera. Adrenaline?" the nurse asks. Adrenaline is the last thing this guy needs. His heart is already near spent as it is. What he needs is the gaping hole in his stomach to be repaired. God knows how many of his internal organs are shredded in there. I'm not going to know until I can open him up properly and clear out all of the blood. Right now, I can't tell a damn thing other than the fact that this guy is going to die unless we do something. And *soon*.

"Let's just get him in the elevator," I tell the nurse. She nods, unlocks the gurney wheels, and is barking orders at her team without even blinking. Grace is a pro. She'd probably be able to save this guy all on her own if she had to. Half the nurses in this hospital probably could if push came to shove. They're all massively undervalued, underpaid, overworked.

Bodies hustle as we guide the gurney to the elevator, my hands still lodged inside the patient. I bounce on the balls of my feet while we watch the numbers count down. I'm not fazed by elevators anymore. Too many trips like this have desensitized me to the cramped space. The hospital's only four stories high, and yet it seems to take an eternity for the damn doors to slide open. Eventually they part and then we're racing against time again.

"Inside, inside! Move!" The intern I sent to warn the OR, Mikey, I think he's called, makes it just in time to catch the doors. "They know we're coming?"

"Yeah."

"He's coding, Dr. Romera." Grace says this as the heart rate and BP monitors start screaming. I pull my hands out of the guy and grab Mikey, shoving him toward the patient.

"Hold him together."

Mikey looks like a rabbit in the headlights when I gesture to the patient's wound. "Wh-what do you mean?"

I take both his hands and place them where I need them. *"I mean hold this guy's fucking intestines inside his body!"*

Mikey may or may not obey the command. I don't waste any more time. I lean as far as I can over the patient and start compressing his chest.

One, two, three, four, five…

The powers that be decided a while back that you don't need to give an arresting patient any breaths. Keeping the heart pumping is the number one priority here. Grace is on it, anyway. She starts bagging him, forcing regular gusts of oxygen into his lungs, and I grunt over my work.

The doors open again.

"Okay, let's move." I can't compress and run at the

same time, so I hop up onto the foot rail at the bottom of the gurney and hitch a ride to the OR. I used to see doctors do this back when I was as green as Mikey, and I could never picture myself composed enough to be that person. A lot's changed over the past four years, though.

Lex's disappearance, trying to find her, has changed me so dramatically that I'm not the same person I was back then. I'm the kind of person I need to be to excel at this instead. Cold. Calculating. I don't buckle under pressure. I get things done. It all started back in that hotel room. I traded a part of myself that night. Extinguished the part of myself that would have prevented me from doing what had to be done.

The very first surgery I performed was on *myself*. I carved out my weakness with a rusty scalpel and reveled in the glorious void that remained afterward.

The nursing team are already waiting by the time we reach OR three. I've been keeping our as yet unidentified patient alive for two hundred fifteen seconds. Time is running out. Dr. Massey is scrubbed and ready to go when we reach the sterile anteroom between the corridor and the OR. Massey's good, a gun with trauma. I'm almost grin with relief when I see his face.

"No ID, MVA, unknown internal injuries. BP tanked between ground floor and level two." Massey nods, face obscured behind his mask, but his eyes are steady. They say he's got this.

"Go scrub, then get your ass in here. This looks like a job for two pairs of hands." The OR nurses take charge of the gurney and disappear through the double doors with my patient. *My* patient. When you've had your hands inside a person, whether they live or die, they become your responsibility.

"Hot damn." Mikey stands next to me, blood mottling his nitrile gloves, soaking his scrubs. It looks like he just went on a killing spree. "That was intense."

"That was *sloppy*," I correct him. "You can't freeze like that, Mikey. You hesitate, you cost someone their life." I feel like I've just kicked a puppy. Mikey's probably only three years younger than me, but in our reality, three years' worth of experience is a lifetime. Him giving me the sad-eye treatment isn't going to earn him an easy ride with me, though. We aren't allowed feelings like remorse. Remorse means we did something wrong, or we didn't do enough. There's no room for wrong or not enough in this hospital.

"Are you going to save him?" Mikey asks.

Can I do it? Can I do for this patient what I couldn't do for my own sister? I tell Mikey the same thing I tell myself each morning before I even set foot inside the hospital.

"I'm gonna try. I'm gonna do my best."

6

SLOANE

WE LOSE HIM.

Sometimes, no matter how much blood, sweat, and tears you pour into someone, your best just isn't good enough. Gary Saunders, twenty-seven, bleeds out on the table, while Dr. Massey and I battle to save him. His internal organs were minced, though, and sometimes that's all there is to it. I've learned to accept outcomes like this. I feel no guilt. I'm a human being, capable of only so much. People forget when they walk through these doors that they're putting their trust in mere mortals. I am not God. I'm not even close to a miracle worker. Some days, there are people you can save, and those are the lucky days. The good days that make it feel like the sun is shining that little bit brighter. But then there are the shitty days, too. Days like today.

I'm in charge of telling Gary's pregnant wife that he's dead. I get landed with this job a lot. My colleagues think I have a skill for breaking terrible news, when really I'm just the same as any of them. It still hurts like hell. The difference between me and them is that I can distance myself from the pain. I'm an expert at distancing myself from pain. If it were an Olympic sport, I'd be a gold medalist. I head to the family room and knock quietly at the door. Inside, a brunette woman with a swollen belly twists in her seat, and my stomach bottoms out. The chart I'm carrying crashes on the floor.

"Lex? *Alexis?*" I realize my mistake a split second after the name tumbles out of my mouth. It isn't her.

This woman is older than Lex would be now. Her eyes are a different shade of brown—slightly lighter, bordering on hazel. She frowns at me. "Do I know you?"

"No, no. Sorry. For a moment I thought you were someone else."

"That's okay. I'm just glad to see another member of the human race. I've been waiting here for hours. No one'll tell me anything. Can I go see Gary now? He's going to be so mad if he has to miss work. He's never taken a sick day in his life." She's rambling. The smile makes a lot of sense—she's plastered it on to keep from crying alone in a this strange room. She can act as easy breezy as she wants, though. She knows. Or she at least *suspects*.

"I'm sorry, Mrs. Saunders. Could I sit with you for a moment?" The charade crumbles. When she slumps back into her seat, she's already entered the first stage of grief: denial.

"No. No, they said he was going to be fine. You've made a mistake. Please...can you go and make sure you're supposed to be here?"

I'm the Grim Reaper. A physical representation of death. My face is one they will forever associate with the worst news they are ever likely to receive. "My name is Dr. Romera, Mrs. Saunders." I close the door behind me, sealing us into the room. "I'm one of the doctors who operated on your husband. I'm afraid I *am* supposed to be here. I'm so sorry, but Gary didn't make it."

7

ZETH

CHARLIE LEFT ENGLAND BACK IN THE eighties, but thirty years hasn't dampened his cockney accent. It took me a long time to figure out what the hell he was saying when I first met him, but now, I understand him perfectly.

"D'you need me to clear out your ears for you, boy? I 'ate 'avin' to repeat myself. My import-export business ain't any of your concern."

Sitting behind his imposing monstrosity of a desk, it's easy to see how he scares the crap out of the younger guys. Even the older guys. He looks like a pumped-up Robert De Niro, except his presence is far more intense. He's in his late sixties but the guy still fucks anything that moves, still snorts anything vaguely white and powdery, and still kills anybody who looks at him sideways. He brought me into this world of violence, though, so it's not in me to be intimidated by him.

It's been three weeks since Matty. Three weeks since I had a slug yanked out of my shoulder by some bumbling moron who was too scared to even look me in the eye. Three weeks that I've had to recover and do a little snooping.

"I didn't even know you had an import-export business, Charlie. Thought you bought your product from the Locklands. The Black Talons when you had to?"

He opens the drawer to his desk and pulls out a small wooden box with a fleur-de-lis engraved into the lid. That box is a childhood relic to me. Charlie used to sit me on his knee and teach me how to roll smokes for him. He's always kept his stash in that box. He hasn't asked me to roll for him since I was ten, though. Twenty-three years have passed since then.

"There are plenty of things about my business you ain't privy to, Zeth. That ain't your fault, I know. When I took you under my wing, I watched you for years, thinking to myself, where will this small boy fit best into my organization when he sprouts hairs on his balls? I watched. I took note, d'in' I?

"If you'd displayed even the slightest scrap of

business sense, I would'a 'ad you involved in that side of things, and you'd know all about my side projects. Everything else pertainin' therein. But that ain't what I saw in you, Zeth, is it? I saw that you were a savage little shit wiv a nasty temper, and I found other uses for you. Other uses that have funded your escapades for quite some time now."

The message is clear: Don't bite the hand that feeds you. Charlie's always liked idioms. Don't shit where you eat. Never look a gift horse in the mouth. You get the picture. I keep my voice low when I respond. "I appreciate everything you've done for me, Charlie. You know that's not what this is about."

He finishes rolling his smoke. Popping it into his mouth, he purses his lips, drawing it out and sealing the handmade. When he lights it, the sickly-sweet stink of the Mary Jane he laces his tobacco with clouds the room. He holds the smoke in his lungs before exhaling, fixing me with razor-sharp, ice-blue eyes. "Then what exactly *is* this about?"

"It's about girls. Kidnapping and selling girls, taking them from their homes."

"I never had you pegged as the sentimental type, Zeth."

"Not sentimental. Just not a monster."

That puts a shit-eating grin on his face. "We both know that you *are*, in fact, a monster."

Maybe that's true, but even I have boundaries. Selling girls for sex most definitely crosses the line in my book. "Just tell me the truth. Was Matty for real when he said you had a fucking shipping container of dead girls roll into harbor?"

Charlie plucks a flake of tobacco from his tongue. Flicks it away. "If you insist on knowing the truth, then yes, okay. Seventeen dead hookers. I had to pay off the port authority to make them disappear. Very messy business."

Even though I'd known it was true before he'd confirmed it, a small part of me had hoped otherwise. I explode out of my chair. It kicks back and falls to the floor with a clatter. Charlie watches my reaction with a blank expression.

"You fucking *lied* to me."

"Am I beholden to you, Zeth?" He asks the question so calmly.

I clench my jaw. "No."

"Do I owe you anything at all?"

"No."

"Then why do you presume that I would submit to this kind of questioning? From *you*? You weren't right in the 'ead when you asked me 'bout the girls last time. You had that fucked-up"—he waves his hand in my general direction, grimacing—"bloodlust in your eyes that you only get when there's something stuck a mile up your ass."

"You had a girl kidnapped. A girl from Seattle, two and a half years ago. Where is she now?" I brace myself by my fingertips against Charlie's desk. I'm doing everything in my power to hold back the wild creature inside of me that's just *begging* to mess him up. Charlie smiles a benevolent smile, like my anger is endearing. Like I'm a puppy baring his teeth. Fucker.

"I don't take locals. And I don't shit where I eat, you know that."

See.

"I thought I knew a lot of things about you. Looks like I was wrong."

"What d'you care 'bout some fuckin' girl that got snatched two and a half years ago, anyway?" He flicks his cigarette into the crystal ashtray that forms the monstrous centerpiece of his desk.

"She doesn't mean anything to me."

"But she means something to someone else, right? That little slut you been shacked up wiv the past little while?"

He knows about Lacey, but he's never mentioned her before. She's too far below him to even be on his radar. "No. This has got nothing to do with her."

Charlie grunts. "Well, either way, I can't 'elp you,

son. I don't know nothin' 'bout some missin' hooker. I'd forget all about 'er if I were you. Sounds to me like you bin carrying this 'round wiv you the past two years. You carry it 'round much longer, I think maybe you and I are gonna develop a little bit of a problem."

I tilt my head to one side, considering the dangerous look on Charlie's face. Oh, we've already developed a problem. He just doesn't know it yet.

8

ZETH

I'VE GOT FIFTEEN MINUTES TO GET HOME before Lacey officially freaks the fuck out. I've been gone all day today waiting to speak to Charlie—the first time I've seen him since Matty laid me up with a gunshot wound—and my codependent houseguest became even more codependent during that time. Like, forget the co. She's just dependent. I'm only just starting to graze the surface on the girl's backstory. She's told me some dark shit that went down in her household as a kid, but I know there's more. She had it way worse than me. Fucked as it may sound to me now, she didn't get lucky like I did. Charlie is a hateful, evil son of a bitch every day of the week that ends in a Y, but he saved me. I'd be dead right now if he hadn't taken me from my uncle when I was six.

You know your problems are bad when you wish a psychotic, drug-pushing Englishman had come to your rescue as an impressionable youth. I don't know if Lace *does* wish for that, though. All I know is that she gets fucking crazy when I leave the warehouse for too long. Jesus If I could go back in time, say, fifteen months and have a conversation with past me, past me would shank me in the ribs for going so damn soft. I mean, shit. I'm rushing home for a woman. And I'm not even fucking her.

Lacey's phone rings out every time I call, and that makes my palms sweat like a rapist sent down the line at Chino. I did a stint in Chino one time. Let's just say I saw firsthand what happens to guys who force themselves on others. Women, kids, animals, doesn't matter. A rapist in a prison like that is a man living on borrowed time.

"Come on. Fuck, Lacey. Pick up the goddamn phone." She *doesn't* pick up the phone. Why the fuck did I even bother giving her the damned thing? I break every speed limit and run every red on my way home, gunning the Camaro's engine to the hilt. It's raining when I finally arrive. The warehouse is a two-story fortress, silhouetted and daunting in the storm-colored evening. The huge steel doorway, covered in blistered red paint, is locked and chained like I left it, but Lace has a key. She could have left if she wanted to. The thumping music coming from inside tells me she hasn't gone anywhere, though. Maybe that's why she didn't hear her phone.

Hope. Hope is a nasty little bitch.

I know I've fucked up as soon as I step through the door. The place is trashed. Broken furniture lies discarded like kindling on the floor. The TV is smashed but still works well enough to produce skull-splitting white noise and a fuzzy, distorted screen. There are shattered beer bottles all over the place and clothes absolutely everywhere, both mine and Lacey's. Shit.

"Lacey! LACE, WHAT THE FUCK?" I charge from the main living space into my bedroom. She hides in my bed sometimes when she's really struggling. I'm never in it, you feel, but sometimes she says it makes her feel safe. She's not in my bed, however. She isn't in hers, either. It's full-blown panic stations when I find her in the bathroom.

She's gone and done it a-fucking-gain.

Her skin is blue and waxy. She floats, fully stretched out in the tub, the overflowing water a deep, offensive shade of crimson. I jump in feet first, dragging her limp body out with me. She weighs nothing at all, so lifeless in my arms.

"Fuck you, Lacey. Fucking fuck you."

She's fucking *mangled* her wrists. I wrap her up in her blanket and dump her ass in the passenger seat of the Camaro, and then I drive. I drive her to the one place on the face of this planet I really don't want to go. The place I refused to go when I was in trouble myself.

St. Peter's Mission of Mercy Hospital.

9

SLOANE

COAT? CHECK.

Purse? Check.

Car keys? Check.

Twenty-hours after the shift from hell began and it finally looks like it's ending. I always feel like a fraud when I put my civilian clothes back on. Like I'm only pretending to be a functional member of society. Someone who shops at The Gap and remembers to color-coordinate their jacket to their handbag. I'm most at home in my scrubs, but people tend to look at you funny if you do your grocery shopping in a pair of blues.

"Night, Sloane. You working tomorrow?" Jerry, one

of the orderlies, is here almost as much as I am. He's a young guy, twenty-two perhaps, with a growing family to feed. Works every hour God sends.

"Sure am, Jer. Catch you for some coffee?"

He grins. "Count on it. I'll need it after tonight."

I'm within sight of the exit when I start to get nervous. This is where it always happens. The fourteen-foot stretch between the reception and the entrance is like some kind of magical hot spot. Nine times out of ten, something or someone will charge through that door while I'm heading for the exit, and I end up having to turn right back around.

Ten feet.

Five feet.

I hold my breath.

I'm at the door. Seattle's autumn wind buffets me, whipping my hair up as the doors slide back to reveal a clear night sky beyond, a bruised shade of royal blue. I breathe a sigh of relief. I did it. I'm free and clear for a whole seven hours. I'm going to spend every single one of those seven hours in bed. It's going to be amazing.

I'm in my car, pulling out of the parking lot, when a souped-up black Camaro screeches around the corner, nearly colliding head-on with me. Shit. Brakes. Brakes! *BRAKES!* We both swerve, and the asshole buzzes my paintwork. The Camaro's horn blares as they speed on by.

I can't see whoever's at the wheel, but they're panicking. There's only one reason a car would tear at breakneck speed into a hospital lot, and that's because there's an emergency. I reverse so hard my tires smoke.

The Camaro roars up to the sliding doors I just left behind, and a wave of regret washes over me. I might as well kiss those seven hours goodbye. Damn it, *why* am I such a glutton for punishment?

Thirty seconds later, I'm parked and back inside the building. A nurse is calling for assistance over the PA system, and a guy dressed in black hunches over a child on the floor. A blood-soaked blanket lies abandoned by his side. He slaps the child, the little girl, in the face, and I drop down beside him, not thinking. Grabbing him by his wrist. I shove him hard enough that he topples sideways and lands on his ass.

"Move away from her. Let me see."

He makes a choking, guttural sound as I quickly assess the little girl. She's not as young as I first thought, but she's tiny. Her pale blond hair is dyed pink with blood. The insides of her wrists are torn to shreds, and it takes me a full second to compose myself. She really meant it when she did this to herself.

"How much blood did she lose?" I check her pulse, bending down to place my ear over her mouth. Any breathing sounds? Faint but there. Pulse is thready but present, too. I look up, still waiting on my answer.

The guy who brought the girl in is propped up by his elbows, staring at me with his mouth open. His eyes are huge, the color so dark it's almost black. Looks like he's in shock.

"Listen, I really need to know how much blood she's lost," I tell him.

"I—I don't know. She was in the bath." He whispers the words so quietly I can barely hear him. The front of his T-shirt clings to him, hugging his chest. So he found her in the tub, went in and fished her out. Suresh Patel, one of the on-call doctors, arrives on scene a second later and we get the girl onto a gurney. Her body temp is low, her stats uneven. She's a coin toss at best.

I'm sucked back into the hospital as I work over the small woman. Hours pass. We replace liters of blood and end up having to wrap the girl in four blankets before she finally picks up enough for us to attempt surgery to fix the mess she's made of her wrists.

It's five in the morning by the time I go looking for the guy who brought her in. I find him sitting in a corridor, elbows resting on his knees, head resting in his hands. He looks up and sees me, and then does the damnedest thing: He gets up and starts to walk away. Fast.

"Excuse me. Hey!" He stops but doesn't turn around straightaway. He waits a beat, like he's building up to it. "I need some details from you about your girlfriend. You can't just leave her here to wake up alone."

Finally, he turns. His jaw is clenched so tight the veins in his temples throb with the flow of his pulse. He just stares at me. His shirt has dried out now, but it's still clinging to him in the most distracting fashion, the arms of the material rolled up one turn to reveal strong, tattoo-covered biceps. Ink in black and blue and red surges down his arms in waves. His almost-black hair is spiked every which way, tousled, still wet. Delectable. I kick my own ass when I realize I'm checking him out.

You're mad *at him, Sloane, remember? He was just leaving. Going to walk right out of the door.*

"You think you can at least give us *some* history before you vanish into the sunset? Or sunrise," I say. He blinks at me, then folds his arms across his chest. He opens his mouth to say something but stops himself. Scowls. He turns toward the door, clearly still thinking about bolting. Bastard.

"On second thought, if this is because of you, then maybe you *should* go," I say. There are no bruises on the girl's body, but I've seen enough cases of domestic violence to know that it's not always physical. A broken spirit can be just as damaging as a broken bone. This guy could have made his girlfriend's life so miserable that she simply wanted to end it. The scars on her arms tell a story, too. This wasn't the first time she's tried this.

Tall, Dark, and Handsome glares at me with a fury that makes me rethink my suggestion. He faces me properly, like he's committing to sticking around now, and finally speaks. "No," he growls. "I'm not her boyfriend. And I'm not leaving her."

My stomach lurches. That...

That *voice*.

Holy...

I press my finger to my lips, scrutinizing every last square millimeter of him. "Do I know you?" I whisper.

A cruel smile pulls at the corner of his mouth. "No."

Relief floods me, but my body won't accept it. "I swear I recognize your voice."

"I was born here. We all sound the same, sweetheart." He continues to deny it, but with every word my stomach twists a little further. I hear that voice in my dreams. I'd know it anywhere. I'm not wrong. I am *so* not wrong. This...this is *him*. The guy who brought in the tiny, broken girl is the very same guy who tied me up and fucked me senseless two years ago. The guy who took my virginity. His brooding eyes burn into me with such intensity that I know he's just waiting for me to realize.

"I—I need to know who your friend is," I stammer, and he smiles. It's a breathtakingly wild and treacherous thing, seeing this guy smile. The gesture's so sharp it could flay a man alive.

"Her name is Carrie."

"Insurance?"

He shakes his head. His eyes never leave mine. "I'll pay."

"You'll need to go speak to reception. Give them your credit card details. And your name."

He smirks, looks down at his shoes, and then raises his eyes to mine again so that he's looking up at me from under those dark eyebrows. "I've got cash. And you don't need to know my name. Better you forget I was ever here."

He steps back, arms still folded across his chest, and I act without thinking. A part of me is already wondering where the nearest phone is so I can call the cops, but the rest of me follows him down the corridor. Damn, stupid body.

"Wait! I—*don'tmakemedothis!*"

He smirks. "Do what?"

"I don't know! I—it was *you*. Admit it. Admit that it was you."

His smirk vanishes, replaced by a cold and calculating stare. "I didn't hurt Carrie."

"That's not what I meant, and you know it."

He pouts, and any remaining doubts I might have had are banished just like that. Those lips—I may not have seen them in the dark, but I sure as hell felt them. He's the guy. He sees it now. Knows that I know for sure. "Maybe I do know what you mean. That doesn't change the fact that you should forget I was ever here. Best for everyone involved. You don't want to know me, sweetheart."

His arrogance is freaking unprecedented. I take four hurried steps and stab my index finger into his chest. "*You!*"

Up this close, he's so tall it's frightening. "*Me*," he agrees.

I ask him the one question that's been burning in my mind for the past two years. "Did you have anything to do with Eli's death?"

He looks away, sucking his bottom lip into his mouth. That's a yes if ever I saw one. "Let's just say… Eli and I had a *disagreement*."

"Fuck! I knew it. Did you take Lex's paperwork?"

He's like Dr. Jekyll and Mister Hyde. One minute he's standing there, watching me like I'm a genie and I might disappear in a puff of smoke any minute, and then he's pure, raw anger. He grabs my wrist and moves lightning fast, shoving me roughly back against the wall. The corridor is empty at this time of morning, so I'm completely alone. Vulnerable. His hand closes around my throat, just tight enough to terrify the shit out of me. "You *like* feeling like this, Sloane?"

Hearing my name come out of his mouth makes my eyes well with tears. He's known who I am all along. I shake my head. "No," I gasp.

"Then you need to treat Carrie. Make sure she gets better. I'll be coming back for her in two days. Don't let the goddamn shrinks near her. Don't let Psych get ahold of her, or I'm gonna be seriously pissed." His body presses up against mine, and he's like a wall of muscle and testosterone. I'm too frightened to do anything but nod. Something changes, then. I could be fooling myself, but I think I see his eyes soften. "Do you remember?" he whispers.

I nod again.

"And when you close your eyes?"

I know what he's asking. "Yes."

"Do it, then. Close your eyes." His grip tightens a little around my throat, making me gasp. I take one long hard look into the bottomless depths of his eyes and then, just like the last time, I do as I'm told. I close my eyes.

His lips brush lightly against mine, and my mind stills. His breath comes fast, ragged, and hot against my mouth. It has the most devastating effect. What the fuck should I do? Should I lean in and *kiss* him? Should I knee him in the balls? He blows all argument right out of the water when his tongue darts out and trails over my parted lips, carefully, lovingly, like he's *tasting* me. I react on impulse. I rise on my tiptoes, leaning in. He doesn't kiss me, though.

"Two days, Sloane. Two days and I'm coming for you," he whispers.

The next thing I know, I'm sinking to the floor. When I open my eyes, all I see are his black boots walking away.

10

SLOANE

THE COFFEE AT FRESCO'S IS PARTICU-larly bad today, but that's no great surprise. Everything here tastes bad. The bagel I forced down my throat for breakfast might as well have been made out of sawdust. It doesn't matter, though. There might be a thousand better coffeehouses in the greater Seattle area, but Fresco's is a tradition for Pip and me.

We've been meeting here ever since we were poor, struggling students and their drip coffee was all we could afford. My best friend arrives looking immaculate as ever. Her hair is swept back into a classic chignon, her pantsuit perfectly creased in all the right places. In my cuffed-up jeans and rumpled long-sleeved T-shirt, I look like I've been sleeping in my clothes the last three days.

Pippa breezes through the café, grinning at Marcus the barista, who will have her regular double espresso on the table precisely sixty seconds after she sits down. She places her Louis Vuitton onto the bench opposite me and elegantly takes a seat.

"Morning, stranger." It's been a week since I've seen her. That's a lifetime for us. She gets comfy, giving me a wink. "What's so urgent it couldn't wait until later? This afternoon's my arson block."

Pippa opted for psychology instead of medicine. We graduated at the same time. She's been certified by the Board of Psychiatric Medicine for the last fourteen months. She works out of an office downtown, dealing with patients sentenced with mandatory therapy in one form or another. Pip's OCD being what it is, she's grouped her patients' appointments in accordance with their crimes. Mondays for domestic violence offenders. Tuesdays for shoplifters. Wednesdays for arsonists. You get the picture. A *lot* of violent offenders walk through her doors. She could easily have chosen to work with Prozac-happy, depressed housewives, but she wanted more. Said it felt better to help those who really needed it.

I stare into the bottom of my empty coffee cup, suddenly doubting whether I should tell her anything that happened yesterday. But...I think I need to.

She's my best friend, but she's also always been able to see things from an unbiased point of view. That's exactly what I need right now.

"If I said I had a patient with an issue they needed to talk through, you'd already know I was talking about me, right?"

"Yep."

"Okay. Well. I won't bother with that spiel then."

Marcus drops Pip's coffee off. She sips from her cup, arching an eyebrow at me. "Would save some time, yes."

"Okay, well..." I just need to spit it out. "I had sex with a guy."

She spits espresso back into her tiny cup. "What? Who? *When?*"

Ahh, shit. This is going to be really bad. Pip often jokes that I'm going to die a virgin. "It wasn't recently. It was... it was two years ago."

Her shoulders stiffen. The incredulous look she was sporting a second ago turns frosty. She's pissed. I knew she would be. She puts her coffee down, staring down at the table. "Why didn't you tell me?"

"It wasn't... it wasn't something to sit around and dissect over a tub of ice cream, Pip. It wasn't something I was exactly *proud* of, either."

"What does that mean? My God, you weren't *attacked* were you?"

"No, no, of course not. But…" This is the part where I either tell her the whole truth or I go for a watered-down version. I'm a coward in the end. She would never think badly of me for what I did, but I just can't bear the shame of admitting it. I sold my virginity for information. Information I didn't even get, which, on other words, means I sold it for nothing. "I didn't know the guy. I didn't even know his name. I…I was drunk. We did it in the dark. I couldn't have even told you what he looked like until yesterday."

Pip closes her eyes and presses her fingertips into her forehead.

Please don't think I'm a slut. Please don't think I'm a slut.

"Sloane. Jeez…" She groans.

"I know, I know."

"I don't even know where to begin with this."

"How about after the judgmental part?"

"Oh, babe. I would never, *ever* judge you. I'm just… I just wanted something special for you. Y'know, romance, red roses, champagne, fireworks…"

I push my bagel crumbs around on the plate still sitting in front of me, pouting. "Oh, there were definitely fireworks. None of the other stuff, but definitely fireworks."

She sighs, then reaches across the table, moving the plate so she can hold my hands in hers. "So this has been playing on your mind for two whole years, and you didn't tell me *why?*"

"Because... it wasn't exactly *normal* sex."

Pippa looks like she doesn't understand, and then realization dawns on her face. "So... you let some guy screw you, and he was into some freaky stuff?"

"Pretty much."

"And, wait, you said you didn't even know what he looked like until yesterday. What happened yesterday?"

"He came into the hospital. His friend tried to kill herself."

She exhales. "I need another coffee for this." She orders one for herself and one for me, and when she comes back, she has more questions prepared. "I just don't get it. How did you know it was him?"

"His voice is very distinctive. I just came out and asked him if he was the guy, and, well, he didn't deny it."

"Okay, so aside from the obvious conversation we should not need to have about you making smart choices, why are you chewing your nails off over this guy? You haven't heard a peep out of him since this happened?"

"No."

"So what?"

"So... he kind of kissed me. Or was about to. I suppose it was more of a... lick."

"He *licked* you? Where? Who *does* that?"

I ignore her sputtering. "And it was kind of while..." I take a deep breath. Here goes nothing. "While he kind of had me pinned up against the wall... with his hand around my throat."

Pippa's jaw tightens. "So he *did* attack you."

"It was more of a threat."

"Why on earth would he do that?"

"He doesn't want his friend placed on a psych hold. Probably thought I could pull some strings and have the whole incident brushed under the carpet."

She snorts. "Well, good luck with that, buddy. Girl tries to kill herself, she gets automatic couch time with a professional at the very least. But anyway, he forcefully *licked* you?"

"No. I sort of... allowed that."

"Fuck, Sloane. I don't know, this almost sounds like grounds to call the cops to me. Why the hell did you let him do that? Is he unhinged? Are *you* unhinged?"

I let out a bitter laugh. "That's a possibility on both counts."

She laces her fingers together, frowning. She isn't supposed to frown. Frowning gives too much away. "You already know what I'm going to say to you, don't you?"

"Yeah. I do." I sigh. The weight of this whole thing is an impossible burden on my shoulders. It feels good to have shared even a small part of it, and I'm not done yet. "There's something else, Pip. He might know something about Alexis."

This information freezes her in her seat. I don't often talk about Lex. I rarely even mention her name, so the fact that I've brought her up now is a really big deal. "How?" I can tell she's doing everything in her power to stay calm. "Did this guy have something to do with her disappearance? Oh my God."

"No. At least I don't *think* he did. I can't...I can't really explain it right now."

She doesn't like that, not one bit. She huffs, staring at me like I have gone mad. "I have a bad feeling about this, Sloane. Aside from the fact that you still know nothing about this guy—" She pauses, as though something has just occurred to her. "Do you even know his name now?" I shake my head, no. She looks mortified. "Okay, well he hasn't offered any information to the cops about Lex being snatched, and you won't tell me how you think he might know this mystery information. That leads me to believe he is probably involved in some bad shit. Up to his neck in it, no doubt. And he tried to choke the life out of you?"

"I know." When she puts it that way, it really does sound pretty messed up.

"I understand that you want to find her, Sloane, but this guy sounds dangerous. It sounds as if he's more likely to stab you than help you find Lex. I want you to stay away from him, okay? Do not have anything to do with him. Please, Sloane? For me?"

I bury my face into my coffee cup. I knew she would do this. I knew exactly what she would say, and I'm kind of relieved, to be honest. I have permission to avoid him like the plague now, even though he might have some idea where my sister is. I should just tell the police that he practically admitted to hurting Eli yesterday, and then they can do all of the questioning. I can stay the hell out of it entirely.

"Okay, yes, you're right. I'll stay away from him," I say. But for some reason, I don't tell her that he's returning to the hospital tomorrow. I don't tell her that he promised he'd come looking for me.

The unsettled feeling that lingers within me is a mix of guilt and anticipation. I've never been one to lie or to hide things. Even to me, it's worrying that the only things I've kept from my best friend relate to this guy. Am I asking for trouble by keeping secrets? It seems futile to even pose that question. Where this man is concerned, I sense that trouble will find me regardless.

11

SLOANE

THE MORNING DRAGS UNBEARABLY AS I try to stretch out my rounds. I do my best to make my other patients' needs more time consuming than they need to be. Eventually I can't put it off any longer, though. I've done everything that needs doing, and since Dr. Patel is off today, that makes the girl *my* responsibility.

Carrie's asleep when I go to her room. She isn't alone. Kim Dixon is there from Psych. She's a lovely woman. Motherly. Warm. She's the first person they send down here when a kid needs assessing. Carrie's no kid, but they must have hoped she'd respond to a maternal figure.

"Hey, Sloane," she whispers, putting Carrie's chart back into the slot at the end of her bed. "Heard you performed quite the miracle with this one."

"Suresh did most of the work." I smile, returning the same warmth she shows to me.

"Poor girl." She looks at Carrie. The girl's definitely a little worse for wear. There are dark purple rings around her eyes, and her skin is still deathly white. "I'm just waiting for her to decide to wake up. Any idea how long I'm going to be hanging around?"

"She's not sedated anymore. Could be a couple of hours. Could be a day or more. She was in a pretty bad way."

Kim wraps her arms around her body and tuts, frowning at the young woman in the bed. She always takes these things to heart, no matter that she has never met the patient before. "People say that suicide's the coward's way out, but they couldn't be more wrong. It takes nerves of steel to commit like she did. It's *good* that she's here now. She can get the rest she needs. Hopefully develop a different perspective on things. She'll have a whole team of people on hand just waiting to help her."

Dark brown eyes flash inside my head. I swallow hard even though there's nothing constricting my airway. *Don't let Psych get ahold of her, or I'm gonna be seriously pissed.*

"She's lucky she came to St. Peter's," I whisper. "She couldn't be in better hands." My mind goes to dark places when I worry. Maybe Alexis *is* alive. Maybe she's been suffering just like Carrie. Who knows what kind of horrific things she's been through. It doesn't even bear thinking about. Maybe *she's* been laid up somewhere, recovering from trying to end *her* life, too. She wouldn't have been taken to a hospital, though. Too many opportunities to ask for help. Too many exits through which to make a run for it.

Lex wouldn't have had a woman like Kim to help her. That thought makes me so devastatingly sad. That guy, whoever he is, is crazy if he thinks I'm going to hand Carrie over to him. Just absolutely fucking crazy.

"Hey, Kim. I really have no idea when her sedative is going to wear off, but I'm done with all my work for the time being. Bar an emergency, I have a little while to sit with her. Why don't you head back to your office? I'll come find you if she wakes up."

Kim smiles at me like I'm the most thoughtful person in the world. "Thanks, Sloane. I have a mountain of paperwork that'll only get bigger if I don't deal with it soon. You got my pager?"

I tell her I do, and she leaves, gently squeezing the top of my arm as she passes me.

The girl is awake. I know she is. Has been for some time, in fact. She's been playing dead, assessing her surroundings, probably trying to decide if it's safe to be conscious. Kim doesn't deal with patients emerging from anesthesia every day like I do. Carrie's breathing is shallow, quiet, and controlled instead of the deep, regular draw of the heavily sedated. I shift the armchair from the window to the bedside and sit myself down. From there I watch Carrie, trying to figure out how best to proceed.

"So. I went and had coffee with my friend this morning," I tell her. "She's prim and proper sometimes, but she's always been there when I've needed her. This morning I told her something dark about me. It was a conversation I'd been considering having with her for a long time, but I'd been waiting for the right time to broach it, y'know? I'm good at making excuses. I've always talked myself out of it. So like with everything else, I left it until the very last minute, until something happened, and I didn't feel like I had a choice anymore. She gave me some solid advice that made perfect sense, and I just kept thinking on my way to work, why the hell couldn't you have just made that decision for yourself, Sloane?" I lean back in the chair, watching Carrie's eyelids flutter. She's listening.

"But...it's hard to do the things we know should do, isn't it? Hard to make the choices we *know* we need to make. We're all so entrenched by our problems that we can never see our way out of the maze we find ourselves in. It's easier to close our eyes and walk blindly because we're too scared to acknowledge the mess we're in. The darkness we create ourselves is better than the darkness waiting for us with our eyes open. At least we feel like we're in control when *we* close ourselves off in the dark."

She doesn't respond. I'm no psychiatrist. I'm not qualified to try to iron the creases out of this girl's life. But I am so curious about her—why he cares so much for her, who she is to him. How it was that he came to be carrying her lifeless body into my ER. "You know, if you're scared…if you're in a position you think there's no escape from, let me tell you now…there is *always* an escape. A way out. If you need somewhere to go, if you need someone to talk to, all you need to do is say so. I can make it all happen."

Carrie's eyelids flutter again. This time, they open. The girl's eyes are pale blue, the color of compacted ice. Like an iceberg. They're filled with tears. Most people would turn to look at me, but she doesn't. She stares at the ceiling, her chest heaving as she battles her emotions.

"I don't need your help. I don't need somewhere to go." Tears streak from the corner of her eyes, chasing each other across her temples and running into her ears. "*I just need Zeth.*"

12

SLOANE

"I CAN'T WAIT ANOTHER DAY. HE wouldn't leave me here if he knew I was awake." Carrie's composure is slipping by the minute; she's so anxious that I'm considering given her another sedative just to calm her down.

"Then give me his number. I'll let him know." Zeth. His name is *Zeth*. It feels strange having a name to put to his face, but then I only got to put a *face* to the *voice* yesterday, so I guess this whole thing is strange.

Carrie gives me a look—*nice try, bitch*. "How about you wheel me to a payphone so I can call him myself?"

"You're not ready for that yet, Carrie. You're too weak."

She looks confused. "Carrie?"

"Yeah, Zeth said your name was—" I break off when I realize I've been stupid. Of course he didn't give me her real name. Why would he? He paid in cash for her treatment (twenty-three thousand dollars) and signed off on her paperwork as K. Vonnegut, for fuck's sake. "What's your real name?" I sigh.

"If Zeth says it's Carrie, then it's Carrie." With her arms folded across her chest, she stares glumly down at her bandaged wrists.

"Well, okay, Carrie, if you don't want to tell me that's fine, but you're not leaving this room. And they're going to be asking a lot of questions when Dr. Dixon comes down here later on."

"She the shrink?"

"Yep. She's going to wanna know why you did this to yourself."

"Who said I did it to myself?" She pouts like a petulant child, but her words set my heart to thrumming.

"Why, did... did Zeth do it?"

"No. Of course he didn't."

The girl is playing with me. Even if I *do* have the time, I don't have the inclination to deal with her today. I'd rather be helping the nurses change bedpans than deal with attitude like this. "All right. Well, whatever. You can tell it to Dr. Dixon when she comes down here."

Carrie stops scowling and sits up, real emotion finally washing over face: fear. "No! Please. I—I can't handle a shrink. Don't leave me. Please." She reaches for my hand, which is gripping the rail of her bed, and weakly she clasps my wrist. It's going to be a while before she regains any strength in *her* hands considering how deep she cut yesterday. "You don't understand," she whispers.

"Dr. Dixon is amazing, Carrie. You should trust her. She might be able to help."

"She can't! Please. Zeth's the only one. The *only* one. I need him. If you leave me with that shrink I—I swear I won't mess it up this time. I'll kill myself. I'll do it, and it'll all be your fault."

I don't usually bargain with patients in this situation. They're hardly ever in a position to know what's best for them, but I can see from the desperation in her eyes that Carrie's telling the truth. She really will kill herself.

"Shit." I exhale, squeezing my hand into a tight fist. "I made a promise when I became a doctor, Carrie. I swore that I would do no harm, and I consider you not seeing Dr. Dixon to be harmful."

"Do you consider me *dying* as harmful? 'Cause that's what'll happen if that bitch comes down here and tries to psychoanalyze me."

Double shit. I run a hand through my hair, trying

to think of a way to convince her that she's being foolish. There'll be no reasoning with her, though. I can see that. But she definitely needs help. I can think of only one resolution where we both get what we want. "All right. I'm not saying that I'm going to help you leave here, because I'm not. That goes against everything I stand for as a health care provider. You still need at least another three days' bed rest, and we need to check the range of movement in your hands to make sure none of your tendons were permanently damaged. But...I will loan you my cell phone, and I will be gone for the next three hours on afternoon rounds. And I *won't* make you see Dr. Dixon, but I want you to see my friend instead. I can ask her to see you off the books, so you won't need to tell her your details."

She's already shaking her head before I can finish my sentence. "They're all the same. Your buddy's not going to make any difference, okay?"

Clearly, I'm not going to sway her. Her mind is so made up. "How old are you, Carrie?"

She answers begrudgingly, but only after considering my question and obviously deciding no harm can come from parting with the information. "Twenty-six."

I nod, thinking this over. "We're the same age, then. And tell me, Carrie...how long have you felt"—*Suicidal. Useless. Crushed by the chaos of this life*—"like this?"

"Always." Her swagger from earlier was pretty transparent, but now she's dropped the act. She's just a broken girl in a sea of hospital sheets, still holding on to my wrist like she needs the physical connection to stop herself from drowning in them.

"So for twenty-six years you've felt a despair so grave that you wanted to end your life because of it? Seems pretty awful to me. When you look to the future, can you imagine feeling like this for another twenty-six years?" Her bottom lip wobbles, but she keeps quiet. "Wouldn't it be better if you saw someone who could help you work past whatever is making you feel like this? That way, in twenty-six years' time, you can look back and see the light you've had in your life, not just the darkness."

Carrie is quiet, gaze fixed on her knees, which are covered by her blankets. If I were a betting woman, I wouldn't be laying down money that my little speech was going to have any effect. But the girl surprises me when her shoulders sag. "Okay, fine. I'll go and see this friend of yours. *Once*. And if she's full of shit, then I'm leaving."

"You promise?"

"I promise. Now hand over that cell phone."

"Fine. Just make sure you leave it in the drawer of

the nightstand when you're done." *When you go.* I can't believe I'm condoning this.

Despite the bad vibe in my gut when I give her my phone, I also feel like I've won three small victories. The first victory: She's promised that she'll go to get help. She might not keep that promise. If she does, I'll have to *beg* Pip to take her. Either way, the seed has been planted in her mind. I have hope that it'll take root. The second victory: She'll be out of here today, a full twenty-four hours before Zeth promised to come looking for me. The third victory: She'll probably be too overwhelmed to realize that she's typing the bastard's telephone number into my cell phone. Having his number will be a huge win. I'll have taken back my power. A small piece of it, anyway. And I'll finally have something over him. Something I can provide to the cops if I need to.

I go on afternoon rounds, careful to avoid the east wing of ICU, where Carrie is being kept. I do *not* want to run into Zeth when he comes to secret her out of the hospital. It's the end of my shift, seven p.m., by the time I head back to her room to collect my phone. Just as I'd suspected, Carrie's bed is empty and her ruined clothes from yesterday are gone. But when I look in the drawer of the nightstand, my precious victories wither on the vine. My cell phone isn't where I asked her to leave it. She's taken it with her.

Fuck.

13

ZETH

Pippa, Rcv'd 11:33 am

I hope you really heard what I was saying, Sloane. Stay away from that guy. I mean it!

I GET TINGLES WHEN I READ THROUGH Sloane's messages. Kinda fucked up, I know, but I *am* that self-obsessed. I get the warm-and-fuzzies when I realize she's been talking about me to her friend. I haven't mentioned her to a single soul on the face of this planet, but then that's what guys do. We hoard our shit. Refuse to let anything slip. Chicks aren't like that. They gossip like mother hens. I'm absently wondering whether she's told this Pippa how big my dick is, if she *remembers* how big my dick is—*of course she does*—when the phone fucking chimes in my hand.

(206) 555-0142, Rcv'd 9:32 pm
    Asshole.

I know it's from her. And I know it's meant for me. I grimace as I reply:

Me: Bitch.

(206) 555-0142, Rcv'd 9:38 pm
    That phone is on a plan. Be good to get it back.

Me: Have to come get it then, won't you?

I'm playing with fire. I shouldn't be trying to get her to meet me. I should be cutting all ties. Since I brought Lace home and corralled her into bed, I've questioned her eighteen different ways from Sunday.
    Did you give her an address?
    No.
    Did you tell her where I worked?

No.
Did you give her your real name?
No.
Did you give her my real name? Lace? *Did you give her my real name?*
Yes.

Well, shit. It's not her fault. The girl was drugged up to the eyeballs and I hadn't had a chance to give her our story, but still...I'm fucking furious that Sloane has my name. Somehow feels like a gross imbalance in power now. I know everything about her. Up until now, she known next to nothing about me, and I've liked being the anonymous party in this shit-fight of a situation.

(206) 555-0142, Rcv'd 9:41 pm
Give me an address. I'll send the cops around for it asap.

She's grown feisty since we met again in the corridor of St. Peter's. It's easy to be shitty with someone in a text message, though. Different story face-to-face. Body-to-body. I'm yet to get a proper read on the girl, but I'm concerned she's not as smart as I think she is. She's a doctor now, so you'd think she had some brains—will let this drop and will forget all about me like I told her to. But I know firsthand how badly she wants to find her sister, and I doubt any amount of time will change that.

Me: Apt. 12c, 515 West Ave. 8pm, tomorrow. Wear something nice and short. And I recommend leaving five-oh at home. We don't play well together.

I smirk as I hit send. That's not the address to the warehouse. That's the address of the apartment downtown where I host my little get-togethers. *Get-togethers* isn't exactly the right term for the gathering, but Lacey thinks it's better than what I'd called it before: the fuck-fest. The first Saturday of each month is always the same at 515 West Avenue, and tomorrow night will be no different. My cock stirs in my pants just thinking about Sloane knocking on the door, absolutely no idea what awaits her on the other side.

I'm taking precautionary measures. If she doesn't follow this Pippa's advice and shows up tomorrow night, I'm going to make sure that, no matter how badly she wants to track down Alexis, she *will* run at the sound of the name she now knows belongs to me.

14

ZETH

I'M PUMPED ALL OF THE NEXT DAY, WAIT-ing for it to be time. I'm always pretty antsy by the end of the month, anyway, purely because the parties take the edge off my more outlandish tastes. I go to nights held by other people—Matty used to host a downright dirty one—but it's not the same. I am in control when that stuff goes down under my roof. I get what I want with whomever I want. The release isn't the same when I'm not the only master to be obeyed. It isn't that I don't let other dudes attend. That wouldn't work. But every guy on the guest list knows who the boss is, and that's the way I need it to be.

It's nearly dark when I drive over to the place in

the Camaro. Lace is laid out on the back seat, sleeping. I'm not leaving her alone for a second, even if that means she has to sit in a room with Michael keeping an eye on her all night. A cell phone alerts, making her grumble drowsily. I remove the one in my left-hand pocket, trying to remember whether this one is Sloane's or mine. It's mine, and funnily enough the alert, an email, is from Michael.

From: mikeywest@webhostprime.com
To: 443232111@connectlive.com
Received: 02/21/14 7:21

Hey, boss, just a quick heads-up. Still haven't found anything on the girl. If Charlie has buried her, he's buried her deep. Got some of Rufus's boys looking, too. They don't know any names. I'll be over in an hour.

I may call Charlie my boss, but there are plenty of boys out there who reserve that title for me. Michael's been on my payroll for the last five years. He's handy with his fists and has nerves of fucking steel. With Charlie's none-too-subtle threat at the end of our last meeting, I know he's probably got people on the alert for me snooping around in his shit. I've always kept Michael separate from Charlie, though. He won't be on the lookout for a six-foot-five motherfucker from Louisiana. I pocket the phone and process the information Michael sent me—he can't find the location of the girl, or even any record to confirm she still exists, but he's on the job. He'll turn something up eventually. It's just a matter of waiting.

We arrive at the apartment not long after that. I park the Camaro in the underground lot and collect Lacey from the back seat, careful not to wake her as I lift her out. She loops her arms around my neck, and I carry her to the elevator. On the fourth floor, the apartment door is open, and Ganya is hefting crates of vodka in from the hallway.

"Thought you liked the girls conscious at the beginning of the night, Zee."

I shoot him a dirty look and head on inside, ignoring the gibe. I go to the end of the corridor on the eastern side of the sprawling, six-bedroom apartment and settle Lacey inside the last room, making sure the door locks properly. We've had problems with unwelcome visitors taking liberties before. It *does* lock, so I leave her while she's sleeping, then I make sure the rest of the place is ready. At the front door, the masks are already set out on a table. The theme for this month is gold, and so most of them are either white or black, coated with gold glitter or whatever that shit is they put on Venetian masks. I pick the ugliest one I can find—a devil's mask replete with horns and down-turned mouth—and set it aside for myself. I'm pleased when I find that everything else has been organized and set in place as well. The lighting is low, a burned, honey yellow that casts as many shadows as it does highlights. Sliced fruit and other treats are laid out for the guests, and silk screen partitions cordon off discreet corners of the various rooms, where people can gain a little more privacy, should they want it. Most of the people who come here don't, but there you go.

Guests begin to arrive, dressed in tuxedos and shimmering evening dresses, hair coiled in sweeping, elegant styles, just begging to be messed up. Names aren't exchanged. Masks are kept in place. I go and get ready, trying to keep my head clear. The fucking thing won't stop racing, though. Will she come? Will she dare? And if so, what the hell is she gonna do when she sees all of this?

15

SLOANE

I MUST BE SICK IN THE HEAD.

Not only have I not spoken to the cops, but I'm on my way to the address Zeth sent me, and I've worn the shortest, slinkiest dress I own. I don't know why, but his text felt like a dare. He didn't think I would do it, which made my rebellious streak stick its middle finger up. It's been a while since that happened. After the worst day at work, being interrogated about Carrie's disappearance—*You were the last to see her, Dr. Romera. Are you positive she didn't mention anything about leaving?*—a fight with this guy is the very last thing I need. I'm not stupid, though. It's probably going to happen, so I'm well primed for one.

I leave my car two streets over and make my way to the apartment building. Should I tell Pippa what I'm doing tonight? If I go missing and am never heard from again, at least that way she could report my last known location. But I can't tell her. One, because I don't have my fucking cell anymore and I'm not a savant with other people's phone numbers, and two, because she will *definitely* tear me a new one for not listening to her.

I press the buzzer for 12C, wondering if the girl is going to be here. I've brought my medical bag with me just in case. If she is, I'll be able to inspect her wounds and change her dressings. I'll also be able to leave her the antibiotics she's *definitely* going to need. A crackle blasts down the intercom, but no one speaks. Whoever is upstairs presses the entry key, and the door lets out an ear-splitting buzz and clicks open.

I climb four flights of stairs before the rumble of music and laughter fills the air. Someone's having a party. A lone guy, suited up with his hands folded in front of him, stands at the end of the hallway, watching me approach. Doesn't take long for me to realize the music is coming from the apartment I'm after, and the guy in the suit? He's standing guard at the door like a bouncer. *What the hell?*

"Can I help you?" he asks in a smooth, low voice. His skin is light brown, his eyes a surprising, piercing light blue. With his shaved head and imposing six-and-a-half-foot stature, he's a refined kind of dangerous. Like a stiletto blade. Slender. Beautifully made... but deadly as can be.

"I'm—Zeth told me to come." Why the *hell* would he tell me to come here while he's having some kind of blowout? It was probably his idea of damage control, make sure there are plenty of people around so I can't cause a scene about... well, everything.

The doorman smiles politely. "May I have your name?"

"Sloane. Sloane Romera."

There's no guest list on a clipboard. No earpiece in the guy's ear. He nods when he hears my name, though—confirmation that I am expected. "Welcome, Dr. Romera. I'm Michael. If you need anything this evening, please don't hesitate to find me." He steps to one side and opens the door behind him, blocking the room inside from view with his body. He gestures to a table behind the door with an open palm, smiling courteously. "Please. Select a mask."

Select a *mask*? My toes curl inside my shoes. The last time I had to wear a mask was back in the hotel when I'd met Zeth the first time. It hadn't mattered in the end because of the dark, but still, the association has liquid dread cycling through my veins.

"Uh, no. I don't think so."

Michael nods understandingly, like he's been through this before. "I'm sorry, Dr. Romera, but without a mask I'm afraid I can't let you inside."

Mother. Fucker. I want my phone back. I want to see if Carrie, or whoever the hell she is, is all right. I want to find out what Zeth knows about my sister. My jaw sets as I look down on the large table. There are six masks left. Four of them are more masculine. The two feminine ones are both black with golden swirls, but a shining, metallic black-purple-green feather plumes from one of them. It's pretty, so I pluck it up, and Michael does me the honor of affixing it into my hair. Seems like the guy has done this before. "Thank you for obliging us, Dr. Romera," he says. And then he moves back so I can see into the room behind him, and my stomach bottoms out.

16

SLOANE

I'VE HEARD THE TERM BEFORE, BUT I'VE never seen it in real life: Orgy. Group sex. Gang bang. My mind shorts out after that. I can't think of any more names for what I'm witnessing.

A large open-plan living room sprawls before me, within which at least fifty people mill around in various degrees of undress. Some men are still fully attired, while beautiful women—dresses slipped down revealing their breasts, ridden up to display shaved pussies—sit on their laps or kneel at their feet on the floor.

Black leather bindings bite into flesh wherever I look. Couples kiss, groping at each other, hands everywhere. On the far side of the room, a man rocks his head back in sheer bliss as a woman on her knees, completely naked, sucks on his rock-solid cock for everyone to see.

My mouth hangs open. I turn around and Michael, still standing there, shrugs. "If you're looking for Zeth, he's in the back room. But you'll have to go through the apartment to reach it." He smiles *ever* so slowly. "Boss told me not to close the front door behind you, though. He doesn't think you'll make it."

Well, fuck me, he was right about that. I don't need this shit. I shake my head, stepping toward Michael and the still-open doorway. Michael lifts one shoulder again. "He said you were a prude. He bet big on you walking out as soon as you saw…" He looks over my shoulder into the room beyond, smirking. "Well…"

"He's an arrogant son of a bitch," I snap.

"He sure is. Leaving won't prove him wrong, though, will it. There's only one way to do that." He winks. "Go rip into him. He deserves it."

I narrow my eyes. "Did *you* bet money on this?"

The left side of his mouth kicks up. "Thousand bucks."

A *thousand* dollars? Zeth's so sure of my reaction to this that he put a grand on the line? That's probably pocket change to him since he paid cash for Carrie's hospital bill, but hell. Surely it would sting to lose it. I take a deep breath.

You've come this far. You've already seen what's going on behind you. All you have to do is go find him.

"Fine." I don't give myself time to think. I spin around and make for the hallway on the other side of the huge room. I'm stepping over bodies before I know it. I do my best to keep my eyes up and front, but I can't help but catch sight of a few things. Things that will be burned into my mind for all time.

When I reach the hallway, there are eight doors, four on either side. Most are open, but a few are closed. Low moaning slides under the wood. Groans of ecstasy and the loud slap of skin on skin. I'm too scared to open the closed doors, so I peek into the open rooms instead, bracing myself each time: a tangle of arms and legs greet me first, four women and two guys so interlaced it's hard to tell where each one of them begins and the other ends. I back the hell out of there pretty quickly. The second room contains a group of men and women all still in their suits and beautiful dresses, watching a couple screwing on the floor. The observers sip politely from champagne flutes while touching each other subtly, a hand slipped up a dress, rubbing at sensitive skin. A manicured hand squeezing an erection over the top of expensive-looking pants. A guy wearing an ornate tiger mask with fierce golden stripes turns and sees me. He takes a sip from his drink, pauses in caressing the exposed breast of his companion, and holds out his hand to me.

Oh, hell *no.*

I backtrack quickly, heading for the last door on the right. For a second I think the door's closed and I'm about to turn around, but then I realize my mistake. The door is wide open. The lights are just turned off.

You son of a bitch.

I grip my medical bag tight around its handle and take another deep breath. I walk inside.

"You're sick, you know that?" I say into the darkness. A soft rustling greets me, followed by the shift of movement. Yes, the lights are off, but the corridor is lit behind me, so it isn't like last time. I can see enough to make out the looming figure that slowly paces toward me.

"I know I'm not *normal*, if that's what you mean." A terrible devil's mask slowly emerges from the shadows. Dressed head to heel in black, the suit Zeth wears is a thing of beauty even in the muted light.

Dark eyes shine from within the mask, sharp and hungry. "You've surprised me, Sloane. I like being surprised," he rumbles.

"Well, you've surprised me, too. Although I can't say the feeling is mutual."

He laughs, voice so deep and powerful I feel it in

the soles of my feet. "You should open up a little. You never know what you might enjoy until you try it."

"I know *exactly* what I enjoy, Zeth, and standing around watching fifty naked people grind on each other isn't it."

The eyes behind his mask flicker with annoyance when I say his name. He stalks toward me and reaches out, tracing his fingertips across my jawline. He seems pensive, intrigued by my stillness—I can't freaking move—as he touches my skin. "If you don't like watching, Sloane, you could always join in."

I slap his hand away, glaring out from behind my own mask. "Give me back my phone."

He watches me for a second, smirking, before sliding a hand into the pocket of his pants and pulling out my cell phone. He offers it to me, and I just *know* he plans on snatching it away from me as soon as I reach for it. I hold out my open hand instead, waiting for him to place it into my palm.

He pouts, game ruined, and does it. I slide the phone into the medical bag I'm still clutching on to for dear life. "I came tonight because you needed to know that I'm *not* scared of you, Zeth. And I want to know what you know about my sister."

"Really?" he eyes the bag in my hand. "By the hand luggage, it looks like you knew all about our little gathering and brought some toys to play with."

I remember his black duffel, the one he'd had with him at the hotel, and I harden my jaw. "Like yours, you mean? *I'm* not the pervert who carries around a stash of bondage gear."

Zeth looks down, a calculated tilt of his head. His bag sits on the floor by the doorway to my left. I shiver when I see it. "My bag of tricks is slightly bigger than yours, Sloane. And there's more than bondage gear in there. Maybe if you're brave, you'll open it and find out?"

Infection is a major problem after surgery. We doctors spend a great deal of time battling to ensure that it doesn't happen, that the wounds we create or try to fix remain clean, but sometimes it just happens no matter how careful we are. A wound becomes infected. Organs become inflamed. The body rejects new limbs. I've watched it happen time and time again, but I've ever experienced it firsthand. Until now, that is. Zeth is performing butcher's surgery on my open chest cavity, and my heart is already inflamed. It pounds behind my ribs, fighting the strange, alien feelings he's infecting me with.

"I'm not touching that thing. And I brought my *medical bag* with me so I could see to Carrie." I emphasize the fake name he fed me so that he knows I've seen through his lie. He doesn't seem fazed.

"*Carrie* is sleeping. But you're more than welcome

to play doctor with me? With the right inspiration, I can be a very good patient." His hand rises slowly—the same way a person might approach a nervous horse. My mom demonstrated it to me when I was little— *Let him see your hand, honey. Let him know you're not going to hurt him.* But I can see from the amused spark in Zeth's eyes that he *is* going to hurt me. One way or another. He wants to tear the bottom right out of my world.

He touches my cheekbone, light as a feather. A far cry from the way he touched me back in the hospital, but his gentleness now doesn't make up for his rough treatment then. "I'm not playing *anything* with you, Zeth. If you care about Carrie at all, you'll let me see her. Her wrists aren't healed. She needs medication, and she needs her dressings changed."

"She's on amoxicillin and her dressings are changed three times a day. More if they need it. She has a drip to help replace the plasma she lost, and she's been restricted to bed rest. And right now, she's *sleeping*," he growls. I've pissed him off, that much is clear. I swallow when he shifts forward, subtly leaning into me so that his body is less than a foot away from mine. Twelve inches has never felt like such a short distance. "Now, Sloane, if you don't mind, I'm hosting a party. If you're a coward and you're going to bolt, then I suggest you do it now before things really heat up."

Before things really heat up? He doesn't think things have already escalated to surface-of-the-sun degrees out in his living room? Maybe he hasn't been out there. Maybe he has no idea what's going on. Maybe he thought his guests would actually use the finger food to... well, eat. My subconscious laughs at me, pointing a finger. *He was sitting here in the dark... waiting for you. He knows exactly what's going on, you stupid girl.*

"Fine. I'll leave. But you have to tell me one thing first. Is she alive, Zeth?"

I don't mean Carrie.

I mean *Alexis*.

My stubborn exterior slips. There are times when I let myself bawl over the loss of Lex, sob until I'm sick, but I won't break like that in front of him. He will *not* see me that weak. Zeth huffs and does something unexpected: He carefully takes off his mask. There's a bed behind him. I can just about make it out as he tosses the mask onto it and his huge hands begin to work at the cufflinks at his wrists. "What... what are you doing?"

"You need to see," he says curtly. The door's still open behind me. I should use it. Turn around and walk right back out of it. But something about the caress of his dark gaze on my face roots me to the spot. Since we met again forty-eight hours ago, our interactions have revolved around theft, threats, and dares, but now it feels like a barrier is coming down and something honest is about to happen. That thought in itself is so confronting that I want to run and hide. His suit jacket comes off, and he hangs it over the shadow of a high-backed chair beside him. He then unbuttons his shirt, which strains against his shoulders, the material drawn tight over his arms as he bends them to free each fastener from the neck down. Underneath his shirt, a black tank top hugs his torso, clinging to every ripped inch of him. He looks like a goddamn UFC fighter. His skin is pale, ivory marked with splashes of black ink. He looks up at me from under his drawn eyebrows and I feel the need to wipe my slick palms against my dress. Hot damn. I hate him, but his larger-than-life presence, his magnetism, the way he looks at me like he's already *inside* me... he slays me.

Moving swiftly, he rips the tank top from his body, tearing it over his head to reveal a wall of muscle that flexes, each individual part of him working together as he moves. There are four or five small tattoos across his chest, aside from the ones marking his arms, but they're tough to make out. A huge fleur-de-lis rides just above his hip, though—that one is easy enough to make out, along with the eagle over his left pec, its wings outstretched. Script writing chains his neck, elaborate wording I can't quite discern. He steps forward, and I step back, holding my breath. I'm hovering in the doorway now, and Zeth's movement has brought him into the light, but only halfway. The front of his body—his chest, his defined stomach, the deeply cut V that slices over his hipbones and disappears down below his belt—is bathed in light from the hallway. The rest of him is cast in shadows.

"This," he says, pointing to his abdomen, "is where I was stabbed the first time." I see the bruised color of the scar he's pointing to, and my body remembers. It remembers his *body*. If I closed my eyes, I would know what that scar feels like. I've relived touching it so many times when I'm on my own in the dark. My fingers tingle with the echo of the memory, how it feels rigid and tight. "These two were the second time," he says, trailing his own hand down over his skin. The scars aren't neat and tidy like the first one; they're jagged-edged and angry-looking, two inches long and almost purple. They weren't stitched properly. It's typical that he shows me this and my inner monologue, ever the professional, critiques the handiwork of whoever saw to saving his life. I would have done a much better job.

"And this is where I got shot." He angles himself so that his upper body moves farther into the light, and I see the red, swollen wound a couple of inches below his collarbone. So close to puncturing his lung. Another inch and it would have caused some serious, maybe irreparable damage. The wound is damned fresh.

Call it professional curiosity. I have to know. "When did that happen? *Why?*"

Zeth takes my hand and draws me forward. My feet try to stay glued to the spot, but the rest of my body sinks toward him like it's been inevitable this whole time. He places my hand over his bullet wound, staring me in the eye. His skin is searing hot, so hot it feels like my hand is on fire. "'Bout three weeks ago," he says softly. "And it happened because the guy I was sent to kill didn't feel like going quietly."

Fuck. I try to pull my hand away, but he clasps hold of it tight, pinning it to his skin. I can't go anywhere.

"This is my world. People get shanked and shot here on a regular basis. It's dark. It's scary. People die. If your sister has been sucked into this world, do *you* think she's survived it?"

Tears well in my eyes. I want to hit him. I want to smash my fist into his face so hard I feel bones break—his or mine, it doesn't really matter. I'm so enraged that I *do* lash out, but with my open palm. I slap him as hard as I can, and his face snaps to the side. My hand stings like a bitch. When Zeth's head rolls back to face me, a slow and considered movement, I've started panicking. A bead of blood pearls on his lower lip where I've split his skin. My heart hiccups, already well aware that I've made a stupid move. A really, *really* stupid move.

"Thought you didn't want to play, Sloane," he growls. Still holding on to my hand, he starts to back into the room, pulling me with him. My heart rate soars. I tug back against him, but he doesn't let go. He moves, bending and picking me up so fast I don't have time to scream. In three long strides, he closes the distance between the door and the bed and dumps me onto it, still picking me over with those almost black eyes.

"I swear to God, if you rape me, I'll kill you," I spit.

Zeth makes a feral snarl in the back of his throat, wild and dangerous. "I don't force women, Sloane. If we have sex, it'll be because you want to."

"Is that why you've just thrown me onto this bed?"

"I threw you onto the bed because you hit me, and that was very bad of you. But I've decided to make you a deal."

I eye the doorway. It's only ten feet away, but I won't make it without him tackling me. "What do you mean, *a deal*?"

He crouches down beside the bed, and I'm transported back to the hotel room again. But this time I see the inquisitive, knowing look on his face. His powerful jawline puts most men to shame. Coupled with the other unique elements that make up his face—dark eyebrows, dimpled chin, pouting lips, a cheekbone structure most women would die for—he is the most beautiful human being I have ever seen. It's not his looks that freeze my limbs to stone, though. It's the way he looks at me, like for this split second I am the sole focus of his entire world.

"I'm going to ask you two questions," he says carefully. "And then you can stay here and do what I tell you to do, or you can leave. You can go home and forget all about this, and me, and what you've seen here tonight. It'll be your choice."

Seems like a no-brainer. I don't think he's lying to me. He *will* let me walk right on out of here. I see it in his eyes. "Okay."

"Okay," he says. A thrill of nerves tingles through me when he rises and sits on the edge of the bed. He leans over and places his left hand beside my head, supporting his weight so that he hovers above me. "Have you fucked anyone since me?"

What the hell kind of question is that? He waits for my answer while I feign anger over the indignity of the question. He doesn't seem to care that he's pissed me off. He just waits. Fine. I have no reason to lie to him. "No. I haven't *had sex* with anyone since you."

Zeth's only reaction to this is a crinkling at the corner of his eyes when he narrows them at me. "Good. Thank you. And now answer me this…"

I hold my breath. This is going to be messed up, I just know it.

"Back when we first met, I told you that you had to own me or I would own you. You've been thinking about what that would be like ever since then."

"No. I haven't." My voice shakes so bad I sound like a terrified little girl. Zeth tuts.

"You did so well just now when you told me the truth. Don't ruin it, Sloane. An, anyway, that wasn't my question. I already know that's true." He lowers himself down as he speaks, until his face is an inch away from mine. He tips his head to the side and dips lower, buzzing his nose along the side of my jaw, inhaling slowly and then exhaling. His hot breath sends a shiver through my body so powerful that I have to lock my muscles to stop it. "You haven't been able to get me out of your head. You think about me all the time, wondering who I am. Where I am. What I'm doing. *Who I'm fucking.*" He breathes that last word directly into my ear, and my legs clamp together. "At night, when you're alone, when you touch yourself, *I'm* the one you're wet for. And this whole time you've been wondering. Wondering what it would have been like to have me own you that night. What I would have done to you. How I would have made you mine. So my last question for you, Sloane, is this: Are you strong enough to admit that this is what you want? Are you brave enough to find out?"

I am stripped to the bone. It's like Zeth has somehow found a way inside my mind and read all of my most personal thoughts. He has no way of knowing those things about me, but he says them with such an unequivocal certainty that I know he believes it's true. And it is. Fuck. I close my eyes, trying to breathe through the panic. Panic due to Zeth hovering over me, pure sex and malice wrapped up in one blisteringly hot, tattooed package.

"I—I do not want that, Zeth."

If he's disappointed, he shows no sign. He sits back, giving me some space. "Fair enough. It's been a very pleasant visit, then, Sloane. But if that's the case, then I think it's time you were going."

I sit up, watching him. He's serious. He's going to let me go. I slowly swing my legs from the bed, tensing, ready, just in case it's some kind of trick. He stands and picks up his dress shirt, slipping his arms back through the sleeves. It hangs open as he collects his cufflinks from a dark, anonymous piece of furniture. The outline of him, the tattoos, the face, the open shirt...he's earned the animalistic and deeply sexual way that he moves. It's not an attitude. I can tell that already. It's just who he is.

"Well?" he asks.

"What…" I can't wrestle the words out. I hate that I'm even thinking them. "What will you do when I leave?"

Zeth walks back to the bed, comes to stand right in front of me. My eyes are level with his belly button, which is just about goddamn perfect. How the *hell* does a man have a perfect belly button? He curls his index finger and tucks it under my chin, lifting my face so that our eyes meet across the length of his torso. "I'm going to go out there and drink some champagne, and then I'm going to find someone who wants to play."

"Play?"

"Yeah. Not fucking chess, Sloane. Someone who wants me to fuck them until they can't see straight. Someone who'll let me sink my tongue into their pussy. Someone who'll let me taste them. Someone who'll let me restrain them and scare the living shit out of them. Someone who *likes* that. I was hoping it was going to be you tonight, but…"

I swallow.

I swallow again. My throat feels like I've inhaled the fucking Sahara Desert. I have to get out of here before I do something stupid. I stand up so quickly, Zeth has to step back to avoid injury. "I—I have work tomorrow. I—" I hurry to the door, fighting for… what? The strength to leave?

"*Ahem.*"

He's washed in pale yellow light when I turn around. "I think you're forgetting something." He bends and picks up my medical bag, holding it out in front of him. He smirks when he sees the look on my face. "Y'know...you *can* stay if you want to, Sloane. You don't need to *say* the words. It doesn't mean you're weak. It means you're strong."

I walk back to him, staring him straight in the eye. I can't...I can't do this. This isn't who I am. Is it? Do I even *know* who I am? He offers me the bag, arching an eyebrow at me. "What's it gonna be, brave girl? You want the bag...or do you want *me*?"

He said I didn't have to say the words. He said it didn't make me weak. But maybe...God, maybe, just for a second I want to be weak. I've been strong for the past two years. I was strong when Lexi was taken. I was strong when I gave up my virginity in order to find her. I was strong when I realized I wasn't going to be able to save her. I am so fucking sick of being strong. I take a deep breath and close my eyes, already regretting what I'm about to do.

I shift around him and sink down onto the edge of the bed.

Zeth's low voice breaks the silence—a rich, electrifying sound.

"Yeah. That's what I thought."

17

ZETH

THIS GIRL'S A TICKING TIME BOMB AND she's about to go off in this bed. I'm gonna make sure of it, if only to reward her for not pissing her pants when I told her I killed someone less than a month ago. Most girls would have reacted, but not her. I'm not blind. I know that I scare her. But that just means she isn't stupid. Only a small percentage of women wouldn't care that I take people's lives, and those women are touched in the fucking heads. Why would I want to fuck a madwoman?

Sloane has a healthy fear of me. That's a good thing. She doesn't know what she's just signed herself up for, though, not really, which positively fucking thrills me. I'm still sticking to my scare-the-living-shit-out-her-so-she-runs-the-hell-away plan, but the greedy side of me wants her to enjoy it a little first. I might just enjoy it a little, too.

I smile like the cat that got the fucking cream when she tells me yes. I knew she would. There is no reality in which she was ever going to say no. She committed to this the moment she decided to come here. I stand up, leaving her rigid on the bed, and walk over to the doorway.

"Stand up," I tell her. She moves slowly, watching me, like she's waiting for me to morph into some kind of monster. Poor pet. She should already know this is what a monster looks like. Once she's standing, I lean against the doorframe and fold my arms across my chest.

"Strip."

She wants to say no. I can see it on her face, but she's trying hard not to upset me, too. She takes a hold of the hem of the tiny, skintight black dress she's wearing and hikes it up enough to show me that she's wearing proper stockings and a garter belt. I'm fucking crowing on the inside. No girl wears that shit unless she knows she's getting fucked. I was right. Sloane can deny it all she likes, but she knew this was happening tonight. Her fingers move carefully over the catches on the suspenders and then she props her foot up onto the bed, gently sliding the stockings first down her right leg and then her left. Her measured movements aren't because she's a master of striptease—they're because she's shitting her pretty little lace panties. My dick throbs in my pants as I watch her, but I don't touch it. I won't touch it for a while yet.

"Now the dress."

She wriggles out of the dress, easing it up over her body, and my hands twitch as I imagine her fingers are mine. I would have removed the dress differently, though. I'd have torn that shit right off her. Her hair tumbles around her shoulders like a goddamn waterfall when the dress comes over her head. I was right about the underwear: Her panties are black lace panties. Her bra matches. That's just too fucking good. Eli, the disgusting shit, had told her to wear black lace when I'd come to her before, told her that's what would make me happy, and here she is standing right in front of me in black lace. Well, well, well.

"Pull your bra down," I command. She looks startled, like she's finally realizing what she's doing and she wants to get the hell out of here. I wouldn't stop her if she tried, but then again, I don't want to advertise the fact. Now that we find ourselves in this position, I need satisfaction. "Do it, Sloane. If you don't, you'll be punished."

Her chocolate eyes, just visible in the light spilling

in from behind me, grow extra round. She doesn't speak. On the inside I applaud her courage as she slips the straps of her bra from her shoulders and pushes the whole thing down to reveal her breasts. They are big, natural, and perfect, just how I remember them from our night together. I may have given her shit for it, but she's not the only one who's coveted our experience in the dark. I might have licked and sucked at those tits, but I didn't get to see them. I've always been sore about that. Until now.

I watch her nipples peak, trying to keep my thoughts from my face. It isn't difficult. I'm a master of intimidation, so this shit is child's play. Her body is incredible, perfect in every way, but I don't let her see that. My role here is to remain as clinical as possible.

"Now lie back onto the bed."

She teeters back in her low heels and sits stiffly back onto the bed. So. She's still uncomfortable. Time to fix that. Time to strip every ounce of self-consciousness from her until she's putty in my hands. There's only one way to accomplish such a feat, and that's to make her body mine, so she doesn't even think of it as her own anymore. There will only be one thought, one desire in her world, and that will be to please me.

I reach out and drag her body toward me, pulling her legs back to the edge of the bed so I can position myself in between them. I sit on my heels, grinning when I see she thinks I'm going to go down on her. *No such luck, sweetheart.*

"Touch yourself, Sloane."

"Wh-what?"

The little mouse is scared. I pinch the inside of her thigh hard enough for her to flinch. "Touch yourself."

I'm astonished when she does as she's told. Her small hand darts between her legs, and she begins to rub herself over her panties. That's good, but not good enough. I growl, pressing my thumb into the skin where I pinched her a second ago. She pauses, and I watch as she closes her eyes. The hand goes underneath the panties this time, and she stifles a whimper.

"Good girl." I pull her panties to one side so I can see what she's doing, and I'm momentarily glad she has her eyes closed, because I slip. For the first time in forever, I slip. The sight of her middle finger working the slick flesh between her legs, teasing over her clit, is enough to make me groan. I have to ball up my fist and bite down on my knuckles to stop the sound from escaping me. A shadow falls across the doorway, blocking out the light, and Sloane's hand freezes. Her eyes snap open, and we both turn—two of my guests have come exploring. A guy in a tiger mask, and a tall, leggy blonde in a sparkly black dress. The girl still wears a golden mask, but the bottom half of her face is uncovered. Her mouth parts into a seductive smile when she sees what's going on inside our little room.

"Oh my God." Sloane scrambles to sit up, but a scenario plays out in my head and has me aching in two seconds flat. I place a hand on her stomach to stop her.

"Lie back down."

"But—"

I harden my gaze, broadcasting my message loud and clear. If she wants to make me happy, she's going about it the wrong way. The indecision in her eyes is interesting. She wages an internal war for ten long seconds. Finally, she eases back onto the bed, observing the couple in the doorway with suspicion.

"Sit down on the sofa. And no touching," I tell them. "Not until my friend says you can." I give Sloane this piece of freedom because she needs it right now. She visibly relaxes, although she still shrinks a little when the couple enter the room and sit down on the two-seater hidden behind me against the wall. I turn my focus back to Sloane.

"Where were we?"

She whimpers but takes the hint and starts touching herself again. She doesn't know it yet, but she is perfect for this. Perfect for me and my dark desires. I run my hands up the insides of her legs, stopping just shy of her pussy, and she rocks her pelvis up in an inviting gesture. *Not yet, sweetheart. Not yet.*

Despite the wide eyes and the hesitancy, she's so turned on I can smell it pouring from her. Her pussy is wetter than wet, and I haven't even touched her yet. She slips a finger inside of herself and stutters out a moan, and the woman behind us pulls in a sharp breath. I can't blame her—she can see what I see over my shoulder, and it's a fucking hot sight to behold. Material rustles quietly as my guests start to move. That's okay, totally allowed. I'll put a show on for them the likes of which they've never seen before.

"Take your panties off," I demand. Sloane responds straightaway this time, shimmying them over her hips and kicking them to the floor. Her eyes close again, which is fine for now, but that can't last forever. "Open your legs."

With her legs spread wide, my cock is straining against my pants, begging to be set free. I'm surprised I'm not lightheaded with how much blood is being diverted to my dick right now. It's time for the bag. I get up, heading for the door, pausing when I notice that our visitors are already thoroughly enjoying themselves. The woman's dress is up around her waist, and the guy's fingers are buried deep inside her. His dick is out of his pants, and he's stroking it slowly, leaning casually back against the chair.

Sloane makes a muffled sighing sound—she's dared to peek and has seen what they're up to. She isn't as freaked out as I would have thought. Such a good girl. I grab the bag and hurry back to the bed, need finally taking over. I take out the items I require—four heavy leather cuffs—and recognition flashes in Sloane's eyes when she sees them. Yeah, she knows these cuffs all right. She's encountered them before. She's very well behaved when I fasten them around her ankles and her wrists, securing her to the bed. Trust, albeit panicked, shines in her eyes, which makes my stomach roll. God knows what I've done to deserve *that*, but it shouldn't be there.

The woman on the couch moans softly, and Sloane turns to watch. The guy has pushed back his tiger mask and is on his knees, going to town between her legs. She palms her own tits, her eyes fixed firmly on Sloane's prone body. I know what this chick is into, know what she wants. I just don't know if Sloane will extend the invitation. I plunge my hand into my bag and pull out the one thing I've been waiting to use since I met her. The one thing I had to fight to put away last time: my knife. Blondie moans again when she sees it, but Sloane goes deadly still on the bed.

"Remember how this works?" I ask her.

She nods just once. "Stay still," she whispers. This is going to be too perfect, I can already tell. Most girls would start screaming around about now, but Sloane seems ready to accept what I'm about to do. I've waited long enough, so I get rid of my shoes, suit pants, and my boxers, and I stand completely naked by the bed. I palm my dick, squeezing it—*that feels fucking good*—and Blondie grinds her hips into her partner's face, mouth gaped open in desire. Sloane's torn between staring at the contents of both my hands—my dick and my knife, like she's not sure which one to be more scared of. I give her my most brutal grin and then climb up onto the bed. Her body quivers when I set the sharp edge of the hunting blade to her skin.

"Zeth," she whispers.

Names aren't a part of this game. I give her a warning look. She bites her bottom lip, nodding to let me know she understands her mistake. I made no explicit promise that I wouldn't hurt her, but I do my best to soften my eyes, so that she knows I won't actually *use* the thing on her. That's not what this is about.

She watches me closely as I trail the sharpened steel over her body. Her breasts, her nipples, down her sides, over her thighs. She shakes so hard I have to be careful not to cut her. The woman on the couch cries out as I do this. She's on the edge, close to coming…and Sloane seems torn between watching that and paying attention to where I'm applying my knife. I flip the thing over in my hand so that I palm the blade, and I close my fingers around the sharp edge. Familiar, blazing pain bites into my skin, and I grin. With the weapon now handle-first toward her, I guide it down, between her legs.

Terror grips her for a second until she realizes it's not the business end. I work the handle firmly into her slick flesh, stroking myself harder when I see the feeling take hold of her. She's scared, yes, but she likes it. She fucking *likes* it. I slide the handle deep inside her, all the way to the hilt.

"Oh, *fuck*." She rocks against it, clasping her hands to reach the sheets on the bed, but they claw at open air, the cuffs restricting her motion.

"That's the hottest thing I've ever seen," Blondie groans. The guy stops eating her out to turn and see what she's talking about, and his eyes flash with something dark and animalistic. He's just like me, this guy. He stands and picks the girl up roughly, guiding her so that she's sitting down on his dick, her back to him. They both watch me pump the handle into Sloane as she writhes and bucks on the bed, moaning. Never in a million years did I think *this* was going to happen. Never in a million years did I think she would let me near her like this. The reality of it is thrilling and also worrying. If she'll let me do this, then where will she draw the line? Because this... this is nothing for me. I withdraw the knife and clasp hold of it hard one last time, enough so that metal digs a little deeper, and then I throw the thing as hard as I fucking can. It needs to be *far* away from me. The knife slams into the wall seven feet away, juddering from the force of the impact.

My hand is dripping blood. Sloane's body arches up toward me, just begging to be taken. I suck on the wound—deep, the length of my palm—and the copper sings on my tongue. I lean over Sloane and place my lips to her ear.

"What do you think, pet? Do you want to play with our friends?"

A guttural sigh stutters from her mouth. "I don't—I don't know."

I give her a one-shouldered shrug. "You might like it." Her eyes meet mine and I see it again: trust. I wish I didn't see that.

"Okay," she whispers. I turn and beckon to the blonde.

18

SLOANE

THE GIRL STEPS OVER HER PARTNER AS though he no longer exists. I fight to maintain control, fight to keep my objections on the inside, while Zeth, completely naked, sits back on his heels.

He runs his hand up and down the length of his shaft, watching me twist on the bed with a stern expression on his face. Most guys would be going crazy right now. Two girls, one of them half-naked, tied to your bed, the other one halfway there and willing to do God knows what? A small part of me shakes its head, sighing with disappointment at the way this evening is turning out. It's the same part of me that also objected to wearing the stockings and the matching underwear.

The rest of me is rejoicing, because I decided this for myself. I wasn't pressured into it because I was after something. I'm doing this because I *wanted* to. I've wanted to relive the night in the hotel for so long, but I've never been brave enough to admit it. Zeth, with his confronting nature, has brought this out of me, though. He is my maker, and he's created a monster. I'm horrified that I liked the knife. The way he used it on me had me vibrating with terror and want. The conflicting emotions had been so powerful that even I couldn't tell whether I was going to lean into the pleasure of it, or run away, screaming at the top of my lungs.

And now this…

I've never been with a girl before. By the way the blond woman crawls up onto the bed, shooting Zeth a possessive look, I'm guessing this isn't *her* first rodeo. Zeth smirks, a deviant smile so sexy it makes my skin burn. He moves back, giving her some room.

The blonde dips down and laps at my pussy, tongue gentle and careful, not like Zeth when he'd done it. He'd feasted on me with the abandon of a lion tearing into his kill. She is more delicate. Her tongue is damn persuasive, though. She watches me as she works, but I'm watching Zeth.

He gives me that knee-trembling smirk and carries on touching himself, completely unashamed. He owns his body, wears his skin with the kind of raw confidence that makes me want to feel the same way.

"You want your hands?" he asks me.

I nod. He gets up and unfastens the cuffs securing me to the bed, leaning over me so that his cock is only inches from my mouth. I want to lick him. I want to suck him. I want to devour him so badly that my lips tingle with anticipation. Making that move feels bold, though, so I angle my head and graze my teeth against his strong thigh muscle. He laughs silently, looking down at me.

"You're gonna have to beg before that happens, sweetheart."

With my hands free, it would only be a simple matter of reaching up and taking hold of him, but I would be asking for a whole world of trouble if I did that. I let my head fall back onto the bed, groaning. The woman licking at my clitoris moans, too, as she slips one of her fingers inside me. The sensation is huge, overwhelming, frightening, and thrilling, mainly because of the way Zeth hovers over me, pumping his cock in his hand as he observes my reaction. I thought I'd been turned on before, but this is something entirely different. This is all-consuming. Such a desperate need to please him. I bury my hands into the woman's hair, grinding my hips up to meet her as she thrusts her fingers inside me.

I've forgotten all about her partner. I'm reminded of the other presence in the room when he approaches the bed, now completely naked. Zeth shoots him a warning glance, fierce and primal, and the guy nods his head, as though he understands exactly what Zeth is telling him. He hops up behind his girl—still totally focused on me—and pushes into her from behind. She cries out, momentarily stopping what she's doing before carrying on. The guy starts fucking her, all the while staring down at *my* naked body.

The blonde lifts a hand and drags her nails down Zeth's side, groping for his cock. He shies back, an irritated look on his face, and then slaps her ass so hard it even makes my eyes water. She cries out again, this time louder and filled with pain.

"Not for you," he growls. He looks back down at me and, fuck, I want him. "Only for her. Only when she *begs* for it."

The woman doesn't seem to mind that Zeth is off-limits. She buries her face deeper between my thighs and sucks at my clit, making my legs tremble with pleasure. It feels incredible, but it's not what I'm desperate for. I am desperate for *him*. I know what I have to do to get what I want, and I've made my peace with it.

He wants me to beg. I'll beg.

He wants me to plead. I will.

Because right now he knows he's got me wrapped around his little finger...and it's right where I want to be. I'm sick. I'm deluded. I'm lost. I'm his.

"Zeth..." The words are like an omen, a bell tolling, sealing my fate. "I want you. *Just* you. Please. Make me yours."

19

ZETH

SHE BEGS ME. I WITNESS THE MOMENT she gives herself over to me, and it's goddamn beautiful. Her tits heave, her eyes wide, her lips bruised and pouting, just waiting to be kissed. I surprise myself by almost breaking my rule and leaning down to do it. I haven't kissed a woman on the mouth in...well, ever. So long that I can't remember the face of the person who last had the pleasure. It's way too intimate. I already came so fucking close back in the hospital that I scared the shit out of myself. I know I'm reckless around this girl. I just have no idea why.

As soon as Sloane says the words, I shove Blondie off her and unfasten her ankles. The guy continues to pound away at the woman. My guests are both lost in the moment, but Sloane is very much aware of what's happening. I pick her up and carry her out of the room, and when her arms lace around my neck, clinging to me, my heart starts thumping in my chest. It's like it's been lying dormant, useless as a fucking paperweight just gathering dust the past thirty-three years, and *this* is the moment it decides to start beating again. Worrying. *Very* worrying. I don't know what to do with the sensation, other than hide from it.

The corridor is all lights and groups of people rubbing up against each other. Sloane sees and buries her face into my chest, like she's worried I'm taking her out here to offer her around. Sure, I've done that before, but that's not happening with this girl. She's *mine*. I carry her to a door opposite, one that always, always, *always* remains locked. This is the first time I've ever taken anyone else inside. I punch in the code for the security pad—handy when you don't have pockets for keys—and the door swings open and we're inside. This is where I sleep when I stay here.

Once I have her inside, things move a little quicker than I might have hoped. If Sloane were some other plaything I was toying with, I'd spend hours drawing this out and teasing her, but I just...I can't.

Scaring the living shit out of her? I'm scaring the

living shit out of *myself* with the way I'm behaving. For starters I don't even tie her up, and that's like a prerequisite for me, but there's something about having her arms wrapped around my neck that's driving me insane. I throw her down onto my bed in the dark, and I do what I've been dying to do since she walked through the door in that little black dress with her medical bag in her hand. I spin her naked body over and draw her hips up to me, grabbing her hands and securing them behind her back. I sink my dick into her so deep she fights for breath.

"Fuck! Zeth!" She screams my name, head turned to one side, pressed into the mattress as I slam myself into her body. I swear to all that is good in this world it's like music to my fucking ears.

There's no holding back after that. I do it. I fuck her so hard that my ears ring. I didn't even know that was possible. The scent rolling off her is pure sex, pure want, so heady and intoxicating that I have to dig my fingers into her body to stop from coming too soon. I feel like howling when I do let go, allowing us both to climax. Instead I roar, a charge of sound that rips out of my chest like a bullet from a gun. Except I'm not the gun. I'm the victim. It feels like I've been shot all over again as I lie, panting over her body. The moment is an out-of-body experience, and she's the only thing keeping me from floating to the ceiling. I let release her hands and fall onto the bed, staring into the darkness in shock.

Sloane rolls onto her side, exhaling in that sated way that tells me I really hit the nail on the head.

And I'm so angry I could *choke*.

20

SLOANE

I WAKE UP IN A BED THAT ISN'T MINE. I curl my toes and flex my fingers, reaching my arms over my head in a satisfying stretch. My body hums, like I went really hard at the gym yesterday, but I couldn't have. I was at the hospital all day and then I—

Oh.

No.

I freeze, suddenly remembering where the hell I am. His place. His bed. His sweat all over my body. And...and *ohmygod*. Some random woman's sweat, too. What the...what the *hell* was I thinking? I sit up, ready to lay into the man who's put me in this position (along with many others last night), but he isn't there. I'm alone in a bed, in a sterile, empty room. Weak sunlight pours in through the windows, and Zeth is nowhere to be seen.

"Motherfucker."

I hurdle out of bed, already half inside my dress before I realize he must have gone and fetched it from the other room. My stockings and garter belt are folded carefully on the chest of drawers at the end of the bed, and my medical bag sits on the floor by the door. I stuff the stockings and belt inside the bag. Where the hell are my bra and panties? Gone forever, probably. I hurry out of the room in a fit of rage.

The apartment is a bombsite. Lipstick-smeared glassware decorates every available surface. Abandoned clothing litters the floor down the corridor. I kick at something sparkly and golden on my way to the open-plan living space, muttering under my breath.

"Stupid...so fucking dumb. Hate him so much..."

The apartment is empty besides the figure standing at the huge bay of windows overlooking the city. *Zeth*. His back is to me, but oh, he's heard me coming. I pick up the first thing that comes to hand and launch it at him. The champagne flute narrowly misses him, shattering against the support beam beside his head. He recoils like a bomb just went off.

A dark fire burns in his eyes when he turns around,

hands turned into fists. "What. The. Fuck. Is. Wrong. With. You?"

I pick up another glass and I chuck it, aiming more carefully this time. Zeth ducks, avoiding some serious facial injuries. "Last night! That's what's wrong with me!" I turn...I need another glass. I find a discarded black patent pump instead. The heel on it looks lethal. I hurl it, grunting with the effort, and it hits him square in the chest.

Zeth is a dark thundercloud, seething, growing angrier by the second. "What *about* last night?" he hisses.

"The bed? The restraints? The knife. The..." I shut my eyes, shaking my head. I can't believe that happened. "The *girl*."

The corner of his mouth twitches, like my freak-out is entertaining to him. He still looks like he's going to brutally murder me, though. He stalks forward, lethal, a dangerous predator, and I snatch up another glass—a rocks glass this time. Heavier in the base. More sharp corners. I throw it at him as hard as I can, but he ducks out of the way, still coming for me.

"Were you drunk?"

"What?"

"Last night. Were you drunk?"

"No."

"Were you high?"

"No!"

"Then stop throwing shit at me. And stop pretending like you didn't enjoy every second of it!"

"I—" My cheeks flood with heat. He's right. He's so right I want to cry, but I can't let him see that. I need to get the hell out of here. "Where's my underwear, Zeth?"

He's three feet away now, slowly closing the distance between us. In a complete about-turn from last night, he's wearing some low-slung jeans and a plain white T-shirt. Somehow, I just assumed he would always wear black no matter what. Black, in keeping with the color of his soul.

"I'll be keeping those," he informs me.

"Uh…I don't think so. They were Provocateur." I shift to the left as he inches closer, putting a narrow ornament stand in between us.

A cold smile unfurls across his face. "Are you denying that you wore them for me?"

He has me there. I shrug my shoulders, trying to remember how nonchalant people act. "So?"

"So when a girl wears something for me, it becomes mine, Sloane."

"Wow. You must have wardrobes full of women's underwear, then."

"Multiple wardrobes," he says. "Many. Full to bursting."

I feel sick. "Forget it. You know what? Keep them. I'm too tired, and sore, and freaked out to be doing this with you right now. I need to go home." I suddenly remember I'm on shift later, and my spirits plummet even further. I'm going to have to spend twelve hours walking around the hospital, reliving every second of last night while Zeth brags to his sick cronies about bagging me again. I'm such an idiot.

"Fucking typical," Zeth breathes.

"What is?"

"You, deflecting your shit onto me. All I did last night was show you who you really are. You can't be mad at me for that."

I can be, and I *am* mad at him. "You're seeing what you want to see. I'm not looking for some sexual awakening. I'm just looking for my sister. I'm done wasting my breath asking you what you know, and I'm done playing these little games with you. Maybe one day, if you suddenly develop a conscience, you'll come and tell me what you know about Lex because it's the *right* thing to do."

I storm toward the apartment door, betting that he won't follow. He doesn't, but he does manage to get the last word in. "A conscience will get you killed in my line of work, Sloane. Doing the right thing often has the same effect."

21

ZETH

I LAST TWENTY FUCKING MINUTES before I feel the urge to smash up the apartment. It's already fucked from last night, though, and Ganya's been shooting me the shittiest looks since he arrived to start the cleanup. Looks like my guests had a blast, not that I would know. I hid in that dark room for hours, waiting for her, not even faintly interested in joining in with them. So unlike me. Ever since Sloane appeared back on the scene, everything's been completely fucked up.

It's all her fucking fault.

And the woman had the gall to *throw* shit at me? I should have tossed her ass out first thing when I'd kicked everyone else out. Nah, scratch that. I shouldn't have let her fucking stay in the first place.

"Is there anything you need me to do this morning, boss?" Michael, stealthy assassin that he is, has let himself into the apartment without making a sound. I drag my hands through my hair, scowling out the window over the city. Why do I do this to myself? I've been just fine. More than that, I've been completely fucking happy. I ran as fast as I could two years ago after I slept with Sloane because I knew. I fucking *knew* this would happen, and now look at where we are.

"Yeah," I sigh. "Send out an email to the group. Let them know all future gatherings have been canceled until further notice."

This is such bullshit. She's ruined the whole thing. Because, now, when I think about screwing someone that isn't Sloane, it feels flat. Pointless. I'm not in love with the girl. I'm not. There's just something about her that I *need*.

I forget about the skyline and focus my foul temper on Michael. He's not big on words. I like that about him. Today he doesn't need to say anything, though. His thoughts are right there on his face, plain as day. Bastard thinks this is hilarious.

"And you can wipe the smirk off your face, too," I snap.

"I'm not smirking, Zee. Just observing something I never thought I'd witness."

"What are you running your mouth about?" I could happily go for a fight right now. Smashing my fist into something would go down just great, but Michael is just being Michael. Besides, we're too evenly matched for a quick brawl. It would take a lot to ground him. He grins at me like he knows exactly what I'm thinking.

"Just this girl. And you. And canceling your monthly parties. Says a lot is all."

"It doesn't say anything. Just quit... quit *smirking*! Have you heard from Rufus?"

Michael buries his smile and becomes all business. "Yes, actually. He said a report came back from one of Jacob Dixon's guys. A girl matching the description you sent out works out of one of the Black Talons' compounds."

"Works?" I know what that means. Jacob Dixon, head of the Black Talons, is one of the biggest pimps in California. His compounds are known all over the country—hell, all over the *world*—for the depraved shit that goes down inside their walls.

Michael nods. "Works."

Present, not past tense.

Shit. I should just unhear this information. Jacob's not a guy to be fucked with, and if Sloane's sister has been based there for the past two years, then she's definitely not the same girl Sloane remembers. She'll be someone quite different by now.

"Benji sent me a shot he managed to snap off when he was there yesterday. Wanna check it out?" Michael asks. Benji used to be one of Charlie's boys before he got sent away in disgrace after royally fucking up an armed robbery he committed on his own time. Three blocks from where he lived. Charlie thought that was stupid. No shitting where you eat and all that.

"He took a picture? Crazy son of a bitch. Jake'll kill him if he finds out he's pulling that shit."

Michael shrugs. "Kid's been working for the Talons here and there. They trust him more than most of the other grunts they've got running for them." Michael talks as he flicks through his phone. He finds what he's looking for and shows me. On the screen is a blurry shot of a young girl with a mass of thick, dark, wavy hair. A loose T-shirt swamps her small frame. Her face is only half turned toward the camera, but it's Sloane's sister all right. I blow out a sharp breath.

"Is it her?"

"Yeah. Sure is."

"How'd you want to proceed?"

"Fucking carefully." Charlie and Jake were rivals once upon a time. About three years ago, Charlie disappeared for a week, told me to stay home, which was weird enough, and when he came back, things were roses with the Talons. I'd been suspicious as fuck at the time. A sudden peace like that is usually birthed out of business, and Charlie's drugs and guns move south, not north. I'm not some stupid kid, though. I've learned to keep my trap shut instead of asking dangerous questions. "We go down there, Charlie's gonna know about it."

Michael considers this. The guy's more than just muscle. His brain is damn lethal, too. I might not appreciate or even like it sometimes, but he always has good advice at the ready, especially when it comes to stuff like this.

"Tell Charlie you're going down there to visit family. Make sure he knows you're not running your parties anymore. Leave it a couple of weeks, and it'll make sense that you go see Jacob. He'll assume you've gone there to get your dick wet."

I grunt. Charlie knows the only family I have in the world is the deadbeat wife of the uncle who used to beat my ass raw. Sure as shit isn't any love lost between me and *her*, but it might work. Maybe. If I can spin it the right way.

"You wanna take a team down there with you?" Michael asks.

"Fuck no. If I show up with a pack of boys, we

won't even get through the front door. No, I need to keep this small."

"You could take a girl?"

I arch an eyebrow at him, pressing my knuckles into my lips. "What do you mean, *take a girl?*"

"He'd be expecting that. Sounds like Charlie sends girls to him all the time. He picks up virgins mostly, but occasionally he'll collect a girl with a little experience. Jacob passes them on for profit down in L.A."

I could say Charlie sent me down there with a girl? I think about that and my stomach twists. The first person that comes to mind is Lacey, but I would never, ever, ever ask her to do that. *Ever.* She's already fucked up enough as it is. No, the only other option would be Sloane, and that's just as unacceptable. Even if it's only an act and no one is supposed to touch her, it's too risky. What if it goes wrong? What if Jacob wants a taste? I wouldn't tolerate that. We'd both fucking die. "Won't work, Michael. We'll need to find another way."

He doesn't argue the point. We stand in laden silence for a moment before he tucks his hand into his pockets. "Okay, then, boss. Anything else for now?"

"Yeah. There is." Fuck. Fuck, fuck, fucking fuck. This is the worst idea I've ever had, but…Nope. I don't even have an excuse. I'm just an idiot. "I need you to go see someone for me."

"The girl from last night?"

"Yeah. Her. I need you to give something to her." I put together what I want Michael to deliver, and he leaves. The moment the front door closes behind him, I want to chase after him and punch him in the mouth for not pointing out how moronic I'm being. He's usually really good at that, but this time he just accepted what I told him and left. What the hell does that even *mean*? Instead of chasing after him, I pull out my phone and call him. I watch him down on the street as he feels his cell ring. He stops and looks back up at the window, pulling his phone out of his pocket and answering.

"Change your mind?"

I clench my jaw, closing my eyes. This changes everything. "No. Just don't leave her side until she does what I have asked, okay? Do *not* let her out of your sight."

22

SLOANE

"DR. ROMERA? SLOANE? HEY, SLOANE."

I shake my head, kicking my brain back into gear. Mikey the intern stands in front of me, wringing his hands. The terror all interns experience is a powerful thing, and it still has Mikey firmly in its grip. He blinks at me, and I realize he's asked me something.

"What's up, Mikey? Have you killed one of my patients?" I probably shouldn't joke about that. It *is* a possibility, after all. Mike is a weird green color, too, which doesn't exactly assuage the sudden suspicion.

"I—there's a guy at the front desk to see you. He's been waiting thirty minutes. The nurses said they wouldn't page you if it wasn't an emergency, and he wasn't family. And then Gracie said she wouldn't page you because she thinks he lied to her when *he* said he was your brother."

I snort when I imagine Zeth trying to pass himself off as my brother. "How did she know he was lying?"

Mikey dithers, turning back down the corridor. He wants out of here real bad. "Mostly because he's black and you aren't."

Black? I put my coffee cup down beside me, my attention suddenly one hundred percent fixed on Mikey. He fidgets, putting me on edge.

"The guy said she should do better and rethink her statement. He said he absolutely *could* be your brother. And then he told *me* that if I didn't come back with you in ten minutes, he was going to torch my Jetta. Sloane, d'ya think… is there any way you could…?" He winces, pointing a thumb over his shoulder.

This guy might not be Zeth, but if he's threatening to firebomb someone's car, he undoubtedly has something to do with him. I groan and get to my feet. This is going to be awful. Mikey jogs back to the reception, pausing to look over his shoulder in case I might not really be coming. When we arrive, Grace glares at Mikey with deep disapproval. He's gone against her. Should have just kissed goodbye to his car, in all honesty. Grace is lord and overseer of this world. He's in for a *world* of hurt now.

On a red fold-down chair in the waiting area, Michael, the doorman from last night, waits patiently, hands folded in his lap.

When he sees me, his icy blue eyes come alive. He stands and approaches, dressed in a beautiful gray suit—no way it isn't designer—that complements his light brown skin tone perfectly. "Dr. Romera." He inclines his head politely. "Mr. Mayfair told me I would find you here."

"*Mr. Mayfair?*"

Michael's eyes flicker—curiosity flaring and then disappearing in quick succession. "Zeth. He asked me to come and give you this." He takes a black envelope from his breast pocket, sealed, and addressed with a sweeping *S* written in gold. I take it from Michael, scowling. Most people would have just sent a text message, but no. Not Zeth Mayfair (surely too ordinary a surname for him?). Michael gives me a friendly smile. How the hell he can set me at ease is a miracle. He's the type of man other men run from, fast, in the other direction, while begging for their lives.

"Do you know what's in here, Michael?" I wave the envelope from side to side. Something heavy and hard slides from the motion, and I can already feel what it is. *That arrogant, manipulative…*

"I do," he informs me.

"Do *I* want to know?"

"Mr. Mayfair insisted I wait here until you've followed the instructions inside his letter." His eyes shine with mirth when he tells me this, like he's enjoying the fury that spreads across my face. I rip open the expensive ridged black paper and tug out the note inside, which is just as thick and luxurious. There aren't many words scrawled on the paper, but they're powerful enough.

Sloane,

Put this with the rest of your keys.
Give Michael the one to your apartment. He'll bring it back within the hour.

Z

Forget being pissed off. Now, I'm livid. Now, I'm seeing red. He thinks he can just demand the key to my *house*? He thinks I'll just hand access to my *home* over one of the most intimidating men I've ever met? I look up at Michael, shaking my head. "Whoa. Pump the brakes. Absolutely not."

He grins, flashing perfect teeth, already laughing under his breath.

"Why the *hell* does he think this is gonna fly with me?"

"Because we heard from one of our contacts this morning, and Zee thinks you might be grateful for the information that contact shared with us. Something about a woman you might be looking for?"

I close my fist around the key still inside the envelope. *Is he for real?* "Not five hours ago, he told me he wasn't going to help me."

"He says a lot of things. Trick is to figure out when he's telling the truth is all. He's been looking for a while now. Not since the hotel, but—"

Oh my God, I think I'm going to throw up. "You *know* about that?"

"Mr. Mayfair told me only what he deemed most important. I needed to know who I was keeping an eye on for him. I'd be grateful if you didn't mention that I told you that, though. I'll be in six pieces and at the bottom of the docks before I can blink if you do."

This is all suddenly very overwhelming. I take a seat on one of the waiting room chairs, covering my face with my hands. My heart pumps with a vengeance. Finally. Finally. Finally. Finally…

Finally.

There's news about Alexis.

Michael sits beside me, letting me digest. I tilt my head sideways, closing my eyes, trying to keep the tears at bay. "Call him," I whisper. "I need to speak to him."

He flashes those perfect teeth at me again. "You

can call him yourself, y'know. He stored his number in your phone before he returned it to you."

I pull my cell out of my scrubs pocket and immediately check to see if this is true. S, T, U, V, W, X, Y… my finger stills over the touch screen.

Z.

There it is. A single letter, followed by ten digits.

My heart. God, my heart doesn't know what to make of that. I hit the call button, eyeing Michael warily. The sound of the dial tone makes my palms break out into a sweat. It rings once, twice…

A pause…

"Did you do it?"

That voice is even deeper from the other end of a phone. Unwillingly, need begins to build between my thighs. *Damn* him. "Do what?" I whisper.

"Don't play with me, Sloane."

I'm pushing my luck with him already, and we've barely said two words to each other. "Fine," I say. "No. I haven't. I can't really say that I want or need the key to your kinky sex den."

"It isn't the key to my kinky sex den." The sound of the laughter in his voice stuns me; it's the most delicious thing I've ever heard. "It's the key to my home. And if you have mine, then it's only right that I have a key to yours."

"And what if I don't want that?"

"I don't know. I don't know what that reality looks like."

Yeah. I'll bet he doesn't. I bet he never even considered I would reject this demand of his.

"Ask yourself the question, though, Sloane. Do you *want* to walk away? Do you *want* me out of your life? Forget Alexis, and Eli, and the way we met. Think about what happened last night instead. You knew who I was, then. *Exactly* who I was. You knew what I liked. And you *chose* to be with me like that."

He waits silently, his breathing slow and measured, sending chills down my spine as I do what he told me to. I consider it. This path can only lead to trouble. A dangerous guy like Zeth, mixed up in God knows what and with whom. He was shot three weeks ago, for fuck's sake. That's not something from his past. That is very much current.

"Plus the kid who was seeing to Lacey's injuries has disappeared," he says softly. "She needs her dressings changed. You don't want me doing that, do you? I have very dirty hands."

"Yes, I know all about your dirty hands," I shoot back, blushing slightly when I remember Michael sitting beside me. "What'll happen if I say no?"

"Then we would have problems. You gave yourself to me. You're mine. That's not something you can undo."

Is he joking? I can't tell. His tone gives nothing away. "I'm sure lots of girls have given themselves to you. You can go back to fucking *them*."

"From here on out, I'm not fucking anyone but *you*, sweetheart."

"Until you get bored, you mean?"

"Until I get shot and it sticks. Until you pack up all your shit and run from me. But let me just say this, Sloane. Don't bother running. I'll only have to come find you. Stay here. Be with me. I'll make it worth your while."

Why, just when it might sound like he's trying to be sweet, does he then follow it up with a threat? And why is the danger of that so thrilling? I feel like I might need a few sessions with Pippa myself. "Okay."

"Okay?"

I blow out a deep breath and then extract the key from the envelope. It's small. Brass. The kind of key made for a padlock. I close my fingers around it, and the sharp ridges bite into my palm. I am a stupid, stupid woman. "Okay, Zeth. Fine. I've claimed ownership of your stupid fucking key." *And you have claimed ownership of me.* I still have no idea why he wants me so badly, but I don't doubt him. Zeth doesn't waste his time. I know *that* much about him already. If he weren't interested, he wouldn't be going to these lengths. I'd be a long-forgotten conquest by now.

"And you're giving yours to Michael?"

"Yes. I'll give it to him, I swear."

A wicked growl travels down the line and straight into my ear. My eyelids flutter closed. I don't know what I've done. I don't know what I've *agreed* to, but I am so, *so* relieved. I've seen terminal patients go through this before. They fight and fight for so long, valiantly refusing to give up, and then, when they're told it's no use and there's nothing more to be done... *that's* when they find their peace. That is the sea of surrender I float in now. It's deep, and it'll be only so long before I forget all about floating and let myself sink. Sink forever.

"Sloane?"

"Yeah?"

"I just thought you should know..."

And then he says the two words I never thought I'd hear. Two words that shatter my heart to pieces.

"She's alive."

23

ZETH

"ZETH! ZETH! WAKE UP!" SOMETHING hard jabs me in the ribs. I flinch, recoiling away from the contact. In the space of two seconds, I spin off the bed, grabbing hold of whoever was touching me and raise my fist, ready to strike. I manage to stop myself just in time—the person stupid enough to enter my room and prod me while I'm sleeping isn't a person at all. It's a broom handle. Fuck me. My knees are exploding with pain from where I slammed down onto them when I rolled out of the bed. My heart is charging like a piston.

It's not him. It's not him. You're fine. Breathe.

I blink at the broom handle, trying to shut down the attack commands screaming inside my head.

"Zeth."

The voice is solid. Calm. I look up from the pale wood at my feet and find Lacey standing in the doorway, her worn, pink terry towel robe drawn tight around her body. It's threadbare, but she will not throw the damned thing out.

Something must be up. She knows not to bother me if I'm in my room and the door's closed. And she's smart. She prodded me from a distance rather than approaching the bed. It's undignified, sure, but I'd rather suffer the indignity of being poked with a stick than hurt her.

Ahh, fuck, I'm naked. Great. Straightening from my defensive stance, I fix a questioning look on Lacey. "What's up?" She doesn't blink at the fact that I'm dressed in nothing but my skin. Then again, she doesn't blink at the fact that I attack people in my sleep, either. We know not to probe each other, to go digging in places we're not welcome. She understands. She has her shit, and I most definitely have mine.

"I can't sleep. I don't feel great," Lace whispers. "Do we have any painkillers?"

When your housemate decides to kill herself, there are certain precautions you take when she comes home. Got codeine in your medicine cabinet? Acetaminophen? Knives in your kitchen? Bleach under your kitchen sink? Yeah, *I* don't. Not anymore. Not until I'm sure Lacey's straight again.

I pad barefoot to my bedside table and grab the pack of Tylenol I keep there to take the edge off my hangovers. They can be brutal sometimes. I pop two pills from the blister pack into my hand and offer them to Lacey, who rolls her eyes.

"Jeez, Zee, you're being an idiot."

"*You're* the idiot." I glare at her. She knows I haven't forgiven her for the shit she pulled yet, but she hasn't said she's sorry. She never will. I'll die holding my breath before that ever happens. I expect a part of her is actually waiting for *me* to say it: *Sorry, Lace. Sorry I dragged your ungrateful ass to the hospital yet again. Sorry for saving your life.*

But you know what? Fuck that. She's being a selfish bitch right now. I watch as she tosses the pills down her throat and swallows them dry. And then I cross a line.

"Why, Lace?"

She foregoes the part where she pretends not to understand what I'm asking. All of those doctors at the hospital, each and every one of them must have asked her the same question. She tucks her crazy hair behind her ear and tugs on the cuff of her robe. I've broken the secret accord between us.

She knows, though. She can't brush me off. She has to tell me something, be it all the truth or just half. She frowns, anger flickering in her eyes. "You know when you wake up in the middle of the night and your heart's pounding? When the dream feels so real your skin is still crawling? When you can still hear it all, ringing in your ears? When you're too scared to close your eyes, 'cause you don't wanna go back there? Not ever?"

I study her, still as marble. I experience that on a nightly basis, but I won't admit it. Shit, no. I will never admit to being afraid again.

Lacey accepts my silence. "Well, I don't feel that anymore, Zeth. I dream...and I wake up, and I'm not...not scared anymore. I've accepted it. My body's accepted it. There's something very wrong with me," she whispers. I understand the horror in her eyes all too well. Whatever happened to her, somewhere along the way, her body has committed the darkest act of betrayal: it started *enjoying* it.

"Dying is the only thing I'm afraid of these days," she breathes. "And I need to be afraid. I need to not feel like...like I do. I'd rather be dead."

She is a lost girl in her grungy robe, with her messy hair and her haunted blue eyes. I look away, nodding. "What do you need?" I can't hug her. Can't hold her. There are some things I can do, and there are some things I cannot. Won't.

"Nothing," she says. "You've done enough." She adopts a vacant stare as she focuses on my chest. "That doctor. She wanted me to go see her friend. Said she would help me."

"And what did you say?"

"Told her the truth. That there's no point. There's no fixing something this broken. I'm not human, Zeth. I'm like one of those statues left behind after Pompeii. The shape of me is still here. The *outline* of who I used to be. But the rest of me is gone. I'll never get it back again. All I will ever be now is ash and stone."

24

SLOANE

THE KNOCK THUNDERS OVER MY MUSIC, even though I have the volume turned way up. I have no neighbors, not for a good mile or two, so I never have to worry about noise complaints.

DUM DUM DUM.

The series of thuds shake the glass in the window frames that overlook the city in the distance, and I pause in folding my laundry. It comes again. *Bang, bang, bang.* Whoever it is, they're getting pissed off.

I immediately think the worst: It's him. But then I remember that Zeth has a key. Surely, he'd just let himself in if he were here. *Why the* hell *did I agree to that again?* I skid down the hallway in my socks, picking up the baseball bat I always keep propped up against the wall behind the front door, just in case. I peer through the spyhole and my stomach drops.

He may have a key now, but for some reason, Zeth *is* hammering on my door at ten a.m. on my only day off this week. Even though the spyhole glass distorts his face, I can tell that he's furious. "Sloane. If I let myself in and find that you're in there, things are gonna get mighty awkward." He speaks in a conversational tone, like he knows I'm standing on the other side of the door, staring at him. He looks right at the spy hole, arching an eyebrow.

Fuck.

I pull the door open, greeting him with a deep-set scowl. "What are you doing here? Couldn't you have sent a text?" The corner of his mouth twitches, and I realize he's trying not to smile. He eyes the baseball bat in my hand.

"I could have. But I didn't."

"Well, you should have."

"I wanted to see where you lived." He smiles a secret smile, and I know what it means. He knew where I lived just fine. He looks ridiculously hot in his tight black tee and leather jacket, his jeans hugging him in all the right places. Dark hair, dark eyes, dark clothes. I'm almost surprised to see him out in the daylight.

"If I don't invite you in, will you be stuck at the

threshold?" I'm pretty proud of that one. Zeth does the eyebrow thing again and steps into the house.

"You think I'm right out of a horror film, don't you?"

"Well, this is hardly a fairy tale, is it?"

"It could be. If you let it."

"Oh yeah? And who are you supposed to be? My Prince Charming?"

He snorts at that. "No, silly girl. I'm the big bad wolf." He looks around with a curiosity that does nothing to dampen his predatory vibe. If anything, it looks like he's searching for the exits, documenting all possible escape routes. Not for himself, of course. For *me*. Wondering which way I will run.

"What are you doing here, Zeth?"

"I told you. I wanted to see where you live."

"No, you didn't."

"Oh? You know me so well already?" He picks up a photo frame, studying the picture of me and Alexis at summer camp. We look like two peas in a pod, smiling, both in braces. He shouldn't be here. He shouldn't be handling my belongings, doing mundane things like flicking through the unopened mail sitting on my kitchen counter.

"Hey. Do you mind?"

"You live here alone?"

"Yes."

"Good." He carries on investigating the place, leaving the kitchen to head through to the living room. The place is pretty empty, just a couple of bookshelves, the beaten leather sofas, a small flatscreen that I never watch. His gaze lingers on my guitar leaning against the wall in the corner.

"You play?" I ask him.

"No." He turns, finally giving me his attention.

"You done snooping?"

"The only room I'm interested in snooping around in is the bedroom, Sloane. Right now I'm just making sure your house is secure. And it is."

"I know. I spent thousands of dollars making sure it was safeguarded against *intruders* when I moved in. Now if you don't mind, I have housework to do."

Zeth smirks, like the idea of me doing housework is the funniest shit ever. "This friend of yours, the doctor," he says. "I want to meet her."

"What?"

"I want to meet her."

"Why?"

"So I can gauge whether she can help with Lacey."

Help with *Lacey*? That takes a moment to sink in. He wants help for his friend? The girl had been so locked down at the hospital, but I'd made the offer. I'd planted the seed and hoped all the same.

"My friend's name is Pippa. And why the hell should I help *you*?"

A reckless smile curves Zeth's mouth upward on one side. "Pippa, huh?" He looks like he's enjoying some secret joke. He stalks slowly across the living room, his face suddenly all danger and destruction. I feel like I'm being hunted. I back up as he gets closer, but the damn wall stops me after three paces. Zeth leans into me and trails the bridge of his nose across my jawline, breathing in deep, inhaling me. "You're going to help me for four reasons." His hands find my hips. He takes his time, reaching into my jeans pocket and pulling out my phone. Meanwhile, I am frozen solid, rooted to the spot. He's *touching* me, and it's broad daylight.

"One," he says, dropping his eye contact to look down at my phone. "You're going to call Pippa because I *asked* you to. That's the only reason you're ever going to need from here on in." He starts keying the buttons, then scrolls across the touch screen, frowning. "Two. You're going to call Pippa because you're a doctor, and it's in your nature to want to help Lacey."

He hits the call button on my cell and holds it out to me. I take it from him, dazed by the fact that the scent of him is making me feel drunk, and from the fact that I *can't* say no. He's already too commanding, too powerful, too confident in himself. I don't have a hope in hell of refusing him. The phone starts to ring in my ear.

"Three. You're going to do what I ask you because I've had a change of heart. I'm going to help you find Alexis." He raises a finger to my lips to stop me from saying anything before I can get a word out—no *thank you*, no *it's about fucking time*. Nothing. "And four…" He bites down on his bottom lip, tugging it between his teeth, and just like that, I'm ruined for every other man on the face of the planet. He leans close again, pressing his lips against the shell of my ear. His hand slides down the front of my jeans, and I start to shake. "Four, Sloane, I'm about to make you come. And you're going to be very, *very* grateful." He parts my flesh with his index and middle fingers, working my pussy lips apart, immediately finding my clit, and I gasp out loud.

"Are you ready?"

Every muscle in my body tenses. A deviant spark flares in his eyes, daring me to deny him. I don't. I can't. He slides his fingers forward, groaning, pushing them inside of me, his gaze firmly fixed on me. I suck in a sharp breath, fighting the urge to let my eyes roll back into my head.

"Sloane? Sloane? Are you there?"

I haven't even noticed the dial tone stopped ringing in my ear. "*SHIT!*"

"Well, hello to you, too." Pippa sounds mildly entertained by my greeting.

Zeth looks about as evil as a man can as he thrusts his fingers inside me even harder. "You want me to stop?" he whispers.

I shake my head.

"Then you'd better get talking."

A wave of pleasure shudders through my body. I can't do it anymore. I close my eyes. This is it. This man is going to be the death of me.

"Pippa, hi. I—I need to ask a favor..."

FRACTURE

25

ZETH

"**OPEN YOUR MOUTH.**"

"No!"

"Fucking *open* it."

Anton Merrin—sweating, hands cuffed behind his back—blinks up at me. The terror he should be displaying is like a drug, one I have a love/hate addiction to, and yet Anton is probably only exhibiting a five on the fear scale—a fact that is downright pissing me off. He's ruining my high. I bring the butt of my Desert Eagle (previous owner recently deceased) down on his forehead, and a river of blood pours down his face. He's a defiant motherfucker, wincing through the pain as he sets his jaw. There's no begging here.

No groveling. No bargaining. Anton is old school. He knows there's a very strong probability that he's about to die, and he's determined not to shit his pants on his way out. I guess I can respect that.

I crouch down so that our eyes are level. Above us, the naked light bulb swings to and fro, casting shadows first over him and then me. We have the same bleak void lurking behind our irises. I recognize myself in him, and I wonder whether he likes hurting people, too. Of course he fucking does. "Where is he?"

"I'm not telling you shit, asshole." He spits blood at me. It sprays down the front of my jacket, over my T-shirt. Sloane thinks I wear black because I'm some kind of nightmarish vision, a creature of the night. The reality of it is much more practical. Black hides the blood. I look down at myself, considering Anton's action while trying to think of something fitting to punish him. It comes to me pretty quickly—a neat trick I picked up in prison. I straighten and turn, surveying the empty room, taking my time. The walls are solid concrete. They're thick. Thick enough to block out a grown man's screams. A rickety wooden table leans up against the wall on the far side of the room. I smirk as I make my way over to it, knowing what I'll need from the black duffel sitting on top of it.

"Hey, fucker! You better not turn your back on me!"

I stop. In the darkness, I smile. I let Anton think for

a moment that I'm going to react to his bravado, but then I continue, slowly walking to the bag and unzipping it. There are so many different utensils inside that it takes me a moment to find what I'm looking for, but I find it eventually: a small black box, about three inches square and another inch deep.

"You ain't gonna get anything out of me." Anton hawks and spits again. "Piece of shit enforcer."

I pace back to Anton, training a blank expression onto my face. "You always have to state the obvious?" I ask him, palming the small box in front of me, making sure that he sees it. On his knees, Anton eyes the box, clenching his jaw. *I will show no fear. I will show no fear.* I'm already inside his head, though. I *see* his fear. It just looks different from most people's. It's dark and tainted, like the rest of him.

"What you talking 'bout?"

"*Piece of shit enforcer.*" I repeat his words as I stoop down. "Back when I arrived at the compound, when you were standing at the gate, you called me the same thing then, too. I know what I *am*, Anton. Do you think that calling me by an arbitrary title will offend me? Do you think you'll get a reaction out of me by implying that I rank *low* in Charlie Holsan's organization?"

"Ain't got nothing to do with how you rank in Holsan's crew, motherfucker. It's about you ranking beneath *me*."

I think on that. While I'm doing that, I tease the lid of the box open just enough for Anton to catch a glimpse of the shiny metal inside. I snap the lid closed. "Charlie's family is organized a little different than most. As it goes, he uses me to do his dirty work, sure. But there *is* no one else above me, Anton. I'm as high as it gets in Holsan's *crew*. If you were one of Charlie's boys, you wouldn't be fit to polish my fucking boots, let alone look me in the eye." But Anton isn't listening. He's staring at the box. Good. I shake it from side to side, scratching at the stubble on my jaw with my free hand. "But right now, we're not here because of who we work for or who's more important. Let's forget all about Jake and Charlie. Right now, I want to talk to you about this box." I hold it five inches from his face, so close he has to tip his head back in order to focus on it. "What can you tell me about this box?" I ask him.

Anton looks at me as though I'm crazy. Slowly, he cranes his neck forward again, widening his eyes at me. "I don't fucking care about your box."

Oh, Anton. Liar, liar, pants on fire.

"Okay, fair enough. I guess we're only wasting time, anyway. It's black, it's small, it's whatever. The most important thing about this box," I say, shaking it from side to side again, "is that right now it's *closed*. It has something inside it that I want. Just like you. *You* have something inside of you that I want, Anton. And just like this box, I'm going to open you up and reach in and take it."

I lift the lid properly this time, wide enough that he can see inside, and I take out a slim piece of metal. A paperclip. Anton's eyes go round. "You're fucking *crazy*, dude. Everybody knows it."

I snap the lid closed again and tuck the box into my jacket pocket. I hold up the single paperclip I took out so he can watch what I'm doing. "I'm not crazy. Crazy people aren't rational. I'm *very* rational. Right now, this situation you find yourself in is rational, too. You tell me where my guy is, and I won't shove this piece of metal underneath your fingernail. And as a result, I won't have to keep getting more paperclips from my box to use on your other fingers until you tell me. Doesn't that sound logical to you?"

Anton looks a little lost, like he's anticipated the pain and already seen himself crumble. "Fuck you, man. This is about loyalty."

"This is *not* about loyalty. There's no such thing."

"Bullshit. You wouldn't be here threatening me otherwise. You're loyal to that English motherfucker. *I'm* loyal to the Talons."

I shake my head, tutting. "Loyalty is another word for stupidity, Anton. Dogs are loyal. You kick a loyal dog, and it cowers at your feet, dreaming of a way to get back into your good graces. Kick *me* and I'll bite your fucking hand off."

He falters. "You ain't here to protect Charlie?"

I shove my face in his, baring my teeth. "I'm here to protect myself. If you're smart, you'll start doing the same."

26

SLOANE

Three Weeks Before

I CAN'T BREATHE. I CAN BARELY KEEP MY legs straight. Can barely concentrate on my surroundings as Zeth growls into my ear. "Then you'd better get talking."

My cell phone is wedged between my shoulder and my ear and Pippa is rambling away on the other end of the line, oblivious to the fact that a dangerous, impossibly sexy, impossibly cruel man has two of his fingers inside me. He works his thumb over the swollen bud of my clit, smirking with a look of dark pleasure that sends vibrations through my whole body.

"Pippa, hi...I...I need to ask you a favor."

"A favor? For my favorite girl? Sure, hon. Shoot."

Zeth draws his fingers out of me and slides them over my pussy, grinning when I twitch. "I need you to see someone for me."

"Like a patient?"

"Like someone who wants to ask you a few questions before you see the—*ah!*—the patient."

"Are you okay, Sloane? You sound like you're trying to do yoga and failing again."

Zeth gently squeezes the tiny knot of nerves at the apex of my thighs, grinning mercilessly. He switches hands and begins stroking me with his left, bringing his right up to his mouth. He slowly slides his fingers into his mouth, piercing me with his gaze the whole time, sucking them clean. Embarrassment floods me, swiftly followed by a crescendo of desire that takes me by surprise. Every single experience I've had with this guy has involved him going down on me or tasting me in some way. As a fairly introverted person, the prospect of someone enjoying the way that I taste is a ridiculous one, but there's no denying Zeth's addiction. He leans into me, pressing his chest against mine, and my heart stumbles in my chest. He's going to kiss me. He's actually going to kiss me...

But at the last moment he angles his head, like he's caught himself about to do something unwise, and nips just below my jawline with his teeth,

"Sloane? Sloane, do you need to call me back?"

"Uh... may... maybe."

Zeth palms my breast through my T-shirt, squeezing painfully. He shakes his head, tutting. "Don't be a bad girl," he whispers.

I am instantly filled with the urge to please him. "I just need you to meet this guy, Pip. He wants to ask you some questions before he sends his friend over to you. Is that okay?"

Zeth nods approvingly, watching me squirm beneath him like a hungry cat might watch a mouse, right before it pounces. Pippa goes silent on the other end of the phone. Even her breathing stops. I can imagine her eyebrows banking into a frown as she sits at her desk.

"Sloane. Please tell me I don't need to have that conversation with you after all."

"What conversation?"

Zeth pulls back, still watching me, backing up toward the kitchen island. He reaches out behind him, barely glancing to locate what he's after, and then my throat swells up. His hand curves around a black handle—the one belonging to the serrated knife that lives in the wooden block on my marble countertop.

My heart doesn't beat once during the long second it takes him to withdraw the blade, always watching me, never taking his eyes off me.

"The conversation I said we'd skip back in the coffee house. The one about you making smart choices. This is about that guy, isn't it? You promised you weren't going to see him again, Sloane. He's dangerous."

He *is* dangerous. He's approaching me with a sharp knife in his hand, and he looks *seriously* fucking dangerous. I press back into the wall, clutching the phone pressed up against my ear. I know he can hear what she's saying on the phone, and Pip's remark seems to have galvanized him toward some outcome I don't even want to think about. "You're wrong," I breathe.

His torturously slow approach hesitates. With his head tilted to one side, only half a degree, he narrows his eyes, studying me.

"He's just looking out for his friend. Why else would he be doing this? How can he be so bad if he cares for her so much?"

"Just because he cares for someone else doesn't mean he won't skin *you* alive and hack you into small pieces. You're being incredibly naïve over this guy."

"I'm not," I whisper. He's closer now, standing right in front of me. He takes hold of the hem of my T-shirt, gathering it carefully in gentle fingers. "I'm just choosing to be hopeful."

"Naïve," Zeth mouths, shaking his head again. I swallow down the building panic that forces its way up my throat, pulling in a deep breath. *This is going to be okay. This is all going to be okay.* A clever person might tell Pippa right here and now that Zeth Mayfair is holding them at knifepoint in their kitchen, but something holds me back.

"Well," Pippa says on the other end of the phone. "I really hope you're not letting your vagina rule your head on this one. If I meet this guy and he's smoking hot, then I know you've lost your mind."

"Don't worry, Pip." Zeth takes the sharp edge of the knife and holds it to my T-shirt, barely touching the sharpened metal against the material. It parts like he's tearing through wet paper. "He's hideous," I say into the phone. One dark eyebrow curves upward as he reacts to that. *Bullshit.*

"Playing with fire," he tells me. I don't think Pippa hears him, though. His voice is so low and laden with desire that I'm pretty sure *I* don't really hear it. I feel it in my bones, burning its way inside me, branding me, charging me with electricity.

"I can see him tomorrow. I have a half-hour spot open at two. If he's late or he doesn't show up, then we're done. I don't trust him, Sloane, and I think you're mad to even be talking with him. If I were you, I'd sever all ties and run like hell."

Zeth has cut a clean line all the way through my shirt. He places the knife onto the countertop beside me and then draws back the fabric, exposing my bare breasts. His eyes feast on me, lighting every square inch of me on fire.

"I don't like your friend," he growls. And then he dips his head and laps his tongue at my nipple, sucking the bud of flesh into his warm mouth. My knees want to buckle, but his solid body presses into mine, holding me up.

"Two o'clock. Got it. I'll make sure he gets the message."

"I'm more concerned about *you* getting this message, Sloane. Please tell me you're hearing me right now?"

"Yes! Yeah…ah…I am, I swear." This is not going well. Zeth seems intent on me giving myself away. His hand finds its way down my jeans again, teasing over my sensitive skin, making me tremble, while his other hand works over my breast, roughly pinching my other nipple so hard that I want to slap him.

"All right, then. Tomorrow. Maybe you should come with him. I don't know if I want to be alone with him either."

"I…I'll do my best."

Pippa hangs up. She's pissed at me. I knew she would be, but for some unknown reason I can't say no to this man. I have a feeling that's a skill I had better learn soon, otherwise God only knows what kind of fucked-up situations I'm going to find myself in.

"You ready?" he asks me. That question has me shivering from head to toe. This is a prime moment to try out that word. *No.* It's just two letters. I can say it. I say it to other people all day long.

Hey, Sloane, you gonna eat that?

No.

What, you didn't remember it's your birthday today?

No.

Can you sign off on my rounds sheet this morning? I know I was late, but—

No.

And yet it's a totally different matter when this man is standing three inches away from me.

"Yeah," I tell him. "I'm ready."

I melt internally when he gives me a savage smile. "Wait here, then." He leaves the kitchen, at which point my common sense returns with a vengeance and kicks my ass. "Stupid, stupid, stupid…" I put down the phone and grab myself a glass of water, downing the whole thing in one long, gulping mouthful. It's so weird how Zeth can make one part of me so wet and then another part of me so ridiculously dry. Has anything ever been as inconsistent as my body right now?

I hear him come back inside the house. I brace myself against the sink, closing my eyes and savoring a deep breath—I need it. Need the oxygen.

"Sloane." My name is a reprimand on his lips, like he's reprimanding a dog that's about to pee on the carpet. When I turn around, he has something in his hand that makes me want to bolt from the room.

The black bag.

Zeth sets the bag on top of my dining table, unzips it, and pulls out a length of coiled rope. "You gonna take the rest of your clothes off or am *I* gonna do it?" he asks. With any other person, I'd probably leap at the second option. Someone slowly, seductively stripping you out of your clothes would probably be incredible, but with Zeth, he doesn't mean it like that. I think what he's really asking me is if I'm going to behave myself. I have yet to find out what happens if I don't.

I pluck up every scrap of courage I possess and walk over to the kitchen table. I position myself right in front of him, so close he can see the *fuck you* in my eyes. I'm doing this because I am evidently addicted to what this man does to me, but that doesn't mean I have to be grateful for it. I lock eyes with him, refusing to look away as I yank my jeans down. I kick them away and shimmy out of my underwear, tossing the items of clothing away like the fact that I'm stripping for him means nothing. Like my heart isn't thundering like a piston.

Zeth nods, appraising me. His half-lowered eyelids give a heavy, sleepy look to his eyes that feels positively sinful. "You're perfection, angry girl. No need to huff and puff. I'm gonna take care of you."

Well, holy shit. I wasn't expecting that. A reprimand, sure. Some sternly worded, poorly veiled threat. Anything but a compliment followed by a reassurance. I open my mouth, but infuriatingly, I can't think of anything to say. Zeth puts the thin length of rope down on the table and slowly shrugs out of his jacket. I catch sight of the impressive bulge pressing against his jeans, begging to be set free, and I can't help my reaction. I blush.

"Angry one minute, coy the next. You're confusing yourself, Sloane." He steps into me, placing his hands on my hips. His grip is strong and masterful. "Pick one emotion. I recommend 'turned on.' If you're not with me on that one, then I can go."

He's been pushy ever since he walked through the door half an hour ago, so I'm not used to this sudden glimmer of compromise within him. A meet-me-halfway, secret side of him that I think he'd prefer to keep hidden away.

The tension that's been drawing me tighter than a bow string slackens a little at the knowledge that it is there, somewhere, hiding within him. Buried beneath ten layers of shit-kicking concrete, but still...

I'm feeling brave, so I do something really crazy: I reach out, take hold of his hand and guide his fingers between my legs. The evidence of my lust is right there for him to judge with his fingertips.

He blinks quickly, enough for me to think I've caught him off guard, and then he moves his fingers, humming deeply. "Mm. I see. Point taken."

My body is jittery, impatient, demanding more than the teasing friction he is applying to my clit. He's doing it on purpose, only giving me enough to make me crave more.

"Sit on the table," he commands.

I do it without question.

"Good girl. Now open your legs."

I do that, too. And then Zeth drops to his knees right there in my open-plan kitchen and begins to trace his tongue lazily up the inside of my thigh.

Let me tell you this: You may think you have been turned on before. You may think you have been ready to beg, to plead, to straight up *murder* to feel someone inside you, but until you've had this. Until Zeth Mayfair is on his *knees* for you...

He looks up at me, eyes still hooded and promising forbidden things.

"I'm gonna do this. And then you're gonna do

something for me, Sloane." He doesn't give me an opportunity to agree to the deal (am I even being asked?). He grabs my hips, pulls me forward, and buries his tongue into the slick heat of my pussy. I'm so ready for him. I feel wanton, totally gripped by my need to drive my hips forward so he can gain better access. He laves at me, drawing his tongue upward slowly and flicking the tip across the charged bud of nerves.

During our encounters thus far, I've fought an inner battle. One that has prevented me from really letting go. From embracing the situation and enjoying it fully. That had a lot to do with fear, which admittedly still remains. But being afraid is overrated. I don't want that anymore. I want to own this. To let it consume and overpower me and wipe everything—all the pain, all the worry, all the regret and guilt—from my mind. I bury my hands in Zeth's hair, and I moan. It's a wild, unfamiliar, carnal sound.

Gonna be cringing over that when you replay this later, my subconscious whispers.

"Fuck you," I whisper right back. With my thighs clamped firmly over his ears, I doubt Zeth heard me, thank God. I'm not even in control of my body anymore. It's liberating, surrendering control to a side of myself I'm unacquainted with. My hips grind into Zeth's face.

He snarls, digging his fingers into my skin, growling into me as he works me over. I fight back when he pulls away, not wanting his attentions to deviate from my sweet spot, but he slaps my thigh so hard my eyes sting. The pain demands an instant reaction. I drop my legs apart, panting for breath. Zeth's chest is heaving, too. And he's wearing that wicked smirk again. Holy fuck, I don't care if he's dangerous. I don't care if he's an *axe murderer*. I'm never letting him leave this house.

"Got any ice?"

"What?"

"Frozen water," he rumbles. "You got any?"

I shake my head, trying to clear it. "Uh, yeah, I think so?"

Straightening, he crosses the room to the freezer and nearly yanks the door off its hinges. I'm still sitting there with my legs wide open, struggling for breath, propping myself up on my elbows when he comes back. There's a mischievous glimmer sparkling in his eye. "Never had you pegged for a freezer pop kinda girl," he says. My stomach lurches. Oh. Shit. I have a thousand of the things stashed in my freezer. Bubblegum flavor—a shade of blue that scientists will probably reveal gave people all over the world cancer in ten years' time. They're my guilty treat. And now Zeth is producing one of them from behind his back.

"Oh boy, you should put that—"

"I know *exactly* where I'm putting it, Sloane." His expression implies that this is way better than the ice cube he had planned.

"I don't know how I feel about that, Zeth."

"I'm gonna make you feel good about it," he says, nodding his head, as though that alone is enough to change my mind. I shake my head, but he drops back down on his knees and presses the offending article against the tender flesh I've left exposed to him.

My brain demands that I close my legs and escape the unbearable cold. "Motherfucker!" I try to kick him, but Zeth grabs my ankle, his eyebrows dipping together.

"*Sloane.*" That reprimand again. "Want me to use the rope?"

I suck my bottom lip into my mouth, biting down on it. Screw this. I should just get up and kick his ass out. It's all well and good when he's doing questionable things that might scare seven shades of shit out of me, so long as they excite me at the same time. But this is just uncomfortable. And sticky!

Zeth's a smart guy—he watches all this play out on my face. "Risk it," he advises me, tightening his hold on my ankle. I hear what he's really saying, though—*trust me*—and that changes everything. He hasn't asked me for that before. I've given him my trust a few times, unwisely I'm sure, but he's never asked anything of me. It feels like a development of some sort. I'm not sure how. It just... *does*.

"Okay. Fine."

He gives me a nod, stern and grim, which is kind of ridiculous since he's holding a fluorescent blue freezer pop in his hand. He traces it down the center of me, watching my reaction with smug appreciation, then dips forward and licks me, still piercing me with his eyes. The switch from cold to burning hot has my muscles jumping uncontrollably.

"Shit!"

Again, he repeats the same thing. Cold then hot. Cold then hot. The pleasure smashes into me over and over, never letting up. Eventually, the cold becomes just as pleasurable as the hot, and my hips are rocking again.

"Your tongue's blue," I groan.

Zeth arches an eyebrow at me. "So's your pussy." He traces the frozen treat downward and hovers a moment over my opening.

I know what he's going to do, and I am not on board. I am *so* not on board. But I'm also too late. He pushes it inside me, growling a warning as I try to squirm away...

It's the coldest fucking thing ever. And then it's not. It quickly turns to heat—the strangest sensation. A burning, stinging warmth that—I hate to admit it—feels good. I gasp as Zeth draws the freezer pop slowly out again, and then does something that shorts the wiring in my brain. He slides it into his mouth, a rumble of approval emanating from his chest as he wraps his full lips around the thing and sucks. I've never been so jealous of a freezer pop in all my life.

"Mm. Bubblegum and Sloane. Best combination," he purrs.

Oh. My. Fucking... I can't think straight.

Zeth rises up my body like a hungry predator, eyes full of fire. I shy back from him until I'm lying flat on the table and he's on all fours hovering over me. The freezer pop makes its way from his mouth to mine. He rubs it over my lips until I open my mouth, and then he slides it inside. The flavor is sweet and sugary, an explosion of chemical goodness. Then he reclaims it again, sucking it, tasting it himself, like he can taste my mouth on it, too. He places it down on the table next to my head and considers me for a moment, his breathing ragged and hard.

"Time for the rope, angry girl."

I haven't forgotten about the rope. Coiled like a snake in my peripheral vision, it's been a danger I've tried not to provoke. Does it scare me? *Hell* yes. But I'm done being afraid. Zeth picks it up, and I brace, readying for the panic. This won't be like before, when he tied me to the bed. This will be hands behind back, ankles knotted together. Who knows? Maybe he'll hogtie me. Sweat prickles in a nervous rash across my skin, and Zeth hesitates. He stops altogether.

Why is he stopping?

He doesn't speak. He jumps down and yanks his shirt over his head in that careless way men do. He looms at the end of table like some rough-hewn monolith, only he is made out of tightly packed muscle instead of stone. Unbuckling his belt, he gets rid of his shoes and rips off his jeans in the space of ten seconds flat, and then there he is, standing naked in front of me. His cock is rigid and hard, the tip level with his navel. I've seen quite a few penises through my training and later through my work, but I've never been possessed with the urge to *play* with one before. In fact, I've always thought they looked pretty comical. But Zeth? No, not Zeth. There's nothing *funny* about his manhood. He is magnificence personified. Christ almighty, I'm staring at him. He stares right back at me, the level of his focus unnerving, but I can't look away. I wouldn't even if I could.

"Stand up."

My legs feel unreliable, and yet they somehow manage. A thousand scenarios run through my head. *Will he bend me over the table and fuck me? Will he grab that knife from the kitchen again? Will he blindfold me and do unspeakable things that I can't even begin to imagine?*

None of those things come to pass.

He snatches me into his arms and hoists me up so that I instinctively wrap my legs around his waist. And then he slams me up against the wall, and pain jangles through my nerve endings like discordant piano chords.

"Ah!"

Zeth doesn't waste any time. He thrusts inside me so hard that my eyes water.

"*Ah!*" I cry out louder this time, and Zeth grunts, too, straining with the effort of pile-driving into me. Hands grasping hold of my hips one second, pulling firmly on my hair, tipping my head back the next, he exposes my neck and grazes his teeth across the sensitive skin of my collarbone. The mix of pleasure and pain is dizzying. I'm pulled into his fever, and the fire inside me sparks and burns. I gouge my fingernails into his back, enjoying the way his muscles tense against the pain.

"Bad girl," Zeth snarls. But he doesn't tell me to stop. If anything, he seems to push back against the pain. I grab hold of a fistful of his hair and jerk his head back just as he did to me a moment ago, and I see the look on his face. He's a man possessed, eaten up by his need. For *me*? This dark, brooding, sexy as hell man wants *me*? Shit. How is that even possible?

Zeth slams himself into me over and over, our eyes locking together. Something...something is passing between us. With each thrust, I'm being drawing closer to something, being pulled in like a boat toward shore. Zeth reaches down between our bodies and starts to stroke my clit, applying a pressure that shows he means business. He wants to make me come. I'm ready to do that. I want to do it for him.

As the pleasure builds to Hurricane Zeth proportions inside me, I feel like...I want to do something I know is stupid. I lean forward and do it anyway, before I can stop myself. My lips meet Zeth's. They crash down on his as he pummels me against the wall, and for one blissful moment I'm in heaven, his lips on mine, full and sweet and tasting like bubblegum and sex. The most divine thing I've ever experienced. And then I'm coming.

Involuntarily, my head kicks back, smacking into the wall behind me as a surge of pure fire ignites through my body. I see stars, from both the pain of cracking my head on plaster and the orgasm that explodes through me. Zeth comes at the same time, roaring out his climax just as he did back at his apartment. His fingers dig into my skin as his movements slow until they stop altogether. He breathes heavily, mouth open, pressed against my neck for a long moment before he lets go of my thighs and slips out of me. A warm, wet sensation rushes out of me, and I realize to my horror that he didn't wear a condom.

Suddenly, the high that I'm floating on pops and fizzles, and I come crashing back down to earth with a thump. Zeth pulls away from me and turns around, gifting me with a glorious view of his perfect ass. He buries his hands in his hair. He's freaking out, too.

I wrap my arms around my naked body, suddenly not so okay with being on show. "It's okay." I have to put his mind at rest, even if the next sentence out of my mouth is going to sound incredibly clichéd. My voice is still low and nervous as I say, "I'll get the morning-after pill. You have nothing to worry about."

He drops his hands to his sides, turning around slowly. His face is a mask of conflicted anger.

"Never do that again," he says. He shakes his head, looking at me like I've lost my mind. "Don't *ever* fucking kiss me again."

27

ZETH

THIS NEWAN WOMAN SAID TO COME BY her office at two, but that's not gonna fly. She asked Sloane to come, but since she's working, the prissy shrink will have found someone else to chaperone our little meeting, if only to prove a point to Sloane: *This guy is* not *someone you should be spending time with.* She's probably right, but it still pisses me off. She doesn't know what I've done so far to keep her friend fucking safe. I'm glad Sloane couldn't come, anyway. After screwing her brains out against the wall yesterday, I've been in a foul mood. I shouldn't have put down that rope. I should have tied her up and done whatever I damn well wanted to her. Used her like I've used every other woman I've ever fucked. And yet, I saw that look of hesitation on her face, and I changed my mind. It's not that I couldn't have done it. I definitely could have done it. I would have enjoyed it more than any normal person would. But I didn't want her to feel like that. And then she ruined everything by kissing me, and I lost my shit and stormed out. Seeing her is the last thing I need right now. So yeah, it's a good thing she's at work and not sitting next to me outside Pippa Newan's practice.

I show up at midday. The building overlooks Greenlake Park. The place is a rainbow of autumnal colors—red, orange, russet, green. Mountains of leaves are banked around the trunks of the trees, ready to be collected. Families walk their dogs. Mothers push their kids on the swings. A couple strolls slowly together, arms linked, thick coats drawn tight. Steam rises from their takeaway coffee cups. This is *not* the ghetto. Sloane tried to make her friend out to be some kind of fucking saint because her client list was comprised mostly of felons. This looks like suburban highlife, though. If I were as judgmental as Pippa, I'd assume she was getting rich and fat from the government stipend she receives to treat these motherfuckers. Her parolees probably *hate* coming to see her, too. Riding the number sixteen bus to this bullshit neighborhood? A neighborhood where they'll never be able to afford a cramped studio let alone a proper home? Yeah, that's a pretty big fuck-you.

I hover outside the building, watching the entrance, smoking my cigarette. This place will have security. Probably a concierge who doubles as muscle just in case the clientele gets rowdy when the good doc won't refill their Valium scripts. I finish that smoke, light another one. The cold sinks through my leather jacket and settles in my bones. After a while, I get up and pace as I smoke, always watching the door. Even though I'm paying attention, I still nearly miss my chance when it comes.

A kid, twenty, twenty-one, low jeans barely hanging off his ass, ball cap peak to the back, jogs up the stairs. I flick the butt, a shower of sparks spiraling upward as I dash across the road. I take the building's steps three at a time. The kid's finger is on the buzzer when I grab him by the scruff of the neck.

"I'm your uncle," I snarl. He spins, ready to swing, face twisted with a snarl of his own, but when he sees me properly, he pulls back.

"What you want? You ain't my uncle, man." It's not my size that makes him back the fuck down, even though I *am* bigger than the little punk. It's the look in my eyes. The *don't-think-I-won't-kill-you-if-you-put-a-foot-wrong-here* look.

"Right now, I'm your uncle. When we walk inside this building and go up the stairs, I'm still your fucking uncle. When we get up to the office, you're gone. I'd better not see you for fucking dust."

The kid hears the warning in my voice, but I'll give him credit where credit's due. He stands his ground. "I gotta see this shrink, dog. I miss my appointment, I'm going inside, and that ain't happening. For real."

"Don't you worry your pretty little head about that. I'll make sure you're square with the good doctor."

"Hello?" The distorted voice of a young woman bursts out of the speaker in the wall. I glare at the kid, making sure he reads how much trouble he'll be in if he fucks up this next part. He shoots me a filthy look and shrugs.

"Yo, it's Mark. I gotta see Doc Newan."

"Hi, Mark. Come on up."

The door buzzes and a catch unlocks somewhere. Mark opens the door, and we walk inside. The mountain of a man waiting for us on the other side is the unfriendly type. He's ex-military. I can smell jarhead a mile off. He's a smart fucker, too. He knows something's off as soon as he lays eyes on me.

"Dr. Newan know you're bringing a guest with you today, Mr. Fletcher? You know how she hates surprise visitors."

"Yeah, Franz. Chill. He's my uncle. She told me to bring him."

The guard, Franz—who the fuck calls their kid

Franz?—gives me the once-over. "I thought your uncle was a resident of the Washington State penal system."

"Just got outta SeaTac," I tell him.

"Yeah. You *look* fresh off the bus," Franz replies. He shoves a tray into my chest none too politely. "You should still know what to do with this, then."

I empty my pockets into the tray, smiling brightly at the guard: wallet, cell phone, and keys. I purposefully left the gun in the car. There's nothing on the phone or in the wallet that could cause me any serious problems. Franz eyes me like he doesn't believe I'm not packing. I hold my arms up at either side: *Search me, motherfucker.* He ignores that and shoves the tray into Mark's chest instead. A grubby bus ticket, a house key, and a crumpled twenty goes into the tray after my stuff. I get the feeling that the contents of his pockets are pretty much all Mark owns in the world.

"Be waiting here for you on the way out." Franz tips his head to the doorway behind him. "Better hurry. You're gonna be late."

The office is on the third floor, pretentious as shit. When we enter, the owner of the bubbly intercom voice is on her feet, bouncing with, what is that? Excitement? She can only be twenty herself, curly blond hair and a tidy body clad in a skirt and blazer right out of *Legally Blonde.* She grins when she sees the kid next to me.

"Hey, Mark."

"S'up, Patricia. This, uh, this is my uncle." There's something going on between these two. The girl practically mounts the little fucker right in front of me. Her smile slips when she looks at me properly.

"Oh, hi, sir. You came to show Mark some support?"

"Something like that."

"Would you like to take a seat?"

"Actually, I was thinking maybe you and Mark could go spend some time checking out the skyline or something. I need to have a word with Dr. Newan about Mark's sessions." A stroke of genius. If the kid heads down there alone, that gung-ho guard will be up here in two seconds flat.

"Uh, I'm not supposed to leave the front desk."

I just look at Mark.

"C'mon, Trish. It's cool." He holds his hand out and my suspicions are confirmed. Trish goes bright red, taking his hand in her own. She edges past me like I'm the devil incarnate. Smart girl. With those two gone, I plant myself in a chair in the empty waiting room and do just that: I wait. The intercom on the reception desk buzzes a couple of times. Seven minutes later, a door down the hallway flies open and a tall brunette in a pantsuit stalks out.

"Patricia, how many times! The buzzer means I'm re—" She sees me. Halts. Places her hands on her hips. It's a defense mechanism. When you're about to be attacked by a bear, you make yourself look bigger.

I smile sweetly at her. She touches a hand to her forehead and looks down at her shoes for a second. Seems as though she's trying to find the right words to say. When she looks back up at me, she's one hundred percent in control again. "She said you were hideous," she announces.

"I'm aware."

"Should I even ask where my appointment and my receptionist have disappeared to?"

"They're fine. On their first date, by the looks of things."

Pippa shakes her head again. "Terrific. Well, I suppose you'd better come with me, then." She isn't even flustered. I like and detest this at the same time. I wanted to catch her on the back foot, but my unannounced arrival has barely made her blink. She gestures into her office. I get up and walk inside. She follows, closing the door behind us. Together in an enclosed space? Alone? Yeah, this chick has steel cojones.

"You're here to talk about your friend." She sits down at her desk, crossing her legs and resting her interlaced fingers across her stomach. The posture immediately makes me angry. Prison counselor pose.

"I'm here to talk about *you*," I correct her. I walk right by the chair in front of Newan's desk and stand in front of the window. If she cares, she doesn't show it.

"What do you want to know?"

"Are you in this for the money, or do you really want to help people?"

She shrugs. "I want both. I have bills I need to pay just like everyone else. But I get to make money by assisting people with their reintegration into society. Helping them isolate the problem areas in their lives and teaching them how to make positive changes."

I hold up my hand—I've heard enough head doctor bullshit to last me a lifetime. It sounds like she's reading from a script. The only reason I haven't walked out already is because of the first part. She admitted to wanting the money.

"Have you ever had a patient confess criminal activity to you?" I demand.

"Yes."

"And what actions did you take?"

"The appropriate ones."

She called the cops. That won't work. I don't know for a certainty what's gone on in Lacey's past, but I get the impression that she did something crazy just before she showed up on my doorstep. And it probably wasn't legal. "What would it take for you to accept Lacey off the books? To keep everything confidential, no matter what she tells you?"

Pippa assesses me, thinking. "I'm a doctor, Mr. Mayfair. I took an oath just like Sloane did. We are both bound by that oath to help people, so under these extreme circumstances I would be willing to help your friend without creating a file on her. I am, however, also bound by the *law*. If your friend confesses that she has caused or intends to cause harm to herself or another person, I can't turn a blind eye to that."

"So your Hippocratic oath will force you to help her, but your sense of civic duty will overrule that and ruin her anyway."

She fixes steel-colored eyes on me. "That's how these things often go."

"And no amount of money will change your mind on that?"

"I'm sorry, Mr. Mayfair."

"Then I guess we're done here." Waste of fucking time. I shouldn't have bothered. I hustle for the exit, unwilling to expend any further breath on the dead-end conversation. There are a million corrupt psychologists, doctors, and police officers out there. I'll just have to bribe one of *them* instead.

"Mr. Mayfair?" Newan is still sitting at her desk. She hasn't flinched. "Against my better judgment, there is one reason that might persuade me to look the other way should your friend admit to something that might normally end in jail time."

"Oh yeah? And what would that be?"

She looks at me blankly, but I can see the worry in her eyes. That part is too difficult to hide. "You can stay away from my friend. Permanently. You can stay away from Sloane."

Well, well, well. Conniving bitch. I definitely don't like her now. "And if she doesn't want me to?"

Pippa looks out of the window, over the park, purveyor of her safe little kingdom. "I suppose if she *wants* to see you, I can't stop her. But then these sessions you need from me? You'll be paying me double. One for your friend, and one for *you*, too. I don't want a mentally unstable man anywhere near Sloane."

28

ZETH

ME AND ULTIMATUMS? YEAH, WE DON'T mix. Give me two options and tell me I need to pick between them, and I'll find a third just to throw up a middle finger. Sloane's friend has thrown me a curveball, though. Try as I might, I can't seem to find a fucking third option here. Newan wants me to stay away from her friend, which I can't do. And so the alternative would be to go to fucking therapy sessions with her myself. Which I also can't do.

The old me would have just said screw it. I'd have agreed to stay away from Sloane, fully intending on seeing her anyway, but if I do that and the shrink finds out, then it's *Lacey* paying the price, not me. The girl needs help more than I need Sloane Romera in my life.

At least that's what I'm telling myself.

Who the hell does this woman think she *is*, anyway? Normally, I'd solve this problem by coldcocking the person responsible for making me see red like this. But I can't. Because she's a smug, in an *I-have-a-PhD-in-psychology-and-you're-one-hundred-differ.ent-kinds-of-fucked-up* kind of way. I'll only be proving her right if I do that. Plus she's a woman. She *is* trying to control Sloane, though. Bitch is probably jealous that her friend is getting laid. I laugh, immediately retracting that thought. The woman oozed sexuality. Not a brand *I'd* ever be interested in, but still. If she wants sex, I'm sure she gets it. She's probably just looking out for Sloane. Does that mean I'll comply with her demands? Nope. Not in the fucking slightest.

I drive the Camaro across the city, headed for Charlie's mansion in Hunt's Point, at the other end of the peninsula. This is one of the most salubrious areas in Seattle. Bankers, golf pros, business owners. Respectable types live here. They wave at Charlie when they're walking their dogs, mowing the lawn. They smile at him as he drives his Lexus down the leafy, suburban streets. They have no idea that he's a fucking serial killer. He's lived there for twenty-five years. The place is sacred to him. He definitely doesn't shit where he eats, and he sure as hell doesn't appreciate when his boys trail their shit to his doorstep on their shoes, either. That means no dealing, no weapons, no grudges, and no shop talk when you step through his front door. Follow those rules, and the man will treat you like a king. Break them, and he'll make you wish you'd never been fucking born.

Shop talk is the reason why Charlie has called me over here tonight, though. The man never married. He has a longtime girlfriend, Sophie, but she's out of town visiting her mother, so the place is empty. No curious ears around to overhear something they shouldn't. I pull the Camaro into the long driveway leading up to Charlie's estate and wait for the gates to buzz open. A burst of static crackles two seconds later. The security guards are well used to my ride. Know not to keep me waiting.

I park and let myself in, not bothering to knock before I enter. Knocking is for people like Karl, and Rick, and O'Shannessy—lower-grade soldiers who've only been with Charlie a couple of years. *I* have my own key. I fucking grew up in this house. I lost my virginity to one of the housemaids who used to clean up after me when I was a snot-nosed teenager. I broke three of my ribs sparring with a martial arts instructor out on the back tennis court. My current digs are humble compared to this monstrosity, but I never felt at home here. I never felt I deserved this. I could never shake the feeling that I still belonged back in the stinking shithole where my uncle lived. Dirt poor, lowest of the low. That kind of poor works its way inside your psyche. No matter how big the roof over your head may grow to be, how many maids you fuck, or how many hundred-thousand-dollar cars are parked in the driveway, you can never really escape it.

The lights are on inside Charlie's place, blazing away, lighting up the whole house. Crystal chandeliers, Persian rugs, antique furniture—the works. The boss may have lived in this country for more than half his life, but the guy still seems to believe he's stuck in nineteenth-century England.

"Charlie!" I make my way through the sprawling ground floor, headed straight to the one place I can always count on finding the man: his study. Just as I predicted, when I push the door back the gray-haired bastard is bent double over his ostentatious desk, snorting a line of blow. He sits up, eyes the size of silver dollars, holding his fingers to his powder-rimmed nostril.

"Well, if it ain't my most entrusted employee." He leans back, wiping his hands on the front of his pinstripe waistcoat, leaving smudges of white behind. "So glad you could join me. Did you lock the door behind you?"

"Of course I did." The very first thing I learned

about Charlie was that security was his number one priority, especially in his own home. Woe betides the person who leaves a fucking window cracked. Ever.

Charlie shrugs a shoulder, nodding. He gestures to the chair waiting for me on the opposite side of his desk. I sit in it like I'm supposed to, making myself comfortable. "Got a job for you, son."

"Uh-huh." There's no other reason for me to be here. Charlie makes nice, pretends that we're family, but the truth of the matter is that I'm his dark and sometimes slightly evil secret weapon. Would he have kept me around if I had been more business minded, utilized me to launder his money or work his contacts like he said he would have last time we talked? Maybe. But even I know I'm more useful to him like this. His savage monster.

"It's Rick." He picks up a razor blade from the desktop and starts cutting another bump of coke for himself. The man is a professional and makes short work of it. Surprised the fucker has any septum left. Once he's done, he points the tip of the razor at me, leaning across the desk. "The little shit's been selling to the bike gangs."

Selling to the bike gangs? I can't help but laugh at that. "His father's president of an MC. What did you expect? I told you your stock would end up in their warehouses if you let Rick anywhere near it."

"Drugs, guns—I don't give a shit about that." He waves his hand in the air. "He can sell those to whoever the fuck he wants to."

"Then what the hell is he selling?"

Charlie slumps back in his chair, eyes wider than they have any right to be. He's gripped by a level ten paranoia. The coke always does this to him. "Information, Zeth." He still hasn't blinked. *Information!* The bastard's been selling information to some small charter in SoCal. Some nobody fucking gang no one cares about. Telling them what we got in our warehouses. When we receive shipments. *Valuable* information, Zeth."

"And have the warehouses been hit?"

Charlie shakes his head. "That's just it. Not a peep."

I'm probably risking my balls by saying this, but the question has to be asked. "Then are you sure the kid's not just talking to family? You know how it goes. One charter and the next, they're all interrelated. All messed up in each other's business, screwing each other's women."

"No! I heard 'im. I heard 'im telling them about the girls from the shipping container. This ain't no family matter. This is about cold, hard cash."

If Charlie wants to ingratiate me to his cause, then he probably shouldn't have brought up that godforsaken shipping container. It's been a sore point between us since I found out the old man was responsible for moving young girls in the skin trade. I still haven't decided if I can overlook it yet without taking some sort of action. The old man probably wouldn't have mentioned it if he wasn't so messed up.

"How did you hear him?"

"On his phone, fuckhead. You think any of my staff ain't monitored? I didn't come down in the last shower. I gotta make sure my interests are protected."

On his phone? What the hell does *that* mean? A listening device? A bug in Rick's phone? And not only in Rick's phone. Charlie just said it himself: *You think any of my staff ain't monitored?*

Any.

My blood suddenly runs hot. I get that hazy blur to my vision that never bodes well. I'm going to flip if he has done what I think he's done. "You got a bug on *my* phone, Charlie?" I ask him quietly. Carefully. The old man has a temper like a lion, but then so do I. I don't want to set him off, especially in the state he's in, without knowing the facts, but it's almost fucking impossible to keep myself in check. Charlie's angry expression fades a little, like he's suddenly realized what he just told me. Like he's just realized what a major fuckup admitting something like that to me would be.

"No, no, not you. Of course not you. You're family, ain't yer." There we go again with the family bullshit.

As if to prove the point, Charlie offers me a small white bump of the coke still scattered all over his desk. "I need you to watch Rick. He's supposed to meet them tomorrow night down on the wharf. They're exchanging something. I wanna know what. You're gonna take back whatever it is, and then you're gonna kill that little shit. You 'ear me?"

I wave off the coke, shaking my head. I'm not buying his vague dismissal of my question. If anything, it's confirmed the worst. Motherfucker. The girls were bad enough, but if he has been *spying* on me? I try to loosen the muscles in my body. Enough so that I won't shake with the rage building inside me. "What time's the meet?" I grind out.

"Seven-thirty. And you make sure you make that little weasel suffer before you dispose of him, all right?" Charlie doesn't seem bothered that I rejected his offer of the drugs. He cuts the bump for himself and then inhales in a sharp blast. God knows how many lines he did before I got here, but that's three in the last five minutes. The old man slumps back in his chair, head tipped back, chest rising and falling slowly as he makes a euphoric moaning sound. I stand up and make my exit, still warring with my need to curl my fingers into a fist and smash it repeatedly into his face.

"I'll let you know what happens," I throw over my shoulder as I leave.

Except I probably won't have to. Charlie will probably be monitoring me somehow. Maybe he'll watch the whole thing via fucking satellite feed. *From outer fucking space.* I tear out of the house before I can do something rash. He still has his security detail on site. If I even so much as lift a finger here, break a vase, scratch the wingback chairs, breathe in the wrong direction, I'm a dead man.

Instead, I jump into the Camaro and lose an inch of rubber off the tires as I scramble to get the hell out of there. Through the gates, out of the suburban headfuck Charlie likes to call home. I'm almost through the other side of Clyde Hill before I pull over the Camaro and get my phone out of my pocket.

It's a smartphone, not the kind of phone you can remove the back from. How Charlie would have gotten a bug inside, I don't know, but if anyone was going to do it then it would definitely be him. I open the security lock and then have the forethought to hit the contacts button to retrieve the one, single most important number I haven't memorized just yet: Sloane's. I scrawl the digits onto the back of my hand, and then I take the thing and smash it against the dashboard. Small shards of glass explode everywhere, into the footwell and all over the leather bench seat. I pry apart the metal casing and catch my breath. There it is—a small, square chip, soldered into place on the main processor. It obviously doesn't belong. The other circuitry is a work of art, neat and meticulously created. This alien chip, this listening device, this act of betrayal, was probably put in place by a very talented hacker indeed. They couldn't replicate the precision of something machine made, though. I open the window on the driver's side of the car and hurl the phone out of it, roaring.

I can't believe he's done this.

Actually, I can *totally* believe he's fucking done this. I just can't believe *I* was stupid enough not to expect it from him. Who's the fool here, me or him?

God knows what the old man has heard me talking about on that cell. It doesn't even bear thinking about. The car engine screams as I gun it, charging in the direction of home.

I'll do this one last thing for Charlie, but not to help him. I'll do it to find out what's going on with Rick. I'll do it to find out what the hell is going on in general. Then, I'm gonna start making some arrangements.

29

ZETH

THE DEAL GOES DOWN JUST AS CHARlie said it would. On the wharf, Rick—built like a tank, tattooed and tagged from the neck down—meets with three bikers from a crew I don't recognize. Their top rockers read "WRECKERS." I arrived early and set myself up on the second floor of the burned-out warehouse Charlie sometimes uses for meets like this, not really believing Rick would be dumb enough to use this place, but the guy shows up like clockwork. The bikers roar up ten minutes late, cursing and swearing about a police tail they had to shake. These Wreckers must be high-end fuckers to warrant that kind of heat. Rick hugs the first guy, a huge piece of work that would tower over me even, and bumps fists with the other two guys.

"What about it, Caleb? How much longer?" Rick says, addressing the guy he hugged.

The massive guy leans back against his bike, hooking his thumbs into the pockets of his washed-out Wranglers. "Three, four days max. Our guy's ready to move."

"And you've got what we talked about?"

"Yeah. Four. Although you could get six on the container. Don't know why you wouldn't wanna maximize your profit."

Rick shakes his head. "You get greedy, you get caught. Four's perfect. And they're all untouched?"

Caleb nods his head. "So our doc says."

"Good."

"More than good, brother. You're gonna wanna fuck this pussy yourself, believe me. They are some fine, grade-A ass."

Rick grins, scratching at his jaw. "Yeah, well, if I sully the goods, they won't be worth much after. I get pussy just fine, anyway. Better to save these girls for Rebel. Guy has more money than fucking sense."

Rebel.

Why am I not surprised? I haven't heard the man's name in a while, though. Maybe not since that bent P.I. nearly sold Sloane to him two years ago. Seems around about time the fucker reared his ugly head. Rick's right. Rumor has it, Rebel's pockets are deep. He also has a very nasty habit of buying pretty girls and using them up until there's nothing left.

"Okay, time to pay up, Holmes," Caleb advises Rick. "And this time we need more than dates and times. We need something solid. Something that'll make the old man happy."

I make a mental note to find out who this old man is, presumably the MC's president. I know every bike club there is to know in Seattle. They don't like it, but they all pay homage to Charlie, be that in cold hard cash or in muscle. The Wreckers are definitely trouble from out of town.

"One-twenty-one South Street," Rick tells him. "Cutting shop. Just getting started. 'Bout half a million bucks worth of coke gonna go through that place in the next month. Gonna get turned into two mil by the time they've bulked it up with talc."

"How many people working the spot?" one of Caleb's associates asks. Caleb casts him a stern look over his shoulder. Clearly, the guys are supposed to be there for backup and not much else. Certainly not allowed to speak. The other guy clenches his jaw, exhaling sharply.

Rick responds anyway, choosing to ignore the tension building within the biker's group. "Four guys.

Armed but entry-level. Kids from the local gangs, mostly. Subcontractors. Charlie don't want his regular guys anywhere near the stuff."

I haven't heard of this cutting shop. Charlie's a dirty crook, sure, but it's a point of pride for him that his products are legit. Guns that work. Drugs that don't fry brain cells. "What fucking use is a dead customer to me?" he always says. "If I fucking kill 'em, then they ain't gonna be around to give me more of their cash, are they, Zeth, my boy?" Apparently, his motto's changed, though. To be quadrupling the weight of the product, some nasty shit must be getting thrown into the mix. With every new piece of information I learn about Charlie, the girls, the cell phone tap, now this, I become more and more unnerved. I wasn't under the illusion that he told me everything, but thought I at least knew the lay of the land with him. Now it seems though I didn't know the lay of the land at all. I didn't even know what fucking *country* we were in.

"So the fifteenth's all set?" Caleb asks.

"Sure is," Rick replies.

"Sweet. We'll see you at the Coal House. Tell your old man Petey says hello, you hear?" Caleb draws Rick into a loose hug, slapping his back before swinging his leg over his bike and grabbing his ape hangers. The snarl of bike engine fills the warehouse. With a deafening rumble, the three men lap around Rick and then burn out of the building, leaving the guy standing below.

This is where I'm supposed to make my presence known. This is where I'm supposed to make Rick hurt and then kill him. But I don't do that. I gather my thoughts as I watch him collect his leather jacket from where he'd slung it over a rusting handrail and put it on. Why the fuck do those guys want to know about Charlie's business operations? Especially if they haven't actually hit any of the places yet? It makes no sense, although they're obviously planning on targeting this cutting shop at some point. They wouldn't want to know how many men are patrolling the place otherwise. And why the fuck is Charlie hiring gang bangers?

A million questions swirl around my head as Rick walks outside. By the time I've decided I want to question the fucker, he's already reached his car—a flashy Mitsubishi Evo with blacked-out windows. He bends, half in, half out of the machine.

"What's up, Rick?"

Rick shits his pants. He jolts, automatically reaching behind him for his gun. He sees the Desert Eagle in my hand before he finds his own weapon, though. I don't point it at him. No need. He knows I don't play with my dick unless I intend to fuck with it. Our eyes lock. "Zeth, man! What you doing out here?" What he really means: *How much did you see? How much did you hear?*

"Oh, you know. Same as you, I guess. Just getting a breath of fresh air."

I heard enough, motherfucker.

Rick sits down on the edge of the driver's seat, sighing heavily. "Charlie sent you with a message, right?" By the tone of his voice, he knows his fate from here on out. Rick's heard about the other guys who were stupid enough to go behind Charlie's back. He *knows* what comes next.

"Yeah," I tell him. "I got a message. But I'm interested in what you gotta say before I deliver."

He looks up at me, a glimmer of hope sparking in eyes that held only resignation a second ago. "What, you wanna know why you're being exed out?"

What? I scrutinize the eager look on his face, studying him. This isn't just random shit. He's speaking the truth. "*Me?*" It hadn't occurred to me, but shit. Hearing *Rick* say it? Fuck, it makes a lot of sense. When Charlie doesn't trust a man, when he's getting ready to kill him, that's what he'll do. He'll ex him out. Exclude him from his dealings. Keep him at a distance. Watch him like a hawk. It all fits into place.

"Charlie found out something about you, man," Rick says. "Something he didn't like. Not one bit. Said you were compromised now, no good to him. He wants you gone. Told the boys to get ready—that he was gonna need a new right hand. The old one was about to get cut off. That's what I heard."

Rick's falling over himself to be helpful. Most men who are about to die do this. Helpfulness sometimes buys a little leverage. He doesn't know that I actually don't plan on killing him, though. I take full advantage of the situation.

"What has he suddenly found out about me?"

Rick shakes his head, shrugging. "Didn't say. Something about your past, though."

Well, that's hardly useful information. Everything up until this very moment is my past. An hour ago. Yesterday. Could be something from last week or ten years ago that's turned Charlie's eye against me. But whatever it is that's soured him, I'm finding it a little hard to believe. Charlie's paranoia being what it is, the guy would have fucking killed me the moment he suspected me of something. He knows everything I know. All of the things he's asked me to do. All of the dangerous things I could let slip should I feel the need.

"I did time in Chino for Charlie," I point out. "He wouldn't cut me off without some colossal fucking reason." *No one* rides out time in Chino without it costing them greatly. To do a stretch for someone *else* is more than a show of loyalty. It's a sacrifice beyond comprehension.

Rick gapes, mouth falling open. "Aw, Zee. Shit. None of us knew for sure, but we figured you must have found out." He smiles cruelly. "Everyone knows Charlie slit Murphy's throat. And *you* were the one who went down for it? You never wonder why?"

The memory of that night resurfaces in still-frame images, blood-splattered and blistered like old film. Murphy O'Shannessy on his knees. Charlie's unhinged expression as he dragged a straight razor across Murphy's throat. The whole thing had begun over nothing—Murphy making some sly remark about the length of Sophie's dress. The comment had passed everyone else by, eliciting nothing more than a frown from Charlie. But then hours later, when the old man had snorted a grand's worth of blow, it was a different story. I don't think about that night too much. Try not to. I've killed, yeah, but always quickly. Knife to the heart, lungs, whatever. Gunshot to the head. Charlie did a hack job on Murphy's neck—on *purpose*—and watched as he'd slowly bled to death. He wouldn't let anybody put him out of his misery.

"I know why," I say. "Cops found the knife in my car. Blood on my shirt. One of my hairs on Murphy's clothes."

Rick nods through this impatiently, as if the information he wants to impart is gravely important. "Yeah, but how did they know to look for the knife in your car in the first place, Zee? How did they know to come knocking on your door?"

I've thought about this. Endlessly, in prison, where there's little else to do but jerk off, exercise, and stew. "I picked Murphy up from his place before we went to the mansion. His father saw us together. Last time Murphy was seen alive by anyone."

"Bullshit." Rick leans forward, face emerging from the shadows. "Charlie fucking threw you under the bus, man. How the hell have you *not* worked that out by now?"

A spiteful burst of laughter erupts inside my head. *Of course,* the voice says. *Father O'Shannessy wouldn't point the finger at you for killing his son. Never. You were best friends for years.*

And then another voice.

Get rid of that mess, Zeth. I'm fucking sick'a looking at it.

An image rises to the forefront of my mind—Charlie grinning madly, unfazed that he'd just brutally murdered a man I called brother right in front of me. Never once had he apologized for doing it, or for the resulting time I spent rotting in a cell for the ruthless crime *he* had committed.

"He wouldn't." I growl. But even as I say it, I feel stupid. Sick to my stomach. Charlie pinned that shit on me. I test the thought out in my head and wither when it rings true.

"He would. He *did*," Rick insists. "We all know it. He barely fucking hid the fact. When you got out, he threatened to kill anyone who breathed a word about it. Him killing Murph. You going away. Him *putting* you away."

Fucking hell. I can't wrap my head around any of this. I keep my face blank—no sense in showing Rick he's riled me. "Doesn't explain why you're selling intel to the bikers."

"I'm as fucked as you are, man." He spits onto the ground. "Cops rolled up on me last month, found drugs I was running for Charlie. Said I could either help them put the old man away or I was gonna land myself inside for twenty. They told me to feed this stuff to the Wreckers."

"And you *agreed*?" I may hate Charlie right now—the taste of his betrayal is battery acid on my tongue—but I hate the cops even more. Power-hungry bastards, every last one of them. I should know. I spent a lot of time with the fuckers after Murphy's body turned up.

Unburied.

And after I had buried him in the one place only Charlie knew about.

Fuck!

"Would *you* do twenty for Charlie, knowing what you know now?" Rick asks the question like the answer is fucking obvious. And it is. I crook an eyebrow at him in answer: *Fair comment.*

"You're gonna do something for me, Rick," I tell him.

He rocks back in his seat, surprise flitting across his face. He really had resigned himself to the idea that I was going to kill him. He thought his revelations about Charlie would fall on deaf ears. Maybe they *would* have if we'd had this conversation six weeks ago, but not after the confirmation that Charlie probably had something to do with Sloane's sister. Not after the cell phone tap. "Sure. I mean...yes. Whatever." Rick looks like he's trying to decide if he should be relieved or suspicious. "What d'you need?"

"Get in your car. Close the door. Drive to Anaheim and wait there for me."

His dark brows pinch into a frown. "Anaheim? What the fuck you want me to go to L.A. for?"

"Because I said so. And give me the name of the officer you're reporting to as well." It's safer to know the name of the bastard who'll be sticking their nose into Charlie's and therefore *my* business over the coming weeks once Rick disappears.

"Ain't just no cop," Rick warns. "Detective Lowell. Denise Lowell. DEA."

That acronym is the worst possible fucking news ever. The DEA looking into Charlie's shit? Catching a crime lord the size of Charlie Holsan would be a career maker. In the very least, a decent promotion. No agent in their right mind would walk away from a fat prize like that. Not if they thought they had a chance of landing him. I need to know everything there is to know about this Denise Lowell. And *yesterday.*

"Give me your cell phone," I snarl. The man scowls but hands the device over. I toss it on the floor and stomp down on it hard. Rick just nods, staring remorsefully at the shattered debris on the blacktop. "When you arrive in Anaheim, Michael will come find you. Stay out of the way. Keep your fucking head down, otherwise you'll lose it for real, you hear me?" I turn and walk away. Rick and I have never seen eye to eye, but he *will* obey me now. Even if he has no idea what I have in mind. The constant wrestling for alpha position—a competition only *he* ever perceived between us—is over. He never stood a chance.

I held his life in my hands, and I let it go.

With Rick about to hit the freeway, it's time for me to get out of town, too. Time for a lot of things. It's beyond time to free Alexis Romera from the cartel. Time for her to be reunited with Sloane and the rest of her family. And I may have somehow made Charlie Holsan's shit list, but the old man's made a big fucking mistake, too. I'm going to show him just how *big* a mistake he has made. Very soon, he's gonna wish he'd left me to rot in the back room of my uncle's shit-infested house all those years ago.

30

SLOANE

IT'S BEEN FIFTEEN DAYS. *FIFTEEN DAYS*, and I haven't heard a peep out of Zeth. I don't know what I was expecting. Him camped out on my lawn, stalking me from my place to the hospital and back every day? Maybe. I sure as shit didn't expect total radio silence. The worst part of it all is that I'm on edge, constantly on the lookout for him. I've played the part of the unhappy victim in our strange relationship for a while now, but the reality of it is…I want to know where he is. What he's doing. And why he hasn't been to see me. I have officially lost my mind. I *know* why he's disappeared off the face of the planet, and I'm aware that it's my own stupid fault. The *kiss*.

I realize now that there's nothing more intimate than kissing someone when they're inside you. And as far as I can tell, intimate is the *last* thing Zeth wants this thing between us to be.

"Urgh. Meatloaf today. Why does it feel like every day is meatloaf day in this canteen?" The interns in front of me, two young women clutching their trays to their chests, whine about the food while I flick through my patient list on my intake tablet. One pelvic fracture, one mystery rash and fever, one gunshot wound to the chest. The last guy was brought into the trauma center under lights and sirens, barely breathing, pulse thready and failing. He's young. Some kid whose brother owns a bunch of fresh produce markets downtown. Or *did* own before his head was blown off. Gang-related, they say. Mob bosses, they say. I have problems believing that, though. Seattle is hardly known for its seedy criminal underbelly. Either way, the kid's brother was killed, and the kid himself almost died. Right now he's sleeping off the anesthetic upstairs in the ICU with a phalanx of cops guarding either end of the corridor. They're either afraid he's going to escape, or they think someone will be along soon to finish off the job. Either way, the police presence makes me anxious. It always does. That uniform. I associate it with one thing and one thing only: *Alexis*. When she went missing, my parents' house was crawling with cops for days. At first, they were serious and determined, assuring Mom and Dad that Alexis would show up, that they'd find her. But as the days ticked by, fewer and fewer cops showed up at our house, and when they did, they told a different story each time.

We have a lot of open cases. Manpower is tight, but your girl is our priority.

We still have good leads. There's no reason to give up hope.

These things take time, Mrs. Romera.

It's been well over a month, Mr. and Mrs. Romera. Alexis's file will remain open, but until we have any fresh leads, there isn't a lot we can do right now. Keep us apprised if you should hear from your daughter.

"Dude. *Tell* me you did not just take the last vanilla pudding." The voice cuts through my thoughts. I turn around to find one of the fresh interns glaring at the pudding cup I just took from the refrigerated cabinet. She looks up, and I gain a perverse sense of pleasure when I witness the realization dawn on her face: *Ahh shit! Resident!*

I know the girl. Jefferies. She's a loudmouth. Thinks she's a contender for a surgical placement. But then again, these walking, talking morons all think they're in the running for a surgical placement.

"Problem, Jefferies?"

She shakes her head. "No Dr. Romera. Definitely no problem here." She squeezes past me, hightailing it before I can give her morgue rounds with Bochowitz for the rest of the week. They hate that punishment. Bochowitz has been working the morgue for the last thirty-eight years. He's impossibly cheerful all the time. Like, *all* the time. He also has an unnerving habit of talking to his patients. They're all dead, of course, so they don't respond, but somewhere along the line, Bochowitz developed a habit of replying for them. It's creepy, yes. *He's* a little creepy, but despite his peculiarities there isn't a single thing Bochowitz doesn't know about the human body. As an intern, I'd keep Bochowitz company in the basement of St. Peters. I had no interest in involving myself in the politics or factions of my peers. But, more importantly, I was also *learning*.

I catch sight of Dr. Patel on the other side of the canteen, eating alone. I haven't seen him since the night Zeth brought Lacey in. He looks up, sees me approaching, smiles…

"Hey, Sloane. What's cracking?" He kicks out the chair on the other side of the table opposite him with his sneakered foot. "Heard you got stuck with the mafia kid with the GSW."

There was a time when we'd have fought over a gunshot wound patient. We've seen so many of them now, though. The outcomes on them are so bleak that a lot of residents will try to pass them off on whoever's standing closest. "Yeah," I sigh. "Guy circled the drain for a moment, but we pulled him back."

Suresh nods, swallowing a mouthful of food. "That kid's got a rap sheet longer than your arm. My mom shops at that store. Keep telling her not to. She used to like chatting to the woman there—what's her name? I can't remember. Anyway, it was her husband Matty who got shot there couple of weeks ago. The wife and the brother, the kid you have upstairs? Both of them know who killed Matty, but neither of them will breathe a word to the cops. Apparently, they're scared shitless."

This all sounds like something that would go down in New York or Chicago to me. I open up my pudding, spooning some into my mouth. "I don't really wanna think about any of that. I wanna think happy thoughts," I tell him, grinning. "When's your wedding again?" I received an invite months ago and mentally filed the event away under the heading "happening too far in the future to worry about." The date must be creeping up, though, because half the hospital's buzzing about it.

"Less than a month now," Suresh says, winking. "Me, a married man. It isn't fair, is it. I'm in my prime. The world's women shouldn't be denied this."

He gestures with his fork down his body, waggling his eyebrows. He isn't what you could term classically handsome, but he has something about him that women really do go crazy for. I laugh off his silliness and shrug.

"You're gonna love it. Rebecca's so excited."

"I know," he says, his voice turning serious. "She told me to tell you that you've gotta bring a plus one. Mandatory, I'm afraid."

I haven't even thought about a plus one. I cower into my seat, eyes down on my pudding. Maybe I could bring Pip as my plus one. People do that, right? Bring friends as dates to weddings? I ask Suresh this and he just gives me a *look*.

"No. It has to be someone you're sleeping with."

Hah! Yeah, right. Like Zeth Mayfair is plus-one material.

"Or someone you intend on sleeping with after you get shit-faced at my wedding," Suresh continues, winking again, just as one of my colleagues, another resident, Oliver Massey, hurries into the canteen. He looks harassed. He spots me, and my stomach sinks when he hurries in my direction.

"Need you upstairs, Sloane. The cops are demanding a play-by-play with the doctors working on the Stanton guy."

Great. I throw my plastic spoon back into my pudding cup. Lunch break over.

"Remember, Sloane," Suresh calls after me. "Someone you're fucking!"

An entire canteen full of people turns to watch me scurry away, red-faced.

31

SLOANE

"**THIS PATIENT WITNESSED A MURDER.** He's under protective custody. It's incredibly fucking important that this guy doesn't get shot to death while in this hospital. You people know what that means?" The detective in the bad suit talks down to us like we're degenerates of the highest order. He's short and bald and walks like an angry Rottweiler. The slender female detective—his partner, I assume—patiently waits for him to shut up so she can speak. Finally, she gets her chance.

"I'm Detective Cooper. I'll be here nights, so I'll be your point of contact. If you see anyone you don't recognize walking the halls, you come find either myself or a duty officer and report it. This is a big place. A lot of people come and go, so we understand that it might be hard to gauge whether you think someone is out of place here. Especially when you're trying to do your jobs as well."

The nursing team, who were previously standing, arms folded, glaring at the fat detective, nod their heads, their expressions softening. The three doctors who are treating Archie Stanton—myself, Hendry, and Oliver—stand at the back of the ICU family room, taking everything in. "What exactly are we looking for here, Detective? I mean, is this some Italian mob thing or what?" Oliver sounds as incredulous as I felt downstairs in the cafeteria. This just isn't something that happens here.

"No, not Italian. We've been investigating a high-level crime boss for some time now. He runs a lot of rackets in the city. Drugs, guns, gambling, counterfeit money. Word has it Matty Stanton dropped the ball on a business deal this guy had in the works, and he paid the price. We know our POI ordered the hit. We just need proof. Matty's brother, Archie, is the key to doing that. We have mug shots of people known to associate with our POI. There are only a few faces on here that you really need to be worried about. I doubt any of them will be stupid enough to come down here." Detective Cooper nods to an armed officer in uniform, who hands out the mug shots to the nursing team.

"How dangerous *is* this situation, Detective?" Hendry demands. "Are we gonna get shot while trying to do our jobs?"

"No. We're here to ensure that doesn't happen. At this stage we're banking on the fact that our POI doesn't even realize he's being investigated. He thinks he's an untouchable, but he's very wrong. We're gonna make sure he goes away for a long time."

Hendry nods, accepts the paper from Oliver, studies it momentarily, and then passes it on to me. "Where do we stand with regard to self-defense? If one of these fuckers *does* come here and attacks us... are we allowed to shoot them up with sedative? Use the defibrillator on them?"

The nurses titter. I glance down at the paper, already halfway to handing it on to the next person, when my breath catches in my throat.

Oh.

My throat begins to swell shut as my mind repeats the word.

Oh.

A mosaic of nameless mugshots stare up at me. Eight photos on the first page. More on the other side. They're all numbered... and at number one, in prize place, Zeth Mayfair stares grimly out at me.

Holy God above, I think I'm going to be sick.

32

SLOANE

IF YOU STAND ON THE ROOF OF ST. PETER'S of Mercy hospital at night, the view is incredible. Back when Alexis and I were kids, my father used to bring us up here sometimes when his shifts were quiet. The doctors would turn a blind eye—Alan Romera was a beloved employee, a radiologist for thirty-five years in the very place where I now work. He moved out to private practice in L.A. long before I ever showed my face here as a clueless intern, but his name still means something in these hallways. He could get away with anything.

His favorite time to bring us up here was when it snowed. A common enough occurrence, but it would still have my sister and me jumping out of our skins with excitement. The soft white flakes spinning dizzily from the vast sky, the thick blanket of cloud that incubated the world...it was thrilling. We would stand for hours, necks burning from craning them back for so long, until our bodies went numb, and Dad would usher us inside before one of us got sick. Memories like that rush back, knocking the wind out of me every time I come up here.

I push them down tonight, though. It isn't snowing, it's raining, and we're waiting on a trauma to come in. It makes me feel sick, the waiting. The adrenaline I need to think, act, move quickly is already pulsing around my body, useless until I can actually see what we're dealing with. The wind howls, driving the rain sideways, lashing our bodies, soaking surgical gowns. Oliver stands with me, waiting patiently. He's a good friend, a good man. Funny, smart, attractive, a terrible flirt. It's a miracle he's single.

In the distance, a volley of mechanical sound reverberates off the city's high-rises. "Hear that? The helo." Oliver nudges me with his elbow. "Can't be more than a mile out. Hit the elevator."

The elevator has been held on this floor for the past ten minutes, doors closed. The nursing team are waiting with a gurney and life-support gear inside, all nice and warm and dry. Time for those bastards to get wet, too.

I jog back to the steel doors and hit the call button just as a powerful gust of wind blows, hurling freezing water into the faces of the three young nurses laughing and joking inside. Mikey the intern stops what he was doing, frozen in place. His hands are locked behind his head, hips thrust forward, bottom lip caught between his teeth.

"You auditioning as a male stripper, Hoxam?" I yell over the wind and rain.

"No. No! Sorry, Dr. Romera, it—"

"Won't happen again?"

"No! No, ma'am. Never."

Ma'am? Fuck me. I'm twenty-six years old, and these idiots think I'm ancient. "Well, when you feel like pretending to be a doctor again, maybe you can move your ass. The helo's on approach."

I'll give him one thing: Mikey Hoxam is either a bag of nerves or a complete goof-off, but he gets a ten out of ten for enthusiasm. He's the first out of the elevator, pushing the gurney onto the rooftop. The helicopter's wheels are on the tarmac by the time we all reach Oliver.

"You ready?" he yells to me.

"Yes, sir!" Mikey yells right back. Oliver gives him a look that would strip paint clean off wood. The intern realizes his mistake and has the common sense to blush. I can't help but smirk.

"Yeah, I'm ready! Let's go!" We rush the helicopter doors. Two paramedics clamber out, lifting a backboard behind them, its cargo small and fragile.

"Maisie Richards, seven years old. Hypothermic. Deep laceration to right thigh. Found seizing face down in the bath. Unconscious. Pulse is still tachy. Coded en route. Shocked twice."

"Okay, let's get her inside!"

Oliver and the crash team hunker down underneath the whipping rotor blades of the helicopter as they take charge of the patient and rush back toward the elevator. I turn back to the paramedics gathering their stuff from the medevac. "Where are the parents?"

The first paramedic, a woman with frown lines carved deep between her brows, sighs frustratedly. "Who knows? Neighbor was dropping food round for the kid. Let themselves in when Maisie didn't answer. Found her in the tub."

"*What?* She was on her *own?*"

The medic shakes her head like she can hardly believe it herself.

"Romera! Come *on!*" Oliver is holding the elevator door open. I run, almost missing the ride down as the doors slide closed.

33

SLOANE

"SHE'S STABLE. IT'S A MIRACLE SHE SUR-vived." I sign off on Maise's paperwork, stabbing my pen into the paper, marking off a series of allergies. Latex. Penicillin. Anesthesia. The little girl might *actually* be allergic to everything. She nearly died four times on the table while we were fighting to save her leg. The wound was deep. Horrible. If Maisie's parents had been here, we would have known not to touch her with our gloves. We would have known not to give her regular anesthetic, and not to give her penicillin once we were done with surgery. As it stands, I'm baffled how her little heart is still beating after all the stress it's been under.

Bemused, Oliver watches as I slash my signature into the bottom of the chart and add it to the towering pile of clipboards for the interns to file. "I'm calling CPS," I tell him.

"Whoa, don't you think you ought to wait for her parents to show up before calling Child Protective Services?"

I have no words. "Did...did you just work on the same seven-year-old girl I did? Because a child, *a little baby*, nearly died just now. She should never have been left on her own."

"I agree with you, don't get me wrong. I'm just saying, you don't know what the circumstances are yet."

I head for the residents' locker room, Oliver following behind me. I slam through the door, tugging my scrubs off over my head. Blood has soaked through them and stains the long-sleeved shirt I'm wearing underneath. Great. I open my locker, using the door to provide a little modesty as I take that off, too, and slip on a clean sweater. When I turn around, Oliver is shirtless, his scrubs top hanging from where he's tucked it into the waistband of his pants, smirking as he types something into his cell phone.

"I can't believe you're even smiling right now," I grumble, pushing past him. Many a resident has been paralyzed by the sight of Oliver Massey's washboard abs, but not me. Not since bearing witness to Zeth

Mayfair's stomach. And definitely not today. Oliver grabs me as I try to make my escape.

"You'd smile too if *you'd* been invited to the interns' party."

"The interns are having a party?"

"Of course the interns are having a party. How many times did *we* get fucked up when we were in their shoes?"

I roll my eyes. "Yeah, well, I do not want to spend a night drinking with those walking liabilities. And, frankly, I have no idea why you'd want to, either."

"Think about it." He grins. "How uncomfortable will they be with their bosses drinking all their beer and walking around like we own their place? It'll be classic."

"Oh, come on!" I laugh. "Which one are you screwing, Olly?"

He looks a little stunned. "None of them!" He does a really bad job of disguising his horror. "I'm not…" He shakes his head, letting go of my arm, and I suddenly realize how close he it. "Never mind, Sloane. Have a good night, huh." He steps back, quickly snatching up a dark shirt from the bench and pulling it on over his head. Impressive. I've managed to piss him off, and I wasn't even trying. Should I say something? Apologize? Tell him I was only joking? Probably a terrible idea. Would only make matters worse, no doubt. He's still getting changed, his back to me, as I exit the change room.

I slump against the wall, closing my eyes. I need a moment. I'm not good at this. Not good at being friends with people, understanding what I should or shouldn't say. I was only joking just now, but I offended Oliver. Fucking a subordinate is just about as unethical as it gets. Talk about an abuse of power. I *know* Oliver wouldn't do that. I should go back in there and tell him that. He shouldn't have to worry about—

Fuck!

Zeth.

I open my eyes, and there he is, leaning against the wall opposite me.

Staring.

"What the fuck, Zeth!"

"You're upset. Why?"

At that moment, the door to the locker room swings open and out walks Oliver. He hesitates when he sees me and Zeth. "Hey." With a stiff smile and a brief nod, he skirts by me, his gaze lingering a second too long on the strange, dark-haired guy loitering in the staffing corridor. Did he recognize him? A tremor of panic lurches through me, but Oliver keeps on walking. No way he would leave me alone with Zeth if he recalled his face from the mug shots. He'd been too busy asking questions to take in those faces properly, anyway.

Zeth doesn't say anything. Doesn't shift an inch. Nothing about him has changed from a moment ago, but I can tell he is boiling mad. "I've had a really bad day, okay," I tell him.

"*Why?*" he grinds out again.

"Because a little girl nearly died, and her parents are nowhere to be found, and I don't know whether I'm supposed to call Child Protective Services on them or wait until they show up looking for her. *If* they ever do. Now, I really just want to go home and have a shower and go to bed, okay? I don't need—"

"Call them."

"Excuse me?"

"What's to think about? Call CPS." His deep voice is surprisingly ferocious. "Some people," he says, prowling forward, "don't deserve to have children. In fact, some people should be chemically castrated and have that privilege revoked."

He raises his hand, and I think he's going to tuck the hair that's fallen from my ponytail back behind my ear. Instead, he rubs the strands between the pads of his thumb and forefinger. "Blood in your hair," he rumbles.

"I'm used to it." I hike my purse strap back onto my shoulder, doing anything to keep myself moving.

"You have a violent job," he observes.

Hysterical laughter rips out of me, echoing down the corridor. "Are you *kidding* me? Zeth, you can't be here. You need to leave. Right now."

"Why? What's going on?"

I spin and jab my index finger into his chest. "Your face is plastered all over the third floor of this hospital is what's going on. The brother of some grocery store mogul was shot the other night. The cops think a fucking *crime lord* they're investigating has something to do with it. And you, apparently, are one of this crime lord's guys! They're betting on you dropping by, and voilà." I scowl at him. "Here you are."

Zeth looks a little puzzled. Nowhere near bothered enough by what I've said. "*Archie's* been shot?"

"Yeah. He's been enrolled in WITSEC or he's under police protection or something."

"If he were under the witness protection program, he'd be long gone by now. Different name, different history, different life."

"Huh. Sounds nice. Maybe I should look into it, see if *I* can get enrolled in the program."

"You're being dramatic."

"Dramatic? *Dramatic?* Really?" My tone borders on hysteria. Meanwhile, he stands there, watching me, taking in my expression and my body language like he can read the truth of things—the truth of *me*—that way. We glower at each other for a moment, neither of us backing down. And then he reaches out and takes both my hands, drawing them behind my back. He does it so slowly and methodically that I don't even think about struggling until he has me firmly restrained.

"The fuck do you think you're doing, Zeth?"

"This isn't about Archie Stanton. Or about some little girl whose parents haven't taken care of her."

"And how the hell would *you* know what this is about?" I snap. With our bodies drawn together, I can feel the heat flowing off him, see the heartbeat pulsing in the hollow of his neck. I try to pull back, but he shakes his head, his expression all blank control.

"This is about the fact that you kissed me, and I got mad at you. And now you're mad at *me*. And," he adds in a quiet voice, "then I disappeared for two weeks, and I haven't called or come to see you."

I try to snatch my hands back, pulling against him, but this only leads to him crushing me to his chest. I pant in two infuriated breaths, then hiss, "Like I care if you haven't been to *see* me, Zeth! Like I give a fuck!"

A half hum, half growl builds in his throat. "Of course you give a fuck."

I scoff at that, but I don't think I'm very successful in convincing him that he's wrong. "So you're telling me that you *do* know you've been a dick, then?"

"I know you're upset."

I want to cover my face, but he won't let me. Fine. I close my eyes. Once I've given myself a second to breathe, I open them again, fixing him with a stony gaze. "Let me go, Zeth."

"No."

I can't believe this guy. "What the hell do you want from me? You've made it abundantly clear that you don't want to be around me, so why—"

He makes a derisive sound at the back of his throat. Couples the sound with a crooked eyebrow. "How have I made that abundantly clear?"

"I think the whole 'don't ever fucking kiss me again' thing and then vanishing for two weeks speaks for itself, don't you? Your *attitude* speaks for itself."

This conversation must be *so* amusing to him. He battles the beginnings of a smirk as he says, "I don't have an attitude. I just have me." This statement doesn't make things any better. I consider hitting him with my purse. "Ask me where I've been the last two weeks," he says.

Damn him. I exhale, trying to keep my temper under wraps. "Where have you been?"

"I've been making the necessary arrangements to go and collect Alexis."

Oh. I stop struggling a little.

Deep, bottomless grief washes over me. It's like a

small part of me has convinced itself that she's dead, and every time he says her name, it's preparing me for the moment he returns without her. The moment when he tells me he was mistaken. That this person he's found isn't my sister at all, and that Alexis is already dead. I let the grief sink into my bones, then I say the only thing I *can* say in light of what he's just told me. "Well. Thank you. I guess."

"You're welcome. Now ask me why I stayed away."

I really don't want to play this game anymore. I don't want to feel so powerless, pinned against him, unable to get away, either. I also don't like how, thus far, he's coming out of this smelling of roses. "Fine." I fix defiant eyes on him. "Why have you stayed away?"

"I stayed away because you needed time to not feel stupid over me rejecting you."

Whoa! What. The. *Fuck?* He is—he is *un-fucking-believable*! "You did *not* reject me. You'd just screwed me, asshole!"

"I'm aware of that. But you *felt* rejected at the time, right? If I'd come to see you two weeks ago, you still would have felt that way."

"So you wait two weeks until I'm fucking furious at you instead?"

He shrugs. "Furious is easier to fix."

I'm going to castrate the motherfucker. I'm going to repeatedly kick *him* in the balls until there's no chance he'll ever reproduce. At least that way, future female generations will be safe from the possibility that there will ever be anyone else as manipulative and clever as him.

He's right. I hate that he is, but he's right. I *did* feel rejected. I *would* have hated to see him fourteen days ago. Urgh. Out of nowhere, extreme exhaustion turns my limbs to lead. "I need to go home, Zeth. I can't do this with you right now."

He doesn't say another word. He releases me, but keeps hold of one hand so that he can guide me through the maze of hallways on the ground floor. The ease with which he does this makes me think he knows this place. Knows it a little better than I might like. He keeps his head down at least, eyes on the floor until we reach the exit. Gracie, the head nurse on shift, gives me a wave as we leave, but apart from that we aren't stopped.

Outside, Zeth leads me away from the brightly lit area of the lot where I parked my Volvo to the dark back corner of the lot where the security cameras don't work.

"What are you doing?" I try to pull my hand free, but his grip is solid. "Zeth. *Zeth!*" He stops. Turns. When I have his attention, I demand the information I need; I can't go a single step farther without it. "Did you shoot that kid?"

"No."

"But you do work for a crime boss, don't you? *Don't you!*"

Zeth just sighs, like I'm trying his patience. "I need you to look after Lacey, Sloane." We glare at one another for a long time while I try to work out if I should be trying to hide with him or calling for help. This is a pivotal moment. He's denied shooting someone, yes, but he hasn't denied being on a seriously dangerous criminal's payroll. I know what that means. Whatever this man may be—murderer, thug, criminal—he is honest. With *me*, I know he is honest. Our conversation in the hallway has only highlighted that. By not giving me an answer, he's found a way around lying to me. He gives me a loaded look. It's almost pleading. And then he actually *does* plead.

"Just...*please*, Sloane. I'm going to fetch your sister. You can do this for me."

"Yeah. About that. Where *is* Alexis? I should come with you. She's shy, Zeth. She won't just leave with you."

He shakes his head. "She's somewhere you can't come. Somewhere dangerous. I want you and Lacey here, where I can have people keep an eye on you."

"Zeth! She's my sister!"

"You fight me on this, I won't bother fucking going at all," he growls. "Either I get her outta there alone, or I stay put and you can keep on missing her."

Oh my God. He *knows* how badly I want to get her back, the scheming bastard. "Okay. Fine!"

He looks away quickly. No expression of relief. No thank-you. No nothing. Walking briskly, he brings me to a matte-black Camaro parked in the darkest corner of the entire lot. Through the window on the back seat, Lacey stares worriedly back at us, knees tucked up under her chin.

"You brought her with you?"

"I'm leaving *now*, Sloane. If the cops think I had something to do with Archie being shot, then it sounds like I'm due a trip out of Seattle, anyway."

I could wrap my hands around his throat—not that they'd fucking *reach*—and throttle him to death. "You're a piece of work, you know that?"

Zeth opens the door to the souped-up muscle car, leaning inside to scoop Lacey out. She looks even paler than when I last saw her in the hospital. Her eyes seem brighter, though. More responsive. He straightens, Lacey's arms looped tightly around his neck, and for a moment he looks torn. He cares for this girl. Loves her in his way. For the fifteen-millionth time I wonder who the hell she is to him.

"I'm tired, Zeth," Lacey mumbles. "Just take me home."

"Can't, kiddo. Gotta leave you with the doc for a while, okay?"

Lacey eyes me suspiciously, then buries her face into Zeth's chest. He gives me a hard look. "Which way to your car?"

I feel like being a dick about it. *You tell me. You're a psycho, right? You've been watching me. You should know where my car is.* But what purpose would that serve? The purpose of *fuck you*, that's what. Still, I turn around and set off in the direction of my car. When we reach it, I open the front passenger door, but Zeth shakes his head.

"She can't. She won't," he says.

Okay. I guess I should remember that. He places her carefully onto the back seat along with a small rucksack I didn't even see him grab. Once he shuts the door, he places his hands on my shoulders. "She needs to see Pippa."

I nod, at least not arguing with him on that front. "I'll make it happen." I open my car door, determined to get in and drive away as fast as I can—*perhaps if karma is on my side, I'll be able to spin up a few puddles of rainwater into his face*—but he grabs my arm, stopping me. *Ding. Ding. Ding.* The door chimes as he stares down at me.

"I'm sorry, Sloane."

I blink up at him, trying to get a read on him. His expression is conflicted, making it hard to decipher his emotions. "You're sorry?" An apology? Coming from *him*? Doesn't seem like something he would do.

He looks back across the car lot, clenching his jaw. "Look. I don't ask anyone for help. But I know I can trust you," he rumbles.

"Of course you know you can trust me. You're using my sister to hold me as an emotional hostage. You know you have me cornered. The question is, can *I* trust *you*?"

Slowly, a crooked smile draws one side of his mouth upward, his eyes sparking with amusement. "*Should* you trust me? Absolutely not. *Can* you trust me?" He lets me wait a moment, still smiling down at me. *Ding, ding, ding.* The car insists that the door is still open. Zeth steps forward, carefully cupping my cheek in his palm. With his other hand, he brushes his fingertips against my temple, leaning into me. Unabashedly, breathes me in. "Yes." He exhales. "You can trust me. You gave yourself to me back at my apartment. I gave myself in return. I may not have *wanted* to, Sloane, but I didn't have a fucking choice in the matter. That means we belong to each other now. It means I'll come back for you soon. I'll do my best to find your sister, and I'll make those bastards pay for what they've done to her."

34

SLOANE

ZETH'S WORDS PLAGUE ME UNTIL I GIVE myself a migraine from overthinking them. I wake before dawn and lie there with my head under the covers, picking at those words like a scab, wondering what the hell he meant by them. *I gave myself in return. I may not have* wanted *to, Sloane, but I didn't have a fucking choice in the matter.* From the mouth of absolutely *anyone* else on the face of the planet, their meaning would be obvious. And yet, from Zeth Mayfair, they could mean everything. They could mean nothing at all. I want to pick up the phone and demand to know what the hell he was thinking, saying something like that to me. My pride forbids it, though. And I shouldn't *want* to know what he meant, anyway. Why am I even *doing* this to myself? Fuck. Okay. I'm going to stop thinking about him.

As soon as the first rays of dawn light force their way through the bedroom blinds, I get up and shower, mentally tidying the whole mess away to deal with another time. I'm good at that. And besides, I have a houseguest to focus on. Lacey is an enigma. She's up before me, sitting at the breakfast bar, spooning Lucky Charms (I don't own any Lucky Charms) into her mouth when I come downstairs. Out of the floor-to-ceiling windows, she watches the city come to life, a lumbering, gray machine, defrosting, remembering its purpose. When she notices me, she goes rigid, her spoon clattering into her bowl.

"Sorry. I used your milk. I was hungry. I brought my own cereal, though." She confesses like she's committed a crime.

"That's okay. Make yourself at home here, Lacey. Help yourself to anything you want." I smile to back up the statement. I mean it. I don't have a clue what she's been through, but it was enough to make her want to die. Repeatedly, in fact. I've seen the scars on her wrists. A lot of them are old. She picks up the spoon again, like I've given her the permission she needs to continue eating.

"You're just a resident, aren't you?" she asks me.

Half inside the cupboard, reaching for a cereal bowl of my own, I stiffen. "Just a resident" is a strange thing to say. Becoming a resident is perhaps one of the hardest things a person can do, and Lacey makes it sound like I'm an underachiever. "Yeah, well, I guess I am," I admit.

"How much money do you earn in a year?" She spoons her Lucky Charms to her mouth. Her teeth clack against the spoon.

"Just over forty-seven thousand," I tell her. Under normal circumstances, I would kick the ass of anyone who asked me that question in that particular tone of voice, but when you have psychological trauma, you get special privileges. Lacey appears to understand this privilege as she continues with her blunt line of questioning.

"So, how come you can afford this place? Up on the hill, out of the city. Killer view."

"My grandmother left me an inheritance. A lot of money, I guess. I sank it all into this place."

Lacey mulls this over. Eats some more of her Lucky Charms. "Are you working today?"

"No. We're going to see my friend Pippa. You remember, the woman I told you about?"

"The shrink?"

"Yeah. She's lovely. You'll really like her, Lacey, I promise." She doesn't look too convinced. She sulks into her cereal while I rinse a spoon, trying to think of something to say to her. I feel like I'm walking on eggshells. I need some common ground with this girl. I catch sight of the cereal box and an idea forms—yeah, I'm pathetic, but what else am I supposed to do?

"You mind if I have some of your Lucky Charms?" Even something this small—if she feels less indebted to me, if she feels like she is doing me a favor—might ease the tension in the kitchen. She looks up at me from drawn brows, and I can tell she's assessing me, trying to work me out.

Eventually, she whispers, "Sure," slowly pushing the box toward me with her elbow.

I pour myself a modest bowl, making sure not to take too much. "This your favorite?"

"Yeah."

"Why do you like it so much?" I pour the milk and take a bite, trying not to pull a face. God, that's *way* too sweet.

"Because of the powers," she says.

I stand up straighter. "What do you mean?"

"The charms. Each one gives you powers." This rings some vague and distant bell in my memory. I look down at Lacey's breakfast and notice that she's separated out all of the marshmallows on the rim of her bowl, stranding them there. Yellow, pink, and green food coloring stains the milk. "All of the charms, they're supposed to be good for something if you eat enough of them," she continues. She leans across the breakfast bar between us and scoops one of the moons out of my bowl and pops it into her mouth. This feels like a breakthrough of sorts. I grin at her.

"Okay, Lacey. Fill me in. What do they all mean?"

She smiles nervously, preferring to look down at the table between us. "Clovers are the one everyone knows. They give you luck, but it's smart because you never know what kind of luck you're going to get. Good or bad, so..." She shrugs. "And then horseshoes, the power to speed things up. Shooting stars give you the power to fly. Hourglass to control time. Rainbows to zip from place to place." She presses her index fingers together and then jumps them apart. "Balloons mean you can make things float. Hearts, you can bring things back from the dead."

I look down and I see all of the charms she mentioned sitting on the edge of her bowl, uneaten. She ate the crescent-shaped charm from my bowl—the only one she hasn't explained. From the looks of things, that's the only one she's eaten from *her* bowl, too.

"And what about the moon charm? What does that one do?" I instantly regret asking. Her face falls, shoulders curving in to form a barrier between the two of us.

"I'm not sure, actually. I forgot." She takes a deep

breath, pushing away from the counter. "You mind if I use your shower? I feel pretty gross."

"Of course. No problem. Like I said, make yourself at home."

She still won't look at me as she washes her bowl and hurries from the kitchen. Once she's gone, I can't help myself. I look it up on my phone:

Blue Moons. The power of invisibility.

35

ZETH

Four Years Ago

Chino

DR. WALCOTT, YANKEES FAN, PROFUSE sweater and prescriber of wonderful drugs, has a nervous disorder. I'm pretty fucking sure he does, anyway. Every meeting we have, he chews his way through at least three pens. Three pens in the space of an hour. That's gotta be costing the state at least a couple of hundred bucks a year, I figure, considering he probably goes through five pens during his sessions with the *truly* scary motherfuckers they have caged in here. Pathetic, really. I mean, why work in a prison if you're this terrified of your patients.

Except we're not called patients in here. We're called inmates. If we were on the outside and sitting in an office with good ol' Walcott, drinking our coffee, he might actually be a good doctor. But with mandatory treatment like this, people tend to be a little reticent. Obstructive. Unwilling to cooperate, if you will. I usually fall into the latter category, but today I'm being forced to sing a different song.

"As you're aware, the appeals board has reviewed your case." Walcott flips through the papers in my file, scanning its contents while somehow managing to keep one eye trained on me. "They rejected your lawyer's request for early release right out of hand. You're aware of that, too?"

"Yeah." Charlie's lawyer, the slick city boy with the immaculate hair, immaculate suit, and immaculate shoes, *did* tell me that. Not like I'd even hoped the appeal would go through, anyway. To be honest, I was surprised the judge had only given me ten years in the first place.

"Given the violent nature of your crime and your

apparent lack of any remorse, they didn't feel it appropriate that you be released until you serve at least half your sentence. Where are you at with that right now?"

"Two years served."

"Well, you've got a long way to go then, Mayfair. At least another three years before any chance of parole unless we do this thing right."

"Three years isn't so bad," I tell him, smirking. But of course it's bad. Three years might as well be thirty in here. Anyone tells you they kicked back and did an easy stint in Chino, they're fucking lying. This place is hell on earth.

Walcott pauses. "Well, what if I were to say you could walk out of here in six months?"

"I'd say that sounds good."

Walcott shakes his head, sighing, looking over my papers once more. "I really don't know how he did it, to be honest. A deal like this frankly shouldn't even be on the table. Your lawyer must be playing golf with the right people."

Hah. Fuck my lawyer playing golf with the right people. The deal the parole board cut me had more to do with Charlie's boys paying a few visits to a few judges' houses. No violence involved, of course. Just bricks of unmarked bills, a few bottles of single malt, and a few choice words whispered into the right ears.

"So this is where we find ourselves, Zeth. If you

work with me willingly, then we both win. I get to help you, and you get to leave. Do we have a deal?"

I feel like I'm giving something away when I reply, "Sure."

He can tell I'm none too happy about it. "Great. Okay. Well, customarily I'd start with the offense that landed you in here, but I think perhaps today we'll go back to the beginning. Let's start off with your childhood." He sits back, the end of the black ballpoint he's been turning over and over in his hand going into his mouth. He just fucking *looks* at me like he's waiting for me to tell him something very terrible and specific that explains exactly why I am the way I am.

"I'm sorry. Did you ask a question?"

"Your childhood, tell me about it."

"What do you want to know?"

"Was it a happy one? Did you have many friends? Did you get on with your parents? You know, that sort of thing."

Typical bullshit psychologist. My chair groans as I slouch back in my chair—I've stacked on fifty pounds of muscle since I was dragged, cuffed, through the gates of this shithole. "It was fucking miserable. When I was four, I went to live with my uncle in California. He was a drunk, and he liked hurting little boys." I suspect not everyone Walcott interviews is quite as blunt as I am. The man blanches.

"And when you say he hurt you, do you mean..." He trails off uncomfortably, gnawing on his pen again.

"No, I do not mean sexually. I mean with a baseball bat. I mean with his steel toecaps. I mean with his fists."

Walcott writes that down. I can practically see it on the fucking paper now: *Beaten as a child. Explains violent tendencies in adult life. An attempt to understand, to control what happened to him in his early years. An attempt to take back perceived loss of power.*

But even as a kid when my uncle was whaling on me and my still-forming bones were snapping like kindling, I didn't feel like I'd lost my power. I was just waiting. Waiting for the day when I was bigger and stronger than he was. Biding my time.

"And what about your parents? Why did they leave you with your uncle?"

"Because they died. My father had a headache. They were going out to a movie. Left me with a babysitter. My mother said she'd drive, but she was pregnant, ready to pop, so he wouldn't let her. Doctors said he had a burst aneurism at the wheel. Wrapped their Chevy around a streetlight."

Talking about my parents isn't something I like to do, but with that six-month-get-out-of-jail-free card on the table, I don't really have much of a choice. I don't tell Walcott about the important stuff. The few hazy, coveted recollections that keep them alive inside me—the smell of my mother's perfume, sweet and light and floral; her dark hair tickling my face when she kissed me goodnight; my father's booming laughter; the *thrum thrum thrum*ming of the baby's heartbeat inside my mother's round belly. I had sat for hours, listening as the unknown creature had flipped and kicked, and my mother had stroked my hair, telling me stories.

"I'm sorry to hear that," Walcott says. He affects a level of sympathy in his voice that almost makes me believe he *is* sorry. "And what about later? After you left your uncle?"

This is now treading into dangerous ground. I won't talk about Charlie. I can't. I'll die in here before I ever get out otherwise. "I lived on the street. I did what I had to survive. Stole, worked casual jobs, moved around a lot. Avoided the system." My uncle kept on cashing the checks the government sent to cover my care until the day I turned eighteen and they stopped sending them. These fuckers have no proof I even really know Charlie. To bring him up now is to open a can of worms marked *Danger: Extremely hazardous to health*.

"I see." Walcott writes all of this down. No fucking point, though. The story I've just given him is a tale as old as time. Within the walls of this tormented place,

I am nothing special. "Okay, Mayfair. Tell me something happy, then. What's the single happiest memory from your childhood?" His pen having caught up with him, the nib hovers over the paper, ready to record whatever profound moment I am about to impart.

"No."

Silence.

"Listen, if you don't plan on cooperating—"

I cut him off. I can't be fucked dealing with administrative threats. I just want this session over. "I'm not being difficult, Dr. Walcott. I can't give you the single happiest memory from my childhood because there isn't one."

"Not even *one*?" He seems doubtful.

I tell him the truth. "Nope. Not even one."

Because even the memories of my parents—the perfume, the hair, the laughter, the *thrum, thrum, thrum*—they are perhaps the saddest parts.

36

SLOANE

IF ANYTHING, LACEY GROWS EVEN QUI- eter as we near Pippa's apartment. It seemed like a bad idea to take the girl to the practice. It *feels* like a psychiatrist's office there, and that's the last thing Lacey needs. Especially given her reaction to her recent experience in a hospital bed. I park the Volvo in the underground lot, and we take the elevator up to the sixteenth floor of Pip's building. A breathtaking vista greets us as we exit the elevator. The Space Needle is a distant gray hiccup in the city skyline, almost swallowed by the other high-rises. Green parkland stretches for miles between here and there, dappled with the bronzed, evolving colors of fall.

When she sees the view from the window, Lacey shrinks into the hoodie she's wearing, two sizes too big and most definitely not hers. I'm oddly uncomfortable about Lacey wearing Zeth's clothes. God knows why.

You're a crazy person, that's why. He's not yours. And you'd be mad to want *him as yours*, the sharp voice in my head advises me. That voice has started to bear a shocking resemblance to Pippa's—a fact that makes me want to punch my friend in the face. I know she's protecting me. I *know* that, and yet I can't help but resent her meddling. I might be cold to Zeth's face, but the truth of the matter is that I can't stop thinking about him. Can't stop thinking about his hands on me. His hot mouth trailing over my skin. His strong hands possessing me, making demands…

"Do we really need to do this?" Lacey's small voice cuts through the silence of the hallway. She looks fragile as lace, just like her name. Mostly, she looks frightened.

"It's gonna be fine," I say. "Think of it this way. You're here of your own volition. We can leave any time you want. You don't have to take any pills or tell Pippa anything you don't want to. There won't be any record of you ever being here, and it's free. There's nothing for you to lose, Lacey. But a lot to gain, right?" I set my hand on her shoulder and gave it a soft squeeze. I haven't touched her at all yet. I expect her to shy from the contact, but she doesn't. Doubtfully, she nods.

"Okay. And we can go whenever I want?"

She needs the extra reassurance. I give it to her, smiling, and guide her to Pippa's apartment.

I rap sharply on the door—my police knock—and not five seconds later, the door opens and there Pippa stands, in neat blue jeans and a crisp white shirt, tucked into her pants. Her casual wear is smarter than something I would wear to an important job interview. Her hair is down, though, flowing to her shoulders, and the effect makes her look less severe. Less doctorly and more soccer mom.

"Hi, girl." She smiles broadly. Her breezy tone makes it sound like we're gathering to watch movies, drink wine, and talk about boys. Absurd, but necessary. Lacey flashes her a grimace that could pass for a smile—a painful one—and the two of us enter Pip's apartment. The scent of lilies and jasmine floats on the air. The place has a showroom feel to it, though admittedly Pippa *has* added a few homey touches here and there. Her couch is the only reason I come over. The thing is huge, the leather grown soft and supple with age. I immediately collapse into it, gesturing for Lacey to do the same. She sits down next to me, tugging a folded throw from the back of the chair behind her and wrapping it tightly over her legs. The action makes it seem as though she wants to bury herself from sight.

Blue moons. The power of invisibility.

Pippa points a thumb over her shoulder toward her open-plan kitchen. "I was just making a cup of tea. Would you guys like one?"

"Be great. It's freezing out there," I reply.

Lacey nods, too, just once. Pippa goes about making the tea, kettle rumbling its irritated rumble, spoon clanking, the bright chime of china clashing against china, and Lacey dips her chin into the throw, staring at the floor. I'm about to ask her if she's okay when my phone buzzes in my pocket.

It's a number I don't recognize. I answer the call, getting up and pacing to the window. "Hello?"

"It's me."

That voice. "Why aren't you calling from your number? And where the *hell* are you?" I whisper.

Silence from the other end of the phone. Perhaps Zeth Mayfair isn't used to people being so hostile with him when they take his calls, but tough fucking luck. If he thinks he can just dump his responsibilities on me and vanish into thin—

"This phone's a burner. Had to get rid of the other one," his gruff voice informs me down the line. "And I'm driving. To California. To try and get your sister back. Forgotten already?"

Well, fuck. I can't really chew him out when he puts it like that. "No, I haven't forgotten," I snap. "It'd just be better under different circumstances."

"You mean if you'd gotten your way, and you were coming along for the ride?" His smirk is the audible kind. The kind I can imagine reshaping his mouth into a bow. I shake my head, trying to dislodge the curve of those full lips.

"Yeah, that's exactly what I mean." Behind me Pippa arrives with three mugs, two of them clasped precariously by the handles in the one hand, the other carrying just the one. I turn my back, whisper-shouting again into the phone. "When are you gonna be back?"

Caring for Lacey isn't a job I would have volunteered for, but my eagerness for Zeth's return also pertains to my sister. Two years is such a long time. It seems impossible that she should be kept away from her home a second longer.

"Need me already?" Zeth growls. "Don't worry. I'll be back to take care of you as soon as I'm done."

My cheeks blush hotly. "No, I do *not* need you to come take care of me!"

"You sure? I think you'll be begging me to use that key the second I hit the city limits."

I hate the arrogance in his voice. Equally, I hate the lie I tell myself when I try to convince myself that it doesn't turn me on. Every dark, hazardous aspect of him turns me on. I'm drowning in the dark, velvet folds of his voice even now, my skin breaking out into gooseflesh at the sexual dip in his tone. *Fucking get a grip, Sloane!* "Just bring my sister home okay, buddy." Buddy? Where the hell did *that* come from? Zeth is a lot of things, but he isn't a buddy. A deep, throaty chuckle meets my ears.

"I'm on it. I just—" A deep inhalation says he is thinking carefully on his next words. "Just keep an eye out, okay? There's a chance someone might be following you."

"Uh, excuse me? Someone following me?" My body reacts like a struck tuning fork. "Why would someone be *following* me? What *someone*?"

"My boss's a little jumpy. He might have put people on me. Could be they saw me bring Lacey to you," he says matter-of-factly. Ice cold dread percolates from my chest and pools in the pit of my stomach.

"Seriously?" I try and fail to keep my voice down. Lacey and Pippa look up from their hushed conversation (a *one-sided* conversation, by the looks of things), giving me quizzical stares. I spin around, turning my back to them. "How dangerous *are* these guys, Zeth? Do I need to call the cops?"

"Fuck no! Just sit tight. I got you covered."

I don't question that. I don't want to know. "Got

you covered" can only mean more shady characters stalking me through the streets of Seattle. "All right, Zeth," I sigh. "Just get your ass back here the second you can. I'm not cut out for this." Which has to be the understatement of the century. Not cut out for waiting. Not cut out for babysitting. My world may seem big to others—the hospital, the scores of patients I see every shift, the responsibility and the weight of all that knowledge pressing down on me—but I have made it small. There are no outside requirements of me. No demands on my life besides being there when I'm needed. *Being there* when a pair of hands are required inside a chest cavity. *Being there* when an arterial bleed needs stemming. But that's physical, logical, manual stuff. I'm hollow enough for all of that. The nerves I experience when I think about Alexis coming home at last? The pressure of trying to be there emotionally for Lacey? Those things, I have no idea how to deal with.

Zeth makes a stiff sound down the phone. "You're gonna do just fine, Sloane," he tells me, his voice softer than I've heard it before. And then he hangs up the phone.

37

SLOANE

LACEY'S STORY MAKES ME SICK TO MY stomach. I plan to leave Pippa and the other woman alone so they can have their session together, but when I try to give them some space, Lacey grabs my hand with frightening strength and refuses to let go. It seems that she doesn't like strangers, and out of Pip and me, *I'm* the familiar face. I plant myself on the other end of the couch, determined to remain impervious to whatever I hear, but that becomes increasingly difficult as Pippa asks Lacey her litany of questions and the girl provides her emotionless answers.

"You were raised by the State. What happened to your parents?"

"They died before I was born."

"But... how could your mom have died before you were born?"

"She was in a coma. Technically, she was dead for the last three weeks of the pregnancy. As soon as her body gave birth to me, they let her go."

"And after that?"

"Foster homes."

"How many?"

"Seventeen. I think, anyway. Some I stayed in a couple of months. Some just days. I stayed in the last one a year."

"Why so long in the last one?"

"Mr. Mallory, Greg, he liked to have me around. I was... useful to him."

"In what way?"

"Cooking and cleaning. Sex whenever he wanted it."

"So you were in a consensual relationship with this man?"

"Not really."

"Not really?"

"No. It wasn't consensual."

"He *raped* you?"

Silence.

Sometimes, a mind cannot bend around a word. *That* word is like a paralytic to Lacey's system. She shuts down, staring out of the window, blinking slowly.

"Was he the first?" Pippa asks.

Lacey's blond hair brushes her shoulders as she shakes her head.

No, Greg had not been the first.

After that, Pippa backs off, sensing that she's on the brink of the girl withdrawing too far. She asks other questions: Why is she afraid to be alone? Can she share why she is so attached to Zeth? But Lacey only shrugs and tells her she doesn't *know* why. After a torturous forty-minute session, Pippa nods and rises from her armchair.

"All right, ladies. I think we should call it a day, don't you? I'm exhausted."

Lacey's eyes flicker back to life, flitting to glance at Pippa. "What, that's it? You don't want me to tell you anything else?"

Pip gives her a friendly smile. "Not if you don't want to. You can tell me anything you like, though."

"No, that's—that's fine." Lacey loosens her grip on the edge of the throw she still has over her legs. "I think I'd like to go now."

"No problem." Pippa holds her hand out to Lacey, offering it to her to shake. Lacey looks at it, full of suspicion. The custom of shaking hands came about thousands of years ago. People did it to prove they weren't carrying any weapons. The same trick works here between Lacey and Pippa—*I mean you no harm.*

Lacey accepts the patiently waiting hand. When she does, a dam seems to break in her, and tears spring to her eyes. Silently, she gets up, tidily folds the blanket away, and exits the apartment, standing on the other side of the open door, presumably waiting for me.

"She's got a long road ahead of her," Pippa murmurs. "She has a lot to work through. I get the impression that she's blocking most of it out."

"What? So the rape isn't the worst of it?"

A sad, pained look develops on Pip's face. "Probably not. Make sure you keep an eye on her, okay? Ideally, she'd be placed on suicide watch for at *least* a month."

I'm already shaking my head, no. "He won't—"

"I know he won't," she interrupts. "But this isn't about *him*. It's about *her*, and what *she* needs. Right now, she's managed to bond herself to this guy, which is probably the unhealthiest thing she could have done. This time with him away is a good opportunity to try and break that connection." She gives me a hesitant look. "And also a good opportunity for you to do the same."

I gape at her. "*I'm* not bonded to him!"

Her lips pull into a tight line: worry. "Not right now, maybe. But it *could* happen, babe. Way easier than you think. Don't forget," she says, pausing, "I *have* met this man."

38

ZETH

I ARRIVE AT JACOB'S COMPOUND AT nightfall. Somewhere in the city, Rick's waiting impatiently for direction from me. Michael is already here, too, having been told to watch the compound since he learned of Alexis's presence. The place is way out in the boonies, skirted with a ten-foot-high concrete wall. It encircles the whole place apart from the front entrance, which bears a fierce-looking wrought-iron gate with formidable spikes on the top. No fucker gets in or out of here, if not without Jacob's direct say-so, then at least without him knowing about it. Two beefy guards smoke joints by the gateway, scowling at me with dark eyes as I pull the Camaro up out front.

Their hands move to the weapons on their hips as I step out of the car.

"Turn around, friend. This ain't the 'burbs. You ain't got no business here," the short, fat one tells me. I arch an eyebrow.

"Sure I do. I got an open ticket with Jacob."

The other man spits on the floor and then draws deeply on his joint. The smell of pot blossoms in the night air. "We ain't got no piece-of-shit enforcers on the guest list tonight, brother. You need to go on home."

I walk up to the gate's railings and lean my face close to the bars. "Better check your list again. *Brother.*"

The two of them look at each other. I'm not driving a Benz, so I'm obviously not their regular clientele. The size of me doesn't seem to be doing me any favors, either. A tense minute follows—them staring at me and me staring right back at them—before the tall one tuts disapprovingly and turns his back, mumbling into a small walkie-talkie. He quickly turns back around and gestures upward with his chin. "Smile for the camera, fuckhead."

A camera mounted to the wall to my right swivels around to capture me. I plaster a fake grin on my face, arrogant as hell, flipping off the blinking lens.

Distorted speech squarks out of the walkie-talkie in the taller guy's hand. The voice sounds angry. Both guards' faces solidify into aggravated steel—*sorry, motherfuckers!*—as reluctantly they open the gate for me. I get back into the Camaro and make sure to spin desert sand up into their faces as I burn past them. Outside the huge, single-story building that lies within the walls, a dark, lithe shape paces down the steps to meet me. The figure of a woman. I park and take a moment to get my story straight in my head: I'm just passing through, looking for a place to crash. Charlie knows all about this.

Charlie has no fucking idea I'm here. Charlie has no fucking idea I've even left Seattle, or that I decided to go against orders and didn't kill Rick like I was supposed to. My mood is still blacker than black over the prospect that the old man might have been the one to tell the police I killed Murphy. If I'd seen his fucking face before I left, I would have beaten down on it until his whole head had caved in.

The woman who comes out to meet me is called Alaska. I remember her from the last time I was here with Charlie. More specifically, I remember her tits. She'd danced for me at Jake's insistence. The girl has beautiful tanned skin and the body of a fucking gymnast. She splits me a wide smile as I make my way toward the building.

"So, you came back to see me, huh?" she laughs. "Only took you four years."

Four years wasn't long enough away from this

place. She places her hands against my chest as she leans up to kiss my cheek. I bear it as long as I can. The woman sells her body at Jake's behest, but that isn't what bothers me. I didn't come here to fuck. And *she* isn't Sloane Romera.

I take her by the wrists and remove her hands. "Sorry. Just came to pay my respects to your boss," I say flatly. She pouts, pretending to be offended by my rejection.

"I'm a lot friendlier than *Jacob* tonight. Come on, come inside. I'll keep you to myself for an hour before you go talk boring business." I just *look* at her. When she reads exactly what I think of her advances on my face, her coy smile fades. "I see. Fair enough." Raising both eyebrows, she cants her head to one side, pointing toward the well-lit building. "He's by the pool. Don't get lost finding it." She turns and storms back into the building, hips swinging, fizzing with fury.

I find Jacob exactly where she said he would be, sitting on a lounger by the pool. He sips from a cut-glass tumbler, grinning when he sees me. He's put on even more weight since I saw him last, and he was already obese to begin with. Probably on the verge of coronary failure by now.

"Zeth Mayfair? Well, I'll be." His accent is thicker than ever; he must have gone home and visited his mother in Tennessee recently. "Why you waited so long to come see me, huh?" He doesn't rise from the lounger. Just holds his hand up for me to take hold of in some semblance of a limp shake. He points to the lounger beside me, groaning as he reaches over himself for a decanter of amber liquid. He free pours three fingers into another glass and holds it out to me. Smells like whiskey. I accept. I'd be shitting on his hospitality otherwise. Bad start to an already precarious meeting.

"Where's that ugly English bastard? He come down here with you?" Jacob asks.

"No, I'm flying solo. Long drive to Las Flores. Thought you might lend me a bed for the night." I am oh-so-casual. "Maybe I'll impose on your hospitality *two or three* nights if you're feeling generous. There are a few old friends I wouldn't mind catching up with while I'm in the area."

Jacob takes a deep sip from his glass, dark brown eyes pensively studying me over the rim of the glass. He probably thinks Charlie's sent me down here to spy on his business. These bastards pretend to be thicker than thieves, but they don't trust each other one fucking iota. Which, by default, means Jacob doesn't trust me, either. "Sure thing, my friend. My house is your house, as the Spanish say." He smiles, but there's no warmth in his eyes.

"You're very kind." I drink from the glass—definitely whiskey—savoring the burn.

"Your timing's impeccable actually," Jacob says conspiratorially. "If you stay 'til Tuesday, you'll be able to attend our little *event*." The emphasis on the final word tells me exactly what kind of an event he's referring to. The kind I used to hold myself until recently. Until *Sloane*. "I got plenty of fresh meat ready to be well seasoned," he laughs, and his belly shakes like a half-deflated waterbed. "This one's a bit different, though. You gotta bring someone to the table. You catch my meanin'? If not for touching, then at least for looking at." He gives me an exaggerated wink, his jowly cheeks swinging like a basset hound's. "I doubt you'll have any problem finding someone to come with you."

Tuesday. If Alexis is here, then she'll definitely be attending a party like that. Today's only Friday, though. I hadn't really planned on staying that long.

I'll just have to make sure I run into the girl before then. I nod, taking a healthy swig from the whiskey. "Yeah. Sounds fun. I doubt I'll have a problem."

SLOANE

The sleek black car follows me from the highway all the way to St. Peter's. Lacey sees it first—I'm having to take her to *work* with me, which is all kinds of fucked—and points it out as I drive. The car passes the entrance to the hospital's parking lot when I pull in, but it draws up on the curb outside the coffee shop across the street, the engine cutting as we get out of the Volvo and make our way to the building's entrance. The generic-looking dark vehicle has blacked-out windows, so it's impossible to see inside, although Lacey seems to have a good idea who it is.

"That's one of Charlie's boys for sure," she announces. She's worryingly nonchalant over this tail. *I'm* on the verge of bolting inside the hospital and hiding in a cleaning closet or something. "Bet they're there when we leave," she adds.

"If they're there when we leave, I'm calling the cops."

She snorts. "Good luck with that."

"What do you mean?"

Pulling one shoulder up to the side, she looks at me like I'm stupid, eyes rolling. "The cops are all in someone's pocket. Mostly Charlie's. They probably wouldn't even show up, let alone do anything about it."

Well, *that's* super fucking concerning. It feels like I've been sucked into a 1950s gangster movie, except this is real. And not being able to call the cops? Just great. Seriously. Just great.

I deposit Lacey in an on-call room. I'm already

nearly late for my own rounds, so I don't have time to baby her.

"Don't step one foot out of this room," I command. "You were a patient here not that long ago. Plenty of people *will* recognize you, and Zeth'll murder me if you get put on a psych hold while I'm at work." Fucking *Zeth*. The guy has done nothing but cause me problems. If he hadn't killed Eli, I might have gotten the information I was after, and Alexis would already be back home. She'd be heading to church with Mom and Dad at the weekend, accompanying the choir on piano and singing along with the parishioners. I try to hold on to my anger a moment, but it fizzles out like an extinguished firework when my mind decides to remember other things instead. Like his painfully big cock, teasing me as he readied to push inside me. His deep brown eyes watching my expression closely as he sank himself as deep as he could, groaning under his breath.

Shit.

Lacey sits on the bed looking anxious as I hurry off to get into my scrubs before nearly *late* transforms into *actually* late. Everyone thinks the interns are under the most pressure to perform, but that's not true. It's just as easy to get booted from the residency program if you're behind in your work. Being tardy is kind of frowned upon. As is bringing a twenty-six-year-old woman who needs constant babysitting to work with you.

I make it through rounds, on time thankfully, and I see the patients who have been admitted on my day off. Punctured lung. Congenital heart defect. Septicemia. Everything is serious today. Serious enough that I have to spend a considerable amount of time with each patient, assessing their progress and filling out the necessary paperwork for their records and meds. It's midday by the time I finally get the chance to lock myself in the bathroom and text Zeth.

Me: Your friends followed me to work this morning.

A minute passes before the phone chimes in my hand.

Zeth, Rcv'd 12:48 pm
What happened?

Me: Nothing. They just followed us. Parked out front. What do you mean, what happened? Is something going to *happen*?

Zeth, Rcv'd 12:51
Doubtful.

And then...

Zeth, Rcv'd 12:51
You okay?

I should tell him the truth: *No, I'm not okay!* But that wouldn't serve any real purpose. Plus, for some reason, I don't want to look weak in front of him. If I admit to being frightened of his thug business colleagues, then it feels the same as admitting I'm frightened of *him*. And no way am I admitting that. He knows I am, but I'll never own up to it. I'm in the middle of typing a long, strongly worded text back to him when the phone starts ringing in my hand. I pick up, frowning.

"*What?*"

"You didn't reply. You told me you were being watched. When I ask you if you're okay, you *answer*, Sloane," he reprimands me in his deep, gravel-filled voice. "Bad things will happen otherwise."

"I was replying to—urgh!" I don't even bother. "What can you do about these guys eating donuts outside the hospital?"

"Nothing." He sounds completely unconcerned.

"What? They're your boss's men, right? Don't you get along with any of these guys?"

That makes him laugh—a rumble that teases its way into my ear and makes me shiver. "We tend to keep out of each other's way. Charlie prefers it like that."

"Well, what am I supposed to do if they follow me home when I'm done here?" The thought of going home and sitting in that big house on the hill with only Lacey for protection isn't exactly a reassuring one.

"You're gonna be fine," he tells me. "I got boys looking after you. Besides, they're just watching. If one of them breaks into your house, just stab them."

Just stab them? My mouth falls open. "I don't go around stabbing people!"

"Got a gun?"

"No!"

"Then you can't really shoot them instead, can you?"

I pinch the bridge of my nose between index finger and thumb, sitting down heavily on the closed toilet lid. "Zeth, can you *please* just get back here as soon as possible. Please."

"Anyone would think you needed me," he says in a low, silky tone. I have shivers again. All over my body.

"I don't!"

"Well, I need you." The tenor of his voice slips into a vocal range I've never heard from him before. It's so deep and rough that my whole body starts to burn. "Next time I see you, I'm introducing you to a few friends from the bag. I'm getting fucking hard just thinking about it. Fuck. There's one toy in that bag that I think you like almost as much as I do."

He's talking about the knife, I know he is. I swallow thickly, shaking my head, trying to push all memories of the last time he used it on me out of my mind. He makes that really hard when he continues talking.

"I wanna slide my hands up those thighs, Sloane. I wanna tear your clothes from your body and make you tremble. I want to dig my fingers and my teeth into your skin and make you scream my name. You want that, too, huh?"

Cold sweat pushes out of my pores, making my skin prickle. I'm a visual person. Say something to me and I instantly imagine it—and at this exact moment in time I find myself visualizing Zeth's impressively big cock straining against his jeans, begging to be freed. I clear my throat, closing my eyes. "That isn't exactly a practical thing to want right now."

"What about me screams *practical* to you?" His voice dips in volume again, so that it's one level above a whisper. It has a flustering effect on me. "Where are you right now?" he asks.

"In the bathroom."

"Anyone else in there with you?"

The question seems like a sensible one. A question any normal person would ask if you were discussing mob bosses, being followed, and stabbing people to death. I duck my head, looking underneath the stall dividers. No feet. No one standing at the washbasins, either. "No. No one else," I confirm.

But with his next words, it becomes obvious that Zeth isn't concerned about people overhearing information our *conversation*. "Good. Put your hand down your pants for me, angry girl."

"What?"

"Do it. Put your right hand down your pants for me. I want to hear you come."

Good God above. "I am not *masturbating* in a public bathroom! You're *crazy* if you think I'm doing that!"

Zeth makes a pleasant growling sound on the other end of the phone. "I'm not asking, Sloane. I'm telling. Touch. Yourself. Now."

"*No!*"

Zeth seems confused by my refusal. "Would you be saying no to me if I was standing in front of you?"

I think on that for a second, imagining it playing out in my head. If he were standing in front of me in this toilet cubicle, I'd do pretty much anything he told me to. God*damn* him. I don't say anything, which makes him chuckle. "I'll make you a deal." He breathes heavily down the phone. "If you slip your hand down those prissy blue scrubs of yours and you're not already wet for me, then you can hang up the phone."

He loves doing this. Turning my own body against me. But not this time. I huff into the handset, smug that I'm about to prove him wrong. I could just tell him I've done it and laugh haughtily as I hang up, but that won't work. But he'd *know*. "Fine!" My hand slides down the waistband of my scrubs, but over the top of my panties—no need to go that far. The smile falls off my face when I realize I'm not only wet for him, but I've soaked all the way through my thin cotton underwear.

"Middle finger first, Sloane," Zeth rasps into the phone. He doesn't even ask if he won our deal. He just knows he has. The bastard. I screw my eyes tightly shut, kicking myself.

"I don't have time. I have patients to see."

"You're catering to *my* patience right now," he informs me darkly. "I wanna hear it in your voice, Sloane. I wanna hear every single agonizing second that you're toying with yourself, wishing that your fingers were my cock."

"You're very full of yourself, you know that?" My breathlessness doesn't do much to make me sound confident.

He tuts down the phone. "Use your middle finger. Slide it inside yourself and tell me that's not exactly what you're thinking. *Wishing* for. My dick, slamming into you. Do it now, Sloane."

I want to laugh. I want to hang up the phone and go on my rounds and forget about this stupid demand he's making of me. But I also want to do it. Zeth doesn't say anything further, but I can hear his laden, heavy breathing still on the line. I spend thirty seconds battling with myself. This is exactly like the situation he engineered back in his richly decorated apartment. He's trying to make me reach this decision by myself. To make me see it's actually what I want. I already know it *is*, so why am I fighting it?

That Pippa-sounding voice whispers in my ear. *Because you don't know him. And what you* do *know is terrifying.* But it's the last two years of my life that have been terrifying. At least I know for a certainty what and *who* he is.

I slip my panties to one side and press my finger into my center, gasping quietly. I'm so wet, so turned on. I've never felt this way when I've done this by myself. But I'm not alone now, am I. Zeth might as well be guiding my hand with his own.

"Good girl, Sloane." He must have heard me gasp, or he's using some sort of that strange psychic power that he's thus far kept hidden. "Is your clit swollen?"

I shut my eyes, trying not to feel absolutely lost and embarrassed. "Yeah. It is."

"Rub it for me." I do. I work my fingers back and forth over the slick flesh between my legs, fighting to keep my breath even. "Does it feel good?"

"Uh-huh." I gasp as a ripple of heat shivers up my spine, burning my ear tips and scorching my face. My lips tingle like crazy. I bite the lower one in an attempt to disperse the sensation, but it only makes it worse. I sigh deeply.

"That's it. Don't hold your breath, angry girl." Zeth's deeply resonating voice is hypnotic now, working into my subconscious. It feels like a physical presence in itself, sending shooting relays of pleasure around my body. "Take your shirt off."

I stop what I'm doing and comply, pushing all thought of objection out of my head. No point now. I yank off my scrubs top and my tee underneath, letting the clothes drop to the floor between my legs. It isn't cold, but I shiver as I shrug out of my bra straps. My nipples are already tightly drawn buds, so sensitive that the still air against them almost hurts.

"Squeeze your breasts. Imagine my hands," Zeth orders. "My mouth."

Squeeze my breasts? That's not something I do when I'm on my own. I never really have. I always reasoned that it wouldn't be the same as a guy doing it, but now when I lightly trace my fingertips across my goose-bumped skin, I am imagining him. I feel the heat of his breath as he stoops to suck one nipple and then the other into his mouth. My own breath catches again.

"Good. That's right," he encourages me. "Put me on speakerphone. You're gonna need two hands for this."

I fumble with the phone, hitting the speaker icon and setting the phone down on top of the pile of clothes at my feet. I'm already too lost to think about what I'm doing. I'm using my own discretion now, touching and stroking where I see fit. I'm panting, too. Lost to madness.

"Now. Slide your fingers inside." Zeth's voice is rougher than normal, and that's saying something. I obey him immediately, slipping first my middle and then my index finger into my pussy. I inhale sharply, the pressure warm and tight and blissful. The forbidden pitch of his words works its magic over me when he commands, "Fuck yourself for me, Sloane. Do it. Fuck yourself hard."

I can't prevent the moans and soft gasps that escape my mouth as I work my fingers inside myself, imagining him on top of me, his rock-hard cock pulsing in and out of me, the sublime burn of his rough stubble on my sensitive skin. He breathes words into the phone, growling and hissing out his approval as I grow louder and louder. I can't focus on what he's saying, though. Soon, a tightening, fizzing sensation grips me. It happens suddenly. A wall of heat crashes through me like whitewater smashing into the wall of a dam, simultaneously rising upward and dragging me down with it.

"Holy...*FUCK!*" The curse rips out of me like a plea for help. My chest heaves as I try to catch my breath, up and down, up and down.

Zeth's lazy, amused laughter echoes around the narrow cubicle. "Sounds like you enjoyed that, angry girl."

"Fuck you," I pant, only half meaning it.

And then I hear something that makes me freeze in place: a toilet flush. Zeth is silent for a moment and then he says, "Let me guess. That wasn't you."

I sit up straight, slapping my hands over my mouth. Zeth just starts laughing. I snatch up the phone and hit the big red end call button, feeling all my blood rush to my cheeks.

Holy. Fucking. *Shit.*

A stall door opens. Not the one right next to me. The one on the very end. A tap squeaks, and the sound of rushing water fills the bathroom. Whoever it is hurriedly washes their hands and then rushes out of the bathroom. I grab up my clothes and dress myself frantically. I need to find out who the hell that was! No. Nooooo, no, no. *Fuck!*

I hastily wash my own hands, and then dash out of the bathroom, chest now heaving more from horror than the orgasm I just experienced. The corridor bustles with nurses, doctors and members of the public. *Members of the fucking public!* I don't know what's worse, the thought of a colleague having just heard that or the poor, unsuspecting family member of one of my patients. My shame becomes absolute when Oliver Massey saunters down the hallway toward me, grinning. He holds up his hand, grinning at me. Without thinking, I respond, giving him a high five as he passes. He raises an eyebrow at me as he continues on his way.

"Scrubs are inside out, Romera," he says, winking. "What *have* you been up to?"

39

SLOANE

IT CAN'T HAVE BEEN OLIVER. THERE'S NO way it could have been him. It was the women's bathroom, for crying out loud. The rest of the day goes by with me feeling flushed and distinctly like I just got caught with my pants down. And my shirt off. While being instructed to do very graphic things to myself.

I want to smack Zeth so hard my palms tingle for the rest of my shift. When it's finally time for me to clock out, I find Lacey asleep in the on-call room where I left her, swaddled in blankets. She doesn't look like she's moved at all since this morning. She blinks groggily at me when I wake her, and we leave St. Peter's via the rear exit, first to avoid the curious eyes of the nursing staff, second so I don't run into Oliver again (just in case), and third so I can try to sneak the Volvo out of the lot without being seen by any mysterious black cars with tinted windows.

Everything goes off without a hitch. No nursing staff, no Oliver, and miraculously no black car. The vehicle isn't even parked outside the coffee place anymore, which makes me feel kind of foolish. Maybe whoever that was this morning just happened to be going the same way as us and stopped off for a quick coffee on the way to work. Both Lacey and I watch carefully all the way home, though, just in case.

I park the car, and we head inside. I make sure all the windows and doors are triple locked just as a precautionary measure. The action brings to mind Zeth snooping around the place, inspecting every square inch to make sure it measured up to his idea of secure. He probably already knew he would be dumping Lacey on my doorstep and wanted to make sure she would be safe. The thought plummets me into an irrationally sour mood.

"I'm too tired to cook. You're just gonna have to make do with takeout." I hurl the words over my shoulder at the girl following behind me, and I immediately regret it. A shutter comes down across Lacey's already wary features.

"It's okay," she says mechanically. "*I* can cook."

"No. Shit, no, I'm—I'm sorry, Lace. I've just had a really long day." I blow out a long breath, pressing my fingers into my forehead as I wince. "But that's no excuse." I haven't had a roommate since college and even then, I didn't do all that well living with other people. I shouldn't be shitty with Lacey because of *him*, though. I definitely should be an asshole to her because I'm jealous of the bizarre relationship they share.

"I don't want you to cook. I really do just want takeout. Is that okay?"

She nods, hanging her head as she makes her way to the breakfast bar. She likes it there. Seems to make her feel inconspicuous. I take the stack of home delivery menus from the drawer next to the cutlery drawer, and I let her pick. She chooses Chinese food, selects what she wants, and to my amazement orders the meals for us, too, giving my address without even having to ask for it. I crack open a bottle of wine (much needed) and offer her a glass. She shrugs—*why the hell not?*—and we settle on the couch, the TV playing quietly in the background while we wait for our dinner to arrive.

There's a bitter taste in my mouth despite the red wine, though. Ahh, to hell with it. I have to know what's going on with them. "So..." I begin—the best way to broach a topic when you don't have a decent segue. "I know you told Pippa you didn't know why you liked being with Zeth so much. But I thought—"

Lacey lifts her glass, holding it with two hands, almost hiding behind it. She chugs the wine *way* too fast. When she lowers the glass, her eyes are watering like crazy. She peers askance at me. From her reaction, I was actually going to let the matter drop, but she chooses to speak of her own accord. "I found him," she says simply. "I was looking for him for a long time, and I found him."

Well, that's a confusing statement if ever I've heard one. "Found him, like...you were looking for *'the one'*? Like, your soul mate?" Holy shit, could I get any more awkward? I sound like an online dating site. Hell, maybe they *did* meet on an online dating website.

Lacey's face is a picture of puzzlement. "What? No. No." She shakes her head violently. "My first foster family told me about him. Told me that he was living north of Los Angeles with his uncle. They said when I was old enough, I could go and live with him."

"Why the hell would they say that?"

Lacey's mouth puckers. She doesn't know what she should tell me. How much she should reveal. Her gaze roves from my eyes to my mouth to my nose and then back to my eyes again. She draws her arms tight to her body, apparently having made up her mind. "He's older than me. My *older* brother. I traveled all over Los Angeles trying to find him when I finally...when

I finally got away from Greg. But he wasn't there." She absently chews her thumbnail, staring into space. Meanwhile, I sit with my hand over my mouth once more, trying to let the information sink in. Sister. She's his *sister*? "I found his uncle, though." She ignores my stupefied look. "*My* uncle, too, I suppose. He said Zeth had moved to New York, so I went there. But he hadn't moved to New York. He was *in prison* there. I didn't know what to do, then, so I left and came here. I'd found out his boss lived in Seattle. I figured Zeth would come back here at some point, so I decided to wait. And then, one day, there he was."

I can't believe it. They are like night and day, one tall and dark, the other tiny and colorless, like a gust of wind. Lacey drinks more wine while I run my finger around the rim of my glass, trying to make the pieces fit. "So...you approached him and told him you were his sister?"

She looks at me, surprised. "No."

"He already knew?"

Another shake of the head. "No. He doesn't know we're related."

"So how did you end up *living* with him, then?" This is getting more confusing by the second.

The girl smiles carefully. "It was raining. I'd been sitting outside for hours, trying to figure out how to introduce myself. I was soaked through. I thought he'd probably let me come in and dry off, at least, once he found out we were brother and sister. But I couldn't find the right way to word it in my head. I passed out from the cold. He was going out somewhere and found me on his doorstep. Nearly tripped over me. He was dressed in this smart tuxedo. He still picked me up and took me inside, even though it got him all wet. He asked what the fuck I was doing outside his place. Did I know him? I said yeah, I did. But then I was stuck again. I still couldn't figure out what to say to make it make sense. He asked me if I'd fucked him. I said no. He asked if I was gonna tell him how I knew him, then, and I said, yeah. At some point. When I'd worked up to it. And then that was that."

"*And then that was that?*" Incredulous, I shuffle closer to the girl. "You said you'd get around to telling him, and you've been living with him ever since?"

She nods, like this is completely normal.

"How long ago was that?"

"Oh, I don't know. Six months or so," she replies.

I have no idea how this man's mind works, or his *sister's*, now that I know that's who she is. But they're both as strange as each other. "So he has no idea? After letting you live with him for six months?"

"I don't *think* so."

Wow.

A knock at the door cuts off further questioning.

I answer—our takeout, finally arrived—and I decide to let the matter drop. We eat in silence, Lacey laughing quietly at the rom-com playing on the television, while I sit and stew on what I've just discovered.

Hah.

The irony of it all doesn't escape me.

I am taking care of Zeth sister, while *he* attempts to take care of *mine*.

ZETH

I can't get that girl out of my fucking head. The sounds she made on the phone, the things I told her to do to herself, and the way she caved like a landslide as soon as I got her past the first gate. Not to mention the horrified silence when that toilet flushed. I'm still pissing myself every time I think about that little gem. Somehow makes it even more taboo. Especially since that sort of thing, getting busted, makes me harder than fucking tempered steel. I'd had to spend half an hour stroking myself before I'd been able to erase the idea of *that* from my head.

Afterward, I spent the rest of yesterday making plans with Michael. He had more photos—confirmation that Alexis definitely is somewhere within compound. The girl was curvier than her sister. Well-dressed. Clearly, she's being taken care of, but there were shadows beneath her eyes. She looked haunted. She's definitely in trouble, but I can't just go sneaking around the compound looking for her today. Far too suspicious, especially after I knocked Alaska back. The woman has been sulking about it all day.

No, today I'm headed to Anaheim to meet with Rick. As well as the photos, Michael had a dossier for me, full of information on the DEA agent who's been snooping around. I plan on taking it with me so I can ask Rick a few choice questions. If he knows anything beyond the details in the dossier, I want to know, too. I also want to know what he's heard from back home. Tossing my phone was smart—Charlie would have found some way of tracking me through it if I'd kept it—but it also means I have no idea what kind of holy hell has been raining down on Seattle since I bolted.

Rick waits in a fried chicken joint for me, a box of cold, greasy fries sitting in front of him, untouched. I picked the place on purpose, just to piss him off. Rick's a big guy, but he didn't get that way through genetics or, gotta hand it to him, steroids. He eats healthy. Like, eats like a fucking chick kind of healthy. Salad and clean protein, all day every day. Even sitting inside this place is probably making him sweat kale extract.

"Took your time," he complains as I sit opposite

him, dropping the file onto the table. He lifts the thing open with one finger, grimacing at the contents inside, then lets it fall closed. "Why the hell am I in Anaheim, sitting in a fried rat shop?"

"Because I told you to be."

He nods, accepting that. "Charlie's gone off the deep end," he advises me from under lowered brows. "Looking everywhere for you."

"The boys know you're alive?" I ask him.

"No. Heard that from the DEA bitch. Gave me a burner back when I started working for her. She. Is. Pissed." He emphasizes each word, just to make sure I understand *how* pissed. "Was screaming 'bout arresting me for reneging on our arrangement and all. I told her I got out of town before I got dead. And I'm no good to her dead."

"True enough."

"She wants to know where I am, though. Wants me to work some of the biker charters around here instead."

"Not happening." I shake my head. "The biker charters that deal with Charlie see you, they're gonna run their mouths and suddenly you're resurrected. Then Charlie knows I didn't do what he asked me to."

"You ran." Rick rubs the back of his hand against his broad, twice-broken nose. "Figure Charlie probably suspects something's up already. Lowell said another guy told her the old man is on the rampage, looking for some girl who was living with you. Wants to lay a few questions on her regarding your whereabouts. The DEA are keen to scoop up this chick, too. Seems they're mighty interested in what you got going on, Zeth."

I had expected the DEA to poke their noses into my business, but I hadn't expected them to go after Lacey. Charlie knows all about Lace. He pretends not to take an interest in my personal shit, but he's up to his sticky fucking coke-rimmed nose in my business by all accounts. Must have listened in on a thousand conversations when the girl was asking me where I was, panicked, begging me to come home. The idea makes me angry.

But then something even worse hits me. If Charlie is serious about snatching up Lacey, then that means... that means he's likely to snatch up *Sloane* at the same time.

My muscles stir, begging for immediate action. I need to hit something. To smash. To pound. I need to make someone *hurt*. The rest of me twitches with unspent adrenaline, lighting firing in my joints, readying them to fight. I've never been this wound up from a single thought. Not ever. I'm worried about Lacey for sure, but when I think about Charlie laying hands on Sloane...

"You okay, man?" Rick stares at the crumpled napkin I have fisted tight in my hand. My knuckles are white. I toss it aside, scowling. This woman is having a seriously fucked-up effect on me. I can't afford to be this distracted by her. She's consuming every single waking moment of my day, and I need to focus. No point in worrying about things that probably aren't even going to happen, either. I've tasked my guys with that one specific job—to watch out for Lace and Sloane, to keep them from harm.

I brush off the freakout, calming myself. "I want you to reach out to this DEA woman. Ask her which bikers she's interested in. I wanna know what information she's got on me, and I wanna know when they plan on picking up Lacey." I scribble my burner's cell number down on another, less crumpled though still greasy napkin and tuck it roughly into the top pocket of Rick's T-shirt.

The guy grunts his assent, although he's clearly none too happy about it. His sandy eyebrows knit together as he thinks about speaking. After a short while, he leans in, saying, "Why d'you care about that piece of ass, anyway? She was sleeping with Georgio Ramerez for months. You know he ain't too careful with his possessions. Word is Matty Stanton had a go at her, too. You never struck me as the kind of guy to be scooping up sloppy seconds from anyone, Zee."

Rick is one lucky son of a bitch. I can't start anything here. Starting something would cause a scene, and there are cameras all over the fucking place. I employ a coping mechanism Walcott used to bang on about in Chino. I imagine reaching for Rick, the tacky Formica table digging into chest. I imagine wrapping my hand around the back of Rick's neck, engaging the muscles in my arm and then smashing his face into the table. In my head, his nose makes a sickening crunch, and an explosion of blood follows right after. It's *vaguely* satisfying. To imagine the action without the follow-through is counterproductive. The goal is to vent the anger *away* from my body, and thinking about it only directs my rage inward.

Rick knows his question was a mistake. I fix him in my gaze, and he shifts uncomfortably in his seat. "Just wondering," he adds.

"Wondering can be very detrimental to the health, I've heard."

"Yeah, well—" Rick looks around, as if searching for a reason to leave. He doesn't need an excuse, though. Our meeting's over.

"Call that number tomorrow. *With* the information." I get up and slide my aviators on, exiting the fast-food place as inconspicuously as possible—a difficult thing to do, when you're six foot three and built like a tank.

40

SLOANE

A CREEPING DREAD WAKES ME. IT SET-tles over me like a blanket, suffocating, as I lie frozen still in bed. The house settles, creaking, sighing, the wind teasing inquisitively at the windowpanes, and I hold my breath. My heart gallops. Moonlight pours through the open curtains at the other end of the room. Outside, it washes over the swaying tree line beyond that marks the border of my property, gilding branches and leaves in silver. I can see perfectly. The closet door. The chest of drawers. The small chestnut wooden blanket box at the foot of my bed. Everything is lit up and where it ought to be. Nothing is out of place.

Perhaps Lacey's presence here, sleeping in the guest room, is enough to set me on edge. I've always been able to sense when I'm not alone, even in a house as big as this. I never sleep well when I have guests. But... *no*. It isn't that. This feels different. Awkward. Tense. There's no *way* I'm getting back to sleep.

My throat feels like the Sahara. Might as well refill my water glass.

I toss back the duvet and tiptoe across the room. No sense in waking Lacey, just because I'm restle—

I freeze, hand still on the door handle, staring slack jawed at the intruders in my hallway. There are two of them. Two *men*, dressed in black pants and T-shirts. They mirror my surprise, locked in place.

They look at me.

I look at them.

I look at the *girl* they're carrying between them. The guy closest to the top of the stairs—the one with a nasty-looking scar twisting his bottom lip—has Lacey's legs. The other guy—a tall fucker with a shaved head—has her arms pinned to her torso, his hand clamped over her mouth. He needn't bother. She isn't even trying to scream. She's stiff as a board. Her gaze meets mine, and the animal terror in her eyes spurs me into action.

"What the hell are you doing?" Stupid question. It's pretty fucking obvious: They're kidnapping Lacey.

The girl Zeth left in my care. *The girl I said I would look after.*

The guy with the scar shakes his head *very* slowly. "Turn around. Go back to bed. You don't wanna make this your business."

My voice quivers with rage "Put her down. Get the *fuck* out of my house."

The two men huff in synchrony. Was I not part of the plan? They must have known I was here. "You wanna die tonight?" the one with the shaved head asks.

The other guy grunts. I don't like the malicious glint in his eyes. "Fuck it. She's seen us now. We're gonna have to deal with her."

Lacey hasn't moved a muscle. She's either been paralyzed by fear or playing dead, but this lights a fire in her. She bucks, thrashing, and manages to free one of her legs. For a moment, the intruders are distracted. They fight to regain control of her, and I move. Lacey's eyes plead with me as I dart back into my bedroom and slam the door closed behind me.

The lock slides home.

I'm not leaving you. I promise I'm not leaving you. Hold tight.

Lacey isn't a mind reader, but I hope she knows I'm not abandoning her. Unarmed, I can't help her, though. I can't reach the only weapon in the house—the baseball bat I keep by the front door—without having to pass her kidnappers, so I go for the next best thing: my medical bag. It's where I always keep it, in my en suite, on the floor beneath the sink.

"Open the fucking door, bitch!" Thunderous hammering rattles my bedroom door. My hands shake like crazy.

C'mon, c'mon, c'mon! Move, *Sloane*.

Boom.

Boom.

Boom.

My pulse is everywhere.

I fumble with the zip, upending the contents of the bag onto the bathroom floor. Blister packs of drug samples, small glass vials, syringes, dressings, tongue depressors—everything tumbles out onto the tiles. I grab a syringe and the first vial I lay my hands on, and then I run for the door. Not the one that leads into the hallway. The connecting door that leads into the third bedroom. I hold my breath a moment, listening.

"...back up for her. We need to get this one in the car first."

"No way. She'll get out!"

"So?" The guy with the deeper voice, the one with the scar, sounds pissed off. "She can't go anywhere. We slashed her tires. She can't call the cops. There's no reception out here. Landline's dead. Internet's dead.

What's she gonna do, send a fucking *smoke signal*? Come on. We'll let her stew a minute."

A few years ago, someone asked me how I thought I'd fare if I suddenly found myself smack bang in the middle of a war zone. Would I fight, or would I crumple under the pressure? I hadn't known then. I do now.

I wait a minute, evening out my breath as the bastards grunt and scuffle, carrying Lacey down the stairs

Then I move.

Thank fuck for trauma surgery.

That's what races through my head as I fly across the landing and down the stairs. If it wasn't for trauma surgery, I wouldn't be able to snap a syringe from its packaging, plunge the needle into a vial, and draw up meds while hustling like my ass is on fire.

The men are at the front door, exiting with Lacey. She's flailing now, finally screaming through the hand over her mouth.

Which vial did I grab from the bag?

Diclofenac.

Great.

25mg if you have bad period pains. 200mg if you wanna send a kidnapper to the back of beyond.

I load the syringe and run.

It's raining outside.

Gravel tears into the soles of my feet.

The guy carrying Lacey's feet sees me coming.

Too late, motherfucker.

I plunge the syringe into his buddy's neck.

The guy with the shaved head sags like I just shot him. *Good.* He hits the ground, all arms and legs. Lacey goes with him, landing heavily on his chest.

"FUCKING BITCH! What did you do?" Scarred Mouth roars. "You killed him!"

Maybe. Maybe not. No time to check for a pulse. He comes at me, a gun suddenly in his hand. "Get in the fucking car," he seethes, jerking his head over his shoulder. The black sedan that followed us earlier is parked to his right, the rear door yawning open, waiting for Lacey. Rainwater pools on the leather, soaking the seats.

The panic hits home at last. I only had one syringe, and now it's stuck in the neck of the asshole sprawled out on my driveway.

Fuck. I should have grabbed the baseball bat from its resting place as I ran past. Not that a baseball bat is much use against a gun, but still.

"Are you fucking deaf as well as stupid?" Scarred Mouth spits. "Get. Inside. The. Fucking. Car."

I've always loved living out in the sticks. No one to harass you. No cars burning by at all hours. No nosy neighbors spying on you from behind twitching curtains.

Now, living so far out of town doesn't seem so

smart. No one to come to your rescue. No cars passing by to flag down for help. No nosy neighbors to witness a berserk gunman and call the police. *Shit.*

This guy could have already shot me. I don't know why he hasn't. I *do* know that if I get in that car, I am *definitely* dead, though.

"No. I'm not getting into the car."

"No?" The gunman's face scrunches in disbelief. "You do see this gun in my hand, right?" He holds it up sideways so I can get a good look at it, index finger hovering over the trigger. He stalks forward, sick of waiting. He's going to force me into the car, conscious or unconscious, dead or alive.

I have no options. Bravado will only get me so far. When grabs me, my show of strength disintegrates into smoke.

Zeth. I *need* Zeth. When I *don't* need him, he's always there, causing trouble, but now that his proclivity for violence would actually come in *handy*, he's a thousand fucking miles away. Of *course* he is.

Scarred Mouth wrenches my wrist like he's planning on breaking it. He's about to bring his gun crashing down on my head when he jerks erratically and stumbles into me. With vacant eyes, he slides down my body, hand locked around my wrist. He isn't restraining me anymore, though. He's trying to use me for balance.

I choke on a gasp when he finally lets go and drops to the wet ground, convulsing. His arms and legs spasm, tendons in his neck bulging as his head trains back.

Lacey stands over him, clutching a gigantic hunk of rock to her chest. It's so hefty that she has to hold it with both hands. Something dark and wet stains its underside. *Blood.*

"Did you just..." I trail off. Why am I even asking?

Lacey startles, as if coming back into herself. She drops the rock, and it lands with a weighty *thud* by her feet, sinking three inches into the mud. She looks at me like *she* has no idea what she just did. "I just—he needed to let you go," she whimpers. "Is he—is he dead?"

"His chest is still moving. He's breathing. He'll be fine, Lacey. But we need to get out of here. Like, *right now*." Am I telling her the truth? I don't know. He *is* still breathing, but who knows how long he'll keep that up for. I don't give a fuck. We've just dodged a bullet, probably literally *and* figuratively. I don't plan on checking in with our attacker to see if he's fucking all right. "Get in the car, Lace." I point to the sedan, indicating which one I mean. We can't take the Volvo, after all. I heard him say he'd slashed the tires, loud and clear.

Lacey complies, hugging herself as she clambers into the back seat.

The back seat? What the *hell* is she doing? But then I remember Zeth's words when he first put her in my car: *She can't. She won't.*

Okay. Fine. So long as she's *in* the car...

I climb in the driver's seat, and panic hits me.

I don't have *anything* with me.

Think, Sloane! Blunt force trauma. Diclofenac. Are either of them fucking dead? How much time do you have? Any time at all?

I can't run upstairs and pack a suitcase. That's out of the question. But we're not going to get very far without money, are we? My bag. It's on the mail stand in the hallway. My cards and my ID are inside. That'll have to do.

"Stay here, Lacey. Don't move."

I risk it. The rain lashes me as I sprint back toward the house. My pajamas cling to my body. My feet are wet when I hurtle through the front door, and I skid, falling, landing hard on my ass in the entry way.

Pain shoots up my spine, making my ears ring. That's gonna leave a bruise. No time. No time. I get up, nearly slipping all over again. There's my bag. I grab it, yanking it open. Gotta make sure...

Yes. My cards are there.

My cell phone is still upstairs, though. I should—fuck. No. I can't. The bag will have to do. I run back to the sedan find Lacey shaking like a leaf in the rearview. Another spike of panic pierces me through the chest when I realize I might have to go fishing in those fuckers' pockets for the car keys. But no, they're in the ignition, thank God. They must have wanted to make a quick getaway.

"Why are we taking their car?" Lacey's teeth chatter when she speaks. She's in shock. I need to get her some sugar, and soon; otherwise, she's gonna crash. Hard.

"They said they'd slashed my tires. Remember?"

She shakes her head, her eyes losing focus. Oh, boy. This is going to be a long night. "Whoever sent those guys knows what my car looks like, anyway. They'll be looking for it when they realize how badly this has gone. Soon as we can, we'll get a rental car, Lace."

No response.

"*Lacey?*"

In the rearview, I see that her knees are pulled up under her chin and she's rocking back and forth. Goddamn it all to hell.

I gun the engine and burn away from the house, leaving the bodies of our attackers sprawled out in the dirt.

41

SLOANE

THANK GOD I GRABBED MY PURSE. THE gas tank is running on vapors by the time we hit the freeway. Who doesn't fill up the tank if they're planning on a good ol' kidnapping? I leave the city limits and find myself on I-5 South without even making a conscious decision. The road stretches out in a never-ending expanse of blacktop now. The road will carry us for roughly seventeen hours in the same direction until we hit Los Angeles. I could have gone to the hospital. I could have gone to Pip, too, but the thought of dragging trouble to her doorstep is one I won't entertain. Same with my workplace. All I know is that the only person capable of keeping us safe now is probably going to be annoyed at our presence. And I have no idea how to find him once we reach L.A.

Lacey eventually falls asleep after we stop at a gas station, and I grab her an overly sweet soda and a couple of PowerBars. A bleary dawn washes the cloudy sky pale pink. After a few hours, I see a sign for Walmart and exit the freeway. I leave Lacey sleeping in the car and go inside to grab us each a couple of changes of clothing. The cashier eyes the fresh purple bruise on my forearm from where the guy with the scar grabbed me earlier and shakes her head, as though the state I'm in, the early hour, and my hastily grabbed stash of jeans, T-shirts, and shoes tells a bleak story. She clearly thinks I'm on the run from an abusive boyfriend or something.

It's amazing, the difference a pair of jeans and some ballet flats can make to a flight of escape. I feel less vulnerable than I did in my PJs, anyway. Lacey wakes eight hours later. She's conscious long enough to tell me that she doesn't know how to drive, before I decide enough is enough and we need to dump the car. We stop in Jackson County, Oregon, and abandon the vehicle in a liquor store parking lot with the keys still in the ignition—someone's *bound* to steal it at some point—and then we traipse five blocks over to a Rest-Eezy Motel, where I check us in under a false name and then pass the fuck out.

ZETH

"What the fuck do you mean, *the place was empty?*" Callum, one of my boys, words the information cautiously, knowing full well how much shit he's in. I set him the task of checking in on Sloane's place through the night, and the unbelievable little motherfucker is only calling me now, at eleven fucking a.m., to tell me that the house was empty when he got there. "When did you last go by the place?" I demand.

He's silent for a long time. And then, "Midnight." I hear the wince in his voice.

I hope he can hear the *murder* in mine. "Say again? Because I swear you just said midnight, when I told you to go by every two fucking hours."

"I know, Zee. But the place is miles from anything, man! Took me an hour just to find it. I figured no one else was gonna be headed up that sketchy road in the dark. It's fucking dangerous!"

"You know what's fucking dangerous?" I growl. "Me. *I'm* fucking dangerous. And right now I'm close to flying back to Seattle so I can *personally* fuck you up. You feel me?"

"I'm sorry, Zee! Seriously, I'm gonna find them, I swear."

"No, you're not. You're gonna tell me what you found when you went up there." My voice grows quieter and lower with each and every word. Anyone with half a brain cell knows that this is not a good thing.

"Well. Her cell phone was upstairs on the nightstand."

"*WHAT?*"

He bulls on, probably afraid to give me chance to speak. "And there were deep tire tracks outside. Not from the doc's car, though. That was still parked there. The tires were cut to ribbons. And there were a lot of footprints and skid marks in the mud. Guess it looked like something had been dragged or some shit."

"*Dragged or some shit?* You are *filling* me with positivity right now, Callum. Do you know what it feels like to have your fingers broken one by one? 'Cause the prospect of showing you is sounding more enjoyable by the second. Where. Are. They?"

"I don't know, boss. I'm gonna find out, though. Right now!"

The line goes dead. I grit my teeth, screw my eyes shut, and squeeze the phone until it creaks under the pressure. I take a moment. Swallow hard. Inhale a deep breath.

Today has not started off well.

I knew something was up when Sloane didn't answer her phone. I fucking *knew* it.

My stomach is twisted in knots, palms sweating, heart thundering. What the fuck is *wrong* with me? I get up, and the floor pitches like I'm standing on the deck of a ship in a sixty foot swell.

Breathe, for fuck's sake, I tell myself. *Fucking* breathe.

Breathing doesn't help. The last time I felt like this, a piece-of-shit warden had just slammed my cell door closed and my new reality had hit home. I was in *Chino*, of all places. Totally fucked. At the will of another man. I hadn't lived like that since I'd fled my uncle. I'd panicked that first night. That was all I'd allowed myself before I'd shut it down. They told me when to eat, and when to shit, and when to clean, and when to work, but they could never tell me how to *feel* about it again. I had taken back control of myself.

Now, there is no control. My insides are flayed raw. My lungs are full of holes.

Completely fucking unacceptable.
I don't know where they are.
I don't know where she is.
I don't know how to get to them.
There's nothing I can do.

But I *need* to do something. I have to. I snatch up my jacket, testing the weight to make sure the Camaro keys are still inside. I'll drive all day and all night if I have to. I'm going to find those girls. My girls. *My girl.*

On the other side of the bedroom door, Jake and

one of the guards from the entrance the other night, the tall one, are heading down the hallway, looking very fucking serious. A serious look on a gang lord is a very bad sign. When Jacob feels threatened, he behaves to the contrary and smiles. When he suspects someone's playing him for a fool, taking liberties, spying, and fucking around in business they have no right to be fucking around in, *that's* when the smile disappears.

"Going somewhere, Mayfair?" Jacob asks. No more *brother*. Open contempt has replaced the show of friendliness he extended when I arrived. The guard next to him carries a gun tucked in the front of his waistband. He hooks his thumb into his belt, emphasizing the fact.

I shrug, casual as you like. "Ahh, y'know, man. Just going to pick up a friend. You said I should bring someone to this event, right?" The event isn't for another two days, but fuck it. It's the first excuse that comes to mind.

"Sure, sure." Jacob scratches at his chin, eying me up and down. "Before you go, come chat by the pool a while, huh?" This isn't the kind of request a man says no to. The fact that he's even disguised it as a request gives me a glimmer of hope that he might not know as much as I think he does. Not yet, anyway. I nod, narrowing my eyes at him. Jacob gestures ahead, signaling that I should go first. After three days casually wandering the halls, hoping to randomly bump into Alexis, I've gotten a pretty good lay of the land within the compound's villa. I head straight for the pool. Outside, a fruit platter waits for us along with fresh juice and beer. Jacob sits on his sun lounger, the guard taking up position standing behind him. I chuckle at the ridiculous punk, who seems to be boiling over the fact that I'm not visibly shitting myself.

"Gonna shoot your dick off with that thing," I advise him, raising my eyebrows at his gun. I pop a strawberry into my mouth, chewing it slowly as I smile a dark smile at him.

Jacob makes a *tsk*ing sound at the back of his throat. "Aw, come on now, Zeth. Be nice to my friends. I'm always nice to yours, true?"

I eat another piece of fruit, rocking my head from side to side—a noncommittal gesture, even though I say, "True."

"I won't keep you long. I just wanted to ask you somethin'." Jacob waves at the guard, who hands over a folded manila envelope that was tucked into the back of his waistband. Jacob slides a piece of paper from the envelope, setting it face down on the table between us. "I've forgotten why you said you were down here in SoCal. You mentioned catching up with some friends on your way to visit family... *right?*"

"That's right." I reply, not blinking at the line of questioning or the piece of paper on the table.

"I see. What kinda friends you got here in Los Angeles, Zeth?"

"All kinds." Another piece of fruit. I gesture toward the ice bucket filled with beers and give him a querying look. Jacob nods, giving his consent. I twist the cap off one of the beers and take a long swig. Jacob does the same, though taking a much more conservative sip from his bottle. "Visited an old high school buddy yesterday. Grabbed some lunch," I tell him. I was careful to make sure I wasn't being followed, but hell. People can be sneaky motherfuckers. Jake could have had me tailed when I went to meet Rick. Better admit to seeing him before confronted with photographic evidence, *if* that's what's on the paper.

"Uh-huh." Jacob rests a hand on his bulging belly, balancing his beer on top of it, too. "This friend of yours. He has a name?"

I give him my best confused look. "Yeah, his name's Rick. Why?"

"Because we caught a guy taking pictures of the girls yesterday from outside the compound. He won't give us his name or tell us why he's here. We thought perhaps *he* might be a friend of yours?"

Fuck. A guy taking pictures of the girls from outside the compound? That sure as hell is someone I know, but it ain't Rick. It's *Michael*. I shake my head, smiling ruefully. "Sorry, man. No idea. Probably just some perv trying get his dick wet, no?"

With a scowl, the guard behind Jacob grunts disbelievingly. "You seriously listening to this, boss? The guy's full of shit."

"Shut your fucking mouth, Anton!" Jacob hisses. His jowls wobble at his sudden spike of rage. Purple-faced, Jacob eyes me in a way that would make lesser men falter. Not me, though. I've dealt with much worse than this and come out the other side smelling of fucking daisies. The other guy usually comes off reeking of sweat and his piss-stained pants. Jacob knows this about me.

"I'm not *accusing* you of anything, Zeth," he reassures me. "I just wanna make sure this man is no friend of yours before I let Anton and his friends get a little more persuasive with their questions. I'd feel bad if one of your employees were to get hurt."

If Michael is somewhere in this compound, then he's keeping his mouth shut tight—one of the reasons I hired him. They have no reason to suspect he's one of mine. This heavy of Jacob's, Anton. He insisted that I'm full of shit just now. *He's* the one whispering into Jake's ear, telling him I'm connected to this in some way.

"Sorry, man. Like I said, I can't help you. Makes

no sense, anyway. Why would I have someone watching the place when I'm already inside?"

Because he could take photos of you fucks while I was gone. Because he could see into the girls' area of the compound from where he was hiding. Because I need to act cool while I'm here and not get caught snooping around like a goddamn spy. There are more reasons, but these are the most important. Jacob's dark eyes laser into me, maybe trying to ascertain the truth of my comment. Thoughtfully, he nods.

"Hmm. I figured as much. But you know how things are with Charlie, huh? We are friends now, but it wasn't always that way. I'm a careful man, Zeth. I always like to be careful."

"Me, too."

Jacob casually flips over the piece of paper on the table, studying it for a moment. When he puts it down again, it's the right way up, and I witness the damage they've already done to my second in command. The dusty jeans and a bloodstained white tank top are a far cry from the immaculate suits he usually wears. His muscles strain as he pulls against the bonds that tie his hands behind his back. There's blood on his forehead, his temple, his shoulder, running from his mouth. They've already worked him over pretty good.

I let it all wash over me. I can't worry about him. This isn't his first rodeo. He can take care of himself. That knowledge doesn't stem my building rage, though. I throw a fire blanket over it, knowing the action won't put out the inferno burning in my chest. It will contain it for a while, at least. I smirk, raising an eyebrow at Anton, who is still running his thumb over the grip of his gun. Twitchy motherfucker. "I feel for you, buddy. Stroking that thing in public and you still can't seem to get it hard? I get it. You gotta make yourself feel tough in other ways, don't you?"

"What the fuck you implying?"

"I'm *implying* that your *dick* doesn't work." The fire blanket isn't working. Oops.

Anton steps forward, mouth turned down—

Jacob holds up an impatient hand, stopping his man in his tracks. "I really wish you would play nice, boys," he groans. "Anton, go see if this guy's ready to tell us what he's doing here. And I know *you* said you were going to collect a friend, but perhaps you'll do me the honor of spending the afternoon with me? I thought maybe some entertainment from the girls perhaps and a few beers in the sunshine?"

For fuck's sake. He wants to keep me close. He may not believe Anton's conspiracy theories, but he also doesn't necessarily believe me, either. I arrange my face into my best imitation of an apology. "Sorry, Jake. I really do need to grab this chick. Maybe tomor—"

He places a firm hand on my shoulder, pushing me back into the sun lounger. "You wouldn't leave me to drink alone, would you? No, Zeth. I don't drink alone. I'm afraid I really must insist."

42

SLOANE

WHEN I WAKE UP, LACEY ISN'T IN THE motel room. The threadbare establishment has an aura of abandonment that gives me chills.

Where the hell is she? My chest is tight. I get up and hurry barefoot across the stained, tacky carpet, flinging the bathroom door open. I expect to find her floating in a tub full of blood-stained bathwater. The stark overhead fluorescent bulb lights up the dingy tiles and the yellowing sink basin, but there's no red in here. No *blood*. My heart rate slows a fraction… until I realize the motel is next to busy road and there's more than one way to get the job done if you've a mind for suicide.

"Lacey? Lace!" Outside, the sky is a wash of glorious blue. In the parking lot thirty feet away, Lacey stands at a payphone, speaking into the handset. I make sure she hears me as I approach behind her.

"...night. Two of them." She nods at me when she notices me arrive. "Yes," she says. "I know. I will, I promise. But right now I just need the address." She bites on her lip, body tense as she apparently waits for whoever is on the other end of the line to respond. Her rigid stance eases when she closes her eyes for a second, exhales, and then goes rummaging for a piece of paper in her pocket. Quickly, she uses a Rest-Eezy motel pen to scribble a set of numbers onto the back of a receipt. "Thank you, Georgio. I'll come and see you, I promise." She slams down the handset, triumphantly holding aloft the dog-eared paper. "I got it. I got the address of the compound where Zeth is right now."

I grab her arm, holding her still so I can squint at the information she recorded. "Those are just numbers, Lacey." I'm screaming in my head, though. Fucking *compound*? A compound sounds dangerous. And why the hell is it that *Lacey* knows where Zeth is, and *I* don't? She's been living with him for the past six months. They clearly share a strong tie. It's an irrational thing to be pissed about, I know, but hell. I must be an irrational creature. I dismiss the petty stab of jealousy, trying to focus on the task at hand.

Lacey tuts, leaning the receipt against her knee to quickly insert some commas, and suddenly the information morphs from a random string of numbers into coordinates. "It's out in the desert," she says, handing over the paper.

"Who gave you this? How do we know this is the right place?"

"Because Zee told me about this place a few times. Never gave me specifics, but my old boyfriend runs in the same circles as Zeth. Kind of. He knew where I was talking about right away."

"Oh God, Lacey." I stare at the coordinates until the numbers start to swim. "This can't be the only compound out in the desert There are probably hundreds of them..."

"Not that charge fifteen thousand dollars a night and are invite only," Lacey argues. Where is the panicking girl who smashed a rock over a guy's head last night? The girl standing in front of me now is barely recognizable. She has a confident spark in her eyes. Even her voice is stronger.

"This *is* the right address." She nods vigorously, as if doing so makes the statement true. "Zeth'll be there. Don't worry. We're gonna go get him, and he's going to make all of this right again. That's what he does, Sloane. He makes everything all right."

43

SLOANE

RENTING A CAR UNDER MY REAL NAME IS a bad idea, but I'm a trauma resident, not a practiced criminal. I don't have the first clue how to bribe someone, and the guy behind the desk at the Hertz car rental doesn't seem like a rule breaker, anyway. He photocopies my ID and has me fill out a mountain of paperwork. I'm surprised he doesn't make me sign over my firstborn. When he asks me if I want to upgrade to something flashy, I politely decline, telling him we'll stick with a sedan, and then we're back on the road.

Lacey is in high spirits as I drive for the next ten hours. Conversely, guilt gnaws at my stomach lining, but it can't be helped. I cannot in good conscience take

Lacey to this compound. Zeth wanted to keep both me and his sister (even if he doesn't know that's who she is) away from the compound, and he's right. She shouldn't be exposed her to that kind of environment. She's too damaged. Anything could happen to her. Technically, anything could happen to *me*, too, but I'm not thinking about that. I'm going to go in there, I'm going to ream Zeth out for completely fucking up my life in the space of a few short weeks, then I'm going to grab my sister and leave. In my head, there is no room for deviations from this plan.

As night begins to fall, we pull into Dana Point, at least an hour from our destination to the northeast. Lacey doesn't bat an eyelash. I have to follow the GPS directions closely. I should know my way from the freeway exit to the quaint little oceanfront house, but in my defense, I've only visited three or four times. With my degree, then my internship and residency, I haven't had much time for visiting. I pull into the driveway, silencing the engine, still waiting for Lacey to realize that we're not where we're supposed to be. She sits on the back seat, staring out of the window even though we're now stationary, not even blinking.

I get out of the car, wondering what she'll do. Without hesitation, she gets out of the car, too, collecting the clothes I bought for her from Walmart. "You all right, Lace?" I ask carefully.

Her eyebrows twitch. "Sure. Why wouldn't I be?"

I can think of a thousand reasons, first and foremost of which being that she may have killed a man with a very large rock yesterday. I keep my mouth shut, though. Instead, I walk up the path to the little house and knock at the door. Nervous energy rolls through me like waves. God knows how this is all going to play out. If I'm lucky, it'll go well. If not, I'll be searching for somewhere else to leave Zeth's sister. Lacey stands next to me, a small smile on her face. The front door opens, and a tall, thin man appears on the other side of it. His eyes widen with surprise, but then quickly soften. He looks older than the last time I saw him. Tired.

"Sloane!" He beams as if discovering on his doorstep in all my disheveled glory is the best thing that's happened to him in years.

I take a deep breath and return his smile. "*Hey, Dad.*"

ZETH

My burner's going nuts in my pocket. There are only five people who have that number, so I know it's fucking important. But can I answer it? No, I fucking *can't.* I'm stuck in a compound full of suspicious Black Talon members, and they all look like they want to beat the living shit out of me.

I'm an arrogant son of a bitch, yes, but there's a reason for my ego. I've fucking *earned* it. I'm not just violent. I'm *trained.* When a situation calls for it, I can hurt a bunch of people in a short space of time. I'm not in a position to hurt anyone here, though. There are three excellent reasons for that, and they are as follows:

Number one: There are too many of them.

Number two: They're toting semi-automatics.

And number three: I'm fucking wasted.

When Jacob said he wanted to have a few beers in the sunshine, what he *really* meant to say was that he wanted to drink a case of beer in the sunshine, alongside three bottles of Cuban rum, and then carry on drinking until the sun went down and neither of us could stand up straight. My only reprieve is the fact that Jacob is as shitfaced as I am, and the sweating bastard didn't end up calling the girls out. No way he could get his dick hard with this much Havana running through his veins. I probably could if I tried, but fuck that. All I can think about is Sloane, and how much I want to kill motherfucking Callum for not watching the house like I told him to.

Occasionally, Michael's precarious situation emerges through the drunken fog of my mind, but I know the guy. He can take a beating when he needs to, Sometimes, he even *enjoys* one, but that's a different story. By the time I figure out where they're keeping him in the morning, he may have a few broken ribs and a couple of black eyes, but Jacob won't allow his men to do too much damage. Not right away. They'll wanna get information out of him first, and it'll take a while for them to realize the stubborn bastard won't give it. Suffice it to say I'll owe him a serious pay raise after this.

"You and me, we—we are fucking dogs, right?" Jacob hiccups. It takes a lot of effort to swivel my eyes toward the great lump of a man, half-reclined, half-slumped on his lounger.

"Speak for yourself, man," I growl.

This makes him laugh. "You fucking are. I am, too! There's…there's nothing wrong with knowing what you are. You were born shit. So was I. But just because…" He pauses, pressing his balled-up fist into his sternum. He waits a minute, eyes watering, and then continues. "Just because we were born shit doesn't mean we stayed shit. We're piranhas swimming around with all the other fish, looking like every fucker else. And then BAM!" he shouts. "We got the nastiest bite around. We're fucking dog *king* fish!"

I grimace at that. "I'm not a piranha. I'm a Great White."

"Whatever, man. You don't know what you're

talking about. You seen those bastards strip—" Another bout of heartburn. "You seen those bastards strip flesh from the bone? It's...fucking fascinating. They're a nightmare."

I sling back another shot of Havana, wincing. "Piranhas live in shoals. They're group...fish. Great Whites are the badasses of the sea. Don't catch them hanging around in groups. They're like...lone wolves."

Jacob throws his head back and howls, mimicking the call of a wolf. "Well, I don't know *what* animals we are anymore, asshole. All I know is that you and I are one and the same. We clawed our way out of the dirt we were born into and carved ourselves out a kingdom. My kingdom's slightly bigger than yours, though, huh?"

I nod ruefully, tipping my glass to him. "Uh-huh. And you don't answer to anyone, too, right?"

Jacob shakily pours some more alcohol into both our empty shot glasses, grinning at me. He suppresses his smile as he says, "From what I hear, *you* ain't taking orders, either." He offers me the alcohol, his eyes more lucid than they were a minute ago.

Well, fuck me. His comment has an instant sobering effect. He *does* know about me running out on Charlie? I clear my throat. There's a lot riding on what comes out of my mouth next. "Charlie's a major pain in the ass sometimes, Jake. We're on a break. I'm sure he'll have forgotten"—I wave my arm drunkenly in the general direction of Seattle—"all about it by next week." Better to make it sound like *he's* mad at *me* than the other way around. Jacob might harbor some sympathy for a payroll guy who's pissed off a boss like Charlie. A payroll guy who's gone rogue and decided to take certain matters into his own hands will look like a red flag. All of these thoughts form through a thick haze of alcohol.

"I see." Jacob tosses back his drink and reaches across the table between us, placing a firm hand on my shoulder, squeezing hard. "I defended you today, Zeth. I chose to give you the benefit of the doubt where my men would have had me kill you instead. I've done this because we're fucking dogs, you and me, and when I look at you I see...me."

Yeah, you wish, asshole. Through the booze, this strikes me as funny, given that I'm twelve inches taller, ten years younger, and a hundred pounds lighter than the sack of man-Jell-O sprawled in front of me. I suppose it's time to thank him now? I breathe deep, willing the fresh air to help me find the right words to convey some self-effacing gratitude. Sadly all I come up with is "*Thanks*."

He offers a one-shouldered shrug. "Don't prove me wro—"

Gunfire.

The compound comes alive.

CRACK! Crack, crack, crack!

Jacob heaves himself to his feet. "God fucking *damn* it!" he roars, throwing his glass on the floor.

I leap up, adrenaline punching through the alcohol. Oh...*shit*. I'm on a goddamn merry-go-round. I follow Jacob as he lumbers toward the villa's entrance. Outside, all of Jacob's guards are bristling, directing their weapons through the fence toward the burning headlights of a vehicle on the other side.

"Back in the fucking car, bitch!"

"Shoot!" a Black Talon yells. "Fucking *shoot*!"

Jacob takes in the scene through bloodshot eyes. "What the hell is going on?" His yell does little to calm the gunmen, although one of them does answer.

"Some bitch rolled up out of the desert. She's a fucking cop!"

A *cop*? No fucking *way*. It can only be that fucking DEA woman, Lowell. That's probably why my burner's been ringing off the hook the whole afternoon. Rick must have been trying to tell me she was coming. For a second, I hope these idiots pull the trigger. But then the figure in front of the car shifts, a slim body falling into silhouette, and I see that I was wrong. It isn't Lowell, or any other cop. It's a doctor.

It's fucking *Sloane*.

I rage past the gunmen, shoving them out of the

way as I charge toward the gate. All I can see is her petrified expression, as she freezes, hands outstretched, as if to ward off the bullets with the palms of her fucking hands. I have to stop when I get to the gate. It's locked. I smash my fist into the reinforced steel, roaring so I hard I taste blood.

"WHAT THE *FUCK*!" I can't even fucking *think*. My hand feels like someone just laid into it with a hammer, but the pain doesn't register. She shouldn't be here. I made plan. Made sure she wouldn't find herself caught up in all this. Wouldn't be in any danger. *She. Should. Not. Be. Here.* "What the fuck?" I ask again, this time growling under my breath, trying to get a handle on myself. Sloane starts shaking, too, hands as they fall to her sides.

"They could have *shot* you," she whimpers.

Distractedly, I register the row of M16s over my shoulder. Jacob's dark bulk wades forward through the sea of muzzles and magazines, one eyebrow raised so high it almost hits his receding hairline.

"Someone you know, Zee?"

Oh, fuck, he is pissed. "Yeah." *Think!* "This is—this is Naomi. She's—my plus one." I face Sloane again, trying to light her on fire with the depths of my anger. "And she should *not* be here."

"You've never been more correct," he replies. His voice is free of the alcohol now, just like mine.. I'm angry with Sloane. Jacob is furious with me. Funny how intense anger can have that effect "You gave a *whore* directions to this place?"

Bile churns in my stomach at the title he just gave Sloane. I want to smash my fist into his face, but instead I say, "Sorry, Jake. My mistake. I was supposed to pick her up, remember. She must have come looking for me."

Jacob shakes his head at me, mouth hanging open. "That was *very* ill-advised."

"I know. Apologies, brother. I didn't think." No way he's buying this. He knows I'm not this completely, utterly, *astonishingly* stupid. You don't give this address to anyone. Especially not some girl you wanna fuck. You blindfold them and lead them here in the trunk of a fucking car, after driving them in circles to confuse the hell out of them first.

Anton appears over Jacob's shoulder, nostrils flaring. But Jacob looks like he's come to some sort of decision. "Get her inside," he says flatly, staring straight through me. "Bring her to the study, Zeth. It's only polite that you introduce me to your friend."

"Jake!"

Jacob pre-empts Anton's objection and spins, stabbing his finger into the other man's chest. "Open the fucking gate, Anton."

Anton looks like he's been sucker punched. He does

as he's told, though. As soon as the gate's open, I shove through and grab Sloane by the arm, pulling her back toward the dusty beast of a car she's rolled up in.

"I'll drive her in," I snap over my shoulder. And then to her, more quietly, "Get in the goddamn car." She's white as a sheet but she opens the door and gets in. I climb in the driver's side, allowing myself the luxury of slamming my fist against the wheel before I start the engine.

Sloane jumps, gasping. "You need to let me expl—" she begins. I gun the engine so loud it screams. She takes the hint and shuts the hell up.

"I don't need to let you *anything*, Sloane. Listen to me. Listen fucking good. You're here as my guest to attend a meeting in two days' time. You're a stupid airhead who knows nothing about my business dealings. You don't know about Charlie. You don't know about your sister. You don't know about Lacey. The only thing you *do* know is that you like fucking me. You got that?" She opens her mouth, indignation flashing in her eyes. Before she can breathe a word, I drive the car into the compound and slam the thing into park beside the Camaro. The others haven't made their way to the car yet, but they're only a few seconds away.

"I'm fucking serious, Sloane. If you want *either* of us to get out of this alive, you'll do as I tell you."

"I'm not some hook—" she starts.

"No, you're right. You're not. A hooker would get paid to be here, and you're doing it for the thrill alone. If you don't do this, we're both fucking dead."

Her cheeks turn a pasty gray color. "All right."

I barely get a chance to breathe a sigh of relief. The doors to the car open from the outside and Jacob stands waiting for me on the driver's side, mouth drawn into a tight line. Anton grabs hold of Sloane, fingers digging into her arm as he drags her out of the passenger side. His dirty fucking hands are all over her as she straightens up. Legs, hips, stomach, arms. He pats her down, palms purposefully grazing her breasts. A red light descends over my vision. *Oh, hell, no, he did not just...*

He did!

That.

Is.

Fucking.

It.

I charge around the other side of the car, finally boiling over. "You did not just fucking drag that girl out of the car!" I roar. Anton reaches for his gun, but he doesn't move quick enough. My fist makes a satisfying crunch as it impacts with his cheekbone. Shouts go up all around us as bodies crowd in. No good, though. Anton drops like a sack of rocks, and I'm on top of him, fists raining down left, right, left, right, hitting him as hard as I can. I have to keep hitting him. I *have* to. Hands tear at me, but they don't do any good. I pummel Anton's head into the dirt.

"Zeth!" The outraged yell finally stays my hands. Standing next to Sloane, Jacob gapes. "The woman's fine! You're gonna kill one of my best men over a fucking *bruise*?"

"I'll kill him for daring to breathe the same air as her," I gasp, chest heaving. "I'll kill him for *looking* at her wrong."

Jacob just shakes his head, astonished. He gestures one of his other men toward Anton. "Get him to the basement." He turns and walks slowly back inside the villa, leaving me and Sloane alone outside with twelve armed and angry Black Talons.

44

SLOANE

WE DIDN'T END UP SPEAKING WITH Jacob. The man had demanded an introduction, but after Zeth had nearly beaten his lacky to death, the large man with the Southern accent had vanished into thin air. Zeth had dragged me through the hallways of the Spanish-style villa toward a bedroom that smelled distinctly like him. He'd shoved me inside, followed after, locked the door, and then placed a chair beneath the handle like in the movies. Following that, he'd stripped down to his boxers, angrily throwing them onto the ground, climbed into the huge king-sized bed in the center of the room, and promptly gone straight to sleep.

Turns out he was mad at me.

I slept in the wingback chair by the window—barely—and woke at the crack of dawn thanks to the bright sunlight eking through the curtains. Since then I've been waiting, stiff and cold, for Zeth to rouse. *Dreading* it. With his eyes closed, he breathes slow and deep, and he looks so vulnerable. His belly and chest, arms and back are solid muscle, but that muscle is relaxed. His knuckles are split open on both hands, but for the first time ever, it seems, they *aren't* balled into fists. I'm too nervous to wake him. I just sit, waiting, hoping that he wakes up in a better mood than he fell asleep in.

I'm also hoping Lacey is okay. She knew I wasn't going to take her with me. God knows how, but she didn't even blink when I said she was going to stay with my folks for the night. Two at the most. The relief on her face had actually been very obvious when I said it wasn't safe for her to come. She'd only become concerned when she'd seen the religious paraphernalia all over my parents' walls: crucifixes, icons of the Virgin Mary, and cherub-faced depictions of Jesus blessing the masses. She'd blanched, picking at her fingernails on their couch, watching my father suspiciously out of the corner of her eye. I don't know what's happened to make her react that way, but it must have been bad. I'm hoping she won't be more traumatized when I pick her up than she was when I left her there.

I'm still thinking about this when, at just after seven thirty, Zeth sits bolt upright in the bed, gasping. He scans the room, sees me, and the next thing I know, I'm being physically lifted and thrown onto the bed. I yelp as Zeth's hand flies, clenched into a scuffed-knuckled fist, down toward my face. He chokes out a shout, catching himself just inches before he makes contact with my face.

"*FUCK!*"

The bed dips as throws himself off me and rolls away.

Jesus.

Breathe.

I hold my hands over my heart, trying to slow it. All of the oxygen has fled the room. I start to shake, and Zeth storms across the room, pressing his back against the wall. For a second, he covers his face with his hands, his ragged breath whistling between his fingers.

"Fuck." The curse is much quieter this time. Eventually Zeth lowers his hands and fixes me a dark, thoroughly unimpressed glare. "You're the *worst* thing that could have happened," he growls.

The statement is so ironic that I almost choke. "Says you! Fuck *you*, Zeth Mayfair!"

"Yeah, fuck me," he agrees. He pushes away from the wall and prowls toward the bed. I kick back against the rumpled covers, trying to maintain a safe distance between us. "You have no idea how complicated you've made things. Why the *fuck* did you come here?" he snaps.

My eyes start to prick. What a ridiculous thing I am, betrayed by my own body. "I didn't exactly have much choice. Your *friends*, Charlie's men, broke into my place and tried to kidnap your—" I stop myself just in time. Zeth's reached the bed now, and has climbed up on his hands and knees, inching closer. His brows furrow. "They tried to kidnap Lacey," I tell him. "And there's no way I'm taking that kind of shit to work. That job means more than anything to me. You dumped Lacey on me and disappeared. I risked everything I have to get her to safety and find *you*, and you're fucking *mad* at me for it!" A tear of frustration races down my cheek, dripping onto my bent knee.

Zeth sits back on his heels, still only wearing his boxers, tattoos shifting as his muscles flex; he doesn't even seem to realize he's tensing them. He's built like a *statue* of a man, not the real thing. He's a portrayal of what perfection should look like. I hate him for looking so good, when I know for a fact that *I* look like shit. And I'm fucking crying. He scrubs his hand across his jaw, scowling. He looked dead set on punishing me for coming here a second ago, but now he seems torn.

"Don't do that," he says in a flat voice.

"Do what? Be mad at you? Of course I'm—"

"Cry," he interrupts. "Don't *cry*. That's a shitty, underhanded trick."

"Trick?" God Almighty, the gall of this man. I've been held up at gunpoint, threatened, driven across three states, shot at and then threatened some more, and he thinks I'm crying to make *him* feel bad. *Asshole!* I throw myself back onto the bed, pulling a pillow over my face, and I scream into it. I do not hold back. Even *with* the pillow, it must sound like I'm being murdered. A large, powerful hand closes around my right ankle, and then I'm being dragged through the sheets. The pillow tears out of my hands. I pause for a moment, glare at him defiantly, and then carry on screaming. He drops down on top of me, clapping his hand over my mouth. He shoves his face into mine, all seriousness and sin.

"Shut up," he hisses. "For the love of all that's holy, *please* shut the hell up, Sloane. You're gonna split my head apart."

I don't stop, so he takes further action and digs his knuckles firmly into my ribs. "Ow! Motherfucker!" I slap him hard, and the impact zips up my arm. Zeth's head kicks to the left. When he turns it back to me, I realize what I've done. His dark eyes are murderous.

"I only *trade* in those," he growls. "And with the hangover I have right now, that counts for two."

Shit. I try to wriggle out from underneath him, but I have more chance of shrugging off gravity and floating off into outer space.

"*Zeth.*" I try a reasoning voice. Like he's a reasonable person and might respond like one. He clenches his jaw, the smooth line of his chin turning to steel as he arches up over me and grabs both my hands.

"You should know better by now, Sloane. You're an angry girl, yeah, but I'm angry, too. And if you plan on doling out punishment, you'd better be ready for it when *your* turn comes around."

The first real spark of panic lights inside me. I buck against him, still trying to get free. A curious smile emerges through the stern expression on Zeth's face. He's not bothered by my thrashing. If anything, my attempts at freedom seem to be making this whole thing more enjoyable for him. At least, that's what the growing hardness pressing against the inside of my thigh would suggest. And yet he nods once, narrowing sharp eyes at me, and then lets me go. He sits back on his heels again, towering over me. I freeze. I should probably bolt, but I know what that will lead to: a chase around the room, broken furniture, and potentially broken bones to match. I clasp my hands over my chest again, fighting to stop myself from glancing down at the prominent hard-on that's pulling against his gray boxers.

He smirks, leaning back a fraction in his straddled position, which pushes his cock closer to my hands. I roll my eyes at this, suddenly a little less afraid. "You have *got* to be joking."

He shakes his head, still very grave indeed. "Not joking, Sloane. You just woke the whole villa, when going unnoticed would really work in our favor." His voice is gravel on gravel, deep and bottomless, filled with clashing desires. He's mad at me, but he also wants to fuck me senseless. "You're reckless," he accuses. "You show up here, without any idea what you're getting yourself *or* me into." He reaches down and palms one of my breasts through my clothes, squeezing hard and eliciting a gasp from me. "I came pretty fucking close to being eighty-sixed yesterday, and the likelihood of it happening today is even higher. You put yourself at risk when I specifically told you not to. And then you go hollering at the top of your lungs at the crack of fucking dawn, reminding everyone that we're here and we're a fucking nuisance. So if you're gonna scream, Sloane, I'm gonna give you a reason."

Still kneading my breast in one hand, he wraps his other hand around his erection through his boxers. I swallow, unable to stop myself from watching as he slowly works his hand up and down, squeezing himself just as hard as he squeezes me. Should I be worried about this? He was raging a moment ago, and now he's ready to fuck me? The possibility that those two factors might be linked is a little concerning.

"I'm not having sex with you," I breathe.

The corner of Zeth's mouth pulls up at one corner—an unbearably arrogant smirk. "Sure you are, angry girl."

"I am not." I squirm pointlessly, but no luck. I needn't bother, though. Zeth does something even more confusing and relinquishes his hold on me, then swinging himself off of my body and leaning back against the pillows. He let me go? *He let me go!* I jump up, spinning around and staring at him incredulously. The seriousness hasn't left his face. His hand hasn't left his cock. He only pauses a second to lift his hips, abdominal muscles flexing tightly, as he hooks his thumbs into the waistband of his boxers and slowly pulls them down. His cock springs free, resting heavily against his belly as he gets rid of his underwear. The sight of him lying there, naked and completely unashamed—Why the hell would he be ashamed? He's magnificent and he knows it—makes my breath catch in my throat. He picks up where he left off, taking hold of himself in his right hand, drawing it slowly up and down the rigid skin. The whole time he does this, he stares at me without a scrap of shame. His eyes never waver from mine.

"You're totally fucked up, you know that?" I fold my arms across my chest. "What the hell are you going for here? You expect me to shed my clothes like Bruce Almighty and jump up on that thing just 'cause you got it out?"

A small smile breaks through the severity of his expression. It tics at the corner of his mouth. "No. I expect you to take your clothes off slow. And then I expect you to climb up on this bed on your hands and knees and I expect you to take this thing"—he squeezes his dick in his hand, making himself shiver slightly—"and put it in your mouth. And then I expect you to suck it until I tell you that you can stop."

"Hah!" I stride across the room, eyeing the chair jammed under the door handle. Great. He wedged in there *really* well. I shove the thing as hard as I can, and voila! I knock it loose. "You are probably the most delusional man I have ever met," I snarl over my shoulder.

Zeth shrugs, pouting a little. Maybe. Maybe not. As if I care. "Where d'you think you're *going*, angry girl? Forgotten where you are?"

He has a point there. *Infuriating.* I slap my hand against the closed door, grimacing. "Fine. Okay. I'm not leaving the room. But I am not obeying you just because you *told* me to."

"Would you prefer to obey me because you're

frightened for your life?" he asks casually. Was that a threat? Damn it, I can't tell. He seems genuinely interested.

"How about this. I refuse to obey you for any reason whatsoever." I pace back to the chair I slept in and slump down in it, making a point of looking out the window. Anywhere but at him and what he's doing to himself.

"Fair enough." Unbothered. Unapologetic. His gaze rests heavy on my skin. The room falls quiet other than the sounds of his palm working his cock and the increasingly ragged sound of his breathing. How can he lie there, jerking himself off, naked, and not even flinch when the woman he's trying to excite seems more revolted than interested? Psycho. I glance at him out of the corner of my eye. His body is a fucking work of art. Especially strained the way it is, locked tight against each stroke he glides up and down with his palm. He grips himself tighter, sucking in a sharp breath, and chuckles slightly when he catches me watching him. I flick my eyes back out the window, cursing. *Don't play this fucking game. Do* not *play with him.*

It's only a matter of a minute before I'm glancing back, though. He lets out a low, hazy rumble from deep within his chest, and it's the hottest thing I've ever heard. My legs start to twitch. The warm, pooling sensation forming between them is intensifying by the second. Bastard. *How?* How the hell does he do this to me? I shift, at war with my body, trying to make it obey *me* and not *him*. But it wants to watch him. God, *I* want to watch him. He doesn't laugh when he sees me observing this time. He just looks down at himself, expression full of sex and invitation. And then he closes his eyes, tipping his head back, and leaves me alone to come to my own decision. His hand works faster, his breath quickening, too.

I'm left wondering what the hell I want to do. But I've had this conversation with myself before, haven't I? He's so smart. He shows me what he could take from me if he wanted to and then turns the tables, making me realize how much I *want* him to have it anyway. I hate that. On principle, I don't want to succumb to the manipulation this time. He needs to know he's not as smart as he thinks he is. Only he *is*. He's an evil fucking mastermind.

I stand up.

At the sound of movement, a broad smile unfurls across Zeth's face, but he keeps his eyes closed. Probably to save what's left of my fragile pride. I can't believe I'm doing this. Every single time we do this, I'm coming to him on *his* terms, I'm pathetic. I lose my clothes slowly, even though he can't see, giving myself time to change my mind. I don't. I crawl up the bed just like he wants me to, and then hover over him as he smoothly works his cock up and down. It's swollen, huge, and kind of... beautiful. I exhale, and my breath skims across his skin, making him shiver.

"I wanna feel those lips, Sloane," he says gruffly.

"Oh, okay. So just so I understand. It's okay to put them on your dick, but not on your *mouth*."

He stiffens at the acid in my tone. Doesn't justify the barb with a response, though. Fucker. I have something in mind to teach him a lesson. I duck down, pulse throbbing in my lips, and I take him in my mouth. I've done this to him only once before. That time, I was on my back. He'd towered over me like a giant, his presence still somehow looming over me in that dark hotel room. He'd tangled his fingers into my hair and guided my head. Now, Zeth doesn't even touch me. At the first contact from my lips, he splays his fingers against the sheets, pressing down on the mattress with all his strength. He's huge, warm, and already tasting musky. I bob my head lower, taking more of him into my mouth.

"Holy shit, Sloane." His deep groan has a rather gratifying effect. He likes this. He likes it, and technically *I'm* the one who's in control right now. Time for a little payback. I duck my head lower, sliding more of him past my lips, until I can't go any farther. *And then I bite down.* Not very hard. Just enough to let him know he hasn't entirely won this round.

The reaction is instant.

He flings me off him so fast I barely catch sight of the ceiling before I'm on my back and then sliding off the bed and onto the floor.

"Oh, no, no, no, Sloane," he growls, stalking toward me. "Slapping's one thing. But that? You're gonna wish you hadn't done *that*." His face is blank. Not a good sign. From my pretzeled position on the floor, legs half on the bed, half over my own head, I should be freaking the fuck out, but I must be crazy, because I'm laughing.

The hysteria lasts all of ten seconds as he gets up and paces to the other side of the room, opening the door to the walk-in closet. My smile dissolves at the sight of the black bag in his hand. Fear, desire. Fear, desire. The emotions take turns electrifying me.

He throws the bag down at the side of the bed and begins to unzip it. "Up onto the bed, Sloane."

"No."

He stops, looks up at me, leans forward, and says, "Do we really need to go through this again? You reap what you sow, Sloane. It's time for you to learn how to behave." He raises his eyebrows in challenge. He gave me a small amount of power, and I abused it. Now, I have to suffer the consequences. And yet, deep down, I think I've been waiting for this to happen. And... *wanting* it to. I ease back up onto the bed as cautiously as I can. Zeth nods once and finishes opening the bag.

"Spread your legs."

I comply. Oh, for the darkness of that hotel room. Zeth has a look of revenge about him as he climbs up over my body. "I'm not gonna tie you up this time. But you should know, you do anything that involves your *teeth* and my *dick* again, and there'll be hell to pay. Understand?"

I nod, wondering what he has in mind. And then I see the small, narrow, tweezer-like instrument in his hand. "What is *that*?"

Zeth grips the device with a level of pleasure that has me squirming on my back, suddenly regretting that I gave in so easily. "This is what you get for being bad," he says.

I quiver as he runs his hands up the insides of my legs, stooping down to lick the sensitive skin just before my pussy. He grazes lips and tongue across my hot skin, licking again and again, but it's all teasing. Nowhere near where I *need* him to lick me. I'm beginning to feel frustrated, angling my hips up to him, opening myself to him, when I feel the cool metal against my core. My body quakes with sudden nerves, but Zeth grabs my hip in his free hand, sending a warning look up my body. "I suggest you stay very… *very* still, Sloane."

The metal instrument in his hand turns out to be a clamp. I know this because he swiftly clamps it to my *clitoris*, causing me to yelp in shock. When he flicks the cool metal, pain tinged pleasure volts around my body.

"*Zeth!*" My cry bounces off the walls. "Oh my God, do *not* do that again!"

He does do it again, a malicious look of glee on his face. My legs spasm, wanting to draw up and protect me—I can't help it—and Zeth shakes his head in mock disapproval.

"Oh, dear," he breathes. "I thought I told you not to move. Looks like you're gonna get punished now." He grips the clamp in his hand and heat explodes between my legs as I try to move away from him. I freeze, understanding all too well now. If I move, the clamp gets tugged. With one arm, Zeth scoops me up from the bed and turns to sit, pulling me into his lap. I instinctively wrap my arms around his neck to maintain my balance. His face is an inch away from mine, the heat of his skin burning into me, the hardness of his erection prodding me between my legs. He's deadly serious when he asks, "You want the belt or my hand?"

"What?"

He gives me a look that tells me not to bother with any theatrics. "The belt or my hand, Sloane? Your choice." He reaches between my legs, fingers finding the place where the metal meets my clit. He rubs softly, massaging the connection, gifting me with more pleasure than pain this time. He smirks wickedly when he lifts his fingers up for me to see that they're slick with the evidence that I'm not hating this as much as I'm pretending to. Not for the first time, he slips his fingers into his mouth and sucks them clean, his breathing fast and labored. "Make up your mind or I'll choose for you." God, his voice is so rough.

"Hand," I whisper. "Use your hand." Maybe if he punishes me with that, he'll go a little easier on me. It will hurt *him*, too. In the blink of an eye, he spins me over on his lap so I'm facing the floor, bent over his knees, my butt sticking up in the air. His hand cups my flesh, squeezing and stroking my ass cheek.

"Perfect," he observes under his breath. Taking a hold of the clamp's handles between my legs, he gives it a gentle tug—a small reminder of the power he holds. Fire pools in my belly, teasing a low moan out of my throat. It feels…it feels amazing. And scary. And painful. And so many other things all at once that I can't bend my mind around all of the things that I'm fee…

CRACK!

My mind goes blank.

A shockwave of pain and surprise rocks me to my core. Zeth brings his hand down on my bare buttocks again, and I see stars. I've always thought that was just a turn of phrase, but no. White, glowing spots dance across my vision as I try to comprehend what's he's just done.

The third time Zeth lays his huge hand to my tender skin, he *really* means it. Yes, it must hurt his hand, too, but that doesn't stop him. He gives me two more painful slaps, each time holding his breath. I do not move. Do not react. He tempers the tingling sting by sliding his fingers between my legs and stroking them over my clit, easing them farther back, so that my wetness saturates my asshole as well. He kneads my tender ass cheeks, then, whispering encouragement.

"There's my brave girl. *So* brave. Are you going to be good now? Have you learned your lesson?"

The whole thing is humiliating. I'm on the brink of tears, but also so desperate for him that I can't stop myself from turning around and launching at him. I make a rasping sound at the back of my throat as Zeth lifts me in his arms and places me back down on the bed.

"That was five," he says, like the pain may have addled my ability to count. "Next time it'll be ten. You ready?"

He expects a response. I nod, just once, and Zeth strokes a hand down the inside of my leg in a soothing, apologetic motion. "Good girl." He bends down and nestles in between my legs, propping himself up on one elbow as he ducks and *finally* sweeps his hot tongue between my pussy lips, pausing to tease the tip of it over my hypersensitive clit. Pleasure rolls up my legs, settling on my chest, making my nipples ache.

"*Ahh!*"

Zeth hums his approval into me as he carries on, working his tongue over my center. He gently flicks the clamp again, but this time the sensation has changed. It doesn't hurt now. Or it *does*, but when combined with the ecstasy of his mouth, the pain becomes intoxicating. It heightens everything until I am drunk on it.

I let go of the bedsheets, but I don't try to stop him; I dig my fingers into the back of his neck and urge him *closer*. Zeth responds in kind by nipping at my clit with his teeth. "Fair turnaround," he growls, and then sets to work.

My back arches up off the bed, mouth falling open at the intensity of the feeling. Am I responding to the stab of pain, or the tsunami of pleasure? They feel like the same thing right now. But when Zeth slides his fingers into my pussy, pumping them slowly in and out, the answer to my quandary becomes clear. This is what true pleasure feels like. It isn't just the softness of a kiss. It isn't just the delicate touch of hands on breasts and tongues on skin. It's the bite of pain.

The threat of danger. The risk taken in dancing with the devil. I come hard against Zeth's mouth. He leans into it, growling and sucking and licking as I scream, his hands locked around my hips, pulling me into his face.

"Fuck, Zeth! Stop! *Please* stop!"

His back hitches as he laughs, still teasing me with his tongue. My legs scrabble against the bed, desperately trying to escape the intense post-orgasm rushes. He gets up after that, raising one eyebrow at me.

"I'm gonna take the clamp off and then I'm gonna fuck you. Are you going to be polite?"

Polite? I'm half fucking *dead*. I lie in a boneless heap as he undoes the clamp and plants a single kiss between my legs. "And, *yes*," he tells me. "Your lips are only allowed on my dick. But mine are allowed on *these* lips, at least."

My body feels like a lead weight as he sits back a moment to inspect my languid state. He seems pretty pleased with himself. With his cock in his hand again, he shifts up the bed and gently brushes himself against my lips. I can't help it—I want to taste him. To feel him fill me in every way possible, even in my mouth. I let my tongue play over the firm hardness of his head, groaning quietly at the clean taste of him. He doesn't touch me.

We're back to where we started, except this time I

don't bite. I lick and suck and stroke, and just when I feel him about to come, I stop.

"That's not polite," Zeth breathlessly informs me.

I give him a half-smile. "I thought you said you were gonna fuck me?" I lay down the challenge this time: *Make me come again. Make me* scream.

Zeth's full lips curve upward. "You asked for it." He shoves my legs apart, growling in that raw, animal way he did when he took me back in Seattle, and then thrusts inside me. Again, again, again, he slams himself home, as though being hip-deep inside me isn't enough. I gouge my fingernails into his ass cheeks as he thrusts, pulling him closer, needing more of him. Harder. Deeper.

We come together. His body locks up, muscles straining, eyes on fire, hands pinning me down as he slams into me one final time. "*FUUUUCCCKK!*" He roars, as though this is his dying word and the whole world needs to hear it, and then falls slack, his head resting on my chest.

For a few moments, we lie there, panting, trying to catch our breath. So strange. With him on top of me, my arms still around his body, it's almost as if I'm cradling him. My skin breaks out in goose bumps when I realize the slow up and down draw of Zeth's index finger over my hipbone isn't by accident. He strokes my skin, soft as a whisper, holding his breath, and my heart starts pounding all over again.

What the hell *is* this?

Hesitantly, I raise a hand and gently trace my fingertips across the nape of his neck. He doesn't move. He doesn't make a sound. He doesn't even breathe. His hand goes still, but I carry on, seeing how far this can go. I venture upward, teasing my fingers through his cropped hair and then down again, tracing the lines of his muscular back, across his shoulder blades.

His hot breath skims across my breasts. "You're confusing me." He whispers so softly that I wonder for a second if I imagined it. I doubt very much that I was supposed to hear those words. What was it he said to me the day he dropped Lacey off? *You can trust me. You gave yourself to me back at my apartment. I gave myself in return. I may not have wanted to, Sloane, but I didn't have a fucking choice in the matter. That means we belong to each other now.* I've tried endlessly not to overthink those words, but now...

Is he just as confused by us as I am?

This is supposed to be just sex. Really hardcore, dominating sex. *Right?* That's all I am to him. And yet, with him lying here on my chest, it—

THUD, THUD, THUD, THUD!

Explosive hammering nearly takes the bedroom

door off its hinges, and Zeth vaults off the bed. He runs his hands through his hair, clearing his throat, and the moment vanishes in the blink of an eye. He doesn't look at me.

"What?" he yells, pacing leonine and incredible, scrubbing his hands over his face and head as if frantically trying to wake himself up.

"Jacob wants you out front," a male voice says through the wood. "*Now.*"

"Yeah." Zeth paces a moment longer and then nods, finally looking at me. "Well, then. I guess it's time to go convince the Black Talons' boss that you're my fuck of the month."

And there we have it. He's not confused at all. He's never lied to me. Never fed me a flowery line about how he's going to take care of me and treat me right. That I'm going to be his only girl, or that he feels *any* kind of affection for me.

Zeth Mayfair doesn't see me as someone to fall in love with. I'm his fuck of the month, and he needs everyone else at this godforsaken compound to see me that way, too.

Well, you know what, buddy? *You want to minimize me? Want me to act like I'm only in this for the sex?*

So fucking be it.

45

ZETH

AS WE WALK THROUGH THE HALLWAYS to meet our fate, I'm actually not all that worried about the head of the Black Talons. I'm not thinking about what'll happen to us if Sloane messes this up. I'm not thinking about what will happen when Alexis spots her sister here, in this hellhole, and gives us both away.

I'm thinking only one thing:

She came to find me.

She was attacked. She defended herself. Saved Lacey. Drove for two days, and then did something completely baffling. She ran *toward* me. She should have run in the opposite direction, but she didn't. She straightlined for me like I'm her goddamn savior. Like I'm capable of fixing everything. Like I'm capable of protecting her. Like I'm whole enough to hold all of her fractured pieces in place. And then she went and held me in her arms like that. Fuck. And just for one terrifying, awful second...

I shake my head, trying not to think it. But it's a dangerous thought, and it won't so easily be ignored.

Just for one second there, it felt like she might be capable of gluing *me* back together, too.

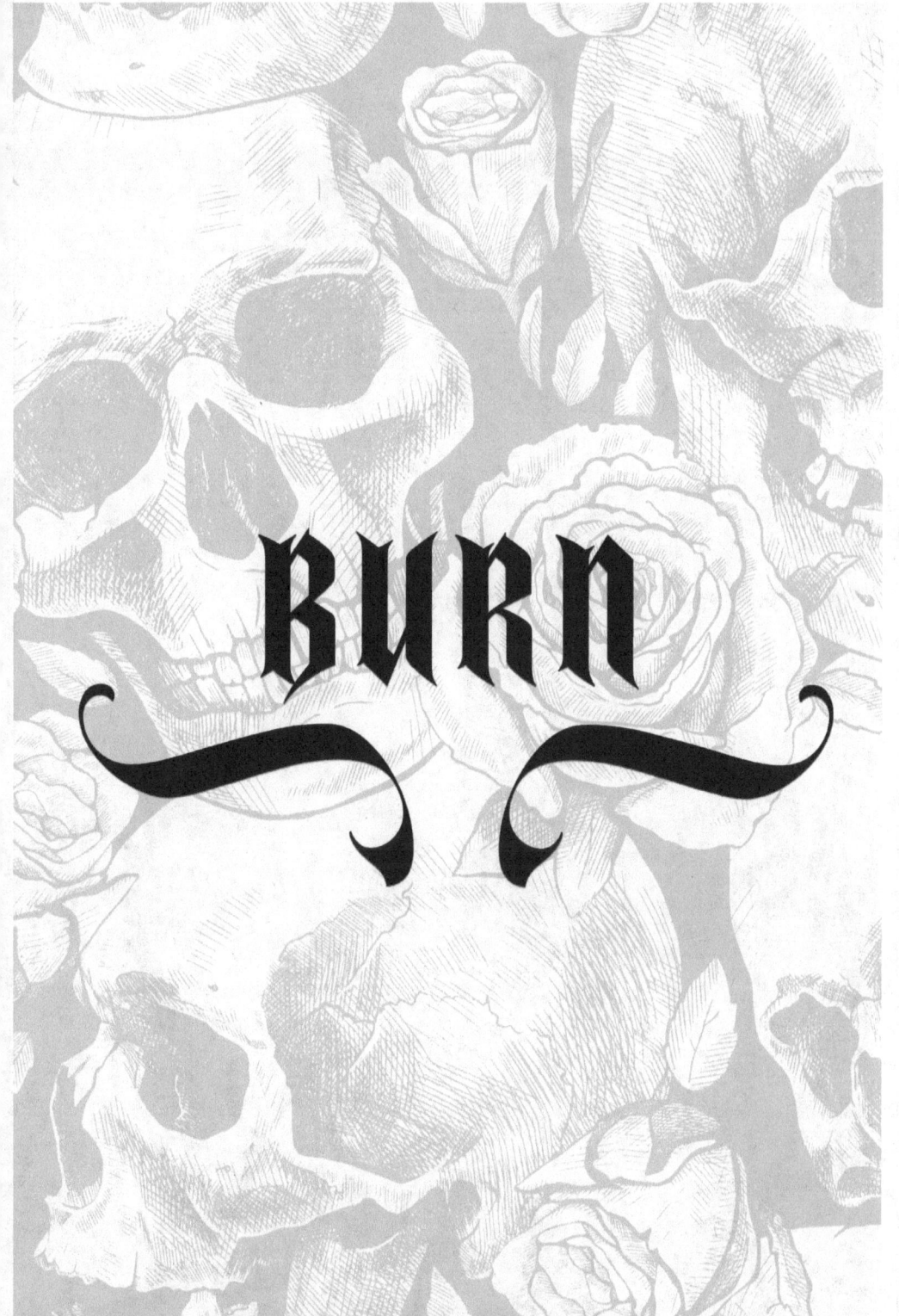

46

SLOANE

JACOB DIXON IS A KILLER.

He may be all smiles and easy talk when we meet in his study, but I see the man for what he is. Perhaps it's spending all this time with Zeth that's done it—I can read the lines of Zeth like the lines of a book—but I recognize the signs now. The two men are cut from different cloth, though. Zeth is dangerous in a primal, instinctive way. It's the foundation of everything that makes him who he is. Jacob, on the other hand, isn't inherently dangerous. He's *chosen* to be so. He's earned the fear of those around him and wears his intimidating persona like a cloak, as if he can take it off and put back on again whenever it pleases him.

I don't know who I should be more worried about: the man who was born into violence, or the man who choose to descend into it.

"And what did you say you do for a living again, Ms. Hawthorne?" Jacob brushes a meaty hand across the polished surface of his desk, sweeping away imaginary dust. He crooks a skeptical eyebrow at me, waiting for me to answer him.

"Uh...I'm..."

"Because you ain't a hooker, obviously," he says, waving hand in my general direction. "Your tits and your ass ain't on show. And I haven't met many escorts or strippers with a name like *Naomi Hawthorne*." He says my fake name like he knows that's *exactly* what it is.

Shit. When he asked for my surname, I said the first thing that came to mind. I should have said Sparkles or something. Lovelace. Symphony. I sound like a fucking dentist. "No," I say. "Not a hooker. I—"

"Naomi's a doctor," Zeth cuts in, slowly craning his head and looking around the room, as if being here is boring him to tears. How he can be so fucking calm? I'm sweating bullets from my forehead. And he told Jacob the *truth*? For crying out loud. As if it won't be easy for a man like *Jacob Dixon* to figure out which hospital I work at. Even in *my* very vanilla circles, I've heard of him. I've read about the Black Talons in the newspapers. If Jacob does some digging and decides I'm not who I say I am, then he won't blink. He'll kill me and bury me in a shallow grave somewhere in the desert. They'll never find my body.

"A doctor?" Jacob looks impressed and confused at the same time. "What kind of doctor?"

"Trauma." I reply without hesitation this time; no point in lying anymore.

"Huh. Interesting."

Zeth snorts. "Is it?"

Jacob looks sharply at him. "Of course! The women who usually end up here aren't usually…"

"Literate?" Zeth's in a bad mood. He's lost the nervous tension he carried in his shoulders as we made our way to the study, and now he just seems pissed off. And bored. I don't know if it's for real or if he's acting, but if he is, he's doing a good job. His quip makes Jacob laugh, though.

"Exactly. They're not quite your… shall we say, *caliber*, Naomi? How the hell did you end up falling into bed with this sick bastard? Something traumatic happen to his dick or something?"

Zeth snorts but doesn't say anything. This one's all on me. A prime opportunity to convince Jacob of my motives in coming here. "I guess you could say that." I smile coyly, glancing at Zeth out of the corner of my eye, as though I'm imparting some salacious secret about him. "I was invited to one of Zeth's parties. I took one look at him and knew what kind of *treatment* he needed. And yeah, his dick was definitely involved. Although I think *I* was the one who suffered the trauma."

Oh. My. Good. Lord.

Where is this stuff *coming* from? Blood rushes to my cheeks and sets them burning. I can only hope Jacob attributes my blushing to the tale I just spun and not embarrassment. A real flicker of amusement flashes in Zeth's eyes. I suddenly realize that what I just said could actually be mistaken for the truth. I did go to one of his parties, and I did sleep with him there. And, in all honesty, he did fuck me ridiculously hard. I do my best not to cringe. I get the feeling Zeth is loving this. He's found a toothpick from somewhere and is shuttling it back and forth over his bottom lip, returning my sidelong glance. Apparently he's no longer bored.

"Sounds intriguing. Did you suck it?"

My head snaps around to look at Jacob. Zeth's eyes travel slowly from me back to the guy with the Southern accent, too, so that he's staring at the other man. He stills the toothpick in his hands, pressing it against his lip. Heat wells in the base of my throat, undoubtedly turning my rosy cheeks crimson. "I'm sorry?"

"Did you suck his dick?" Laughing, Jacob asks the

question like it's nothing. Like it isn't weird as fuck that he would ask that.

"Well, yeah, of *course* I did." I don't pull off "seductively amused" as well as I would have liked. I sound more like a flustered schoolgirl than someone who shared a bed with Zeth Mayfair and kept up with him. How the hell did I think I could do this? I am not going to be able to pull it off. The knowing look in Jacob's eyes confirms this. Zeth slouches in his seat beside me, rocking his head back to stare up at the ceiling, toying with his toothpick again. "Are we nearly done here? I was hoping I could grab a little of that dog that bit me. My head's fucking pounding."

"I tell you what's good for a hangover, brother," Jacob says, turning his attention to Zeth. "Getting your dick sucked."

Zeth's head rolls forward. He doesn't look impressed. Thankfully, Jacob's too busy gauging Zeth's reaction to catch *mine*. He wants me to do it? Now? In *front* of him? This is definitely a test. Zeth smiles, and the smile is a silk wrapped threat. "I just fucked the girl two seconds ago. Didn't you hear?" He points the toothpick over his shoulder, gesturing not only into the corridor but into the recent past, when he had me bent over his lap and slapped my ass raw.

Jacob shrugs. "Sounded like you were killing the woman, sure. But this pretty piece of ass is still sitting here, twirling her pretty hair around her pretty fingers, so we all know *that* wasn't the case." He grins at Zeth, leaning forward across his desk. "What's the matter, man, huh? Can't get it up again so quick? I know it ain't cause you're shy. I seen you fuck plenty of girls under this roof."

My hands curl involuntarily, the tips of my ears burning. I choose to get upset over *that*, and not the fact that a lowlife piece of shit criminal wants me to drop to my knees in his office and blow Zeth right in front of him? Stupid.

Zeth nods, seeming to consider this. "Guess so. But that was a while back. I'm a little more restrained these days."

"Bullshit!" Jacob laughs, but his whole face is turning red, highlighting the spiderweb of burst blood capillaries in his cheeks. Here is a man who drinks too much. Gets mad too much. He probably gets his own way too much, too. But not today.

"I'm sorry, Mr. Dixon, but I'm not gonna give you a private show this morning. You've already established that I'm not like your other girls. If you're after some cheap entertainment, then by all means go ahead. Bring one of your other girls in here. But I'm not some performing show pony, to be gawped at by strangers. I think I'll go read by the pool."

I'm standing up. I don't know when I did it, but

I'm on my feet. I straighten my shirt, trying to fix what I hope is a cool look on both of the startled men. Zeth looks like I've just thrown a bucket of cold water over him. Jacob's mouth hangs open, eyes narrowed in confusion, as though the words I just spoke were in a foreign language and he didn't understand a one of them.

The panic rolls in quick. Not even Zeth, who isn't afraid of anyone, refused Jacob's wishes so bluntly. Jacob clears his throat, looking back down at his desk for a moment while I try to prevent myself from succumbing to the titanic swell of alarm building behind my breastbone.

"So, you wouldn't care if I asked another woman to come in here, Ms. Hawthorne?" Jacob asks the question slowly, showing considerable restraint.

"Of course not. Why would I?" Despite my clammy hands and the color still rising in my cheeks, I know I've nailed it this time. I've managed to affect an air of complete indifference toward Zeth that makes me fist-pump on the inside, while all that shows on the outside is one gently raised eyebrow. "I'm afraid you seem to be confusing the dynamic of my relationship with Zeth, Mr. Dixon. I'm not the one on my knees, begging for snippets of his affection. It's entirely the other way around."

Zeth coughs violently. Just once. I've startled him

with my comment as much as I've startled myself. I try not to react as I calmly exit the room. The door is barely closed before I slump against the wall in the hallway, my pulse pounding in my ears like gunfire. Shit, shit, shit. The meeting was *not* supposed to go like that, but, boy, did that pig make my blood boil. He clearly holds women in low regard. And to be told so casually to degrade myself in front of him? On *no* day of the week was that going to happen. Thanks to my quick temper, I've just created a problem, though. I was supposed to make Jacob believe I was the one desperate for Zeth's attention. Now, it seems as though I've just implied Zeth is on his knees for *me* instead.

47

SLOANE

I DON'T SEE ZETH FOR THE REST OF THE day. I don't see anyone. No girls. No guards. No one at all. Everyone seems to have vanished. The villa has the feel of the *Marie Celeste* to it—meals half eaten and abandoned on the kitchen counters, television sets switched on, playing cheesy soap operas to an invisible audience. Something's going on, and I don't have a good feeling about it.

I go out by the pool and read like I said I was going to, but my eyes skim over the pages, the print morphing into black squiggles as I rehash the past twenty-four hours.

I've been on the run. I've dealt with seeing my father

for the first time in twelve months. I've been threatened at gunpoint, suffered the wrath of an angry... what, *boyfriend*? Associate? I've been spanked mercilessly for my disobedience, and now, to top everything off, I've informed a the head of the Black Talons that *I'm* the one calling the shots with Zeth Mayfair. Nothing could be further from the truth. Jacob must know I was lying out of my ass. I mean, all you need to do is take one look at Zeth, and it's obvious that he isn't the sort of man to bow down to anybody. Let alone someone so physically inferior. Me. *A woman*.

It's past four o'clock by the time I see another soul. The woman is tall and willowy, with hair the color of copper and cinnamon. She struts across the courtyard, eyes hidden behind huge, darkened sunglasses as she makes her way toward me with a pronounced swing of her hips. She wears a one-piece, but the cut-out sections at her sides expose most of her skin regardless. Her boobs are the kind you see on music videos. The kind you like to tell yourself are plastic, when you know all too well that they're real. They bounce impressively with each step that brings her closer. When she's standing right in front of me, her hands move to her hips, and she sticks one leg out to the side in a classic runway supermodel stance. Her expression is at once intimidating and hard to read, especially with those huge sunglasses hiding her eyes.

"Marica Dela Rosa," she says.

"Marica Dela Rosa?"

"Yeah." The redhead sits down on the sun lounger in front of me with the elegance of a crane folding itself neatly into its own body. "Jacob's mother. She was an actress in the fifties. She used to sing opera, if you can believe it. Had the clearest Casta Diva going at the time. *She* was the last person to piss off Jacob like you did this morning." She takes out a cigarette from the small swim bag on her hip and lights it, lips forming a perfectly round *O*. "That was seven years ago. And he still gets mad about it even now."

"And what did Marica Dela Rosa the opera singer do to upset Jacob so bad?"

"Well, she *died*, of course." The redhead pulls at the cigarette, holds the smoke in her lungs for a moment, turning her face up to wash it in sunlight, and then exhales. Wispy tendrils of smoke curl from her mouth and nostrils, like a ghostly hand caressing her face. "Jacob loved that old bitch. I think he intended her to live forever. *She* probably did, too, now that I'm thinking on it." The redhead grunts, smiling briefly. "I guess the universe disappointed them both. She had a massive heart attack at breakfast one morning and face-planted into her French toast." At this, she erupts into laughter—a laughter so perfect and feminine that, again, I instantly think it's fake. I mentally chide myself for being so ungenerous.

The woman is friendly, if a little abrupt. She nudges her sunglasses down her nose, revealing slightly angled, dark blue eyes. Cat's eyes. And such an odd color for someone with such red hair. "I'm guessing you don't know who I am?" she says.

"Unfortunately not." Should I shake her hand or something? Is that something sex workers do? *Is* she even a sex worker? Jacob implied that the girls at the compound weren't exactly free thinkers, but this woman seems bright and smart. She angles her head, appraising me from head to foot. "I'm Alaska. I'm Jacob's mistress. You'll be the crazy interloper who showed up in the middle of the night, trying to get herself killed, I assume?"

I laugh, too, lifting one shoulder in an attempt to brush off perhaps one of the most terrifying moments of my life. "Yeah, that'd be me. Pleased to meet you."

This small attempt at politeness seems to surprise her. "*Are* you?"

"Absolutely. Since I've arrived, you're the only person who hasn't screamed at me, shoved a gun in my face, or asked me to perform sexual acts in front of them."

Alaska doesn't laugh at this. An amused smile does tug at her lips, though. She takes another drag from her cigarette and dispatches the smoke in my direction. "Oh, honey. Just give it time." She pulls a face, then, glancing disgustedly at the cigarette in her hand before flicking it into the pool. It hisses when it hits the water and goes out. "Too fucking hot to smoke, anyway." She stands up, shoving her glasses back up her nose, hiding those intelligent cat's eyes of hers. "Jacob says you're free to decline given your arrangement with Zee, but me and the other girls are all beginning to prep for the party tomorrow. If you're not an asshole to them, they'll play nice. Entirely up to you." The change in her tone is subtle, but I hear it. *She* isn't pleased to meet *me*. She definitely isn't happy about my *arrangement* with Zee. Perhaps she heard about me claiming ownership of him this morning. Perhaps she just thinks I'm his piece of ass. Either way, I'm smart enough to know she doesn't like it.

"We're meeting in the ladies' house around back after dinner. Tell the guards Jacob's okayed it before you go over there, though. They'll shoot you if you don't." Before I can reply, she pads over to the pool and dives in, her body curved into a perfect arc so that she doesn't make a splash.

I pick up my book and I head back inside before she can swim the length of the pool. There's something about her I don't like. I get the feeling I haven't met the real Alaska yet. I very much doubt that the real version will be an improvement on the version I was just introduced to. After all, she said it herself: *Oh, honey. Just give it time.* And I can totally picture the redheaded Alaska with a gun in her hand.

ZETH

There are few things in life that put me on the back foot. I've come to expect shitty things from shitty people, so it's no surprise when one of Charlie's boys, or even one of my *own* boys does something fucked up. But Sloane? Shit, Sloane keeps on surprising me. Sometimes in really entertaining, really fucking hot ways. Sometimes in desperately stupid, idiotic ways. I haven't decided which category her little stunt from this morning falls under yet, but when I do, I'm gonna make sure she pays for it. She needs to know she can't pull that shit here. Not if she wants to survive. And I may not be much, and I may not *have* much, but I'm kind of attached to my life. I'd like to keep a hold of it for as long as I can, too.

I'm not gonna tell her about Jacob's reaction after she left his study. She'll think it's okay to speak to him that way, and it's *so* not okay. It's not okay for me. Not for Alaska. Not for Charlie. Not for I straight up thought he was gonna pull out his gun and go shoot her in the back of the head, but instead he'd laughed like a fucking drain. Told me he understood why I was fucking her and then some.

"She wears you out, man, you send her straight to me, okay? I wouldn't mind being toyed with by a feisty piece of pussy like that."

It had turned out that Sloane was only half the issue with Jacob, and once he'd decided she wasn't a threat, he'd moved swiftly onto his other concern: Charlie.

"I'm gonna need you with me today, Zeth. I need you to explain *exactly* why you've run away from home like a dog with its tail tucked between its legs. Plus, your help wouldn't go amiss. I have some business to attend to."

There wasn't much I could do or say to refuse him. If I had, it would only have made me look guilty as fuck. "Fine. Happy to help." *Happy to bury a bullet in the back of your head. Happy to set this place on fucking fire and dance around the inferno like a madman.* "What kind of business you got?"

"Is there more than one kind?" he'd said, shrugging.

And that's how we ended up in his basement.

I've never been down here before. A man hides his darkest shit in his basement. You end up somewhere like this, you're either inner circle or you're royally fucked. I'm hoping for the first, but in all honesty, the latter is more likely. It's clear what goes on down here. Below the compound is a series of small rooms. Bare concrete boxes with no furniture and naked light bulbs dangling from the ceiling. There are large drain grates in the cracked floor of each cell. Easier to hose away the debris.

In the third room we pass, a hospital bed has been set up, and Anton Medina is laid out on it, hooked up to an IV with his right arm in a cast. He's watching television, his face is set into a permanent scowl. He's *definitely* still mad that I kicked his ass. Didn't know I'd broken his arm, though. That makes me deliriously fucking happy. Bitch should never have laid a finger on Sloane. Anton notices us passing and tries to sit up, but too late. We're already gone.

We pass more open doorways until we reach one at the far end of the corridor that's locked. I already know who's inside this room. I'm praying to all that's holy that Michael is still alive, or I'm gonna blow my cover right here and now and kill every last motherfucker within reach. I'll die trying to do that, anyway, and then everything really *will* be fucked. Sloane. I won't be able to protect *her* if I'm dead.

"Clark, get the door," Jacob orders the other guard who was with Anton when I arrived at the compound.

Clark isn't like Anton, though. He does as he's told without voicing his fucking opinion over every little fucking thing. And he doesn't seem to hate me the same way Anton does. He just does his job and keeps his mouth shut. This might make him seem less of a threat, but the opposite is actually true. Anton has shown me his hand. I know what's going on in that dumb motherfucker's head every time I fucking look at him. I have no idea what's going on in *Clark's* head. He's an unknown. A threat.

He's all business as he opens up the door, and I brace myself for whatever might be waiting on the other side. Jacob's bulk blocks my view for a second, but then I see.

Michael sits on an armchair, hands cuffed in front of him, watching television. The room is empty besides the chair and the television, which rests on a splintering wooden stand. My second in command doesn't look up at us when we walk in. He focuses on the screen.

The photos Jacob's guys had taken of Michael shortly after they'd captured him had shown him with a black eye and a split lip. I'd assumed he'd be in far worse shape by now, but looks as though I was wrong. He's fine. Okay, not *fine*, fine, but they haven't roughed him up any more. The bruise underneath his right eye is vivid purple against his tawny skin, but the outer edges are starting to yellow, and his lip has had time to scab over. Jacob lumbers into the room, pausing to take a moment to assess the TV set.

"*America's Next Top Model*, huh? You gay, asshole?" Jacob asks in a conversational tone.

Michael, my boy, my right hand, smirks out of the corner of his mouth and raises an eyebrow. "Yes. That's why I was checking out all those girls you have locked up here. *Because I'm gay.*"

Jacob snorts, nodding slowly. Michael finally peels his indifferent gaze away from the TV and sends it our way. His expression doesn't falter when he sees me, and I cheer like a fucking moron on the inside. Seriously. Most people would twitch or something—would show *some* sign of recognition—but not Michael.

"Well," Jacob says, "I suppose it's a good insight into how chicks' brains work, I guess. You learned anything interesting yet?"

"That they're all vicious and competitive?" Michael rubs his nose with the back of his hand, at ease in his surroundings. He'll have been like this since they put him down here, which has undoubtedly been driving them all mad. The problem is, a random perv busted for spying on chicks taking a shower wouldn't react this calmly. They'd probably be shitting their pants. The Talons may not have anything on Michael, but his attitude is telling them enough all by itself. He's not just some pervert. He's *someone*—a someone who will eventually be missed. Jacob walks to Michael's chair and picks up the remote. He switches off the set, and Michael sucks in a tired breath, pivoting in his seat so that he's finally facing us.

Our eyes meet for a split second, and I get nothing. Not a warning. Not a flicker of recognition. Nothing. I'm itching to send him some sort of message, but no. I do that and we're both dead. "You brought in the heavy artillery, I see," he says.

Jacob snaps his fingers and Clark hurries out of the room. "Yeah. I brought in the big guns just for you, buddy. We gave you some time to think about what you've done and why you're here. Now we've come to chat. Anything in particular you'd like to talk about, asshole?"

Clark reappears with a wooden stool in either hand. He sets both of them down in front of Michael. Jacob sits on the first. The other is apparently for me. I sit, trying to figure out how the hell this is all gonna play out. Badly, I'm guessing. Really fucking badly.

"Not particularly," Michael says, letting his head fall to one side. His shirt is filthy, covered in blood. Not *his* blood. His lip wouldn't have bled that much, and his nose is just fine, which means it must it must have belonged to someone else. I get a kick out of that. My boy Michael is fucking dangerous when he needs to be.

Jacob isn't at all impressed with this show of nonchalance, though. He leans forward, chair creak underneath him complaining loudly as his body weight shifts. "I ain't got time for torturing people right now. I'm gonna ask you two questions, and then after that we're not gonna use words anymore. You hearin' me?"

Michael looks at Jacob, then at me, and then at Clark, as if considering his options. Even I know they look pretty fucking bleak right now. But Michael also knows I got his back. I won't let things go too far before I step in. "Sure," he says. "Ask away."

"You see this man?" Jacob points his thumb to his right. *At me.* Michael nods, and an unhinged smile spreads across Jacob's smug face. "Great. You ever seen this man before?"

"Nope."

"You sure? You've never heard the name Zeth Mayfair?"

"Never." Michael is a brick wall as he denies knowing me. We've been friends, business associates, drinking buddies for close to eight years, but from looking Michael straight in the eye, you would never, *ever* suspect him of lying. You could hook this guy up to a lie detector and he would charm the pants off the thing. Jacob's a persistent bastard, though.

"You ever heard the name Charlie Holsan?"

"Nope."

"So you weren't hired by anyone of that name? To follow this man to my home? To disturb the peace here?"

Holy shit. Jacob suspects Charlie sent Michael here to spy on *me*? I guess in Jacob's head that's the only thing that makes sense. It never occurred to me that he might come to that conclusion. I've been too busy worrying over the real reason to consider that. Jacob has no cause to suspect I came here to steal a girl from him, though. I mean, why would he? That wouldn't only be dumb. It would be fucking suicide.

"I told you. I don't know this guy, and I don't know those names. I got laid off from my job with a nice fat payout." Michael rolls his eyes, as if he's told this story before. "I knew about this place from my cousin. He said you had top pussy here, so I thought I'd pay you guys a visit. I wanted to see the girls first, though. No crime in *that*, is there? Why should I waste my money if the product isn't as advertised, y'know?"

Shit. He had money on him when they found him, then. A lot of money. I know because I gave it to him to pass on to Rick. Too much money for your average person to back-pocket, but enough to have in your possession if you plan on renting a girl or two from Jacob Dixon. The only problem is, the people who know about this place also know that you can't just turn up looking to hire a girl without an invite. *That's* suicide, too.

Clark scowls, brows banking together as if he's thinking the exact same thing. Jacob nods, considering Michael's lie. Maybe not *believing* it, but definitely considering it.

"Who's this cousin of yours, then? He someone who comes here often?"

An important question. If Michael doesn't tell Jacob his cousin's name, he's dead. If Michael makes up a fake name and Jacob knows he's lying, he's dead. I have no idea how he's going to get out of this one. I straighten on my stool, readying myself. If I see either Jacob or Clark reaching for their weapons, my ass will be up and charging before they can manage to pull off a round.

Hopefully.

Michael still doesn't look bothered by this situation. I've gotta admit, I knew Michael was stone cold, but I can see his slow, steady pulse beating in his neck, and it's barely fucking there. Even I would be sweating a little if I found myself down here, cuffed, and forced to watch *America's Next Top Model*. "Well, my cuz is a regular here by all accounts. I could tell you his real name, but he won't be happy with me."

Jacob's the one who isn't happy. "Now is not the right time to be fucking around. Understand this. You are on the verge of being skinned alive and left out in the desert for the vultures. I invite you to act accordingly."

Michael smirks at that. "Then I accept your invitation. My cousin's real name isn't mine to give. But you've heard of *Rebel*, right?"

Jacob wheezes like Michael's just sucker-punched him. Clark steps forward, clearing his throat nervously. He wants to shoot Michael, or at least he wants to know if *Jacob* wants him to shoot Michael. Jacob gestures with an urgent flick of his wrist—get back. "You're Rebel's cousin?"

Michael smiles like the cat who got the cream. "His father is also my godfather, if *that's* not enough of a commendation for you?"

"Did you happen to mention this to Anton when he brought you down here?" Jacob's turned a queasy greenish color. He's sweating, too, which makes him look decidedly unwell.

"He didn't ask." Michael raises both shoulders and eyebrows at the same time, a picture of indifference. "He seemed more interested in using his fists on me. There wasn't much time for talking."

I've sat through this whole exchange on the edge of my seat. Michael's a grade-A moron of the highest order to concoct that kind of lie. This is the point in the proceedings where Jacob calls Rebel and asks him if he's sent his cousin Jacob's way. And Rebel's response? "No, of course not. Kill the lying little fucker."

You don't want to cross Rebel. He's the kind of guy who makes people like Jacob quake in their boots. He has enough power to shut down any organization he sees fit. As head of the largest motorcycle gang in California, Washington, and New Mexico combined, Rebel *also* happens to be the same vile piece of shit who bid to buy a night with Sloane two years ago. He's a violent motherfucker with a penchant for girls in the skin trade. After *he* spends a night with them, they tend to disappear. That's why I stepped in when I found out Eli was about to sell Sloane to him. And Michael's just claimed that he's related to the guy?

Jacob doesn't seem to know what to do with himself. He leans back, scratching his belly, then sits forward again, scowling. "And how do you propose I verify this claim of yours, then? Because that is one motherfucking crazy-ass claim. If you're lying to me, you know it won't just be a simple case of killin' you now? I'll have to have my boys to beat the living shit outta you. Then they'll have to bring you back from the dead so Rebel can kill you himself for using his name."

He's absolutely right. Rebel *will* want to kill him

personally. Michael doesn't blink at the description of what will happen to him if he's caught in this lie, though. He's calmer than fucking ever.

"I tell you what, *Jacob*." Michael peppers his tone with just enough disrespect to make me cringe. "Why don't you take a photo of my handsome face and send it to my cousin? He'll tell you straight up if we're blood."

The cogs inside Jacob's head grind in protest as he works this one through. Eventually, he takes a picture of Michael and types a quick message. His cell makes a dinging sound: *Sent*.

The next few minutes are brutal. Jacob's cell phone sits on his knee, while Jacob stares down Michael. He may be past his prime, but there's no doubting the threat in his eyes. I've always known I'll die a grisly death at some point—you can only dodge bullets for so long before one of them eventually hits something vital—but I have to admit I never thought it would be in a Black Talon brothel. And I never thought I'd be so afraid for the safety of the woman I'll be leaving alone in their midst if I get—

Bright white light illuminates Jacob's cell screen, and the thing almost jumps off his leg when it starts vibrating. He's calling. Rebel's actually *calling*. A text would have done it. But no. A phone call? What the hell does that mean?

Michael eyes the phone, arching an eyebrow. "If you know my cousin, then you'll know how he dislikes being kept waiting."

A sneaking suspicion begins to develop in the back of my head. No *way* Michael would be this sure of himself right now. Not unless... not unless...

"Rebel, my friend." Jacob answers the call gingerly, as though he's working his way toward the same conclusion I am. "Thanks for calling. Sorry to bother you with such a—"

The rumbling voice on the other end of the line cuts him off. Jacob's eyes grow round as he listens, the fingers of his free hand tapping distractedly at the side of his chair. "Well, I didn't order *that*, I assure you. I'm—" Jacob exhales, pinching the bridge of his nose between two fingers. "I know. I'm—" Doesn't look like Rebel's in the mood to let Jacob fit a word in edgewise. The head of the Black Talons pales as he listens to whatever the man on the other end of the line has to say for himself. "Yes, I agree. I *totally* agree. It's unaccept—"

A roar erupts out of the cell phone's speakers, and then... nothing. Jacob lowers his phone in order to look at the screen. Unaccustomed as he is to having people hang up on him, the look on his face is hilarious.

"How goes my cousin, Jacob?" Michael asks.

So it's true then. I can't believe Michael's been keeping that shit under lock and key for so long. And why the hell has he been working for *me* when he could be a big fucking deal in his cousin's organization? The smug bastard does a good job of hiding his smirk, but the tone of his voice is too satisfied to conceal. Jacob's just the sort of person to kill someone for being a cocky shit, and yet he doesn't kill Michael. Thoughtfully, he sets his phone to one side.

"He was unhappy about the bruise on his only cousin's face," he says slowly. He meets Michael's gaze. "I have to apologize for the mistreatment you've suffered at the hands of my men. If I'd known, then..."

Michael just nods. "An easy misunderstanding." He holds up his hands, jerking his chin toward the restraints. "I'm assuming you have no problem with removing these now, though? They're a little tight."

Jacob goes purple. With horror, embarrassment or fury, I don't know, but he signals to Clark all the same. "Uncuff him."

Clark, the ever-obliging employee, does as he's told. Michael massages his wrists, that smug fucking look still on his face. "I wonder," he says. "If you might have a bathroom I could use? I've been stuck down here for three days. A shower really wouldn't go amiss."

Most men would flee for their lives after escaping an ordeal down in Jacob Dixon's cellar, but not my guy. By the glint in his eye, Michael seems dead set on sticking around. Jacob's double chin wobbles. He's mad as a grass snake, but what can he say? "Of course, my friend. Of course." He stands and gestures toward the door, still twitching with what I can only imagine to be affront.

Michael goes to follow, but first he turns to me, offering me his hand to shake. "Sorry to hear about your trouble, man. If you need any help with this Charlie Holsan guy, just let me know. I'm sure I could pull a few strings."

I wanna slap the cheeky fucker upside the head. If I'd have known he was Rebel's cousin, I may have asked him to pull hard on those fucking strings a while back. Maybe not, though. Dancing with Rebel is like dancing with the devil. I wouldn't want to owe the man a thing. I shake Michael's hand, squeezing way harder than necessary. In return, Michael provides me with a saintly smile and saunters out of Jacob's killing room like he just enjoyed a pampering weekend at the Ritz.

48

SLOANE

"WHAT THE HELL WAS THAT?"

When Zeth comes back to the room later on in the day, he doesn't look happy. In fact, he's furious. He's had nearly eight hours to calm down since Jacob's office this morning, but from the storm cloud over his head, he's been itching to ream me out ever since. He stalks into the room and stands in front of me where I'm lying on my stomach on top of the bed, new phone in hand. He leans down, placing his hands either side of me, glaring at me with a level of intensity that makes goose bumps break out across my skin.

"What are you *doing*, Sloane?"

"I'm texting my dad to make sure your friend is still alive. That okay with you?"

The anger temporarily fades from his eyes. "And is she?"

"Yes."

"Give me the phone."

"What?"

"Give me the phone."

He tries to take it from me, but I sit up, holding it protectively against my chest. "I don't think so. I've had enough of you stealing my phone."

"Sloane, just…" He stops himself. Scrubbing his face with his hands and then his head, he growls under his breath. "Just tell me what she's been doing."

"She's been helping my dad prepare for his church youth camp."

Zeth's face goes slack. I think I've just broken his brain. "Sorry, *what*?"

"Church. Youth. Camp." Those are the three words that matter, I think. I haven't told him that my dad's planning on taking Lacey *with* him to the camp yet. I don't know how well that will go down.

"And she's okay with that?" Zeth asks.

"She says she is in her text message."

"Oh my God, just give me your fucking phone!" He lunges for it again, and this time I let him have it. He seems genuinely worried about the girl, and me being pissy with him is only making matters worse. I shouldn't do it. I should be doing everything I can to soothe him after the stunt I pulled earlier, but instead I feel like baiting him. Pissing him off some more. Seeing just how far I can push. The problem is *I'm* still mad at *him*. Because of this morning, when he showed a side of himself I didn't think could exist. A sweet, vulnerable side that made my chest hurt.

"You're confusing me." That's what he'd said as he let me stroke his back, his hair. As he'd held on to me, still inside me, after we'd just had crazy, confronting sex. And then he had promptly dragged that side of himself back into the dank, dark dungeon where he keeps it locked up and has gone back into asshole mode. And I know I didn't imagine it. Zeth Mayfair *does* have a vulnerable side.

I watch him as he scrolls through my messages to both Lacey and my dad, observing his reactions. I know what he's reading:

Lacey:
You used to really like pink, huh?

Me:
Yep. I also used to like NSYNC and dungarees.

Lacey:
Yeah. Your mom showed me pictures.

Me:
She refuses to let me live that down! I'm gonna burn those pics.

Lacey:
Don't. She'll be devastated. She's really lovely. Your dad, too. He's got me pitching tents with him all day today.

Me:
Make sure he's not using you for slave labor, Lace. If you leave, just let me know and I'll send in a rescue, okay?

Lacey:
It's fine. I like it. It's fun. Say hey to Zee for me?

And then, of course, there are the messages from my dad.

Dr. Sloane, MD:

Your mother caught her crying in the bathroom this morning. You didn't tell me, so I won't pry, but this girl seems a little broken?

Me:

A little, yes. But don't go trying to fix her. She's already seeing someone for that.

Dr Sloane, MD:

They aren't doing a very good job.

Me:

Just keep her busy, okay?

Dr Sloane, MD:

Already on it, kiddo.

I thank the stars that Lacey didn't write "say hey to my *brother*" instead of *Zee* in her message. That would be a rough way for him to find out the truth—that the young girl he's been watching over for the past six months is actually his blood relative. His *sister*. Zeth looks adorable as he frowns over my phone, rereading the texts. Adorable, in a terrifying kind of way.

"Is he gonna try and convert her?" he asks.

I shrug. "He might ask her what she believes. He won't push, though. He's not like that."

Zeth just nods at this. I can't tell what he's thinking. He's withdrawn to some place deep within himself. Somewhere I'd have trouble reaching him. And then, just as quickly, he seems to realize what's happened and he surfaces again, tossing back my phone. "You didn't answer my other question. What the hell did you think you were doing this morning?"

I'm beginning to think this guy is bipolar. He swings so wildly from one attitude to the next. I didn't see it at first. He just seemed arrogant and pissed off all the time, but I've begun to realize something: His negative emotions are his anchors. They keep him from drifting off someplace he doesn't want to go. Maybe the place he drifted to just now? Does he know he's developed this coping mechanism? I doubt it.

"Jacob knew I wasn't some single-brain-celled idiot, Zeth. There was no point in lying to him about it."

"So you lie to him about me instead. He *knows* me. He knows I would never..." He starts pacing, working on wearing a hole in the polished floorboards.

"You would never what?"

"I would never submit to a woman. Not like that."

"That's bullshit. You told me to own you when we first..."

Zeth raises an amused eyebrow at me. "Fucked? See, you can't even say it. That's why I told you to own me. Because having you try was just too delicious. You're so uncomfortable in your own skin. I just wanted you to break free from that. If I played a little game with you so you could do that..." It's his turn to shrug now.

I glare at him, my temperature rising. "*I'm* not uncomfortable in my own skin. Out of the two of us, *you're* the one who isn't at home in his own body."

A shit-eating grin spreads across his handsome, incredibly annoying face. "Have you seen me, sweetheart?" He spreads his arms wide. "I look like a fucking Abercrombie and Fitch model."

Oh, the smug, smug bastard. "No you don't! You look like a fucking criminal. You *are* a fucking criminal."

"A criminal who models for Abercrombie and Fitch?"

"Urgh!" I contemplate throwing my phone at him but then think better of it. I hurl a pillow at him instead, and it hits his head—way less satisfying than the phone would have been. He's too busy laughing at me to care, anyhow. I suddenly realize what he's doing.

He's actually laughing. Laughing, like a normal person. My anger vanishes. I sit in silence, stunned over how surprising the moment is.

He picks up the pillow from the floor at his feet, still chuckling a little. He tosses it back on the bed, unaware of the reaction he's caused in me. "Well, regardless of the why, you've landed us in a mighty fucking awkward situation now, Sloane Romera. You should have just blown me and had done with it."

"What?"

He paces to the closet where he packed away his black duffel this morning, and surprise, surprise, pulls the damn thing out again. My palms start sweating at the very sight of it. "We have to figure out how to make Jacob believe you're as ballsy as you made yourself out to be, otherwise we're both in a lot of fucking trouble, aren't we? He's already suspicious as fuck about me. Especially now he knows Michael isn't here spying on me for Charlie."

"Wait, what? Michael's here? *Your* Michael?"

Zeth snorts, carrying his black bag to the bed and unzipping it beside me. "He's checked into the room two doors down from us, swanning around like he owns the place."

"I don't understand."

"You don't need to." Zeth's amusement levels seem to have evened out again. He turns to face me, done fiddling with his duffel of tricks. "All *you* need to do is take something out of this bag and use it on me. And make me believe it."

"Uhh..."

"Right now."

"I...I can't. It's not that simple, Zeth. I can't just decide to—"

He lunges for me, placing a hand over my mouth. "Stop talking." He climbs up onto the bed, hovering over me, his face a short inch away from mine. "Stop. Talking. Start. Doing."

Despite his command, I see in his eyes that he thinks I will fail at this task. This is exactly the same thing as him telling me to own him. He thinks I'm too self-conscious to do it. Well, fine. He wants me to start doing? I'll give him what he wants, and he will *not* fucking like it. His hand's still over my mouth, so I turn my head and bite down on his index finger.

"Sloane."

I bite harder, staring him straight in the eye. His mouth twitches, but he doesn't say anything else. I have to release him for the next part. There are small red wheels on his finger as he pulls his hand away. Good. It's about time I marked *him* for once.

"Get off me," I command.

He narrows his eyes. "Why?"

"Don't ask questions. Do as you're told."

He smiles, wolfish and dangerous. I take that smile straight off his face when I slap him with my open palm. *Hard.*

"You need me to ask you again?" I demand. My cheeks are burning so hot that I must look ridiculous, bright red and flustered, especially with my chest rising and falling so quickly. Zeth isn't looking at my chest or my cheeks, though. He's looking me straight in the eye, transfixed. I can see him warring with himself over what I've just done. He hates me slapping him. I already know that from past experience. And yet, this is his own doing. He's *told* me to do this.

He straightens slow as honey, still staring at me. Once he's moved away, I sit up and slide off the bed, trying not to let my nerves get the better of me. I can do this. I just need to maintain my resolve. I can't think about what this will cost me later.

The duffel's already unzipped. I draw it open so I can get a better look inside and almost lose it on the spot. I've never seen anything like it before in all my life. It's part sex shop, part hardware store in there. God only knows whether the coils of strapping or the sheathed knives are meant for work or play, and frankly I'm scared to find out. There's other stuff in there: ball gags, handcuffs, lengths of rope, a sleek silver bullet vibrator, still sealed in its box. Alongside all of that, there's a knuckle-duster, a gun, and a Taser.

The roll of duct tape really finishes the whole thing off for me.

This is a stark reminder that Zeth is not a fucking Boy Scout. He's dangerous. *And he's never pretended to be anything else*, a small voice in my head reminds me. I glance up to find him watching me closely, hands clenched by his sides. It's almost as if he's done this on purpose. He's *made* me look in the bag. To see who he is. He must think I'll run. He must be waiting for it to happen. But I am not reserved, timid Sloane anymore. Even if I find Alexis and bring her home, it will be impossible to go back.

I take the gun out of the bag. "Stand up."

Zeth couldn't look more surprised if I'd already shot him with the damned thing. "*Sloane…*"

"I said stand up." I check the clip, take the safety off, and aim the thing at his chest. I'm still panting like crazy, still red in the face, but something has shifted inside me. I'm not nervous anymore. Not with this weapon in my hand. Zeth stands up slowly, never taking his eyes off me.

"When I told you to take something out of the bag—"

"Yeah, I get it. You didn't expect me to pick this. Now take off your shirt."

He does it, slipping the clothing over his head quickly, as though he doesn't want to take his eyes off me even for a second. I want to take a moment to appreciate the beauty of the half-naked man in front of me, but I can't let him know what he does to me. Instead, I point the gun at his pants, raising my eyebrows. He gets my meaning: *those, too.* He kicks off his shoes and loses the pants, all without looking away.

"Now what?" he asks.

"Shut up. Come here." He makes his way around the bed and looms over me in his boxers. He's trying to intimidate me with his size, but it won't work. Not this time. That must come as a shock to him. I get the feeling he's relied on his stature to scare the living shit out people for a very long time…and I'm about to take that advantage away from him. "Get on your knees."

He doesn't obey straightaway. I shove the muzzle of the gun into his chest, pressing hard enough to depress skin and muscle. He gets the picture and sinks to his knees.

"Now put your hands behind your back."

He does that, too. I skirt around him, still aiming the gun at him, until I reach his duffel. The duct tape comes out next. My heart hammers as I pull out a length, my hands shaking like crazy as I bind his wrists together. I keep expecting him to whip around and grab me, but he doesn't. He lets me do it, although his breathing has kicked up a notch, coming faster and louder.

I pause behind him, taking a moment to regroup. I know *exactly* what I'm going to do to him, and the prospect is at once thrilling and terrifying. I bury my fingers into the hair at the nape of his neck, grabbing hold of it and pushing his head forward. He grunts but doesn't react. Not until I press the gun against the back of his head. He stops breathing. I know his eyes are open because his long, dark eyelashes are visible from this angle, but he doesn't blink. Doesn't move. He just stares at the floor, holding his breath.

"Tell me what you're feeling," I demand.

Zeth blasts a full lungful of air out of his nose. "Oh, really? We're sharing our feelings? Right now? Come on, Sloane."

I cock the hammer on the gun.

"Fuck! Okay. Okay. Well, I guess you could say I'm wondering if you're gonna blow my head off. Happy?"

"No. That's what you're thinking, not what you're feeling. How do you *feel*?"

"What the fu—"

"You're kneeling on the floor with a gun pressed against the back of your head, wondering if you're about to die. Don't fucking tell me you're not feeling anything, Zeth."

"Alright, I'm fucking shitting my pants. I'm losing my shit. Is that what you want to hear?"

"Yes."

He lets out a scathing laugh. "Wonderful. I'm glad I'm not the only sadist in this relationship."

"I'm not a sadist. And neither are you."

"Then what the fuck are you *doing*, Sloane?" He sounds exasperated.

I put the gun back into the duffel, remembering to snick the safety back into place first, and then I kneel down behind him. Carefully, I stroke my fingertips down the defined groove between his shoulder blades, taking great pleasure in the way he shivers at my touch. From there, I lace my arms through his so that I can run my hands over his chest and his abs. I'm so close to him, my chest pressed to his back. His skin smells of outdoors and the faint tang of masculine sweat. I can't stop myself; I press my lips against his shoulder blade, closing my eyes.

"God, Sloane," he whispers. Nothing else. He doesn't ask anything else. He just trembles as I trace my fingers across the planes of his stomach and downward, to the tops of his thighs. I kiss his shoulders, running my tongue over his heated skin, licking and biting at him, gently this time. Not hard like before. My knees hurt, but it's worth it if only for the way his body comes alive against me, twitching and reacting to each considered stroke.

The anger that I felt just now eventually turns into something more heady, sexual and basic. The power that I have over him is incredible. I could do anything I wanted to him and... and realistically he probably *could* stop me. He's still kneeling where I told him to because he wants to, not because I'm forcing him. But still...

I slide my hands lower, then lower still until I find what I'm looking for. His cock is rigid, straining against his boxers. He sucks in a sharp breath when I take him in my hand and squeeze, the way he did to himself back in his apartment the second time I slept with him. No, not *slept* with him. He was right earlier. I *fucked* him.

"Do you want me?" I whisper, grazing my teeth against his ear lobe.

"Yes."

"Are you going to behave if I let you come play with me on the bed?"

Zeth makes a low, guttural sound. His breathing comes fast and uneven. He's never been like this with me before. Control is a big thing for Zeth. He's *always* in charge, always handling what's happening between us, but not now. I don't think he's even realized himself yet.

I stand and let him rise as well. His eyes are hooded by his half-lowered lids. I take the knife from his duffel and cut the duct tape, freeing his hands, wanting him to be able to participate in what I plan on doing next.

He hooks his thumbs into his boxers and strips out of them without me asking him to. And then, not two seconds after thinking that he's actually giving himself over to me, I realize my mistake. I scream when he rockets forward and grabs me by the waist. "*ZETH!*"

In a flash, his lazy, sex-doped expression is gone. He's lit up, fizzing with fury. "You're fucking crazy, you know that!" He has me off my feet, practically over his shoulder. Three long strides and then he throws me forcefully onto the bed. I hit the mattress with a very unladylike *Ufff!* as the oxygen leaves my lungs. I lash out with my feet, trying to push myself up the bed and away from him, but it's no good. I'm all arms and legs, panicking, and Zeth is a practiced predator. He has my arms pinned over my head before I can scramble my way off the bed. "Stop struggling."

Oh, I want to, but my natural instincts are warning me not to trust a man who carries a Desert Eagle around in his sex kit. He huffs impatiently and then lowers his body weight on top of me, pinning me to the bed. "Sloane, stop fighting me."

"Get off me and I will!" I regret pulling the gun on him. Massively. I have no idea what kind of retribution he has planned, but I'm sure I'm not going to like it. "You told me to do it, Zeth! You can't hurt me for doing what you told me to!"

He lifts himself a fraction, rearing back to get a

good look at me. The anger on his face has morphed to something else. "*Hurt* you?"

"For the gun!" I have to get him off me. I need to. I buck against him, but the bastard doesn't shift an inch. He's a dead weight on top of me.

"What do you mean, *hurt* you?" His voice is cold. Detached.

"I don't—I—" The disbelief on his face finally hits home. He doesn't look like he's set on killing me. If anything, he looks horrified.

"I would never hurt you, Sloane. You honestly think I would?"

A small voice immediately answers yes, but it doesn't belong to me. It belongs to that treacherous Pippa impersonator who lives inside my head. My panic subsides, leaving me exhausted underneath him. I stop struggling. "No. I..."

Zeth sees the flicker of doubt in my eyes before I can rein it in, though. His jaw tightens. "Have I ever raised a hand to you? Have I ever..." He trails off, exhaling sharply. He looks away for a second, and when he turns back to me, his gaze pierces me through. "I don't hurt people who can't defend themselves. I don't hurt girls. I will never hurt *you*."

"I'm sorry, I shouldn't have said that." But even as I'm saying this, the Pippa voice is back and on a mission. *The guy's pinning you to the goddamn bed, Sloane!*

Like, right now! What the hell is wrong with you? It's almost as if Zeth can hear that voice, too. He carefully lifts himself up a little, removing most of the pressure he was exerting on me with his body. His hand stays locked around my wrists, but the tension eases a little, making my fingers throb painfully as the blood rushes back into them.

"I might stop you from going nuts on the odd occasion, Sloane. I might spank you, but I would never harm you like that. I thought you knew that."

I've reclaimed my cool now. He's not overly mad about the gun—I can see that—but he's still not overly *happy* with me, either. "I just thought…"

"That I'd rip your head off for threatening to kill me? Yeah, well…" He shifts, pressing down on me again. The subtle weight transference seems to wake up my body. I realize my legs are spread, knees drawn up, feet flat against the mattress, and Zeth's huge and powerful body is between my thighs. And he's naked. He's not shy with his body, but his confidence has nothing to do with his physique. It's something else. Something I haven't quite been able to put my finger on just yet. Whatever it is, he's still lying on top of me, and my jeans and T-shirt are the only barriers between us. Zeth rumbles, as though he's been waiting for me to notice our tangled position.

"No, you threatening to kill me wasn't exactly what

I was expecting," he says. "But you did look incredibly sexy with a gun in your hand. Do you know how to use it?"

"Yes."

"Then that's even sexier." He dips his head down and grazes his teeth against my neck, surprising me. His warm breath causes goose bumps to break out down my arms and legs, as well as the sensitive area below my ear. My nipples tighten automatically. My body is way ahead of my head right now. I'm still trying to come to terms with the fact that I just held Zeth Mayfair at gunpoint—that it felt *good*—but my body is craving his touch. I want to feel him everywhere all at once. A few moments ago, Zeth's weight was crushing, and now...now I want him to smother me with his body, so that the only thing I can breathe and see and feel and smell is him.

I think there's something wrong with me.

"You got any more ideas about how you're gonna make me your bitch?" The words vibrate through the muscle and bone of his chest, sending chills through me.

"No."

"Good. Because you won't be able to threaten me with weaponry tomorrow night. And besides..." He grabs hold of the hem of my T-shirt, pulling it roughly upward with his free hand. "You like this better, *don't* you? You *like* obeying me. You like feeling defenseless.

You like that trickle of fear, lighting up your insides. It makes you feel alive."

He's right. He's always fucking right. I hate that he is, but it also saves us a lot of hassle. I enjoy my work. I pay my bills. I keep my shit clean and tidy. But I haven't had to make a tough decision in a long time. Nothing has been life or death. But choosing to continue whatever this is with Zeth, choosing to follow him down here to L.A. to find my sister, choosing to let him touch me, to lick and suck and bite at my skin, to obey him? Choosing all of that has felt like choosing to *live*.

Zeth pulls the cup of my black bra down, exposing my breast. His eyes feast on the expanse of pale skin on show, focusing hungrily on my pale pink areola. He makes that delicious, toe-curling sound at the back of his throat, like a starved animal, and then he ducks down and takes my nipple into his mouth. At first, he runs his tongue around and around, playing with the tightened bud, but then he uses his teeth, nipping hard enough to make my back arch up in a mix of pleasure and pain.

"You want me inside you, angry girl?" He pulls down the other side of my bra, freeing my other breast, and then he traces his tongue up the swell of my flesh and takes that one into his mouth, too. A stuttering sigh escapes me, ruffling his short, disheveled hair.

"Yes. I want you in...inside me."

He chuckles at my lightheaded response, and then he tilts forward, grinding himself against me. His cock is hardened steel, pressed up against my inner thigh. I pull in a quick breath, closing my eyes. I want him. I want to feel his skin against mine. I want to feel his cock rubbing up against my clit so badly that I push back, rocking my hips up to meet him.

"You hungry, Sloane? You want me that bad, huh?" Ohhhh, that smile. Slow as honey. Suggestive as sin. Adrenaline and endorphins collide in my bloodstream, tilting the room. I need to be naked right now. I try to communicate this, but all that comes out of my mouth is a frustrated groan. Zeth's eyes dilate, zeroing in on me. He tugs his lower lip between his teeth, his breath catching, as though he enjoys that sort of reaction out of me. Does he? Do I inspire the same need in him that he kindles in me?

He pushes up against me, and I gasp, my eyes rolling back into my head. It feels amazing when he does that. I'm burning, desperate to be touched, but...why am I still *dressed*? It's a fucking travesty. Zeth's mouth twitches. Rocking back onto his heels, cock rigid and brushing up against his belly, he takes the ankles of my jeans and pulls without even bothering to undo the button or fly. They don't come off easily, but he isn't about to be thwarted by a pair of fucking pants.

"I'm gonna try something different with you, Sloane. And you're gonna like it, okay?"

By the dangerous lilt in his voice, this information is a warning and not reassurance. "What are you gonna do?"

With a final rough jerk, he tears my jeans off my body. "Wait and see." My T-shirt goes next. He grabs me by my hips and pulls me toward him on the bed, drawing me upright so I'm sitting, and then he rips it over my head. He falls on me like a man possessed. My bra straps have fallen down over my shoulders, and my breasts are still free; Zeth cups both of his powerful hands over them, my nipples throbbing in time with my pulse,

"You're tits are amazing," he whispers. "But I wanna see them up here." He picks me up and holds me like I weigh nothing at all. On his knees, he grabs my thighs and pulls one up over his hip, indicating what he wants me to do. I'm all too happy to oblige. With his cock trapped between us, every movement he makes sends fire licking up my spine. He kisses and licks my breasts, his hands gripping me tightly around the waist as he arranges himself in a sitting position with me sitting over him.

I'm still wearing my panties, but that's no hindrance to Zeth. Carefully, he gathers the material together and tugs it upward, so the bunched lace applies intense pressure on my clit.

"*Ah!*"

"I hope you're not overly fond of these," he says, doing it again. "They're not gonna last long."

My breath saws in and out. My cheeks are flushed. Hell, my whole *body* is flushed. A primal, animal part of me takes over as I begin to rock against him, angling myself so that our hips are in alignment, pushing and rubbing and grinding. Coupled with the fact that he continues to tease my underwear, pulling it taut as I move, my head starts to swim. I'm out of breath. Delirious. I don't exaggerate the cry that comes out of me when he slips his fingers *beneath* my panties and strokes the slick heat of my pussy. I'm too far gone to be embarrassed by how wet I am. How wet he's *made* me. I just accept it and grind harder into his hand.

Zeth props himself up on one elbow and reclines, assessing me from head to toe as I set my body free, letting it do whatever it wants to do. I lean forward and place my hands on his chest, tracing my fingertips across the dark spill of tattoos across his pecs and his shoulders. The bruised purple of the scar where he was shot just below his collarbone nearly two months ago now. The graceful, packed lines of his solid muscles. I'm learning every single last line of him, committing him to memory and enjoying the process immensely. I'm drunk on him. And not *beer* drunk. I'm fucking *tequila* drunk. Sideways. Gone. *Blind* with how badly I need him.

"You're fucking amazing," he rasps. My ears are filled with the sound of my roaring blood and our combined panting, but, fuck, *Zeth* sounds drunk, too.

He slides a finger inside me and I'm done for. It's no good. His fingers aren't enough. I want all of him, buried balls deep inside me, pounding into me until all I see is stars. I reach down, and a whole new fire ignites inside me when I close my hand around his swollen cock. He's huge, rigid and smooth as warmed marble. He feels like silk wrapped steel as I slowly pump my hand up and down his shaft.

"*Fuck*, Sloane." His body locks up, his muscles vibrating as they strain beneath his skin. "Fuck!" He can't wait any longer, either. He grabs me, falling forward so I'm on my back again, and then he's on top of me, guiding himself into me so slowly, taking his sweet fucking time over taking me.

There's a safe site at one of the free clinics I volunteer at. I've watched users shoot up and seen nirvana take them as the drugs have soaked their blood. I understand now. My eyelids flutter as I'm washed away on a tide of pleasure. My body stretches around him, accommodating him as he languorously claims me. He lets me float for a second, his dark eyes devouring my expression as I shudder, trying and failing to breathe...

And then he *fucks* me.

He's ruthless as he slams himself into me again, again, again, impaling me on the end of his cock. "Oh, shit! Zeth!"

"You okay?" he growls.

I nod, digging my fingers into his back. The sharp bite of pain encourages him, and he powers on, slamming into me over and over. I hold on to his shoulders, clinging on for dear life, and he... he ducks his head and kisses my fingers. Everything slows. He... *he kissed my fingers?* Holy shit. Surprise prickles over my skin, fueling my building orgasm. I tremble, wrecked, as Zeth drives himself into me, my synapses flaring like stars being born and dying in the blink of an eye.

"How bad do you need to come, Sloane?" Zeth pants.

"Oh my God, *please*." If this is his payback... If he pulls out and leaves me like this...

But Zeth has something else in mind. He slides his hand up my body and doesn't stop until he reaches my neck. Once he's there, he curls his fingers around my throat and squeezes, applying the *tiniest* amount of pressure. "Do you want this?" he pants.

The memory of the belt in the hotel room takes me

out at the knees. It had scared me, but also *seriously* turned me on...

His grip tightens the tiniest amount, his eyes narrowing at the same time. "You safe," Zeth rasps. "I'm gonna make it feel good. I've got you."

The surrender. The loss of control. The vulnerability. It stirs something strange inside of me...

"Say the word, Sloane. I'll stop. I *promise*."

I don't hurt girls. I will never hurt you.

Medically, I know how dangerous this is. I've seen all kinds of damage caused by breath play. Cervical spine damage. Brain damage. Death. Jesus fucking *Christ*, why am I even *considering* it? But...

That's the whole *point*, isn't it. The stakes are high. He's testing the ground between us, seeing if it will hold the weight of whatever this might become.

I nod. *Do it.*

Zeth bares his teeth, victorious, as he grips my throat and fucks me like he means it. He leaves me *just* enough room to breathe.

"Ride it out, angry girl. That's it."

I slide hands slide up to Zeth's torso, shivering at the wall of heat and muscle beneath my palms. Zeth raises his eyebrows, smiling open-mouthed: *You* like *that, Sloane Romera?* He thrusts himself deep, grinding hard against me, making sure I feel every inch of him as he works his cock in and out of my pussy.

I'm not afraid anymore. I'm dizzy, sure, but the sensation is heady. And he *will* stop. One tap from me and it ends. My senses fire into overdrive, heightening, the colors in the room flaring vivid, bold, bright. Zeth's touch leaves sparks in its wake, and I revel in the chaos.

We are one carnal creature, moving in unison, working together to reach the same finish line. It's fast approaching. I can feel it building, cycling around my body, growing and pulsing…until…until…

"Shit. Shit! Oh my g…fuckimgonnacome, Zeth!"

He said he was going to make it feel good. This is better than good. Forget fireworks. A nuclear fucking bomb goes off in my head as I climax. I try to bite the scream back, but I can't keep it in check. Zeth's hand loosens, but even so, I barely make a sound.

"Holy fuck. Yes. Keep going, keep going. Come for me, Sloane. Come hard."

From the strain in his voice, he's holding himself back. That doesn't last long. I make sure of it. I reach down between our bodies and find what I'm looking for. I take hold of his balls and squeeze gently, grabbing his ass with my free hand and pulling him into me even deeper. I'm a hollow shell after that orgasm, but I manage to open my eyes enough to watch him get his. It's a beautiful thing to witness. With bared teeth, he slams himself inside me and roars.

A high-pitched hum fills the bedroom.

Zeth holds himself up for all of a second before collapsing on top of me, breathing hard.

That was...*fuck*, there are no words to describe what that was. We lie there, pulses flying, chests pumping like billows, skin cooling, hearts slowly easing, breath slowly deepening...

Room...

...slowly fading...

49

SLOANE

IT'S DARK WHEN I WAKE UP. REALLY dark. Like, *middle of the night* dark. I'm late for something. I'm late for work? I'm *really* fucking late. Night shifts turn you around something fierce. I often wake up once the sun's gone down, not knowing if I'm coming or going. But then I realize I'm not alone. Someone's in the bed with me. That part is *definitely* out of the ordinary.

Zeth Mayfair lies on his back with one arm thrown up over his face. The other arm is folded across his body, fingers splayed against his stomach, and the bedsheets are twisted around the lower half of his body in a tight knot. With all of our energetic exercise earlier, the fitted sheet has disappeared somewhere, and I've been sleeping naked and coverless on a bare mattress.

"Oh."

It's all I've got right now. The digital clock on the nightstand blinks 6:42 p.m. at me in stark red numbers. What time did Zeth come in here looking for me? I can't remember, but we must have been sleeping for hours. I sit up, careful not to make any noise, and tiptoe my way to the en suite. It's only when I stand that I feel the slick stickiness between my legs, and a rush of alarm floods me. No condom. We didn't use a condom. *Again.* Since our slip back at my place and the subsequent humiliation of a morning-after pill, I've been taking the pill, so there's no risk of me getting pregnant. But still...I'm a doctor for crying out loud, and Zeth Mayfair is a man whore extraordinaire. I should know better than this. Nasty shit will happen to your lady parts if you're reckless with them. I like my lady parts. I don't want them all funked up with chlamydia, or worse. Zeth and I need to have a chat about that.

In the meantime, I take a hot shower and get dressed. I don't really have time to do much but towel-dry my hair and apply a small amount of makeup—I'm supposed to meet with Jacob's girls at seven thirty for a pampering session, and I can't afford to be late. Despite how distracting being here with Zeth is, I haven't forgotten who *else* is here. Alexis is in this same compound, and I'll be damned if I don't finally get to see her. We won't be able to get her out until tomorrow night. Zeth explained earlier that with everyone distracted by the party, it will be the perfect opportunity to slip out without being seen. Plans aside, I'm so nervous I feel sick. I haven't seen Lexi in over two years. I've changed a lot since then. I'm guessing she has, too.

Zeth's still asleep when I leave the bathroom. He's in exactly the same position I left him in. The man sleeps like the dead. I sneak to his side of the bed, and then I lay my hand flat on his chest, snickering to myself, knowing how cold my hands are.

The reaction is instant. And violent.

"*Motherfucker!*" He's lying still as the dead one minute. The next, I'm pinned against the wall by my throat and Zeth's fist is sailing toward me. I turn my head just in time, narrowly avoiding the blow, but he's already pulling back for another try.

"Zeth! Zeth, *STOP!*" My windpipe being crushed for real this time. Makes it difficult to scream.

"Sloane?" Shock registers on Zeth's face. He drops me immediately, and I slide down the wall into a boneless heap at his feet. "Oh fuck. Fuck. I'm..." He rushes to the door and switches the light on. "Are you okay?"

I eye him uncertainly, rubbing my hand over my bruised esophagus. "Oh, yeah. I'm *great*. You did just try and stave my face in, though. And after swearing up and down you'd never hurt me, too. *That* was pretty rude."

"I'm sorry. I fell asleep. I shouldn't have done that."

"Sleeping makes you homicidal?"

He tries to speak but chokes instead. He tries twice more before the words come. "Waking up somewhere strange…with someone lurking in the dark…makes me homicidal."

I raise an eyebrow. Pippa would be having a field day at this admission, but I'm not stupid enough to ask what his deal is. I suspect this is the one thing Zeth Mayfair will not explain to me. I don't have to be a psychiatrist to know when someone has completely shut down. He tenses, naked, eyes empty, clearly waiting for me to ask him what the fuck that was. When I don't, he holds out his hand, offering to help me up. "I'll find somewhere else to sleep tonight. That way you won't have to worry about me attacking you at three a.m."

I accept his hand, grateful that my heart has dislodged itself from my throat and returned to its rightful place behind my breastbone. I don't like the thought of having to sleep in the room all night on my own. He's right, though. I don't like the sound of being strangled to death in the early hours of the morning, either. "I could just coldcock you with that gun."

Zeth sits back down on the bed, staring at the floor. He's forgotten how to blink? "You're not gonna say anything about that, then?" he asks.

"Do you want me to?"

"*No.*"

I shrug. "Well, then."

He grinds his teeth, nostrils flaring, not looking at me. "You've got to say something."

"What do you *want* me to say?"

He rubs his eyes—such a normal thing to do for such an abnormal human being. "Anything. The gun. Why did you take *that* from the bag earlier and not something else?"

A distraction, then.

That's what he needs.

I sit beside him, then let myself fall back into the rumpled sheets. They smell deliciously of him. "Well, you were right before. I've been holding myself back my whole life. You constantly push me to free myself. But *you* aren't as free as you think you are—"

He laughs abruptly, a cold, hard sound.

I carry on, regardless. "You're *sexually* liberated, yes. But I've never met anyone so emotionally shackled before. You'll run a full-length marathon before you let yourself experience an emotion. So I took that from you. I picked up that gun, and I made you *feel* something."

He stares at me, eyes narrowed into slits, the adrenaline of what he nearly just did all gone now. "What, you think that just because you successfully scared the shit out of me, I'm suddenly fixed and I'm gonna fall in love with you now or something?"

That earns him a cold laugh in return. "Oh, no, Zeth. You don't have to worry on that front."

"And how's that?"

"I'm a game to you. An experiment. A broken toy to play with until you achieve whatever you're hoping to accomplish, at which point I'm assuming I'll no longer be of use to you and you'll go find someone else to warm your bed."

He twists to look over his shoulder at me. The muscles in his back contort beautifully as he shifts his weight. "There are plenty of girls out there more broken than you, Sloane Romera. And I have no interest in *experimenting* on you."

"Oh, really? Then what the hell are you doing with me?"

"Is this a '*where do you see our relationship heading*' conversation?"

"God, no! *Relationship?*" Even I can hear the bitter edge to my laughter. "We know nothing about each other. You're the guy who shows up on my doorstep and screws me senseless whenever he feels like it. And I'm the girl stupid enough to let you do it." I choke on the words, hating them but knowing they're true. Zeth's expression is blank as solid stone. He stand quickly, pulling on his clothes, and when he looks up at me, the conflict warring in his eyes takes me by surprise.

"I know plenty about you, Sloane. All I *need* to know. If *you* know nothing about *me*, then that's on you and no one else. All you've ever gotta do is ask. And you're not the girl stupid enough to *let* me do anything. You're the girl stupid enough to not see what's standing right in front of her."

He snatches up his shoes and he doesn't even sit down to put them on. He takes them and storms out, closing the door softly behind him. It would have been better if he'd slammed the door. At least then, I'd know he wasn't working so hard to stay calm.

What... on *earth*?

What *was* that? Was he... was he actually *hurt*?

Did he actually just admit that he thinks we are in a relationship? That he *wants* to be in a relationship? No. That can't be true. The man won't even let me *kiss* him, for fuck's sake. I—

URGH!

I slump back into the bed, body sore from our earlier

activities. But my *heart* is sore now, too. Because he's right. I *am* the girl too stupid to see what's standing right in front of her. I'm too stupid to understand *any* of it. Zeth is emotionally stunted—there's no doubting that—but it turns out I am, too. How is it that a man like *him*, a man forged over a lifetime into a weapon of mass destruction, has seen more in us than *I* have?

50

SLOANE

THE SKY LOOKS LIKE A PHOTO I SAW once in *NATIONAL Geographic*. Without the light pollution from the city, the stars are spilled diamonds on black velvet, pinwheeling across the night with a blatant disregard for how suddenly *unsafe* human existence seems. My breath fogs on the desert night air, and for a second it's as though I can feel the earth spinning beneath my feet. Like I'm a tiny speck of sand balanced on the tautly stretched drum skin, and I could go flying off into space at any moment. I am small and meaningless against the vastness of that sky, and yet I'm paralyzed by its beauty. I haven't spent time in the desert since I was a child, camping with my parents, too young to appreciate the experience. What I wouldn't give to stare up at the sky a little longer now... but I can't.

"Come on. Move it."

Clark shoves me in the small of my back with the butt of his gun. I've known the man for all of five seconds and I can safely say that I do *not* like him. I'm glad it's him taking me across to the girls' building in the compound and not Anton, though. The guard at the gate was beaten within an inch of his life technically because of me, so I doubt he's be harboring any affection toward me. Rumor has it his arm is broken and he can't even walk, anyway. If luck works in our favor, we'll be in an entirely different state by the time Anton can walk again. Zeth, Alexis, and I—all three of us, long gone. God, *Alexis*. My heart hiccups when I think about seeing her again. It's about to happen, and I'm unprepared. She's going to freak out when she sees me. I hope she keeps it together long enough to rein in her surprise and not blow my cover. There's a lot riding on this first meeting. If anyone notices tension between us, or the fact that I look an *awful* lot like my sister, then who knows what they'll do.

Clark gives me another firm shove of "encouragement," and I respond. The girls' house is a large, two-story Spanish-style building with a wraparound porch. It looks pleasant. The sort of place a family would vacation, perhaps. Nothing about it screams *den of iniquity*, that's for sure. From the desert flowers and succulents growing in blue pots on the steps, to the clean and tidy entrance porch, this place is evidently maintained by a woman's hand.

The ground floor is lit up, blaring soft light out into the darkness. Inside, the chatter and laughter of female voices can be heard. I hesitate. What the hell am I doing? I can't go in there. What if she's sick or something? What if they've beaten her? What if they've given them all drugs to keep them compliant, and my sister's now a junkie with track marks up her arms? I've seen it all before. I don't need to imagine how easy it would be. God, I *can't* go in there. I—

"I got food waiting for me back indoors, woman. You done staring at the front door or what?" Clark spits on the ground, jerking his head toward the front door.

Indecision tears at me. But it isn't really indecision. It's cowardice. I'm afraid of the condition I might find my sister in. And I'm afraid I won't be able to fix whatever they've done to her. She's alive, though. I need to hold on to that. Whatever else happens, she's still drawing breath, and she *needs* me.

"All right, all right. I'm going."

I walk up the steps and go inside.

51

SLOANE

"WHO WANTS *TEQUILA*, ASSHOLES?"

Since Alaska invited me to this thing, I've been imagining a gaggle of women reluctantly beautifying each other like sad geishas, so that a horde of unwashed men can take their fill of them. The scene that greets me inside the girls' building is about as far from that as you can get. It's more like a sorority party.

"Shots! Shots! Shots!" A group of girls is gathered around a marble island in a very expensive-looking kitchen, clapping like idiots as a brunette girl with her hair in rollers free-pours Patron into shot glasses like her other job is bartender at Coyote fucking Ugly.

"Who's got the lime?" she shouts, casting heavily

mascaraed eyes around the group. She sees me—I know she does—but her gaze passes straight over me like I don't exist. "C'mon, girls. Line 'em up! Line 'em up!"

The girls—there are seven of them—lick salt from their wrists, down the shots, pinch wedges of lime into their mouths, then start giggling all over again.

"So you decided to grace us with your presence after all, then?" The cool voice comes from behind me: Alaska. She stalks into the room with a glass of red wine carelessly cupped in her hand. She's wearing more clothes than the other girls—a tight black dress that barely covers her ass and shows off an awful lot of cleavage. The other women are all in booty shorts and tanks, like they're having a freaking sleepover. So far, none of them have turned out to be my sister.

"Yeah, well, you said to come, right?" I've never felt so out of place. The girl who poured the shots may have ignored me a moment ago, but it seems Alaska's presence has electrified the group, and now everyone is suddenly interested in the stranger who's invading their space.

Alaska sniffs, looking down her nose at my jeans and T-shirt as she sips delicately from her wine. "I did. But then, I assumed you'd be too busy with Zee to grace *us* with your presence."

Seven pairs of ears perk up at this comment. One

girl—a short blonde with innocent blue eyes and not-so-innocent fake tits—squeaks like a mouse. She hurries over, clasping her hands and bouncing on the balls of her feet. "Did you just say Zee? Like, as in *Zeth*?"

She looks starstruck. Like the grumpy bastard who stormed out on me earlier is some kind of rock god who she'll do anything, just *anything* to meet. Alaska raises narrow eyebrows in a bored fashion. She takes another sip of her red. "Yes. Like, as in *Zeth*." She mimics the girls broad Cali accent, but the blonde is too excited to notice.

Alaska doesn't seem impressed by Zeth's presence at all. The other girls all exchange excited glances, though. One of them even grabs hold of another girl's arm, apparently unable to contain herself.

What. The. Hell?

A cold realization washes through me, chilling me to the bone. Oh, God. He's been here before. He and Jacob know each other well. I showed up halfway through one of Zeth's own *"events."* How did I not consider this? He's probably slept with some of the girls here. Hell, he could have slept with *all* of them.

As reactions go, I'm not proud of the way I handle this thought. Once the dizziness and the mouth sweats calm down and I know I'm *not* going to throw up, I smile weakly at the blond woman who's just spoken to me.

"I'm sorry, what?"

"I asked if he's coming here tonight? I want to get a look at him. Georgia says he's fucking massive!"

"Uh…"

Another girl with brunette ringlets steps into the conversation. "I heard that he's got gnarly face tattoos. Is that true?"

I inch backward, trying to put a little space between me and the other women. They're approaching as a pack now. A hungry one. "No, why the hell would he have—"

"And what about his dick? You came here with him, right? You're his girl. You must have seen it. How big is he? I heard he fucked a girl so hard that he put her in the hospital. Split her right open or something."

"No, dude. That was *Rebel*." The girl with the rollers joins the debate, correcting the other girl's wild statement. "Zeth's the one who let that homeless girl move in with him, remember? Benji told us."

The bouncy blonde widens her eyes at me. "Ooooh, you were homeless? What was that like?"

"Uh, I wasn't ho—"

"But you *do* live with him, right?"

Alaska casually puts her wineglass down and clears her throat. All talking in the room ceases. With a dismissive clap of her hands, she takes control of matters. "Naomi wasn't homeless. She does *not* live with Zeth.

Zeth *is* massive. His dick *is* pretty fucking big, but not the biggest dick in the world. And now it's time for you all to shut the hell up." She looks sideways at me through partially narrowed eyes, not even trying to hide her displeasure. "Regardless of what you have heard about Zee, he's brought Naomi here as his partner, not as his blind."

A chorus of unhappy gasps go around the room. They all seem horrified by this information, and I'm standing here gaping like an idiot because I don't even know what it means. "His *blind*?"

Alaska rolls her eyes. "Like in poker. In order to play, you have to bring something to the table. You have to buy your way into the game with a bet. A blind. We're all blinds here, sweetheart. We get passed around like delicious little canapés, so our masters can enjoy the gifts brought along by the other guests."

"But...I'm Zeth's partner, so I *won't* be passed around?"

The girls hear the anxious note in my voice, and they don't take it well. "Trust me, honey. You're the one who's losing out," Rollers says. "We make ten grand a pop on a night like tomorrow. What do you get? Five hundred if you're lucky. I bet Zeth Mayfair's not dropping serious coin on one skinny bitch."

"Zeth isn't paying me *anything*."

That stuns them all into silence. They look at each

other, engaging in a silent conversation that I'm not party to. Alaska shoots me a smug smile, collecting her glass again and tipping it in my direction. "And didn't I tell you not to be an asshole to them?" She laughs at this, and then turns and leaves, singing under her breath.

It takes forever for the girls to get over the idea that I'm not a sex worker. It takes even longer for them to forgive me for my disgusted tone when I'd told them that Zeth didn't pay me for my services. It's only after the tequila starts flowing again that I convince any of them to talk to me, and that's only by participating in three generously poured shots and whooping like a moron whenever they do. I skipped this part of college for a reason. I'm no good at being a girlie girl, and it shows. It makes other girls nervous. Especially ones who paint each other's toenails and squeeze each other's boobs to check out their "work." Rollers, whose real name is Dani, gets a good handful of mine before I realize what the hell is going on.

"Hmmm. Real, huh? They're nice. Good size. Not too small, although your silhouette would look much better if you went up a couple sizes."

"Yeah, I didn't look right in my clothes before I got these," Sara, the girl who asked about Zeth first, says, cupping her giant double Fs. They're the biggest boobs I've ever seen. I'm half tempted to tell her that she probably wasn't dressing for her body type, but I bite my tongue. That wouldn't go down well. And besides, I'm not here to talk about plastic surgery or how to dress. I'm here to find out where Alexis is.

The grooming part of the night begins after the fourth shot of tequila. Cosmetic kits come out, as big as workmen's tool kits and just as heavy, and the girls begin to fuss over each other, giving advice on skin care and practicing the makeup they plan on wearing tomorrow night. The event has been a secondary consideration, tucked away at the back of my mind, but now it comes roaring to the forefront. An event. Like the one Zeth held. But this time, there won't be any dark rooms to hide in. I'm going to have to participate, out in the open... and I'm going to have to make it look convincing, for both my and Zeth's sakes.

Future Sloane can worry about that, though. I have to focus on the task at hand. I start with general questions, waiting for an in to discuss other matters.

"So, is it just you guys who live here? The place seems really big for just seven of you."

"Oh no, there's usually ten of us altogether," Sara says. "Kady's gone into the city to get a nose job. Jacob paid for that. Can you believe it? He said it was putting people off and no one was gonna fuck her if she had a hooked old-man nose. He shelled out for the whole thing. The surgeon. The hotel. Expenses. Everything." She sounds jealous. I'm getting the feeling Sara had to fund her boob job personally. "Anyway, one of the other girls, Chloe, went with her to keep her company. And Sophia's the other girl. She's gone to meet with one of the groups of guys who are coming here tomorrow. She'll be back tomorrow afternoon, I guess. Chloe and Kady, too, although Kady won't be working. She's gonna have two black eyes, I bet. Can you imagine how bad she's—"

Sara keeps talking, talking, talking, not even pausing for breath, and I run through this new information in my mind. Chloe, Kady and Sophia. No Alexis. But then again, I *know* she's here. Zeth told me Michael took pictures of her before he got caught, so they must have changed her name or something. She's not Kady, that's for sure. Alexis is even more fine-boned than I am. No one would ever accuse her of having a hooked old-man nose. That leaves Chloe and Sophia. My heart sinks when I realize I'm not going to see Alexis until tomorrow night now.

And what if I can't even speak to her properly then? What if we're surrounded by people all night long and the opportunity doesn't present itself? I'll just have to make it happen. Come hell or high water, I *am* getting my sister out of there.

52

ZETH

"WHY THE HELL DIDN'T YOU TELL ME you were Rebel's cousin?"

Michael's out of his dirty, blood-stained clothing and back in a well-tailored suit, the way I'm used to seeing him. I've thought about laying the motherfucker out for keeping something so huge from me, but it's wasted energy. He has a right to keep shit like that under lock and key. And making him bleed would only mean he'd have to go get changed again.

"Not my call, Zee. I'd have told you way back when, but Rebel doesn't want people knowing about family, y'know? Thinks it's a weakness to have people out there worth kidnapping and torturing. Bad for business. Especially if you're in the kind of business he's in. He has enemies. Scary ones."

I grunt, knocking back my beer. "Makes sense. Still…"

"Yeah, I know. I know. I could have trusted you with it. I *should* have."

Michael knows Rebel bid to fuck Sloane in that hotel room. He also knows how I feel about sick motherfuckers who kidnap girls and rape them against their will. I'm quiet about most things, but this is perhaps the one thing I *have* been vocal about. Maybe he thought I would have judged him for his blood.

"You heard from him since Jacob's call, then?" I ask.

Michael nods, collecting a beer from the ice bucket by the pool and sitting down to join me. "That's why I came to see you. He's coming here."

I point to the floor at my feet. "Here? Rebel's coming *here?* Why?"

"For the event? To fuck with Jacob? To screw some girls? I don't know. He just told me to expect him."

This is fantastic news. Fan. Fucking. *Tastic.* At once, a parade of problems present themselves, giving me an instant headache. Will he recognize Sloane? Eli, the PI I killed, must have shown him photos for him to have bid so fucking high on a night with her. Will he behave himself? Will he do something that my temper will not fucking tolerate?

Alongside all of that, small advantages present themselves, too, though. If Rebel *is* here, Jacob's gonna be on his best fucking behavior. He's gonna be distracted, trying to shove his nose so far up Rebel's ass that he won't be paying attention to me. Or Sloane. Or one of his girls being snuck out of the place. Plus… I've never met Rebel. I've only heard his name spoken among the bike gangs and the cartels, whispered like the man's a fucking god or something. This is a prime opportunity to meet the guy and see what he's like for myself. To put a face to the name. And commit it to memory for later so I can beat him to death, should the need arise.

"You listening to me, man?" Michael's already downed his beer and is holding out a fresh one to me, too. "I thought you were leaving Lace with the doctor? Where is she?"

"Oh. With Sloane's parents." I pull on my fresh beer, mulling that one over. The whole thing is kind of ironic. And worrying.

"Aren't they super religious?"

"Yeah. Her dad's a minister. Doesn't get more religious than that."

Michael smiles politely, although I can tell the fucker's grinning on the inside. "And do they know about Lacey's girl-on-girl tendencies? Or the fact that she's dead set on killing herself at the earliest available opportunity?"

That last comment sparks panic in me. Lacey may have taken to playing with the odd girl here and there, but she isn't gay. Wouldn't matter to me if she was, mind you. And I get it. Eating pussy's addictive. But Lacey's only been toying with the fairer sex of late because she's afraid. Afraid of *guys*. Women are softer. Kinder. There'll come a time when Lace'll go back to fucking men, I think. No, my panic has everything to do with the other thing. The *dying* thing. Sloane may have told her parents to watch Lace like a hawk, but they don't have the first clue how messed up the girl is. They don't *know* her like I do. She's committed to this course of action. I need to speak to Sloane. Scratch that. I need to speak to Sloane's fucking *dad*. If she dies on his watch...

Michael brings me back from thoughts of murder. "Does Sloane have a problem with Lacey?"

What a weird fucking question. My beer bottle only makes it halfway to my lips. "What? No. Why would she?"

This has Michael chuckling, shaking his head. "You're so clueless. You're fucking Sloane, yet you're so protective over Lacey. The doc's gonna assume you're fucking her, too. Or that you *used* to fuck her."

I love Michael like a brother, but sometimes he's a stupid shit. "Sloane doesn't care about my exes. She probably wouldn't care if I *was* fucking Lacey. She's not that kind of girl. All she cares about is finding her sister. I'm a means to an end."

Michael looks at me like I'm the stupid shit. "Seriously?"

"Yeah. Well, she's not asked me for anything." And they all ask me for something. A phone number. A second date. A marriage proposal. Meanwhile, Sloane has repeatedly asked for me to get the hell out of her life.

Michael reaches over and slaps me on the back. He looks oddly bemused. "If you believe that, my dear friend, you're the dumbest motherfucker alive."

53

ZETH

I HAVEN'T FOUND ANYWHERE ELSE TO sleep. I really, really should, but I haven't. I'm waiting for her when she comes back from her pajama party with Jacob's girls. Her eyes grow round when she sees me sitting at the small table by the window, cleaning the Desert Eagle.

"What are you doing here?" she asks. She's wearing some of the heaviest makeup I've ever seen. She's got that smoky look thing going on with her eyes, which makes them pop like crazy.

"Same thing you've been doing, I presume? Preparing for tomorrow night."

"You're bringing the gun?"

"Fuck yeah. And whatever else I can use to kill a man."

"Ahh, well, Jacob better watch his silverware, then."

"The silverware's safe. I'll use my bare hands if things get that bad."

A flash of concern transforms Sloane's face. "Are you *expecting* it to get that bad?"

"No. Maybe." I snap the action of the gun home. "Better to be safe than sorry. Did you see your sister?" This is a dangerous question. I can't tell by looking at her what's gone down at the other house. I'm assuming if it had gone badly, she'd be bawling her eyes out, but with Sloane you never know. She's far more complex than other women. Far more intelligent. And far more fucking confusing.

Sloane comes and sits at the table opposite me. The cloud of perfume that follows her is enough to make my eyes water. No surprises there, though. Jacob's girls are heavy handed with everything. Makeup, tans, tits, the whole nine yards.

"She wasn't there," Sloane informs me. "She'll be back tomorrow afternoon, in time for the party."

"Oh." That's not great, but not terrible either. Our plan will still work. Sloane looks troubled, though. "What's up?"

She runs her thumb across her lower lip, staring at me. I'm about to tell her she's making me really fucking uncomfortable, when I realize no girl has *ever* made me feel fucking uncomfortable. I'm damned if I'm gonna admit something like that to her.

"I've been thinking about something. And I don't want you to get mad."

Well, that is a fucking promising opening to a conversation. I sit back in the chair, putting the gun down on the table. She glances at it, and then takes a deep breath. "I want to know if you're clean."

"Wha—if I'm *clean*?"

"Yeah." She shifts uncomfortably. "Y'know. We've had a unprotected sex, and I want to know that you've not given me some disgusting, life-threatening disease. You've slept with all these women, and—"

"Whoa, what the *fuck*?" I'm replaying the last words to come out of her mouth, trying to process them. "I've slept with all *what* women?"

Small knots of muscle jump in her jaw as she clenches down. I've made her angry, but then so fucking what? She's made me angry, too. Her eyes are blazing when she says, "I thought you were always honest with me. You can't tell me you haven't slept with sex workers before."

"I *have* slept with a lot of women, Sloane. But I've never *paid* for sex." She lets out a snort that says she doesn't believe me. "I have nothing against it, Sloane. It's an honest fucking trade. Paying for sex is *not* something that attracts me, though. *At all.* Everyone I've ever slept with has done so because they wanted to. Yourself included."

My temperature's on the rise, but so is Sloane's. Her cheeks have turned a bright red. "Oh, really? So I lost my virginity in a hotel room in the dark to a complete fucking stranger because I *wanted* to?"

"You—" I bite back what I really want to say. Fuck! That *night*. It's gonna haunt us for the rest of fucking time. "I bid on you to save you from someone who would have *really* fucked you up. And Eli told me you were experienced. He told me you were into kink. I thought I was doing you a *favor*, Sloane. I hate that I took your fucking virginity, I really fucking do. I'm sorry for that at least. But I did *not* force you, and I did *not* pay you."

"No. But *Eli* was supposed to pay me, wasn't he? He was supposed to tell me where my sister was. *That* was the payment, but then *you* killed him before he could do it. So you're right. I guess I *wasn't* compensated for bleeding for you."

She jumps up from the table, shaking with rage, and I follow suit, taking hold of her arm. She spins and slaps me. I let her have this one. I deserve it. I probably deserve a whole lot more from her. I embrace the sting, waiting. Has she got more in her? Doesn't look like it. She just stands there, shaking.

"I'd have found Alexis a lot sooner if *you* hadn't interfered, Zeth," she hisses.

"Wh—wait. You're blaming *me* for the fact at she's been stuck here all this time? You wouldn't have found her. Eli didn't have any information to *give* you, Sloane."

"Bullshit! I went into that office. I found him sitting there with a goddamn letter opener sticking out of his chest. I found the file he had on Alexis! It was right there, in his filing cabinet. Except *you'd* taken all of the information out of it, hadn't you!! Why? Why did you *do* that?"

I'm trying my best here, but she is *not* making this easy. They taught anger management techniques in Chino, but I was too pissed off to pay attention. Fuck it. She wants to rehash this? Let's go.

"That file didn't contain a single thing about Alexis, Sloane. It was all you. Eli had all your personal details in there. He had photos of you at work, in your car. At *home*." I wait, letting that hang in the air a second, so she can fully comprehend the implications of the information.

"*Me?* What do you mean, photos of me at home?"

"I mean photos of you in the shower, in bed, walking around naked. He had video files of you fucking *touching* yourself, Sloane."

"What?"

"I went there to get everything he had on Alexis, but he just laughed. Said he'd tricked you. That he'd heard on the grapevine a dark-haired girl had been taken by bikers, and she was working for them now, but that was it. And he wasn't even gonna tell you that much. He was gonna feed you some shitty line that would end up being a dead-end lead, and you would have had to go back to him again for more information. And guess fucking what? You would have had to fuck *three* guys to get *that* fake piece of info. And on and on it would have gone. Around and around we go. And then I saw the other files on the other girls he had in his office. Did you bother looking at those?"

"Yes! I—" She stops, though. All her fury is gone. She stares at the floor, tears trembling on the tips of her eyelashes, while her brain works overtime. "I saw them. I looked through a few. They were all…" She swallows hard. "They were all normal. Regular cases. Adulterers and broken bail bonds."

It's my turn to shake my head now. "No, you didn't see the files. because I took them, too. I took *all* of them. He was doing the same thing to at least twelve other women, pulling their strings, puppeting every one of them. I destroyed the photos, the thumb drives, the discs, everything. And you're right, I *did* kill Eli. I killed him because he stabbed me first. Here. You want fucking proof?" I tear my shirt over my head, twisting so she can see the two inches of scar tissue where Eli Horowitz stuck me in the side with his stupid fucking letter opener. I mean, what kind of PI doesn't have a proper fucking knife? Or a *gun*, come to think of it?

"Zeth..." She shakes as her fingers hover over the scar, but she doesn't touch me. *Ohhh*, no, no, no, this isn't what she wants to hear. She pulls her hand back, shaking her head. "You had those scars before. In the hotel. I felt them."

"I had *these* scars." I point to the three jagged marks across my torso—some of my many souvenirs from Chino. "But *this* was after I saw you at the hotel."

"Oh my God." She backs away, as if the truth won't find her on the other side of the fucking room. When she backs into the bed, she sits down heavily on the mattress, shaking her head. "I had no idea." She covers her mouth, breathing noisily through her fingers.

"And in response to your earlier question, Sloane, I *am* clean. I've only ever slept with you without using protection. I figured it was safe, since I'm the only guy you've been with. But still. I needed a good STD accusation to really round off this super shitty day. So fuck you very much."

If I could, I'd storm out and tear the goddamn door off its hinges as I went. I've been bailing a lot recently, though, and we can't afford to keep yelling at each other here. Jacob's patience is paper-thin already.

He'll gladly kill me if we keep disturbing the peace. Instead, I turn my back on her, pressing the heels of my palms into my eye sockets, and take a breath. It would be so unwise to go to war with her, but *fuck*, am I armed and ready. She—

Her hand rests lightly on my back. I didn't hear her coming. "Why did you do all of that?"

"Which *part*?" I snap.

"All of it. Why intervene in the first place? How did you know Eli was...was *selling* me?"

It's easier to answer these questions with my back to her. Eas*ier* but not *easy*. "My uncle, Carl." That's how a lot of stories in my life have begun. With *him*. "When my parents died, Carl took me in. He was a piece of shit. Used to beat me. He wasn't *all* bad, though. He'd wait long enough for me to heal from the last one before laying into me again. And he hardly ever broke bones. *That* was a small mercy, I guess. Things got real bad when I was about eight. He started drinking more. Whatever. So I learned how to distance myself from it all. Carl was an open wound that wouldn't fucking heal. I didn't want whatever *he* had infecting *me*, so I shut it down. All of it. Until nothing he did affected me anymore.

"Anyway. The fucker was murdered three years ago. Someone cut him up real fucking good. I had to go to the hospital to ID him, and that's when I saw you. You were waiting for an elevator. I was just sitting there, soaking it all in. That he was dead. That I wouldn't ever have to think about him anymore. And you... I took one look at you, and I saw that we were the same. Shut down. Closed off. You were walking around, acting and sounding just like everyone else, but you weren't. You'd retreated inside. And I..." God damn it, this fucking sucks. Every word is a razor blade, flaying my throat as I speak it into existence. Now's about the time I'd normally try to put my fist through a wall. The pain won't temper the chaos this time, though.

Again, something warm touches my back. and I exhale shakily, looking up at the ceiling. It's her lips. She's *kissing* me, and it feels so fucking good. She freezes, as though waiting for me to walk away. When I don't, she steps into me, her chest flush with my back, and hugs me from behind.

Shit, fuck, motherfucking *bastard*. Can this get any more difficult? I grind my teeth, taking a beat until I'm ready to continue. "And... I needed to know what had hurt you so bad, Sloane. So I made up my mind to find out. Didn't take long. And then Michael followed you when you went to see Eli that first time. And now here we are."

This *is* going to scare the shit out of her. And it *should*. I fucking watched her like a psychopath and had Michael follow her. I brace for the fireworks, but Sloane just leans her forehead against my back, her shallow, warm breath fanning across my skin.

Nothing?

Seriously?

The only person who knows anything about this is Michael, and he only got the raw instructions: Follow the girl. Find out what she's doing. Don't let her see you. That kind of thing. I never told him why, and he never asked.

Eventually, Sloane stops breathing, like she's concentrating very hard. And then…

"How? How can you be so good and so dangerous at the same time, Zeth? You're a contradiction."

Laughter boils up and out of my throat before I can stop it. "There's nothing *good* about me. I watched you. I followed you. I worked out what made you tick. I made plans to infiltrate your life and manipulate you just like Eli did. I'm no better than he was."

Her forehead rolls left to right as she shakes her head. "You are. You're better than you think. You outbid someone because you were worried he'd hurt me. You emptied all of those files. Protected all those women—"

"You're projecting what you *want*—"

"Why don't you want to admit it? You *can't*, can you? Not even to yourself."

There are a lot of things I can't admit to myself. A *lot*. But being good isn't one of them. I know what kind of man I am. I see the monster staring back at me when look in the mirror. "Just don't get your hopes up, Sloane. I'm not waiting to be redeemed. There's nothing here for you to try and fix."

Women never want to hear the truth. They always think they can change you. Iron out the creases in your screwed-up life. Waltz in and light you up so brilliantly that they chase away the shadows.

But ever so quietly, Sloane whispers, "I don't want to fix you. But… I would like to try and *understand* you."

Fuck, she's going to need a crystal ball if she wants to accomplish that. *I* don't even understand me. This is awkward as hell. I try not to feel her heat behind me. I close my eyes and try not to feel *healed* because it.

"Zeth?"

"Mm?"

"I need you to do something for me."

Oh, here we go. The needing part. *I* need a stiff drink. "What?"

"Turn around and put your arms around me."

The thing about Sloane is, she never says what I think she's going to say. She wants me to hold her, but holding someone in your arms, the way she's holding me? That isn't about sex. That's about something else, and I'm not sure I have it to give. I implied the exact opposite this morning. I know how it sounded. *You're the girl who's too blind to see what's standing right in front of her.* Well, she's throwing it right back at me now, isn't she? She's telling me she does see, and she *wants* it. I should have listened to the voice in my head hissing at me shut up and done precisely that.

I reel off every curse word I can think of, and Sloane patiently waits.

She doesn't panic.

Doesn't run.

She's braver than I give her credit for. Far braver than *me*. So I turn, and I put my arms around her, and I hold her.

54

SLOANE

ZETH SLEEPS THE FLOOR, ON THE OTHER side of the room, about as far away from me as he can get. I know he's unconscious from the slow pull and draw of his breathing, deep and regular. I, on the other hand, cannot sleep. Tonight didn't pan out the way I expected it to. I saw a side of Zeth that terrified me. He also made me feel like an asshole for holding him accountable for Alexis's time here at the Talons compound. To be honest, I hadn't realized that I was blaming him. Not until I went and hung out with those girls.

After some initial awkwardness, they were sweet and seemed happy, but their lives aren't what I pictured for Alexis. She wanted to study psychology. She wanted to create beautiful art for people. Instead, she's probably been drinking herself into oblivion just so she can forget what happens to her body afterward. God, why did I think that? The idea of it makes me feel sick. I need a coffee. I need Pip. I need the safe little bubble I've created for myself back in Seattle, but there *is* no bubble anymore. It's well and truly popped, and I'll probably wind up dead if I go back there now. I have no idea when I'll even be able to go home. Or *if*.

I pull out my cell phone from underneath my pillow, needing to do something. I automatically head to the messages app and hit compose.

Me:
You awake? I need a mental assessment.

A few moments later:

Pippa:
Yeah. As if I would EVER be asleep at 2 a.m. What's up? Your vacation not as relaxing as you imagined? Book a massage with a hot guy. That'll fix everything.

I hate that I've lied to Pippa about my sudden disappearance, but she would have a fit if she knew where I really was. And who I was with. And what I was planning on doing. All of it, basically. The whole arrangement would make her head explode.

Me:
A massage! Yes! Totally planning on one of those. But as for relaxing...

Pippa:
Yeah, yeah. I know why you can't sleep. And you know I don't approve.

Me:
I can't help it.

Pippa:
Find someone else to distract you. Flirt with a Hawaiian surfer.

Me:
And if I don't want a Hawaiian surfer?

I can't type the next part. To actually admit it to myself. *What if I only want* him?

Pippa:
Then we're all doomed.

Pippa:
Look, don't worry. In the end, as much as I don't like it, I'll support you no matter what. But he doesn't deserve you, Sloane. He is no good for you. That's it. I won't say it again. Just try and get some sleep, okay?

I spend the next half an hour clutching my phone, wondering if she's right. Am I doomed if I go down this path? He said it himself. There's no fixing him. And if he hadn't told me about Eli and his plans for me, would I be feeling this way right now? Would I still want to get out of this bed and go and curl up next to him on the floor? God, why can't I just even be honest with myself? Yes, I would want that. I *would*. I've wanted to be that way with him for a while now. And now that things are a little clearer…

Hah! The ridiculousness of that thought catches me off guard. Yeah, things are as clear as mud.

I tuck myself into a ball, hugging my knees to my chest. I need sleep. Pippa's right about that. I close my eyes and try to *make* myself pass out, but it's no good. Especially when the bed begins to shake. The sound starts as a rumble, out in the desert. It grows quickly, louder, deeper, more resonant. *Thunder?*

"Open the gate!"

"Fucking *move*, dumbass! They're *here!*"

Outside, shouts echo into the night. I climb out of bed, pushing the blinds down, and find that the window pane is buzzing in the frame, distorting the view.

I see enough, though.

Motorbikes.

Scores of them stream through the open gate into the compound, so many of them that I lose count. The sleek black machines snarl like mad animals as the sound of raucous laughter fills the courtyard. Jesus Christ. My pulse pounds like a drum beneath my skin.

"Rebel. That's his crew." The timbre of Zeth's voice is as deep and menacing as the bikes' engines. He watches me from his makeshift bed on the floor, his chest bathed in the bright white light from the bikes' headlights cutting through the window.

"Who's Rebel?"

Zeth closes his eyes. "Someone very bad. Someone you do not want to know."

55

ZETH

SO MUCH FOR BEING CAREFUL AND SET-ting myself up on the floor. I shouldn't have bothered. My thoughts keep me awake, hurling endless possibilities at me as dawn incrementally lightens the bedroom. Eventually, I abandon the idea of sleep and get up, leaving the bedroom quietly and heading outside.

It's hot as fuck during the day, but at night, the desert is frigid. My breath clouds in great plumes as I take a quick walk. The line of bikes propped up alongside the villa is worrying. I count them off, one through eleven. *Eleven* fucking Widow Makers. I'd banked on a lot of things, but Rebel showing up with his boys never made it onto my list of inconvenient shit that might go down while I was here. The Widow Makers are based out of New Mexico. Rebel must have set off as soon as he'd ended that phone call with Jacob yesterday. They rode all day and halfway through the night until they got here. Not a good sign. Thirteen hours with your balls crushed up against a gas tank is gonna make anyone cranky. And from what I've heard about Rebel, he gets cranky easy.

But, then again, so do I.

Back in the room, Sloane's still asleep. Her hair looks like a bird's been nesting in it, and there are weird crease marks on her cheek from the pillow. She's fucking beautiful. I feel like a spare part standing there staring at her, so I stomp around the room, making enough noise to wake the dead.

"Zeth?"

I pause my task, letting the duvet drop back to the floor, and there she is, half sitting up and blinking at me through huge, sleepy owl eyes. "Sorry. I didn't mean to wake you." *Yeah, I totally meant to fucking wake you.* "But since you're up, we need to talk about tonight." Tonight. Jacob and Rebel, two big dogs, trapped in a small building with a bunch of other criminals, all of whom are up to no good. And then me and her in the middle of it all. Yeah, I'm a sick motherfucker. Why? Because there's a good chance Jacob's gonna murder my ass. And an equally good chance that Rebel will recognize Sloane. And yet my dick is still getting hard when I think about taking Sloane to this event.

"Yeah? What's the plan?"

"The plan is that you get your ass dressed and come for some breakfast. No one's gonna be up yet. We can talk and eat." My stomach's complaining like it thinks my throat's been cut. I need sustenance, and I need to leave this room before I forget all common sense and climb up in that bed with Sloane.

She pats her head and must get a sense of what's going on with her hair. Her eyes widen, but she just shrugs. I love that about her. She doesn't give a fuck about her appearance.

"Okay," she says, climbing out of bed. She's wearing a long T-shirt and panties, and the sight of bare skin makes my dick stir in my jeans all over again. Girl's got legs for days. "Will there be coffee?" she asks.

"Hell yes. I'll make sure of it."

56

ZETH

I WAS RIGHT. THE OCCUPANTS OF THE villa are still slumbering as I make my way to the dining area just off the kitchen. Jacob's maids are the only ones up and about, setting up food for the houseguests and undoubtedly preparing finger food for tonight's little show. I grab two cups of coffee, a plate of sliced fruit, and some toasted bagels and set up at a small table in the corner of the room, waiting for Sloane.

She doesn't take long to get ready—another thing I like about her. The last chick I waited on took over an hour to fuck around with her hair and makeup. Sloane only takes fifteen minutes before she comes to find me. If she's wearing any makeup, it isn't much.

Just a little mascara and some lip gloss. Her hair is wet. She looks like she's towel-dried it some, but the wet ends have made dark, see-through patches over her tits where the water has seeped through her shirt. Shit, she looks hot.

"Ohhh, coffee." She groans as she takes a sip, closing her eyes. I wonder if she realizes that's a total porn move. I can't picture her watching much in the way of porn, but who knows. I've been so wrong about her before. Regardless, the situation in my pants worsens as my cock stiffens all over again. I'm fucking *raging* this morning.

"So, what?" she asks. "How is tonight gonna go down?"

"Well." I shift in my seat. Pick up the saltshaker. Put it down again. "There are going to be a lot of people here. We're gonna find Alexis, and then we're gonna get the hell out of here while we can. We're gonna leave your car here and go in mine."

She shakes her head. "That's my dad's car. He'll kill me if I don't take it back."

Sloane's worried about her dad's Oldsmobile, and we're surrounded by unhinged sociopaths? Nice. "I'll give you a thousand dollars if that car can get up to sixty," I say.

"Oh, it definitely can't."

"Right. Plus it has wood paneling."

"And what does that mean?"

"It means I'm not driving a fucking car with wood paneling is what it means."

She shrugs off the critique, smiling as she sips her coffee. "Well, I suppose Dad will have to be happy to get his daughter back instead then, won't he?" She looks so fucking elated that my stomach clenches. She hasn't even laid eyes on Alexis yet, but she has absolute faith that she's going to be leaving here with her sister tonight. I, on the other hand, have a few doubts.

"Shit'll get nasty real quick if Jacob lays eyes on us. We have to keep to ourselves. Try and be invisible."

She seems entertained by this notion. "It's sweet that you think that's possible. With *you* here. You didn't hear those girls talking last night, though. They're desperate to see you." The tone of her voice turns sour, betraying how she feels about that.

"So that's why you asked if I was riddled with disease last night, then?" Last night is pretty much the last thing I want to talk about, but this is too delicious. "Were you jealous, Sloane? Hm?"

Sloane squirms in her seat, cheeks flushing. "No, I was *not* jealous! I was worried for my own safety!"

Such a liar. Oh, well. Let her pretend if she wants to. "Yeah, well like I said. I don't pay for sex."

"What about Alaska? She doesn't count because she's Jacob's mistress?"

"*Alaska?* Alaska doesn't count because she's a crazy bitch. I've turned that girl down more times than I can count." Sloane raises her coffee mug to her face, but I can see the crinkling at the corners of her eyes. She's smiling. "Why? Did she say I'd fucked her?"

"Oh, she implied it, that's for sure. Some of the girls were speculating over, um..." Her eyes travel south, staring straight through the tabletop, lasering right into my crotch.

"My *dick*? They were talking about my dick?" Oh, this just gets better and better. Sloane's face is a bright shade of red now.

"Alaska said it was big, but she'd had bigger."

"I've never fucked Alaska. She's probably seen my dick, though. And I'm sure she *has* seen bigger. Alaska used to work in porn. The guys who work in that industry are normally way above average."

"Well, I'm sure you *could* work in porn, then." As soon as the words leave her mouth, Sloane starts choking on her coffee. Ahhh, poor woman. She did *not* mean to say that out loud. I bite back the urge to grin.

"Sloane Romera. Did you just compliment my cock?" She wheezes, trying to breathe, but I can't help it. This is just too easy. "I have to say, I'm almost flattered."

"I meant that—ah, forget it. Yes, I did. It's massive. Are you happy? Do you feel validated as a man now?"

She's doing a valiant job of trying to own this, but she's dying of embarrassment. "I'm already validated as a man, Sloane. I feel like a man every time I make you scream. No, fuck that. I feel like a *king* every time I make you scream."

She stops spluttering and rearranging things on the table and just looks at me. It's the look in her eyes that does it. I can't stop myself. There's only so much a guy can take, and having her look at me like that is my limit.

"Stand up, Sloane."

"What?"

"Stand up. Follow me." I get up, abandoning my coffee and my untouched breakfast, holding out my hand. She hesitates for a second before taking it.

"Where are we going?"

We make it as far as the hallway and give up my original plan. We're not going to make it to the bedroom. I duck into the first alcove we pass, lift her up and pin her against the wall, slamming my body up against hers.

"Zeth!"

"Yeah, just like that. My name on your lips—*that's* what makes me feel like a man," I growl. Her wet hair brushes my face as I kiss her neck, her jawline, her collarbone. She tastes fresh and clean and uniquely her. My cock throbs in my pants, so fucking hard. I have to have her. I can't fucking wait.

I rip the T-shirt over her head and immediately bury my face in her cleavage. The. Most. Amazing. Tits. Ever. I pin her with the lower half of my body, her legs wrapped around my waist, and from there, I can then grab hold of those beautiful tits and squeeze. Sloane gasps, her head rocking back to expose more of her neck. I don't have enough fucking hands. I want to be stroking and touching her everywhere.

"Damn it, girl." I huff against her skin, grinding my dick against her. It feels amazing; I want to push harder, to sink myself so deep inside her that she screams. Forget worrying about her waking the house. I want to make her scream loud enough to wake *the dead*.

She's incredible. I take both her tits and push them together so that the pink, tightened nipples stand erect, begging me to play. She makes stifled moaning sounds as I lick at her, sucking each nipple in turn and then biting down just hard enough to make her hiss. Her head kicks forward and a memory come crashing back to me—her kissing me the last time I fucked her like this. How she just leaned forward and smashed her lips against mine, digging her hands in her hair. How it set me on fire. I can tell she's thinking about that kiss, too. It would be the most natural thing in the world to kiss her now. It would be easy. Suddenly my heart is slamming inside my chest, each and every beat chanting, I can't. I can't. I can't. I back off and let her legs slide down, so that her feet are on the floor.

"What's—"

I unbutton her pants before she can finish. She's going to ask what's wrong, and I don't wanna hear it. I don't wanna hear about right and wrong. This whole situation, her and me, none of it qualifies under either heading.

I rip her pants down, smirking a little when she has to put her hands on my shoulders for balance. I'm not gentle. I tear them off her body, taking her dainty little leather ballet flats with them.

She stands in her panties, hands twitching at her sides, trying to decide whether she wants to cover her chest or not. She's all curves and soft lines, slim yet feminine, shy but completely unaware of the sexual energy she exudes.

I have to fuck this girl.

Right fucking now.

"Turn around, Sloane." She gives me a guarded look, but her chest is heaving. She's as turned on as I am. She'll do anything I ask her to right now, and that thought is like kindling to a flame. She shoves away from the wall, turning slowly, giving me a hesitant last glance over her shoulder.

I take one look at her ass in the black lace underwear she's wearing, and I'm done for. Three seconds later, I'm out of my clothes. I run my hands down the toned lines of her back and then cup her ass cheeks, sucking in a sharp breath through my teeth. I can't wait. I can't fucking wait to slam home on that thing. It takes monumental restraint to gently push Sloane forward, so that she's bracing the wall. Perfect. This is exactly what I was going for: Sloane, hands planted against the wall, bent over at the waist, presenting her ass to me. It's the most beautiful thing I've ever seen.

She's trembling with need. I wasn't joking before—I feel like the motherfucking king of the world when I do this to her. I slide my hands over her sides and curve myself over her, reaching to palm her tits. They hang down, heavy and full, so amazing. I feel like a kid in a playground, and her body is my own personal ride. I thrust my hips against her and nearly explode right there and then when she bows her back like a cat and pushes back.

"Fuck, Sloane."

"Fuck *me*," she returns. "Fuck me now. Please. Please..."

Her breathless pleading like music to my ears. She's already wet for me—I can feel it through her panties, already soaking my dick—so I'm not gentle. I can't be. I have zero restraint. I grab hold of those pretty panties and I rip them, not even a little remorseful about the waste. I'll replace them. I'll buy her thousands of dollars' worth of black lace in exchange for this one pair. It's the fairest trade I've ever made. Sloane cries out. I can tell she's trying to stop herself, but she's far from succeeding. I crow like a fucking cockerel in my head over that.

I grab hold of my dick and squeeze, my muscles tightening at the pressure, sending a burning wave of adrenaline around my body. I don't sink myself into her right away, though. I ease my fingers over her soaked pussy and work her clit, working my dick at the same time. With every little stroke and flick of my fingers, Sloane becomes more breathless. It takes her by surprise when I slide my hand back and I use the slick moisture on my fingers to touch her ass. In fact, she nearly jumps out of her skin.

"Trust me, Sloane?" It's a risk, asking for her trust outright. I won't break it, though. Not now. Not with this.

"Uhhh…"

"*Trust* me." I rub my dick against her pussy, causing friction in just the right places, using my fingers to tease and stroke and knead her ass at the same time. She may never have thought she would react this way, but before long she's pushing back against me again. *Enjoying* it. Presenting herself to me, allowing me to apply more pressure every time she rocks her hips.

I push a touch harder this time, inserting my finger

just a little, and Sloane cries out, her body shaking hard against me. "You like that?" Not a throwaway comment—I *need* to know. If I think for one second she's not enjoying it, I'll pull the pin on this immediately.

"Yes. Yeah. Yeah…" Her voice is hazy, as if she's drunk. But she isn't, she's sober, and she's rocking against me like she's asking for more.

I've waited long enough. I take hold of my dick, and I slide it inside her, pushing so hard that my balls clench. I want to be rough with her. I wanna bruise her, leave my fingerprints all over her, but I don't. I gather her hair and wrap it around my fist, jerking on it hard enough that her head pulls back. With it, her body bows again, far enough for me to lean forward and bite her shoulder.

She gasps through the pain. "Oh, *fuck*!"

I pull her head to one side, so that her chin tips back toward me, and there it is: I'm not overstepping any boundaries. Far from it. Sloane's eyes are rolled back in her head, her bruised lips swollen and parted as she pants out my name over and over again each time I force my way inside her. She's so fucking tight, gripping me from the inside like a glove.

I risk applying a little more pressure to the fingers still playing with her ass, and she sighs, pushing back against me.

"Oh my God, Zeth. Yes. Please. Please…"

Yep. That's what I thought. It's game on. I'm not a fucking douchebag, though. I've shown her. I've shown her that she *likes* it.

"Please…"

Shit. Well, I'm not a fucking douchebag, but I'm no saint, either. I thrust my dick into her as deep as I can, and I ease my finger forward at the same time, going slow so that I can stop as soon as she wants me to. Her legs wobble, and I can tell that she's fighting it, but she doesn't tell me to stop. Her panting and whimpering are thanks to pleasure, not pain. I can feel my dick inside her through the wall of her pussy, and it's… it's just… I can't…

I fuck her. I fuck her *hard*. I gauge her reaction and act accordingly. When it looks like she's tilting, when the pleasure is turning to pain, I stop playing with her ass altogether and grab her hips with both hands. With the added leverage, I pound myself into her even harder than before, my blood singing through my veins.

I can tell when she's about to come. She starts to shake, her muscles straining, trying to keep her upright. I don't have a hope in hell of holding back. We come at the same time, and neither of us is quiet. I slowly pump myself in and out of her, catching my breath. I must be a freak, but I take a great and perverse pleasure in rubbing my cum through the slick folds of her pussy and into her asshole.

"Bravo! Bravo!"

Sloane rockets off my dick like someone's just thrown a bucket of ice-cold water over us. In the hallway, leaning up against the wall opposite our alcove, a guy with a torn black T-shirt and ripped black jeans claps, grinning ear to ear. I don't recognize him. He's young. Like, early twenties. And he's a *Widow Maker*. "Good show," he says, still clapping. "Didn't think the fun started 'til tonight. Obviously, I was wrong." Sloane scrambles for her clothes, swearing under her breath—her panic is nowhere near as funny as it was when someone busted her in the toilet. Now, it makes me angry. I turn and angle myself in front of her, blocking her from view.

"Usually polite to announce your presence, asshole," I snarl. Fuck that I'm naked. Fuck that Jacob will be pissed. I'll break this kid's jaw if the next words out of his mouth aren't *I'm sorry*.

Lucky for him they are.

"Sorry, bro. My bad." He's not laughing anymore. He holds his hands up, looking suitably concerned about my reaction. He must have thought I'd be embarrassed, but living in prison takes all that away from you. Your modesty, your humility, everything. "I didn't mean to come up on you like that, man," the kid continues. "But shit, dude. You *were* fucking in a hallway."

We were. But I still think I should hit him. My knuckles are already cracking when Sloane grabs my arm. "It's okay. He's totally right."

She sidles out from behind me, fully dressed now though looking mighty disheveled. Despite her crimson cheeks, she manages to look the kid in the eye. He blanches when he gets a proper look at her. "Holy. Fuck. *Me!* What the...?" He looks like he's seen a ghost.

"Mal, what the hell are you—" An annoyed voice comes from behind us right as another Widow Maker rounds the corner. Black boots, black jeans, black tee, finished off by a leather cut adorned with a VP badge over the top pocket. The guy stops dead in his tracks when he sees me, and this time it's my turn to look like I've seen a ghost. Because he *is* a ghost.

Motherfucking *Cade Preston.*

He stares at me, his own shock rippling across his face before he says, "Zee?" And then, brow furrowed, "Why are you naked?"

I can't think of anything else to say, so I settle for the first thing that comes into my head. "Never mind that. Why the fuck aren't you *dead*?"

57

ZETH

Four Years Ago

Chino

"THIS FOOD TASTES LIKE SHIT, MAN."

"Mm. Yeah, I'd say there's a pretty high ratio of shit to food in here."

"Fuck a high ratio, dude. This stuff all be shit. That brown mushy stuff be dog shit. That bread be horse shit. And that pudding is bird shit, dude, straight up. I seen the wrecking crews scraping that stuff off the roof."

I prod the brown slab of reconstituted meat on my tray with my plastic fork, eyeing it dubiously. Marco sees me do it. He makes a derisive *tchhh* sound through his teeth. "Zee, man, that's the worst shit on there. That's Colossus's own personal brand of shit. He's back there in that kitchen laying tracks all day long. That's why none of us eat the meatloaf, motherfucker."

This is how mealtimes play out every day in prison. We complain about the food, and then we eat it anyway because we have no choice. But meatloaf day is especially bad. Colossus, the huge Russian guy who was convicted of killing his wife and kids, also happens to be the cook, and he delights in burning everything he sends out of the kitchen. His dry meatloaf is disgusting.

The canteen hums with chatter and raucous banter between the inmates, everyone segregated into their appropriate racial stereotypes. It doesn't matter if you're not a neo-Nazi, a gangbanger, a coke dealer, or Mafioso on the outside. Inside walls such as these, your heritage is your creed. The system is based on hate. The Black gangs hate the white gangs. The Italian gangs hate the Mexican gangs and the Black gangs. The Mexican gangs hate the white gangs, and the white gangs hate everybody, including other white gangs if they piss each other off.

Cast adrift in the middle of this sea of hatred, I

sit at a table with Marco, who just so happens to be Black, and Leroy, who just so happens to be Mexican. There's an empty chair next to Leroy, awaiting the fourth member of our group: Cade. Cade's white like me, but neither of us is "white" (read: evil) enough to join the Klu.

They call the four of us the UN—a term that even the guards find funny. We're outcasts. We eat together, shit together, shower together, run the yard together. The only time we're not watching each other's backs is at lockup, when it's just us and the guy we bunk with. Our cellmates know better than to go toe-to-toe with any of us at close quarters, though.

"Where's your boy?" Leroy hacks at his food with the side of his fork. You get good at that when the only tool you're given to cut through Colossus's food is a blunt plastic fork.

Marco chews, open-mouthed, fork hanging loosely from his hand. "Dunno. He's out, though. Hadley saw him in with the nurse an hour ago."

This is news. News that makes no sense. "The nurse? Why?"

"He got busted up talking back to one of the guards on his way outta the SHU. They were gonna throw his ass straight back in there, I think, but they done needed the cell for Barteaux. Crazy motherfucker shivved himself again."

Usually, you worry about by other people shivving you in prison. Not Barteaux. "That is the third time he's done that."

"I know, man." Leroy laughs. "Dude reckons he's gonna get his ass transferred outta here if the administration thinks he's being targeted. Someone really oughta tell the guy not to keep stabbing himself in front of the cameras."

Marco pauses laughing, pointing down the far end of the canteen. "Ho. Hold up. I see our guy."

Sure enough, there's Cade making his way through the tables, tray in hand. He's a big guy, almost as big as me. Dark haired and covered in tattoos. We could be brothers, but we're not. He got sent away to serve a bullet—a year's sentence—for a crime he won't talk about. Day one of his stretch, I saved his ass from a severe beating being served up to him by the Klu, and ever since then we've been friends. When Cade rocks up and slaps his tray down on the table, Leroy prods his finger into the seam of angry-looking stitches running from Cade's temple down to his cheekbone. "What d'I tell you about the clavo, knucklehead? You don't wanna be keeping that shit in your cell, man. They gonna put your name above the fucking SHU, the rate they keep throwing your ass in there."

Cade's a repeat offender for contraband, or *clavo* if you're Leroy. So far, he's been thrown in solitary for weed, a knuckle-duster, and a cell phone. Fuck knows how he got *that* in here. Cade scowls, smacking Leroy's hand away.

"Fuck you, man."

I pass him a pack of smokes, raising an eyebrow. "What was it this time?"

Cade opens the pack and takes three, tucking them into the top pocket of his jumpsuit for later. "Lewd images of a graphic and sexual nature," he recites, spooning food into his mouth.

Marco erupts into hails of laughter. "Porn? You got busted for a week for lookin' at pussy?"

Cade just shrugs it off, swallowing down his meal. "They'll screw me for anything. You know that."

"Yeah, man, we do. They still riding you hard?" Marco asks.

Cade casts a suspicious glance around the tables, eyes narrow. He blows out a deep breath. Ever since he's been in here, he's been the target of attacks from the Aryans, the Mexicans, *and* the prison guards, although no one is saying why. Least of all Cade. The prison admin wants him to spill his guts over something, and the gangs are afraid he will. So far, he's refused to even tell *us* why his life is being threatened on a daily basis. "Offered me WITSEC this time," he admits.

Leroy thumps his arm. "Damn, dude. You know

they give you a salary for life when you join WITSEC? Free money. You don't gotta do nothing for the rest of your days!"

"Apart from look over your shoulder," I say. Cade gives me a nod—I understand. The others are petty criminals. Leroy broke into a hardware store and stole a power drill. That crime would have landed him in Lompoc instead of a super-max if the stupid fucker hadn't bludgeoned the security guard who caught him half to death. Same story with Marco. He was a small-time dealer on the outside, probably would have scored twelve months in minimum security if he hadn't assaulted a cop trying to escape. These guys have no idea what it's like working in organized crime. I do. Cade does, too. He doesn't need to tell me he's in some deep shit. WITSEC is nowhere near as safe as the cops and politicians make it out to be. There's always a way. A person to be threatened. A computer to be hacked. And then you're dead. We eat our food, and we don't talk about it anymore.

In the end, worrying about a flawed witness protection system doesn't really matter. Cade doesn't get to join WITSEC. He doesn't even make it out of Chino. Three weeks later, during one of the rare moments the UN aren't in session, an Aryan named Spider stabs my friend three times in the back. Kidneys. Liver. Lungs. A professional hit. The guards carry his limp body down the gangway, past the open door of my cell, where I'm doing chin-ups, leaving a river of blood behind them. He doesn't come back.

The official line is that Cade Preston died of his injuries.

58

SLOANE

THIS GUY, THIS *STRANGER*, LOOKS dangerous.

Zeth freezes in the hallway, staring straight at him, jaw clenched. And he just accused him of being dead? An awful sinking sensation pools in the pit of my gut. Zeth looks like he put a bullet in this guy and buried him, only to find out that he resurrected himself and dug his way out of a shallow grave. Fuck, is out-and-out warfare about to be unleashed? Zeth just picks up his clothes and gets dressed, frowning slightly.

"Hey, Mal, why don't you go see if the boys need anything, huh?" The stranger asks the guy who was watching us have sex just now. Mal looks mildly put out, but at a stern look from the dark-haired guy down the hall, does what he's told and leaves.

Now that he's fully dressed, Zeth seems to have gathered himself together a little. "So, you're a Widow Maker. I guess that makes sense," he rumbles. He sounds...I have no idea how he sounds. I can't figure out what's going on with the stormy expression he's wearing. Cade scuffs the toe of one boot against the heel of the other, nodding.

"I guess it does. You're probably very confused right now."

"Could say that."

The tension between these two is stifling. Cade looks apologetic, while Zeth seems wired to blow a fuse.

"They moved me after the stabbing. I got put in solitary for the remainder of my sentence."

"They put you in solitary for *five months*?"

"Yeah, man. They pushed pretty hard. And then they pushed harder. I wouldn't give them what they wanted, so they left me in there to rot. Said I knew where to find 'em if I changed my mind."

So, prison. That's where Zeth knows this guy from. And by the sounds of things, Zeth thought he'd died inside. I clear my throat—a timely reminder of my existence. Cade glances up at me, shocked to find me still standing there. Apparently, Zeth feels the same way. "Uh, Naomi, why don't you go get ready for later? I need to have a conversation with this guy."

A *private* conversation, then. Fine by me. If Zeth thinks I shouldn't be present for whatever these two have to say to each other, then I'm inclined to listen. Plus the heat has receded from my cheeks, but I am still very aware of the fact that we just got caught fucking in the hallway. I need a shower, not to mention a moment to regain my dignity.

I leave them and hurry off down the hall, questioning my own behavior the whole way back to the room. Who *am* I? Suddenly so ruled by hormones and a level of stupidity that frankly borders on insanity. I don't recognize the person I'm becoming. I'm sore as I strip and take my second shower of the day. I crank the temperature control all the way to the right and let the blistering hot water slough off two layers of skin, disconcerted when I realize that my *shame* has remained intact.

The door starts hammering not long after I step out of the steaming bathroom.

"Hawthorne! Ms. Hawthorne!"

Hawthorne? Oh, yeah. Right. That's me—Naomi Hawthorne. The door bulges, about to come off its damned hinges. What the *hell* is going on out there? Kicking my way into a pair of jeans, I throw on a fresh T-shirt and answer the door, panting from the exertion of trying to wrestle on clothing when still wet.

A short, portly guy stands on the other side, chest heaving, with a gun in his hand. Oh, hell no. Absolutely not. I am *not* getting shot to death in the bathroom of a Black Talon brothel. I try to slam the door closed again, but the guy jams his foot into the gap.

"Ms. Hawthorne! Please. Come with...me. We need your...help."

My help? *Crap.* Zeth did want to beat that guy to death after all. They must have gotten into it as soon I left. I let go of the door, shoving past the short guy. "Okay, where is he? Show me." He's probably killed that Cade guy by now. I don't know why they think *I* can stop him from fighting. Ironic, how he's been telling *me* we need to keep our heads down, and now he's—

Outside, the morning sun bakes the courtyard flagstones, making the air dance. I stop dead, trying to piece together what I'm seeing. The girls I met last night are standing in a circle, holding each other and crying, and a man on his knees is performing CPR on a body, laid out on the ground. A woman. White sneakers on her feet. Faded blue jeans. Red shirt. No, not red. Her shirt is white; the front of it is just drenched in blood. The guy performing CPR stops, gasping, looking down at his hands like he doesn't know what to do, why the girl's not waking up when he presses down on her chest. Instinct kicks in then. I sprint across the courtyard and shove him out of the way, not paying any attention to the gasps from the onlookers as he falls sideways. I drop to my knees and lift the girl's shirt.

The source of all the blood is instantly visible: a gunshot wound, just below the underwire of her bra. I roll her toward me, craning over her to check her back—is there an exit wound? No. No exit wound. Shit. And she's been shot in the worst place possible. These days, bullets are designed to shatter inside a body, breaking into pieces to cause maximum damage to internal organs. And the internal organs close to this wound are the most important ones them all: the heart. The lungs.

"We need to get her inside. On a table." I look up to find a dozen strained faces watching my every move. On the outskirts, I register Michael, lost in the bustle as three men, members of the biker gang that rolled in late last night, hurry forward to get the woman inside. I still haven't even ascertained whether she's alive. I hold her by the wrist, searching for a pulse as they take her inside. There. I find it, weak and tachycardic but *there*, and then—

All my worst nightmares coalesce into one awful moment.

I see the small star-shaped birthmark on the inside of the girl's wrist. I know that birthmark. It features in nearly every one of my childhood memories. I'd recognize it anywhere.

I never looked at the woman's face, but I know it's her. It's Alexis.

59

SLOANE

THEY LAY ALEXIS OUT ON THE MASSIVE kitchen table. Maids run back and forth, squealing and crying. The guy from before, the one who was performing CPR on her, stands beside the table, preparing to begin compressions again.

"Get the fuck away from her!" I bulldoze my way through the people who have followed us in and shove the guy away. "She has a pulse, you idiot!"

"But she isn't breathing!"

"She *is* fucking breathing. She's unconscious because she's lost too much blood."

The guy staggers back, running his hands through his hair, smearing blood all over his face. "Jamie's gonna kill me. Jamie's gonna *murder* me," he says, over and over again. He's distracting the shit out of me.

"I need..." Fuck, I have nothing that I need here. I left my medical bag at home.

"What? What do you need?" White as a sheet, Alexis's would-be savior can hardly speak. "Tell me, and I'll get it for you. Come on!" He's panicking, just like me.

I take a deep breath and force myself to focus. "A plastic bag. Duct tape. A sewing kit. I need alcohol, prescription drugs, boiling water, towels, tweezers. The sharpest knife you can find. *Go.*"

Back-alley surgery on my dying sister—that's what this is turning into. There's a reason why doctors never treat family members. Trauma surgery is an art form. Not many people can do it. You have to stay calm in the face of extreme pressure. You have to block out the chaos, the shouting, and everyone else's panic. Your hand has to be steady one hundred percent of the time. No margin for error. Right now, my hands are shaking so badly, I wouldn't trust myself to hold a fucking *pen* steady.

"Tell me what happened. Tell me *exactly* what happened so I can visualize." The guy has already sprinted off, on a mission to find the items I asked for. Another guy steps forward, late twenties, wearing a smart shirt and a tie. He's also wearing skinny jeans, which seem out of place next to his other business casual attire. "Soph got shot," he mumbles, scrubbing his palms against his jeans. His hands are covered in blood. I want to smash him in his face.

"I can fucking *see* she's been shot, asshole! What kind of gun was she shot with? From how far away? From what *angle*?"

The guy just looks at me blankly. A tall blond woman with piercing green eyes steps forward and answers. "We were at a meet. It went bad. We copped heat and had to run. Soph got hit with a Glock 22. A .40 caliber. The shot came from about twenty feet away, from the side, like this, but from high up." She moves to my left, lifting her hand in the shape of gun, aiming it directly at my chest.

So she was shot from a distance, down and to the right. The bullet could be anywhere, could have torn absolutely anything apart. A sense of hopelessness washes over me. If we were in a hospital, if I had a surgical team, if I had a sterile environment, and life support machines, and time, there might be a chance I could save Alexis. But I am in a domestic kitchen with none of those things…

"Here, I got everything you asked for." The guy returns, carrying all of the items I've asked for in his arms. He dumps everything out on the table next to Alexis, whose shallow, rapid breathing has quickened since she was brought inside. She's in shock. And if I cut her open, I'm about to make it ten times worse. It will probably kill her. The alternative is that I leave her to bleed out on this kitchen table, and that definitely *will* kill her.

"Naomi?" Zeth's larger-than-life frame fills the doorway, his face unreadable as he surveys the scene in front of him. A number of the people in the kitchen turn to see who this newcomer is, but the others remain staring at Alexis. *Soph*, the guy called her. They all know her as Soph. The girls from last night called her that, too. "What's going on?" Zeth asks. His voice is a grounding rod. His presence brings with it a sense of calm that blunts the edge of my hysteria. My hands quit shaking so hard.

"I need the room to be cleared," I announce. Zeth nods, and I turn to my patient, snatching up the plastic bag and the duct tape. I tear the bag using my teeth an lay a square patch of it over the wound in Alexis' chest. I fix it in place, making sure the plastic and the duct tape form a perfect seal.

"This is her, isn't it?" Zeth's voice is the only one in the room now. I hadn't noticed everyone leave while I worked, but suddenly the silence is deafening.

"Yeah. This is her." I quickly tell him what the blonde told me, while I hold my hands over my mouth, watching and waiting. I count to twenty, with my hand resting on Lexi's chest, checking to make sure she's still breathing.

"Sloane? What are you doing?"

"I need to know if her lung's been punctured. If it has, air will seep from her lungs. The plastic bag will inflate as it leaves the wound." Another five seconds. Ten. Alexis is still breathing, but the plastic doesn't inflate.

"Her lung's fine." I rip the plastic bag and tape from her skin. Shame I can't do a similar triage test to tell if her *heart* has been grazed. The tachycardia could mean that it has, but it could also just mean that she's in shock. Which she definitely *is*.

"Now what?" Zeth is steady. Focused. Alert.

"Now, I have to try and find the bullet." I press down Lexi's stomach, waiting to feel the firmness that might indicate internal bleeding. Her abdomen is soft, though. If fate is on our side, I might be able to use the tweezers the Widow Maker brought back with him to extract the bullet. Alexis's odds will increase a hundredfold if I don't have to open her up.

Zeth reacts swiftly and decisively, handing me what I need when I ask for it. I run into problems immediately. The tweezers are too short. They're regular cosmetic ones and only reach a couple of inches into the wound. The alcohol they've given me to sterilize with is fucking *schnapps*. I have to send Zeth in search of something cleaner. When he comes back with high-grade Russian vodka, I could kiss him. But then, Lexi worsens, topping everything off with agonal breathing—a sign that her heart is under massive strain or that her kidneys or liver are failing.

"I don't know what to do. *Fuck!*" I'm cracking. I can't fucking do this. She's going to die. I've worried for years that she's dead, but she been alive. And now she's dying in front of me, and I can't save her?

Zeth takes the tweezers out of my hand and stalks around the other side of the kitchen table, grabbing me by the shoulders. "Sloane. Sloane, look at me."

I don't. I can't. I stare at baby sister's ashen face as death closes its fist around her. I'm crying, but I can't feel the tears. Can't feel my rasping breaths. Grief consumes me as I watch the worst thing imaginable unfolding on the kitchen table in front of me.

"Sloane!" My head cracks to the left, my ears ringing. Zeth slaps me so hard I see stars. His expression is all granite and grit when he says, "She's dying, Sloane. *Think*. What comes next?"

"I don't know which part of her is damaged inside. It could be...it could be her heart. But then it could be...her liver. Or her kidneys. I don't know."

"Okay. Let's use logic. Her lips are turning blue. What does that mean?"

"Hypoxia. Lack of oxygen to the brain."

"What causes that?"

"Cardiac arrest. Punctured lung. Massive strain on other organs." Anything. It could be *anything*.

"It's not a punctured lung. We already know that. And trajectory of the wound is down and away from the heart, so it's unlikely to be damage there, either. Cardiac arrest could come from damage to the liver and the kidneys?"

"Yes. Caused by excessive bleeding."

"Okay. So either way we need to open her up, Sloane. We need to see what part of her is bleeding, and we need to fix it." He hands me the knife the kid found for me—mercifully it's a scalpel. And a sharp one at that. God knows who it belongs to or why they have it, but it's a small mercy. If the only instrument available to me were a vegetable knife, I'd give up here and now.

"You can do this, Sloane."

"I can't! I—"

He shakes me. "I've watched you. I've seen you perform what other doctors have called miracles. You're *better* than this. I *know* you. You're an excellent surgeon, and you are *not* going to let your sister die."

I glance wildly around the room, trying to disassociate and find a way to not be here, but Zeth takes my face in his hands and holds me still, locking me in his steady gaze. "You've *got* this," he says.

There isn't a shadow of doubt on his face. In this moment, he believes in me more than anyone ever has...and a flicker of hope kindles in my chest.

I can do this.

I have to.

A weak gasp from the table steels my nerves. Alexis is fucking *dying*. She was taken, and I couldn't do anything about that, but I *can* do something about this.

"Okay. Okay, all right. I'm ready."

The next few moments happen in fast-forward. I drench my hands in the alcohol, and then I turn Alexis, giving her back one last look to make sure I haven't missed the exit wound.

"Holy shit!" Zeth hisses.

It's a good job I've checked. Since bringing her in, a massive, violent purple bruise has bloomed all over her back. Total renal failure. Definite internal bleeding. In the weak yellow light from the pendant in the kitchen, I haven't noticed a discoloration of her skin, but when I lay her flat and check her eyes, the jaundice is clear.

"Kidneys," Zeth says. It seems he's not *completely* unfamiliar with the workings of the human body. I nod, relief making my legs weak. At least when I cut now, I know *where* the hell I should be cutting now.

I make the incision—a bold, deep line about four inches long— horizontally across her abdomen on her right-hand side, and everything changes. This always happens when I operate. The world narrows to a pinpoint. Everything else fades, leaving a cold, clinical calm in its wake.

It takes time to inspect Lexi's abdominal cavity. There's a lot of blood, and I have no nursing team to provide suction or swab. I have Zeth, though. He moves unhesitatingly, bolstering my confidence. When he applies pressure with the torn shreds of towel, clearing away the blood so I can see what the hell I'm doing, I'm not worried that he'll damage her. In another world, in another entirely different reality, Zeth would have made an excellent surgeon. He is completely fucking bombproof.

I soon begin to find shrapnel. The relief is like a punch to the gut. I could cry as I tweeze the sharp shards of metal from my sister's stomach. As soon as I lay eyes on her right kidney, that relief vanishes, though. This is where I remove the largest bullet fragment from her body. It's nestled in among the ruins of the organ, completely and utterly destroyed.

"Fuck. Fuck."

Zeth holds his hand over mine, fixing me with that look again. He can see the mess just as well as I can, but he's not frozen with fear. "She's still breathing, Sloane. She has a heartbeat. And she still has another kidney, right?"

"Right." But it's not as simple as that. Removing a kidney is a massive surgery. People die on the operating table all the time during this kind of surgery, and that's under sterile, controlled conditions, too. But what choice do I have? None.

So I do what I have to do. I remove the mangled organ, stitching it neatly with a regular needle and thread from the sewing kit, and then I cauterize the wound. After that, it's a case of cleaning out her abdominal cavity and sewing her back up. I take a look through my supplies, and I don't find what I need now.

Zeth watches me search, expression even. "What is it? What do you need?"

"I need to find something to use for a blood transfusion. We're the same blood type. She lost so much. She'll need more blood if she's going to make it to a hospital."

Zeth just grunts at that. "They're not gonna let you take her to a hospital, Sloane."

I stop rifling and look up, my heart lurching into my throat. "What the fuck are you talking about?"

"Your sister was shot. Hospitals are obliged to report gunshot wounds to the police."

"Yes, I'm well aware of that, Zeth. I work in a fucking hospital."

"Right. So none of the people here are gonna want

that kind of attention. If your sister talks, the cops will come down on this place in two seconds flat. Jacob'll never allow that. They're gonna want her to recover here. If she gets an infection—"

"THERE IS NO *IF*, ZETH!" I grab the first thing that comes to hand—the vodka—and hurl it at the wall. The glass bottle splinters into a thousand pieces, detonating like a grenade. Zeth doesn't even flinch. After everything I just did? After Alexis pulling through all of that? "There is no *if*. There is only *when*. They need to open her back up and fix the hack job I just did on her insides! If she survives *that*, she's gonna need nuclear-grade antibiotics, a whole mountain of painkillers, and at least two blood transfusions. Otherwise, all of this has been for nothing." I cover my face with bloody hands, trying to catch a breath. "And as for drawing the cops' attention, I think it's a little late for *that*."

Zeth comes to me, placing his hands on my shoulders. "What do you mean?"

"She was shot with a Glock 22. A .40 caliber. You know who uses guns like that, huh? I'm sure you do. You've probably had a couple pointed at you in the past." I shove him away from me, dragging my hands through my hair.

Zeth narrows his eyes, staring me down. "Yeah. Cops."

"Not just cops. The *FBI* carry Glock 22s. The *DEA* carry Glock 22s. I see them on the hips of nearly every agent who walks through the hospital doors. If these friends of yours have that sort of attention already focused on them, *if federal agents have been fucking shooting at people*, then they're already looking for Jacob and this fucking MC that's just rolled up out of nowhere."

"You're exactly right, darlin'."

The voice startles Zeth almost as much as me. Our reactions couldn't be more different, though. I flinch away from the stranger in the doorway. Zeth pulls a gun on him.

The stranger—a tall, lanky guy dressed in leathers—doesn't seem to mind. He takes a slow step into the room. "The cops *are* looking for us," he says. He peers past me, looking at Lexi, lying in a pool of blood on the table. "Is she alive?"

Zeth looks like he's about five seconds away from shooting him in the face. I move in between the two of them—one GSW victim in this kitchen is enough for today. "Yes. But barely. She needs proper medical attention. Do you know her?"

The guy shrugs. He must be in his late twenties, early thirties, dirty-blond hair, and obviously not one of Jacob's men. He's from the MC, then. He confirms this when he walks further into the room, going to stand by Alexis, and I see the embroidered patch on his jacket. *Widow Maker.* The icon stitched into his leather is of a woman, head bowed, crying. She looks like some grunge version of the Madonna. "Yeah, I know her well enough," he says. "I should. She is the boss's girl, after all."

60

ZETH

ALEXIS ROMERA HAS BEEN DATING the president of the Widow Makers. This information is more than a little surprising, but hey. Nothing should surprise me anymore. Carnie, the guy who nearly gave Sloane a heart attack with this news, tells us that Jacob's expecting us in his study. Outside the kitchen, a dozen people lean against the walls, sitting on the floor, all pale and anxious looking. A tall blonde beelines for Sloane as soon as she sees her, and grabs her by the elbows.

"Is she okay? She's fucking dead, isn't she? She's fucking *dead*!"

Sloane extricates herself from the girl's grip and

guides her toward the kitchen door. "She's not dead. Sit with her and come tell me right away if her breathing changes. Check for her pulse every few minutes, too."

The blonde heads into the kitchen, gasping when she sees all of the blood. Carnie escorts us through the hallways, giving the impression that Jacob told him we were to come or else he was to *make* us come. Hilarious. I'd like to see the bastard try to move *me*. And if he even *touched* Sloane...

"In there." Carnie jerks his head into Jacob's study. On the other side of the door, Jacob, Michael, and Cade sit awkwardly around a large, polished oak table. Cade and I barely got to speak before all hell broke loose earlier, but he did have time to tell me that Rebel is his friend. That he's been a Widow Maker his whole life. I have no idea what to make of that. I've thought we were on the same wavelength, Cade and me, but this revelation turns that concept completely on its head.

"Come join us," Jacob says, gesturing to the empty chairs at the table. There are three of them, one each for Sloane and me, and then an extra one. "I hear you've had quite an eventful morning, Ms. Hawthorne?" Jacob asks. He bridges his hands in front of him, spearing Sloane through with an arctic gaze.

"You could say that," Sloane answers. She looks

like something out of a fucking horror show. There's blood all over her hands and up her arms, and speckled all over her face. It's down her shirt and in her hair, too. The clipped, dry response she shoots at Jacob doesn't hide the fact that she's not impressed by his glib remark. "We'll be leaving soon. To take the girl to hospital."

"Oh, I don't think so, Ms. Hawthorne. Sophia's a strong girl. She'll be just fine."

I was right. I knew he'd say that, of course, but I'd hoped I was wrong. I catch the look of fury on Cade's face, and goddamn—he's so angry that his neck has broken out in a splotchy, crimson rash.

"The girl *is* going to the hospital, Jacob."

The Black Talon tilts his head toward Cade, smiling ever so slightly. "You are just a mouthpiece, Mr. Preston," he drawls. "Please remember that you are a *guest* in my home."

"I may be a guest, but Rebel's on his way. What do you think he's going to say when he gets here and his girl's dead?"

Ahh. Rebel's not here yet. But on his way. This could be a good thing. Sloane sees the opportunity, too, and grasps it. "If we leave now, we can get her to a private practice in San Bernardino. I know them there. They'll keep her off the books if I ask them to."

Jacob plants his hands palm down on the table,

considering them for a moment. When he looks up, the malice in his eyes that makes me think he doesn't give a shit what Rebel is gonna do to him when he arrives. But I'm mistaken. This look isn't about Rebel. The look is all for me. "You lied to me, Zeth. I had a very enlightening conversation this morning with an acquaintance of yours." Jacob nods to Clark, who does as his master bids him and brings a single sheet of paper to the table. He puts it down in front of Jacob.

"This acquaintance of yours told me some very interesting things about you. See, I thought you were here to spy for Charlie this whole time. I didn't suspect that you came here to steal my property."

Jacob slides the paper across the table, and this time, there's no point in bullshitting. Rick, who I left in Anaheim fishing for information on the DEA bitch investigating Charlie, is tied to a chair, while the fuzzy silhouette of a man partially out of shot lays into him with a tire iron. I push the photo back to Jacob, raising my eyebrows.

Shit. Shit, fuck, shit. I don't care all that much about Rick taking a beating, I have to say, but this means everything is over. The whole ploy goes up in smoke. "You got me." I hold up my hands. "I wanted to take one of your girls. She's dying in your kitchen right now, though, so you might as well let me have her. I'll take the whole mess right off your hands."

"You're not taking shit from me, asshole." Jacob nods to Clark, and the guy comes and stands behind me, gun held loosely in his hand. In a moment, Jacob will tell him to blow my brains out. I have to admit, Clark lurking behind me with a gun is a whole lot less fun than it was when Sloane did it. "Sophia isn't my mess. Rebel bought her from me years ago, and she's been sticking her nose into my business and riling up my girls ever since. If she dies, it'll be because she's a nosy bitch who gets caught up in things that don't concern her. *You*, on the other hand, are going to wait here with your fine little piece of ass until Charlie arrives. Then I'm gonna let *him* take care of you. He seems highly motivated toward that end. He was especially pissed off when I sent him a shot of your little friend here."

He gestures to the image of Rick. Fucking perfect. Charlie's probably had plenty of time to put two and two together, but seeing the physical evidence that Rick's living and breathing after he betrayed Charlie to the Wreckers... the guy's gonna be fucking raging.

Michael has watched all of this play out nonchalantly. I'm not fooled by the facade, though. He's a viper, not a rattlesnake. With him, you don't get a warning. He stands up and casually takes a throwing knife from the waistband of his pants. Jacob gapes up at him, face drawn into an angry scowl.

"Sit down, man. This doesn't concern you."

Michael disregards the command, flipping the knife over and driving it through Jacob's hand with lightning speed, pinning him to the table.

"Motherfucker! Clark, kill him!" Jacob's cry is loud enough to alert the whole fucking house. Perhaps Clark's too stunned by Michael suicidal actions, but he makes a mistake—he *hesitates*, and that hesitation gives me enough time to spin, grab hold of his M16, and punch the guy square in the throat. He crumples to the ground like a ragdoll, fighting to breathe. I collapsed his esophagus, though, so he won't be doing that again any time soon. Sloane screams, jumping up, and now it seems like *everyone* is screaming. We're about to have fifteen angry guards storm this room.

I shoot Michael a displeased glance. "Real smooth, man."

Michael braces against the table and jerks his knife free from Jacob's hand, then lays it against the big man's throat instead. The leader of the Black Talons stops yelling and freezes. As though thanking him for his silence, Michael gives him a friendly pat on the arm. "*You* didn't hear what he was saying before you came into the room, boss. He was gonna let Anton cut your dick off. At least that's what I thought he said. It was in Spanish."

Cade nods. "Yeah. That was pretty much the gist of

it." He gets to his feet, coming around to take a look at Clark, who is lying still and silent on the floor.

Sloane only has tear-filled eyes for me, though. "Did you have to do that? You crushed his windpipe."

She wants me to defend my actions or make her see the sense in what I've done. To make it *okay* in her eyes. I can't do that for her, though. She needs to decide for herself. Gently, briefly, I cup her cheek in my hand. "Why don't you think about it and make up your own mind." Then, I turn to Michael. "We need to get the fuck out of here."

"Agreed. What about him?"

"You motherfuckers seriously think you can pull this shit?" Purple as a beet, Jacob spits everywhere as he shouts. "You are fucking dead. All of you!"

I stalking toward the two of them. "Hey, Michael, how many times can a man die?"

"Just once, boss."

"Yeah, that's right. Just once." I take the throwing knife Michael offers to me and I hold it in front of Jacob's face. "Charlie's already called dibs on *my* death, motherfucker. Sorry to disappoint, but you aren't gonna get a look in. Now..." I trail the knife down Jacob's cheek, watching the metal reflect his wide-eyed terror back at him. "We're both big fucking dogs, Jake, remember? You see yourself in me. We've both come from shit, as you so kindly reminded me the other day. So ask yourself this." I bend down, bracing my hands on my thighs and giving him a thoughtful shrug. "If we're so similar, what would *you* do in my position right now?"

"You can't kill me, Zeth. You wouldn't fucking *dare!*"

Cade has joined Michael behind Jacob now. He looks grim, but he gives me a hard nod—*I'm with you, brother.*

"Oh God, this isn't happening." Behind me, Sloane looks like she's going to throw up any second. She turns around and leans her forehead against the wall, hyperventilating and covering her ears with her hands.

Jacob smirks when I face him again. "I'm *unarmed*, Zeth. You gonna show your woman what kind of monster you are by slitting my throat in front of her?"

I rush forward, shoving my face into his. "*Yes.*"

I lash out with the knife.

But the steel doesn't strike flesh.

A wet stain soaks the front of Jacob's pants as I signal to Cade: *Finish the job.* The Widow Maker flips his gun and brings the butt down on the back of Jacob's head, knocking him clean out.

Hah. Slumped in his chair, unconscious, sitting in his own piss—exactly what the cocksucker deserves. I allow myself all of a second to feel smug, but only the one. "Come on. He won't be out forever."

Sloane's been mumbling, cursing by the sounds of things, but her diatribe trails off as she turns around. "You didn't kill him?"

I wrap an arm around her waist and guide her out of the room. "Jacob Dixon is an evil son of a bitch, Sloane, but he was right about one thing. I won't kill an unarmed man."

61

ZETH

JACOB'S GUARDS DIDN'T COME RUNNING at the sound of their boss's cries for a reason. They didn't *hear* them. In the compound's courtyard, countless Mercedes, Lamborghinis, and Harleys compete to snarl the loudest in the front courtyard as people burn in from the desert for tonight's gathering.

Alexis is a cold, limp weight in my arms. The blonde hadn't wanted us to take her from the kitchen, but a few sharp words from Sloane and the bitch backed off. We spend a full thirty seconds out in the open, looking for my car. Michael locates it parked to one side, covered in dust from being exposed to the desert for four days. I deposit Alexis in the back seat, and Sloane gets in after her, cradling her sister's head in her lap.

I take the driver's side, and Michael gets in on the right. Cade stands at the window, eyes searching the crowd of people, looking for a way out. "You'll need to be quick, bro. I'll call Jacob's boys inside, and then we'll be right behind you."

I start the engine, revving it like crazy. We're set to go. Cade holds out his knuckles and I bump fists with him. He's about to head inside when a piercing scream tears above all of the noise and Alaska comes barreling out of the villa.

The engines drown her out, but one of the guards hears her well enough and signals the others. They charge inside, guns at the ready.

"Better go now, man. We'll catch up." Cade thumps the side of the car and runs back inside the villa. We do as he suggests and get the hell out of there.

62

SLOANE

IT TAKES THREE HOURS TO REACH THE hospital in San Jacinto. Jacob knows about the hospital in San Bernadino, so we have to take a detour. Alexis nearly dies a total of seven times on the journey. Her pulse is barely there anymore, weak, irregular and thready, and I am numb. Heavy silence reigns supreme inside the car as Zeth drives, and I try to forget where I am. To forget everything that's happened since I woke up this morning.

It's pitch black by the time we pull up outside the hospital, and just the sight of the place has me in tears. The ambulance parked out front, and the lights blaring from the building's many windows, promising help, is more than I can take. We got her here. Somehow, she made it this far.

Zeth collects Alexis from the back seat again, and we run inside. Michael stays with the car. Michael takes the car away. I don't know what happens to Michael. All I care about is Alexis.

The nurse on duty at reception drops her pen when she sees us. We must look like hell, covered in blood and dust, carrying a half-dead girl between us. I'm rattling off Lexi's stats before the girl can even process what she's seeing.

"Gunshot wound to the abdomen. Severe kidney damage, hemodynamically unstable, tachycardic, and hypertensive. She needs to be booked into an OR now!"

The nurse responds quickly, sending out an emergency page for all available bodies. A crash team and two doctors arrive within seconds, taking Alexis without so much as a backward glance at me and Zeth. The nurse sticks around, though. What's happened to her? What's my relationship to the patient? What treatment has she received? Allergies? End-of-life, do-not-resuscitate wishes? I answer everything through a daze of exhaustion and a toxic level of adrenaline.

After that, it's just Zeth and me. Alone. In a hospital waiting room.

"Sloane?"

I can't look at him. If I do, I'm going to start cr— ah, shit. Too late. He holds me tight, arms wrapped around me, and I bawl my eyes out for God knows how long, feeling utterly weak and useless. The likelihood of Lexi making it is so slim that I can't even calculate such low odds. And what happened back at the compound? Zeth killing Clark?

"She's going to be okay, Sloane. It's all gonna be okay."

"How can you say that?" I push him away, batting the tears out of my eyes. *"How?"*

Throughout this entire nightmare of a day, Zeth has been composed. He reaches out and sweeps my hair out of my face, shaking his head, still in total command of himself. "Because she's your sister, angry girl. If she's half as strong as *you* are, then she's gonna be just fine."

God, he really *believes* that? I stand up on shaky legs and start pacing, my arms wrapped around my body. "I hesitated. I took too long. She's probably gonna die now, and if I'd acted quicker…" I pull in a deep breath, fighting against the tears. How many times have I told interns you can't hesitate? *How many times?* And then the moment when I need to concentrate the most, *I* freeze. Lexi needed me, and I froze. My legs are like rubber. I'm going to collapse any second. As if he knows this, Zeth comes and stands behind me, placing his arms around me, giving me the support I need to stay upright.

"You were brave. And you were fucking strong. You did what you had to do." The bass timbre of his voice rumbles through his rib cage and vibrates into my back. I was *scared* of him when he attacked Clark back at the compound. It all happened so quickly. He went from dormant to lethal in the space of seconds, right before my eyes. It was a terrifying thing to witness. But his words have been playing in my head ever since I asked him if he'd *had* to kill Clark, and sick as it may sound, I understand why he told me to work it out on my own, now.

In between freaking out, thinking that my sister was dead on the way here, I've run the scenario through my head over and over. I've watched it play out a thousand times, and I've imagined every single outcome I can: Zeth not acting, and Clark shooting Michael; Zeth taking the time to try to wrestle the gun from the guy and getting shot himself in the process; Zeth attacking him in a million different ways, and each time the outcome is the same. Someone dies. I'm a terrible person, but I've come to the conclusion that he did the right thing,

By letting *me* figure it out on my own, he knows I *know* it's the truth. A guilty man will plead innocent until he runs out of breath. That it was all an accident.

That it was someone else. That he had no other choice. I wouldn't have accepted Zeth telling me that he'd had no other choice. I would have just been afraid. And I still *am* afraid... just not afraid of *him*.

I place my hands over his, folded on my stomach, and I let my head fall back against his chest. He's got me. He's got me now, and he had me back in Jacob Dixon's kitchen, when I needed someone the most. *He* was the one who got me through it.

"You did what you had to do as well," I whisper. "I know that." I don't explain what I'm talking about. Zeth knows, and his deep sigh tells me he's been waiting for me to make up my mind on that front.

"Thank you," he murmurs.

I shake my head, closing my eyes, determined not to cry anymore. "No. Thank *you*."

Whoever Zeth is at his core, he's killed to protect me, and he helped save my sister, for however short a time she may live. He's going against every single instinct he has even remaining in this hospital right now, knowing the sort of questions that are going to be asked. And he's doing it all for me. He can hide behind the violence of his past all he likes, but I'm beginning to see the *truth* of him, and the *good* that he so desperately wants to hide.

We stand for a long time, not speaking. Just waiting, Zeth supporting me against him, breathing softly into my ear. Two long hours later, a doctor comes to find us. She's young, a resident like me, wearing the same businesslike expression I wear when I come to deliver bad news. My throat closes up at the sight of her, my legs finally buckling.

"Ms. Romera? You're Alexis's sister, correct?"

I nod, unable to get any words out.

"Alexis is in the ICU right now. We repaired two slow bleeds to her stomach and small bowel, but for now, we've done everything we can. There's a massive risk of infection from the first time she was opened, but we're confident. If Alexis makes it through the night, there's a good chance she'll survive."

A good chance. Doctors don't use those words lightly. I have never said them. The danger they will backfire is just too high for me. This woman is either one hundred percent sure my sister will survive and is simply covering her ass, or she's grossly negligent. I pray with everything I have that she's covering her ass.

ZETH

Neither of us sleep.

Neither of us eat.

We wait for the dawn, holding our breath. *If Alexis*

makes it through the night, there's a good chance she'll survive. When the sun rises and we haven't had any bad news, Sloane loses her fight against exhaustion. She passes out on the uncomfortable hospital chairs and sleeps like the dead.

The nurse comes back at ten to tell us Alexis's stats are improving. She's still unconscious, but they're hoping she'll wake up in the next few hours. I have to say I'm Sloane's husband before the nurse will tell me any of that without waking Sloane up, though, and that feels... *awkward*.

At midday, Cade appears through the glass window of the family room. He sees me, sees Sloane still passed the fuck out, and gestures for me to come to him.

"Dude, we've been looking for you everywhere. This was the sixth hospital we tried before we saw your man outside."

Michael's waited for us. Goddamn hero. "You get away from Jacob's without a problem?"

Cade rubs the back of his neck. "There was a bit of a stand-off. None of the boys got hurt too bad, though." He turns and tenses as he looks back over his shoulder. Three Widow Makers are coming in hot, and the one at the front looks ready to kill. "Oh fuck. I said I'd come find you first."

I stand my ground, squaring off, ready to start

throwing fists if I have to. After everything that's happened, I don't give a shit that we're in a hospital. I could really use the chance to break someone's face.

The guy in front's a monster. His hands are scuffed and already bloody. Looks like he's started the fight without me. To Cade, he growls, "This him?"

Cade nods. "Yeah, this is Zeth." He turns back to me with a look of apprehension on his face. "And this is—"

"Yeah, I know who this is," I reply. "You're Rebel."

The guy nods. He's wound up tighter than a fucking bowstring. He shakes as he takes a deep breath and says, "Thank you, man. Thank you for helping my wife."

63

SLOANE

MY SISTER IS A MARRIED WOMAN.

A million thoughts go through my mind when I learn this. The first and foremost of these thoughts is Hell. To. The. Mother. Fucking. No.

My sister was kidnapped. *Kidnapped*. And then, more than two years later, she turns up *married*? A large part of my brain is assuming that this marriage was forced on her. The remaining part of my brain is dedicated to imagining brutal and painful ways I could kill this Rebel guy without being arrested for murder. I'm a doctor. I have access to any number of substances that could cause lethal damage to the human body. Or in the very least, there are a number of items in Zeth's duffel bag that would fix this situation very quickly. While shooting Rebel with a Desert Eagle won't undo the damage that's already been done, it would certainly free Lexi from future torment. But my homicidal plans are brought to a halt when I meet the guy. He saw fit to leave the hospital when he learned that Lexi was still asleep, but he returns a couple of hours later, when we're waiting for permission to go and see her.

Cade seems as on edge as I am. I can only imagine how worried he is over what Lexi will say if I talk to her before Rebel has a chance to intimidate her into saying something else. However, his nerves only seem to grow when a tall, dark guy with arms full of tattoos saunters down the corridor toward us. Zeth leans against the wall opposite me, his own arms crossed and eyes fixed firmly on me as I watch the guy approach. Cade rubs his hands on his thighs, sucking in a deep breath.

"He's left the other guys outside, sweetheart. Just go easy on him, okay?" he says to me.

"Go easy on him? I'm gonna tear his fucking balls off."

Zeth's mouth curves into a positively evil smile.

Cade, on the other hand, doesn't seem to think this is a funny prospect. "Soph's gon' be pissed at you if you do that."

"My sister's name is *Alexis*. And this bastard's probably brainwashed her, haven't you, you fuck?"

The guy arriving in front of me reels back, eyebrows rocketing up his forehead. The most annoying thing about him, aside from the fact that he's incredibly good-looking in a rugged, bad-boy kind of way, is that he has the gall to look shocked at my accusation. He gives me an irritated look. "The hell you talking about, woman?"

"I'm talking about you forcing my sister into doing God only *knows* what against her will. You do realize that a marriage isn't legal unless it's overseen by a State official, right?"

Rebel snorts. "First, you're wrong. Carnie got certified online. He married us back in New Mexico, and we sent off the paperwork. Recognized by any court in America. Second, what the hell do you mean? Soph said you gave us your blessing. She also said you were too busy being a fucking hotshot doctor to come to your own sister's wedding."

What the actual...? I close my eyes, I'm shaking my head. "You're such a fucking liar."

Zeth snorts, eyes glinting with mirth, and suddenly I'm itching to punch him in the face. "What, you think this is fucking *funny?*"

He shrugs, shoving off from his leaning post

against the wall. "Not at all. I've just never heard you swear this much. Not even at *me*."

If he thinks my language is bad right now, he should lock me in a room with this punk and see what I say to him then, with no innocent bystanders around to hear it.

"I'm not lying," the guy says simply. "I'm telling the truth. Not that I have any reason to justify myself to you, *Dr.* Romera."

"What do you mean by that?"

"What?"

"*Doctor* Romera? You say my title like you're trying to swallow down liquid shit."

"Oh, nothing. I just don't get why you haven't spoken to your sister in so fucking long. She needed you, y'know. And where *were* you, huh? Your fucking job's been too important. Your fucking patients have been too important to leave, even for a goddamn weekend?" He doesn't turn red as the temperature of his tone rises; he turns a pasty white, which makes his frosty blue eyes seem even cooler.

Well, fuck *him*. Of all the messed-up, delusional things to accuse *me* of. The guy's lost his freaking mind. "You are off your meds, asshole." I prod him hard in his chest, hoping it hurts him as much as it hurts my goddamn finger. "My sister was taken from her home and her loving family, and you bought her from a fucking pimp! Like she was fucking takeout! You don't get to lecture *me* on how much I care about my sister. I have been looking for her every single day since she went missing!" Nope. The finger stab wasn't enough. I slam my palms into his chest, shoving him as hard as I can. I don't even get to see how far Rebel—who the fuck is called *Rebel*, anyway?—staggers back. A solid band of muscle locks around my waist, and my feet are suddenly a clear six inches off the floor. Zeth's voice is in my ear, dark and deep and hypnotic.

"Come on, now, angry girl. Less of the angry."

I struggle, but it's pointless. The man's arms are made out of reinforced steel. "All right. All right, okay. All right, I'm fine. Jesus!" I *must* be mad. I don't believe in the church anymore, but I still have a lifetime of my father's anti-blaspheming lectures under my belt. I think I was twelve the last time I said Jesus without it being in between the words *in the name of our savior*, *Lord*, and *Amen*.

Zeth puts me down, though he lingers behind me, ready to grab me if I look like I'm going to start throwing fists, no doubt. I try to shake off my rage, but it spikes when I see that Rebel *isn't* on his ass three feet down the hall. He's standing right where I left him, with a crooked frown on his face. "So...Soph didn't tell you she was okay?"

"No! Probably because she *wasn't* okay!"

"She told *me* you didn't wanna know her anymore."

"I—that—" That makes no sense. I want to accuse him of lying again, but this look on his face...Rebel isn't a master of concealing his emotions like Zeth is. Or maybe it's just that I've become very adept at reading people, having so little to work off with Zeth all the time. Either way, I think he's actually telling the truth.

Over Rebel's shoulder, a nurse is walking toward us with purpose. Her skin is a pretty taupe color, two shades lighter than Michael's. "What the hell's going on here? No bickering in the hallways. It's a rule! Sick people are trying to get better here!"

"I'm sorry, I—" Urgh, I'm *not* sorry. I still want to kill this guy. The nurse gives me a *look*, daring me to cause trouble, but...

Cade steps in, his leather cut creaking as he folds his arms across his chest. "Sophia ready to see people now?"

The nurse shoots him a filthy look, then shares it around our group, making sure she levels it at each of us for an awkward amount of time. "I'm not letting *troublemakers* into my patient's room."

I hold my hands up in surrender; in this hospital, this woman is God. "Look, I am sorry, okay. I'm just worried about my sister. If you could just let *me* see her—"

Rebel holds up a hand, too. "*I'm* worried about my *wife*. I should go and see her first, just to let her know—"

"Shut up. You can both go in and see her. Together. Sophia can choose which one of your asses she wants to kick out all by herself. You two," the nurse says, pointing an authoritative finger at Zeth and Cade. "You two are gonna wait here."

Zeth and Cade do as they're told and wait in the hallway, and I follow the nurse down the corridor, Rebel jostling at my elbow, into an elevator, up three awkwardly silent floors, and then into the ICU. I should feel at home here—the majority of my trauma patients either start off or end up in a ward just like this one at some point within the length of their treatment—but I don't. I feel sick. The smell of disinfectant and the chorus of life support machines blipping from behind closed doors ignites the kind of panic I've only ever experienced once before, in Jacob Dixon's kitchen. The nurse guides us to a room and opens the door, giving both Rebel and me a glance of warning before disappearing. Rebel walks in before me, his hand covering his mouth.

Alexis is bundled up in the hospital bed, thankfully not hooked up to life support, but she looks bad. Her face is drawn, and her eyes are bloodshot. But, most importantly, her eyes are open. She sees us the moment we enter the room, and her mouth falls open. "Oh my God," she whispers. *"Sloane?"*

I've imagined this moment a thousand times. A million. And in none of my imagined moments where Alexis and I are reunited does she look horrified. She's overwhelmed, deliriously happy, crying with tears of joy. Not gripping her blanket so hard her knuckles turn white. She swallows, looking from me to Rebel and back again. "What are you doing here, Sloane?"

"What am I *doing* here? What the hell am I..." I can't. I can't even...

Rebel, a towering pillar of muscle and tattoos, moves around the side of her bed and sits on the edge of it, taking hold of her hand. "Are you okay?" he asks softly.

Alexis's gaze flickers to him. She nods, the gesture robotic, as if she's at a loss for words.

"Good. I'm glad you're okay," he says carefully. "Babe, remember when we got married? And you said it would have been the most perfect day if only your sister could have been there? Well, about that..."

Alexis tries to pull her hand away, but Rebel has a decent if cautious grip on her. "I'm sorry, baby," she says. "I just...I didn't..." Tears well in her eyes. Alexis always *was* one for crocodile tears when she wasn't getting her own way, but these look genuine enough. She's shaking. "I swear I didn't mean to lie to you. And I swear I'll tell you everything. But... can I just have a moment with her?" With *her?* Alexis sees how black my mood is becoming and amends her words. "I need a moment with my sister."

Rebel grunts, stands, and then places a kiss on the top of her head. "Be careful," he says to her. "Dr. Romera attacks when provoked."

He leaves the room, winking at me as he goes. I think about Zeth and how he would react to something like that. Probably smash his head through the observation window or something. If only I had Zeth's body mass.

"You can stop looking at him like that."

Alexis's voice is a little stronger now, but it's still shaky. "How the hell *should* I be looking at him, Lex? Should I be warmly embracing my new brother-in-law, the human fucking trafficker?"

"Yes. No, wait. He's not... He isn't what you think, Sloane."

I can barely believe my own ears. He has brainwashed her. She has Stockholm syndrome. This is a classic presentation. "So you *weren't* kidnapped from outside college? And this guy *didn't* force you to marry him?"

Alexis sighs and falls back against her pillows, wiping her face with the back of her hand. The tears are falling now. "Yes, I was taken. But it wasn't by him.

He helped me." She sets her jaw. "And he didn't force me to marry him, Sloane. You have to believe that."

"Then why on earth did you marry the president of a motorcycle gang? Because I'm really struggling to understand any of this."

She sniffs, swatting the tears from her cheeks. "I married him because he's the other half of me, Sloane. The slightly grumpy, slightly scary, deeply wonderful other half of me. I married him because I love him."

This is all too much to take. So, it's all true. She told Rebel I didn't care about her. That I couldn't be bothered coming to her wedding. I need to know why, but right now I have a more pressing need, and that is to get the fuck away from her. After all this worrying, all of the nightmares about my poor baby sister being used and abused, she's blissfully happy. And married.

Fucking *married*. I can't breathe. I need time to think. To process all of this properly.

I turn, and I walk away, and I do not look back.

I make it down to the ground floor, back to where we were waiting earlier before—

"Hey, Sloane!"

It's him. the tattooed bastard, following me down the corridor. I try to power-walk away, but he grabs my arm. I spin around, ready to lay into him again, but he lets go of me, holding his hands in the air.

"Don't be mad at her, Sloane. She's been through hell and back."

"And was it *you* who put her through it?"

He clenches his jaw, eyes narrowing. I wasn't paying attention before, but the color of his eyes is so blue they look like flints of ice. *"No."*

"Then how the hell did she end up with you?"

"Maybe that's something *she* should tell you. You can probably hazard an educated guess, though." Pulling on his leather jacket, he smirks infuriatingly as he jerks his head down the hallway.

Toward Zeth.

He's watching us. He cuts an imposing figure, standing there like he's carved out of rock. Rebel's smirk morphs into a grin. "You both have similar taste in men, after all, sweetheart. You *both* like us dark and dangerous."

Zeth and Sloane's story continues in

Blood & Roses Vol. II

Coming in 2027!

About the Author

Callie Hart is the #1 *New York Times* bestselling author of the international phenomenon *Quicksilver*, along with many other bestselling dark romance and dark academia titles. A British expat now living in California, Callie can most likely be found sequestered away in the corner of a library, fantasizing about exciting new realms and the brooding antiheroes who occupy them.

You can learn more at:

calliehart.com
Instagram @calliehartauthor
TikTok @calliehartauthor